Jesus the King

A Paradigm for Liberation
(Christology of Luke's Gospel)

Jesus the King

A Paradigm for Liberation
(Christology of Luke's Gospel)

Sam Christopher

2019

Jesus the King: *A Paradigm for Liberation (Christology of Luke's Gospel)* —
Published by the Rev. Dr. Ashish Amos of the Indian Society for Promoting
Christian Knowledge (ISPCK), Post Box 1585, 1654, Madarsa Road, Kashmere
Gate, Delhi-110006.

ISBN: 978-81-938241-9-1

Laser typeset by

ISPCK, Post Box 1585, 1654, Madarsa Road, Kashmere Gate, Delhi-110006
• *Tel:* 23866323/22

e-mail: ashish@ispck.org.in • ella@ispck.org.in
website: www.ispck.org.in

Dedicated
to
My beloved parents

Rev. A. Daniel (late)
and
Mrs. D. Annilet (late)

Contents

CHAPTER - 2
Kingship Motif in the Infancy Narrative   ...   52

Acknowledgments

This book, *Jesus the King: A Paradigm for Liberation*, is the outcome of my doctoral research under the title, "The Motif of Kingship in Luke's Gospel and its Significance for a Reconstruction of Lukan Christology." The dissertation has been accepted by the Senate of Serampore College for awarding the degree, Doctor of Theology.

I am thankful to God for his Grace; various persons and institutions for their invaluable help and support during the period of my research. I am grateful to Rev. Dr. J. G. Muthuraj, New Testament professor at the United Theological College, Bangalore for his supervision during my research period. I am indebted to Rev. Dr. C. I. David Joy, New Testament professor at U.T.C. for his timely help in accomplishing the dissertation as well who has written the preface to this book; Rev. Dr. J. R. John Samuel Raj, Principal of U.T.C. and Rev. Dr. Santosh S. Kumar, the Dean of Doctoral Studies for their encouragements to complete the dissertation.

I am grateful to Professor, Rev. Dr. David Fergusson, Principal of New College, (School of Divinity) Edinburgh, who arranged the Exposure programme and to Dr. Helen K. Bond, my supervisor during the period of my stay over there. I am grateful to all the librarians and the library staff of the libraries who helped me a lot to get access and avail the materials: The United Theological College, Bangalore; St. Peter's Pontifical Institute, Bangalore; Dharmaram College, Bangalore; South

Asia Institute of Advanced Christian Studies, Bangalore; School of Divinity, New College, Edinburgh; and, the Tyndale House, Cambridge.

I am grateful to both CWM and Global ministries for their financial support to meet the expenses of my research as well, my travel to Edinburgh. I am grateful to Rev. Arun Kumar Wesley, Bangalore for having gone through the script of my thesis. I am indebted to my wife and children for their constant support during the entire period of my research. Finally, I express my thanks to ISPCK for their readiness to publish this book.

Preface

Rev. Dr. D. Sam Christopher's book *Jesus the King: A Paradigm for Liberation (Christology of Luke's Gospel)* is an upgraded version of his DTh thesis. It is a well crafted work with the support of relevant arguments and significant bibliography.

He studied the socio-political context of the Gospel of Luke very well by citing the social communities in a systematic manner. This work seems to be attractive and important as it offers afresh understanding about the socio-cultural undercurrents of the early church.

The King title ascribed to Jesus here refers to the liberation of the subaltern communities of that era. It has been argued well the place and location of the imperial affairs in the Lukan world. Sam Christopher could handle the linguistic dimensions of the text in a deeper manner and that sounds the strength of the book.

In addition to this, the author could compare the King title with other gospels in order to bring out the distinctiveness in Lukan studies. I am indeed delighted to recognize the use of latest and current Lukan scholarship by the author in presenting his arguments.

In order to update its implications in our context, Sam Christopher could present many directive comments for discussion. I am sure this book will enable many researches to explore further to understand the hidden dimensions of the early church and her comprehension of the title King of Jesus Christ.

Rev. Dr. C. I. David Joy
Professor, New Testament
UTC, Bengaluru.

List of Abbreviations

1) English Translations of the Bible

NAB	New American Bible
NRSV	New Revised Standard Version
RSV	Revised Standard Version

2) General Abbreviations

Antt	The Antiquities of the Jews
ATLAS	ATLA Serial
BCE	Before Christian/Common Era
BJ	Benjamin
CE	Christian/Common Era
cf.	compare (confer)
ed.	editor/edition/edited
et al.	and others
f.	the following verse
ff.	the following verses
Ibid	same source/same work as cited in the immediately preceding foot note

i.e.,	that is to say
Jub	Book of Jubilees
LXX	Septuagint
Macc	Maccabees
Ms, Mss.	Manuscript/ Manuscripts
Pss. Sol.	Psalms of Solomon
passim	here and there (at various places in the same work)
Syr.sin	Sinaitic Syriac version
T. Benj.	Testament of Benjamin
tr.	translated
v.	verse
vs.	versus/against
vv.	verses
vol.	volume

Qumran Scrolls

CD	Damascus Document
QH	The Thanksgiving Hymns
QM	The War Rule
QS	The Community Rule
QS[b]	Blessings

3) Books of the Bible

Gen	Genesis
Ex	Exodus
Num	Numbers

Deut	Deuteronomy
Jos	Joshua
Judg	Judges
Sam	Samuel
Kgs	Kings
Chr	Chronicles
Ps	Psalms
Isa	Isaiah
Jer	Jeremiah
Ezek	Ezekiel
Dan	Daniel
Hos	Hosea
Ob	Obadiah
Mic	Micah
Zeph	Zephaniah
Hagg	Haggai
Zech	Zechariah
Mal	Malachi
Mt	Matthew
Mk	Mark
Lk	Luke
Jn	John
Col	Colossians
Tim	Timothy
Phlm	Philemon

Introduction

L uke, the author of the third Gospel is recognized as a historian, a theologian, and an artist primarily because of his literary skill in composing the Gospel. As with Luke, the Gospels in general center around the saving work of Jesus. The form critics agree that the Gospels contain the proclamation of the saving events of Jesus in view of each evangelist's own theological emphasis. In view of that, Lukan Christology and theology can be seen from the way by which Luke's Gospel is structured and composed out of his use of traditional materials in accordance with his theological purpose.

Concerning the source materials used for Lukan composition, scholars by and large differ in their views: J. J. Griesbach says that Luke used Matthew as his source, which was later advocated by W. R. Farmer. There is also another view that Luke followed John. But, generally it is accepted that Luke used Mark along with Q and L, despite the speculations of B. H. Streeter, followed by Vincent Taylor, F. C. Grant and others that Luke is the first written Gospel. However, in this book, the generally accepted view that Luke added Q and L to the Markan frame work is considered. On the basis of Mark, Q, and L as the sources of Lukan composition of the Gospel, this research intends to explore and investigate the motif of Jesus' Kingship and attempts to reconstruct the Christology of Luke, which is woven around the title, 'King.'

Kingship of Jesus has been problematic as a theme and idea, and a notion in Luke as scholars differ on that. For example, M. Dibelius, A. Nolan, J. R. Donahue, O. C. Edwards, C. H. Talbert, M. A. Powell, J. B. Green, G. Theissen et al. view the crucified Jesus in Luke's Gospel as a Martyr. U. Wilckens, H. Conzelmann, E. Käsemann, C. H. Dodd, H. Marshall, R. Kereszty, W. R. Farmer, S. M. Heim et al. view him as a Saviour.   H. Flender, J. Neyrey, Powell, S. R. Garrett et al. view him as a New Adam who has overcome temptations. J. A. Fitzmyer, V. Taylor, J. B. Green, J. Kurichianil et al. view his death as an act of obedience to the will of God and a divine plan. And, by and large, almost all the New Testament scholars focus on Jesus as per the Christological titles given in Luke's Gospel as: Son of God, Son of Man, Son of David, Christ the Messiah, Innocent One, and so on. But they have not given any serious attention to the title King, which was accorded to Jesus at the time of his death, as Luke portrays in his Gospel, along with the nuances of political and non-political Kingship.

Even though, a few scholars like N. A. Dhal, F. J. Matera and Fitzmyer recount the Kingship of Jesus, the Lukan motif of Jesus' Kingship is not yet explored fully: Dhal sees the prominence of the Kingly aspect in Jesus' death recorded in the Gospels of both Mark and John than in the Gospels of both Luke and Matthew; Matera considers the Kingship of Jesus only in relation to the Passion Narrative of Mark; and, although Fitzmyer speaks of Luke, according to him, the Lukan account of Kingship emerges only in the Passion narrative and it has no real significance in the rest of the Gospel except for one reference in 1:33, in the Infancy Narrative. But it is observed that the Kingly character of Jesus becomes not only more prominent in the Passion Narrative of Luke's Gospel, but also, this royal motif pervades the entire stream of Lukan Christology throughout the Gospel along with its political overtone than the other Gospels.

Further this study explicates the compositional skill of the author Luke and the Christological significance of the Gospel, which connotes the people-centeredness of Jesus' Kingship, i.e., a reversal of power and authority, a reordering of a privileged position etc. along with the concern: how did Jesus' socio-economic and political attitude knock down the dominant values of imperial oppression and empower the alienated vulnerable Lukan community. It may be distinguished that the historically and culturally conditioned Lukan Christology seems to have its own specific significance for the people-centered Kingship of Jesus in challenging the liberation theology that deals with an option of life for all humankind and all of nature along with the rebuilding of hope for the poor, the outcast, as victims of oppression, and ethnic, racial and gender discrimination.

On the other hand, the title 'King' given to Jesus was misunderstood and misused down the ages. Even the title 'Christ' was misunderstood as the dominant ruler such as King, conqueror, or even colonizer instead of its sacrificial overtones. Also, there was an abuse of Jesus' title 'King' by the leaders of the church to exhibit its power in spite of the humble image of Christ which is weak in power. However, Lukan Jesus carries neither glory nor respect, rather a mark of mockery and humiliation and dishonor as the King of the Jews as Liberator and Savior, a King who subverts the rule of Caesar.

Although the Acts of the Apostles is also from the same author and Luke has further developed the theme of Kingship in Acts in the ongoing mission and life of the early church, this research is limited to Luke's Gospel that records of the earthly ministry of Jesus. This study uses the method of Redaction criticism to seek the author's message and purpose in Luke's Gospel. The method of Composition criticism stance views the Gospel as a whole, enabling a transition from the editorial redaction to thematic pursuit of the Gospel which paves the way for a holistic interpretation of this Gospel by examining the motif of the Kingship of Jesus, introduced in Luke's theology of Jesus' death that runs throughout the Gospel. In order to seek the composition of Luke further, Source Criticism, which helps to identify the Lukan sources, will be employed in this book.

In addition to these, Sociological criticism will be used to elicit the geographical, sociological or even ideal or typical contexts in which the evangelist places the source materials to construct his theology.

Sociological criticism unlike the social scientific method, social historical method is used to analyze the social matrix of early Christianity. This is employed as it may help to elicit the meaning of Jesus' death in terms of Kingship as it was understood by the evangelist not only as the fulfillment of scriptural prophecies but also, from the living experiences of early Christianity. Along with all, an exegetical study of relevant texts will be carried out in Chapters two to four. Moreover, the method of *anumana* of Saiva Siddantha, which means inference, confirming the fact by assumption from one's previous experience will also be used.

As the first step of this investigation, in the First Chapter, a survey of the use of the title, βασιλεύς in various social, historical, political, and biblical milieu will be dealt briefly in order to explain its meaning as Luke has used it in the context of Jesus' triumphal entry as well in the Passion Narrative. Besides, the socio-political reality of the first century Palestine, especially during Jesus' and Luke's time and, the community's need for anticipating the Christocentric, Messianic King, out of the long entrenched tension between theocracy and human Kingship, the Saviour who brings peace to the nation will be explored.

In the Second Chapter, the Kingship motif of Luke will be explored in the composition of the Infancy Narrative, which is considered as the introduction to the entire Gospel. Along with the study of the special material and his artistic composition, the way by which Luke introduces Jesus as the messianic, anticipated King through the historic present which signifies imperialism; the scene of Jesus' birth against the backdrop of emperor Augustus; the step parallelism connecting both John and Jesus; with reference to the Davidic descent; the usages of courtly languages; the political overtones of power and the reordering of position through the canticles; and the portrayal of Jesus at the age of twelve in the temple, will be dealt with.

In the Third Chapter, the Kingship Motif of Luke in the Life and Teachings of Jesus is explored through the Lukan composition along with the triple tradition sources, Q and L materials. His skill in establishing the Kingship motif through the peculiar geographical structure of Jesus' journey from Galilee to Jerusalem through Samaria; the socio-political context in the backdrop of his baptism; temptation; Nazareth manifesto; his miracles; table fellowships with tax collectors and sinners; his purpose of choosing the disciples; the theme of conflicts; the event of transfiguration; reason for rejection at Samaria; teachings along with parables including his own L parables; concept of the Kingdom of God; triumphal entry; Temple and it cleansing; the issue of paying taxes to Caesar; and, the desolating sacrilege with nationalistic sense, will be dealt with in order to find the oppressive structure as well as the imperial theology against the Jewish nation.

In the Fourth Chapter, the Kingship motif is further explored in the Passion and Resurrection Narratives, which seem to be the culmination of Lukan portrayal of Jesus' Kingship. It will be dealt in two sections: Passion Narrative and the Resurrection Narrative as, how Luke weaves the motif through indicating Rome as Satan; Jesus' prayer at the Mount of Olives; tribulation as the power of darkness; Peter's denial which depicts a threat of Rome for survival; the accusations in the trial which imply the cause for his death either religious or political; the events of crucifixion; the mockeries which reveal his Kingship; his death; his burial; resurrection; commissioning of the disciples; and, ascension.

In the Fifth Chapter, along with the discovered Kingship motif in the composition of Luke's Gospel, Lukan Christology of Jesus' Kingship will be reconstructed, redefined, rearticulated and reassessed as People-centered, Messianic, Alternative, Crucified, and, Victorious King who is a paradigm for liberation which is relevant not only to our nation India but also to everyone in the entire universe.

Chapter - 1

Anticipation of the King in the Socio-Political World of Luke

A brief survey of the use of the title, 'King' in various social, historical, political and biblical milieu becomes essential at the first stage of investigation. The title, King, accredited to Jesus towards the end of his life in Luke's Gospel, invites us further to explore the socio-political world of Luke to find out its context and the anticipation of the community for a King. In other words, the *Sitz im leben*, the life-setting of Luke's Gospel, i.e., the social matrix the early Christianity in which the text had emerged, will be of immense help in understanding the eagerness of the society to have a King to redeem them from the state of oppression and the existing social unrest,[1] which is assumed as the hub in the portrayal of Jesus' Kingship by the author.

In order to explore the fact of anticipation of the King, in this chapter, an attempt is made under four heads, namely:

1) Kingship of Jesus: A Messianic Hope, in which, the evolution of the concept of Kingship from various cultural, social, political milieu will be analyzed including the idea of Kingly Messianism in the Old Testament; 2) socio-political world of Luke, in which, the socio-economic, ecological, political, and cultural factors that created the eagerness amidst the people to have an alternative King will be viewed;

3) Q and the socio-political world of early Christianity, in which, how the Q passages exhibit the context of early Christianity will be seen; and, 4) Lukan special material and the socio-cultural and political factors.

Kingship of Jesus: A Messianic Hope

When Luke seems to portray the image of Jesus' Kingship in his Gospel, it gives the clue that the Kingly idea was prevalent among the Lukan community. It may not have been a sudden surfacing, but the idea of a King and Messianic hope had been prevalent probably then. This status of Kingship perhaps had acquired different connotations and had evolved out of the tension between theocracy[2] and human Kingship, as a Messianic hope in various cultural, social, and political contexts of the Old Testament times, later in the Intertestamental period and then recognized in Jesus during the New Testament period. This evolutionary idea of Messianic Kingship or the Christocentric understanding of Kingship raises the questions, such as: What was the image of a King in the Old Testament times? What was the image of the Messiah portrayed in the Old Testament? Whether the Messianic ideology and the royal ideology of the Old Testament interrelated? Was the Kingly aspect present in Intertestamental Literature? How did Luke understand early Messianism and portray the Messiahship of Jesus in juxtaposition to secular Kings? Was it an alternative model of political Kingship against the Kings of the world? While the secular Kings rule the nation, what was the need to expect a messianic King to be an alternative in the socio-political world of Luke? etc. So, in order to have a glimpse of these issues before dealing with the socio-political world of Luke and its anticipation of a King, we need to look at the concept of a King and its evolution in the past through the idea of Kingly-Messianism and its application to Jesus by the Lukan community.

Connotation of the Noun 'King'

In secular Greek, βασιλεύς denotes royal sovereignty, royal dignity, royal office or monarchy,[3] and lingually means a King or chief who is a lawful ruler of the people,[4] a head of a state, a sovereign, a monarch and by extension a representative of a group.[5] But, in Hellenism as well as Asian countries,[6] it denotes divine Kingship, i.e., God-King, who is above human and a shepherd, who sustains the life of the subjects as a benefactor by his own will without a particular geographical stretch and law.[7] The connotation of a King, in Judg. 9:2f refers to one man who rules over a specific group as understood and expected by the Hebrews. According to Josephus, "King was not defective in any virtue, but was religious towards God, and righteous towards men, and careful of the good of the city."[8] Besides, a King takes care of the temple, builds great towers and protects his people from his enemies so that they could live happily.[9] However, since late Bronze Age, the Hebrew term, מֶלֶךְ with a broad and comprehensive semantic horizon, refers to diverse monarchical forms of rule from municipal Kingship to national Kingship and vast empires, and acquired concrete meaning in particular contexts.[10]

In the New Testament, usually, βασιλεύς is used both in secular as well as religious sense. Among the 115 occasions, although the secular sense[11] predominates in many places, in a few occurrences God and even Christians are referred to. However, it is significant to note that within the 38 references to Jesus,[12] which are both religious and political, 26 are in the Passion Narratives of the Gospels and seem to have political nuances.[13] Besides, in relation to West Asian[14] and other cultures, the twentieth century research on Kingship has distinguished it as divine and sacral.[15]

Concept of King in West Asian Civilization

In Egypt, the King was understood as the one who appears on his throne as the ruler who brings order in the land, and the representative, indeed an incarnation of the deity known as son of god. As a caretaker of his people, he was considered as a shepherd and greeted as a deliverer with rich harvests, good fortune, and joy throughout the land, who had the responsibility of establishing and maintaining the temples.[16] In Mesopotamia, prior to the origin of Israelite royal ideology, Kingship was understood as a divine institution. Akkadian royal inscriptions note the King as god's special creature albeit he is given birth through his mother's womb.[17] In Babylon as well in Assyria, the King was considered as a son of a god, who is god's messenger and rules with divine authority.[18] In ancient Sumer, the King was considered as a descendant from heaven, who is wise, just, hater of the wicked and one who maintains law and order; protector of the destitute, and the shepherd who is responsible for the maintenance of the cult and temples.

In Babylonian New Year Festival, every year it was celebrated that the King ought to atone either by him or by a substitute in order to renew his Kingship.[19] Afro-Asiatic inscriptions adduce the image of a King as the one who is installed by gods to be responsible for the construction of temples and be just. An ideal king is distinguished by his performance of justice.[20] The pseudoprophecies of Egypt also provide evidence to the characteristics of an ideal King. For instance, the prophecy of Neferti (Nefer-Rohu) reads:

> Then a King will come from the South,
>
> Ameny, the justified, by name,
>
> Son of a woman of Ta-Seti, child of Upper Egypt...
>
> Rejoice, O people of his time,
>
> The son of man will make his name for all eternity!
>
> The evil-minded, the treason-plotters,
>
> They suppress their speech in fear of him;
>
> Asiatics will fall to his flame,
>
> Rebels to his wrath, traitors to his might,
>
> As the serpent on his brow subdues the rebels for him...
>
> Then Order will return to its seat,
>
> While Chaos is driven away,
>
> Rejoice he who may behold, he who may attend the King![21]

In addition to these concepts of an ideal King which were prevailed in the West Asian civilization that a King is a divine being, a shepherd, and who cares for the people, in the history of the people of Israel the idea of Kingship had evolved out of the tension between theocracy and human Kingship as it is seen in the Old Testament.

Concept of King in the Old Testament: Theocracy vs. Human Kingship

In the Old Testament, the term מֶלֶךְ is used in both religious as well as in political sense: religiously, Yahweh is referred to as the King[22] and politically, at the outset of the monarchy in Israel, Saul and then, his successors are addressed as Kings.[23] But, the human King is considered as Yahweh's anointed one and his functions are accounted in accordance with the will of Yahweh to deliver Israel.[24] It is clearly seen in 1 Samuel chapters 8 & 12, cf. Deut. 17:14f, that when the people of Israel wanted to have a human King instead of theocracy, the supremacy of God is well established in appointing the King with his consent albeit Yahweh says that he was rejected by the Israelites.[25]

In the farewell address of Samuel, recorded in 12:6ff, he furnishes that Yahweh was with the Israelites from the time of their ancestors and brought forth them from Egypt and rescued them from their enemies. But at last, when the king of Nahash of the Ammonites came against them they had opted for a human King by rejecting God's Kingship. But in 12:13-15, he portrays the supremacy of God saying,

> See, here is the King whom you have chosen, for whom you have asked; see, the Lord has set a King over you. If you will fear the Lord and serve him and heed his voice and not rebel against the commandment of the Lord, and if both you and the King who reigns over you will follow the Lord your God, it will be well; but if you will not heed the voice of the Lord, but rebel against the commandment of the Lord, then the hand of the Lord will be against you and your King.

The supremacy of the rule of Yahweh is not only reveled during the appointment of King Saul, but also prevalent throughout the Old Testament. For instance, the Royal Psalms: Ps. 95:3 says that Yahweh is the great God and the great King above all gods; and, 96:10-13 and 97:1-6 portray him as the King of the world and the judge of the nations. J. J. M. Roberts says about the supremacy of Yahweh and human Kinship as,

> 1) Yahweh is the great King...not only over Israel but over all the nations and their gods; 2) Yahweh has chosen the Davidic house as his human agents for the divine rule and has confirmed that choice with an eternal covenant; and 3) Yahweh has chosen Zion as his royal city, as the earthly dais of his universal rule.[26]

Concerning the ideology of theocracy in the Old Testament it may be identified from the pre-exilic period albeit it is disputed as it was shaped later. In a few pre-exilic passages like Ex.15; Pss. 24, 29 & Isa. 6, the Kingship of Yahweh ideology is presented in connection to the Zion tradition. According to Von Rad, Yahweh is understood as King of Israel in the pre-exilic period; and, King of the world in the exilic and post-exilic period.[27] Whereas, Wellhausen says that the ideology of the Kingship of Yahweh was a later theological concept and may be dated from the post-exilic cult of Jerusalem during the priestly aristocracy legitimatized the position of the High Priest as the leader of Judah, as it is echoed in 1 Sam. 7-12.[28] According to prophet Jeremiah 8:19, the people's cry for help reveals this Zion ideology: "Is the Lord not in Zion? Is her King not in her?" In their distress, people cried for the help of Yahweh, the supreme ruler even though they had a human King. Isaiah also anticipates a renewed Zion along with an omnipotent as well as a just King.[29] The ideology of the supremacy of Yahweh is predominant in Deutro-Isaiah.[30] This Zion tradition also seems to have influenced the evolution of the royal ideology in the prophetic texts, concerning the supremacy of Yahweh: Jer. 3:17; 10:7, 10; 17:12; 51:57; Ob. 21; Mic. 2:13; 4:7; Zeph. 3:15 & Mal. 1:14. It might be Deutro-Isaiah's accommodation of Deuteronomistic historian's vision[31] and the theocratic ideology of the Chronicler, i.e., the notion of the throne of God and the house of David.[32] Further, it indicates the longing of the Israelites for Yahweh, the great King's providence in their affliction *ipso facto* the existence of the Royal ideology of Davidic monarchy from the pre-exilic period.

Messianic King: Magna Charta of the Davidic Monarchy

The term הַמָּשִׁיחַ appears 38 times in the Old Testament, mostly in connection with the Israelite royal ideology where the King is called, the Anointed one of Yahweh.[33] Quite a number of times, it is used to denote the promised King in Davidic lineage. Concerning the promise of Davidic rule, there are two ideologies of Deuteronomistic history prevailed in ancient Israel: 1) unconditional promise of eternal dynasty of David portrayed in 2 Sam. 7 and echoed in Pss. 2, 89 & 110; and, 2) conditional promise of the eternal dynasty portrayed in 1 Kgs. 2:2-4; 8:25 & 9:4-6 and echoed in Ps.132:11-12; Isa. 9:6f; Jer. 17:19-27 & 22:1-5.[34] However, the origin of the messianic idea is generally traced from 2 Sam. 7:11-16, the prophecy of Nathan, which states the promise of God in restoring Davidic rule in Israel.

It may be said that the Messianic idea in Israel originated within Judah out of the Magna Charta of the Davidic monarchy, developed in the prophets of the Southern Kingdom and continued in the post-exilic Jewish community along with the expectation of the Davidic Messiah who would redeem them from their misery.[35] During this period, while the prophetic criticisms seem to be antimonarchic, they exhibit the anticipation of a King yet to come: Isa. 7, 9 & 11, the establishment of Davidic Kingdom in future; Jer. 22:15; cf.21:11-14, future King against Zedekiah; and, in Judah, after Zerubbabel, a future King for the restoration of David's dynasty. It envisages the promise of an eternal dynasty, a New David and a New Exodus. The prophecies in Jer. 23:5-8; 30:8-11; 33:14-26; Ezek. 17:22-24; 34:23-24; 37:24-25 37; and, Hos. 3:5 envisage the expectations of the New David to the re-establishment of Israel, against Josiah's reign. In Isa. 40-55, the messianic exodus is focused upon both Cyrus and the loyal servant.[36] This messianic reading might have occurred in the exilic and postexilic period due to their oppressive state.

Brown brings forth the development of the royal Messianism in three stages:[37] 1) before 8th century BCE: for instance, the Royal Psalms, in particular, 2, 72 & 110 were composed and recited in relation to Davidic King on the occasion of the coronation to portray the King as God's representative, priest-King and saviour; 2) from 8th century BCE to the Babylonian Exile: during that period, the restoration of David's dynasty was expected against the Assyrian threat along with the messianic hope as envisaged in the prophecies of Isaiah, Micah, Jeremiah, Ezekiel and Zechariah;[38] and 3) from Exile to New Testament times: then onwards the expectation began to move toward an indefinite future.

Swanson, Brown and others observations of the existence of the Messianic King ideology from the time of exile indicates that in the state of utter hopelessness, the Israelites hoped for the restoration of Davidic dynasty. It may be seen in Ezek. 34 concerning the idea of Yahweh as shepherd and New David, and in Isa. 40-55 about the message of hope and the description of the servant figure in relation to the Messianic King.

The hope of restoring the Davidic dynasty, according to C. Guignebert, is based upon two histories: 1) based on the glories of Israel during the rule of King David, who was the unifier of nations; and 2) related to the brilliant triumph of Maccabaean revolt against the Seleucid monarchs.[39] It may be understood that as an impact of past histories and amidst the anguishes, in the long run, as an eschatological hope, the concept of Kingly Messianism seems to have developed along with both political and religious ideas. However, it is essential to see whether there is any perception of the Messianic King in the documents that preceded and surrounded the New Testament during the Intertestamental Period such as, Qumran documents and other so-called pseudepigraphal texts.

Messianic King in the Intertestamental Literature

The discoveries of the Dead Sea Scrolls and manuscripts, which are deuterocanonical and pseudepigraphal, considered as Jewish and pre-Christian, help us to understand the prevailed concept of the Messianic King between the periods[40] of both the Old and the New Testament. It must be noted that there is no integrated concept of Messianic King in the early Jewish Pseudepigraphal writings. But, at the same time, it cannot be brushed aside that there is no Messianic idea in those writings; because, not only there are different usages and meanings of the title Messiah but also there are interweaving ideas of Messianic King which developed later.

The expressions like: the anointed of the Lord, his anointed, and my anointed in the Old Testament are considered as the general references to the kingly offices with prophetic and priestly dimensions, or sometimes to a particular king like Cyrus and Zerubbabel who were anticipated to rescue the nation from anguishes. Even though the term Messiah is not used in a technical sense to refer to an eschatological saviour or a redeemer, the subsequent crisis in the history of Israel such as the exile, and persecutions gave impetus to the Messianic idea. Subsequently, during the time between the two Testaments, known as the intertestamental period, the oppression of Antiochus and Rome caused Judaism, Christianity and the Essenes seem to develop the Messianic ideas taken over from the Old Testament. It may be evidenced from Levey's depiction that one of the Eighteen Benedictions of the daily liturgy of Jews, dated to the 3rd century B.C.E., includes a prayer for the advent of the Messiah.[41] So, it is vivid that the in the intertestamental period the concept of Messianic expectation prevailed as a legacy from the Old Testament.

Further, the concept of Messiah in the apocalyptic literature during the intertestamental period seems to be the amalgamation of the two eschatologies: the eschatological beliefs of Jewish religious thought and of the dualistic concept of Persia regarding the world of this age and the age to come. It leads to the concepts of the Messiah of expected King of the immediate future and the eschatological King. D. S. Russell points out Movinckal's observation that the expected Messiah of this-worldly, national and political was developed later predominantly transcendental, eternal and universal and culminated in the usage of different titles, Messiah and Son of Man though it is originally distinct, yet related concept.[42] So, it is agreeable that the Old Testament concept of Messiah as the leader of the coming kingdom persists in the intertestamental literature in its developed form.

However, it is to be noted that while considerable number or writings during this period imply the messianic hope, but, the title of the Messiah is not mentioned. Particularly, Tobit, the Wisdom of Solomon, Judith, Ben Sira, Jubilees, I Enoch 1-36 and 91-104, the Assumption of Moses, 1 Baruch and 2 Enoch.[43] On the other hand, in the parables of I Enoch the titles of Messiah get significance.

Messianic King in the Parables of Enoch

1 Enoch is known as the book of parables because 37-71 are considered as a collection of three parables.[44] In these parables, the titles: Chosen One, the Son of Man, the Righteous One, and the Anointed one are used. Son of Man is identified as the Chosen one, who is the servant of Yahweh. In 48:10 it is acknowledged as the Anointed One and portrayed with futuristic function:

> And on the day of their affliction there shall be rest on the earth,
>
> And before them they shall fall and not rise again:
>
> And there shall be no one to take them with his hands and raise them:
>
> For they have denied the Lord of Spirits and His anointed.
>
> The name of the Lord of Spirits be blessed,"[45]

It speaks of the salvation of the righteous. In short, it is that the kings will be punished by the Chosen One. 61:6ff depicts the Chosen One's enthronement as an eschatological judge. The kings and the powerful were considered as evil because of their experience of colonialism and imperialism. The colonial experience is explained by R. M. Victor as it was not changing from ancient days until today. In all ages, subjugation, oppression and exploitation are common in their attitudes as well in the cultures.[46]

Nevertheless, while considering these four titles used in the parables which are not in other parts of Enoch: Astronomical, Watchers, Visions, and the Epistle of Enoch; as well as in the early Enochic materials: the Genesis of Apocryphon, Jubilees, Book of Giants, and 2 Enoch,[47] raise an issue that whether they refer to four persons or only one. According to Y. Collins, the four terms of messianic figure used in these parables refer to the same figure.[48] S. Chiala sees common elements between the Son of Man portrayed in Dan. 7 and in the parables of Enoch. In Enoch, it is portrayed that the Son of Man strips the kings from power, whereas, in Daniel, the power is conferred upon the one who is like a son of man.[49] However, the power is entrusted on the Son of Man. 46:4f reads,

> And this Son of Man whom you have seen will rouse the kings and the powerful from their resting-places, and the strong from their thrones, and will loose the reins of the strong, and will break the teeth of the sinners. And he will cast down the kings from their thrones and from their kingdoms, for they do not exalt him, and do not praise him, and do not humbly acknowledge whence (their) kingdom was given to them.[50]

Besides, in some quarters the traditional idea of the Jewish Messiah prevailed and in other quarters it is transformed into Son of Man and probably denotes two separate strands of eschatological expectation and two distinct accents of messianic hope.[51] It shows that the concept of the Son of Man and the concept of Messiah are different in their origins. H. H. Rowley points out that there is no evidence of the identification of the Son of Man with the Messiah until the time of Jesus and it is to be found in Jesus' use of titles in associating them to himself in order to avoid the title Messiah until he confessed it during the trial. He preferred to use the title, Son of Man along with the concept of suffering servant.[52] However, it could be noted in the parables of Enoch that even before the time of Jesus, the title Son of Man is related to the Messiah's work as we have seen in 48:10.

The title Servant is used in 2 Esdras and in 2 Baruch to describe the Messiah from the seed of David. In 2 Esd. 7:29, the Messiah is described by God as 'my servant' and his death at the close of the interim kingdom and in 7:30ff, his resurrection follows and will continue his work as God's servant. But, Russell argues that in no sense it is associated with the Suffering Servant of the Lord.[53] Russell's argument cannot be pleasing, because in Targum of Isa. 53, the suffering servant is identified with the Messiah. Targum of Is 53: 13 reads, "Behold,

My Servant the Messiah shall prosper; he shall be exalted and great and very powerful."[54] 53:2 reads, "The Righteous One shall grow up before Him..."[55] It gives the picture of the suffering Servant as the national and political figure of the Davidic Messiah in the Old Testament who is later understood and read as the Servant Messiah by the Jewish people.

Messianic King in Pseudepigraphical Writings

The author of the Psalms of Solomon dated late in the first century BCE expected the arrival of the Messiah to purge Jerusalem[56] as a Zadokite priest or a Davidic King.[57] The Magna Charta of Davidic Kingship here indicates the Messianic rule and theocracy. It may also be understood that the psalmist of Solomon is concerned with the actions of the Anointed One and his dependence upon God.[58] It can be seen in 17:21ff,

> Behold, O Lord, and raise up unto them their King, the son of David,
>
> At the time in which Thou seest, O God, that he may reign over Israel
>
> Thy servant.
>
> And gird him with strength, that he may shatter unrighteous rulers,
>
> And that he may purge Jerusalem from nations that trample (her)
>
> down to destruction.[59]

The Apocalyptic Pseudepigrapha, Book III of the Sibylline Oracles speaks of two Messiahs namely, the Messiah of the line of Levi, and a subsidiary Messiah of the line of Judah. This thought might have developed during the 2nd century BCE along with the idea of priestly origin of the Levitical Messiah as opposed to the priest-Kings of the Hasmonaean dynasty.[60] It might have been a dual expectation in terms of Levi and Judah motif and seems to be a future ideal priesthood and an ideal kingship.[61] It is to be noticed that *the Testament of Levi* from the *Testament of the Twelve Patriarchs* describes the priestly Messiah.18:2, thus:

> And then the Lord will raise up a new priest
>
> to whom all the words of the Lord will be revealed.
>
> He shall effect the judgment of truth over the earth for many days.[62]

2 Baruch, composed from earlier Jewish traditions also gives evidence to the anticipation of the messianic King: 29:3 speaks of the passive role of the Messiah as he is revealed; 30:1 speaks of the eschatological hope of the Messiah; and 40:1 speaks of Messiah's active part in the annihilation of God's enemies and foresees the revelation of the Messiah, his appearance as a militant warrior, and the recovery of the righteous from the last evil leader. J. H. Charles explains it as a final conflict between the Anointed One with the last ruler.[63] 70:9 states that the one who escapes the last wars and disasters will be delivered into the hands of God's Servant, Messiah; 72:2f and 73:1 says about the Messianic rule with peace. According to Klijn and Bogaert, 72:2f and 73:1 of 2 Baruch are inconsistent with one another but the author of Baruch tries to say that the time of the Anointed One belongs to the world of corruption and by his rule he changes it.[64] In general, 2 Baruch deals with the messianic hope in terms of annihilating the evil kings and evil doers through the Servant King Messiah.

2 Esdras 7, 11:37-12:34, 13:3-14:9 discuss the functions of the future Messiah. In 7:26-30, 'my son the Messiah' is mentioned.[65] 12:31-34 speaks of the absolute use of the Anointed one along with the emphasis of judgment, rule and heavenly origin. Although T. F. Glasson points out the inconsistency in 2 Esdras concerning the rule of Messianic King and M. De Jonge, says that it might be the impact of messianic age description, influenced by Daniel,[66] it is vivid that the Pseudepigraphical writings underline the idea of Messiah and Messianic rule.

Messianic King in Qumran Scrolls

In the battle between 'the sons of darkness' and 'the sons of light,' at Qumran, Messiah was expected to deliver the sons of light.[67] Leivestad argues that the Qumran community expected a Messiah, and a Messianic King. But, de Jonge disagrees with it saying that the Messiah in Qumran documents is not clearly Davidic. On the other hand, Leivestad argues that in several documents at Qumran there is an expectation of a Davidic Messiah. For instance, 1QSa and

CD vii.20 ought to be noted.[68] Knib points out that there a priestly Messiah is given importance than the Davidic Messiah.[69] According to M. de Jonge, the Qumran community awaited the coming of a true priest and a true king and that some scrolls state of a prophet.[70] However, it cannot be plainly said that the Davidic line is totally absent in the Qumran documents.

In Qumran scrolls, references to Yahweh's supremacy had prevailed: 4Q 510:1; 4Q 511:52-59 III 4 & 4Q Flor 1:3, the temple scroll speaks of God as: the King of glory; 1QH 10:8, the ruler of all creatures; 5Q 10:3, great King; 4QM 1:13 & 1QM 14:16, King of Kings; and, 1QM 12:14 & 19:6, Kings of the nations. As per 1QS 9:11-12, the Messiah was considered as a political King as well a priest King. 4Q 285 identifies Messiah as "the Branch of David" and "the Prince of the Congregation." The concept of a political Messiah existed after the Hasmoneans adopted the title, King. In Qumran documents, the function of the expected King is found to be identical with the high priest along with the idea of 'the Messiah of Aaron.'[71] The expected priestly leader is called "the anointed of Aaron" in 1QS 9:11. At the side of this, the ideal priest stands as "the anointed of Israel, the Davidic Messiah. Later there seems to have been a fusion between the coming priest and the Davidic anointed one into one messianic figure in which the priestly features tend to dominate."[72] By and large, the ideology of a priest-King was rooted deeply in the eschatological thought of the Qumran community along with the concept of the Messiah who is the Davidic King.

On the whole, the Messianic idea of the Old Testament is developed during the intertestamental period in the struggles and survival of the community. The titles, Anointed One, Messiah, Servant, Chosen One, Son of Man, and the Righteous One are used in line with the Magna Charta of the Davidic Kingship. Mostly all the titles refer to the expected eschatological King. Particularly, the title Son of Man is related to Messiah who is a Servant King. In other words, it may be said that the ideology of a future Kingly Messiahship either by the impact of West Asian civilization or by the background of the Old Testament ideology of theocracy against the failure of human Kingship, the community lived during the intertestamental period developed it in the expectation of the Messianic King as an eschatological hope of Davidic rule as it prevails in the intertestamental literature. Later, during the New Testament times, the Christians might have recognized it in the person and work of Jesus as the fulfillment.

Messianic King: Christocentric Understanding

Concerning the Christocentric understanding of the Messianic King in the New Testament, N. Walter argues that while looking at the Intertestamental literature one tends to connect Jewish Messianism with Christology, whereas, in early Judaism 'the things to come' is the important concept than the one who is to come.[73] It may be true, but Jewish Messianism's eschatological hope and the titles mentioned in it, such as: Anointed One, the Messianic King, etc., are related to the Magna Charta of Davidic Kingship. The terms: Messiah and Messianic in the Old Testament and the Intertestamental literature seems to be sensible to the New Testament Christocentric understanding, only when they are understood as eschatological expressions. Becker says, Old Testament references are the "pedestal of the Messianic expectation."[74] Klausner says that the Messianic expectation can be understood as "the prophetic hope for the end of this age, in which there will be political freedom, moral perfection, and earthly bliss for the people of Israel in their own land, and also for the entire human race."[75] In general, the Messianic prophecies of the Old Testament and Intertestamental literature are understood that they have fulfilled in the life of Jesus as recorded in the Gospels in the New Testament albeit they are not viewed as messianic until the last two centuries BCE.

The Old Testament texts which deal with the Anointed one of Yahweh are viewed as Christocentric passages in the New Testament time seem to be an anachronism. It raises the issue that whether the authors and audiences of the texts truly understood them as messianic. For instance, the passages: Gen. 3:15; 14:17-20; 49:8-12; Num. 24:17-

19; Deut. 18:18-19; Ps. 2 & 110; Dan. 9:24-26 etc. Becker rejects the view of the existence of an explicit expectation of a Saviour in the pre-monarchic period and defines Gen. 49:8-12 and Num. 24:15-24 as fictive prophecies of the Davidic monarchy.[76] E. F. Scott gives a secondary place to the Messianic idea of the Old Testament.[77] Levey exposes that in Targum, these passages are interpreted as Messianic.[78] However, it is evident that it had been referred to Jesus in the New Testament to portray him as the Messiah.

Particularly, Luke in his composition of the Gospel depicts the messianic activity of Jesus through the words and deeds of Jesus as the fulfillment of Old Testament prophecies. For instance in 4:18ff, the messianic programme of the historical Jesus is cited from Isa. 61:1ff; in 24:25ff, the disciples of Jesus understood the Christocentric interpretation of the risen Jesus about his death and glory; the forerunner, John the Baptist cites Isa 40:3ff, while announcing the messianic age in 3:3ff, etc. Besides, it is evident from the Gospels that the impact of the life and teachings of the historical Jesus made the early Christian community to identify Jesus as the Messianic King as foretold in the Old Testament prophecies.

It is discerned by Best that the Kingship of Jesus seems to be a momentous one in the "living experiences of the early Christianity."[79] Briggs says that till Jesus' birth no one could be discerned as the Messianic King; no one accepted the hardship of a suffering Messiah as he did; and advanced the throne as the reigning Messiah. All the phases of the Old Testament Messianic prophecies are realized in his unique personality, work and Kingdom values.[80] It is obvious in Lukan writing that after the resurrection of Jesus, the early church confirmed the Messianic Kingship of Jesus by the preaching of Peter, in Acts 2:36, "Therefore let the entire house of Israel know with certainty that God has made him both Lord and Messiah, this Jesus whom you crucified." Hence, it could be understood that the Lukan composition of the Gospel along with the motif of Jesus' messianic Kingship revolved around in history and the same was realized in his person and work during his life and confirmed after his resurrection by the Lukan community.

Along with this view we need to further explore the Lukan socio-political world in order to see whether the Lukan community expected a messianic King. In this instance, Moberly says that the Gospels portray the hopes and expectations of the Jews of Judaea that they were reluctant to the Roman power and longed for another powerful Davidic King to set free from the oppression of Rome.[81] To ascertain the anticipation of the Messianic King in Luke, we need to explore the socio-political reality of that time and its need in anticipating a messianic King.

Socio-Political World of Luke

C. W. Hedrick notes, "...when the synoptic evangelists selected material for their portraits of Jesus, each evangelist chose, so far as can be determined, from among undifferentiated traditions about Jesus in the context of a given confession, i.e., in accord with a given 'cover story' of faith; that is to say, in accord with a given community image of Jesus."[82] So, it is significant to identify the words of historical Jesus, the community's faith and how Luke redacted it in his Gospel. According to E. Boring, environmental criterion is one of the criteria for authenticating and assessing the Jesus tradition.[83] The *Sitz im leben* of the episodes may be helpful to identify that. Concerning this, Robbins says, "...'sapiential' sayings of Jesus suggest that many of the 'aphorisms' of Jesus not only require a concrete context in order to be understood, but apparently arose out of and addressed a situation of conflict as well."[84] Besides, the sociological studies[85] of the New Testament put forth the emphasis on the social contexts of the community in addition to the image of community's faith.

In exploring the socio-political matrix, in this research, Lukan authorship will be maintained for the third Gospel as accepted during the process of the canonization of the New Testament as well by many scholars.[86] Concerning the date of composition, it will be maintained as a post-war composition.[87] Concerning the place of composition, it may be accepted as outside Palestine,[88] and the Lukan community, may be the Pauline community, identified as Jesus' movement.[89] While acknowledging this as a post-war composition and from Pauline community, there is a possibility of contextual impact of Luke's time. In other words, certain elements of anachronism are apparent in the portrayal of Jesus by Luke in his Gospel. Bearing these in mind, let us try to explore the anticipation of a Messianic King in the socio-political world of Luke, which includes the context of Jesus' time, the time of Luke and the early church as: how did they view Jesus through his action? And, how did the situations naturally amplify the need of an alternative King in Lukan socio-political world? In order to investigate that, initially we need to have a glimpse of the Roman rule during the first century Palestine.

Roman Imperial Rule of Palestine during 1st Century CE

During the time of historical Jesus and Luke's time, Roman rule was imposed on Palestine. Even though the Jewish religion was allowed, religious leaders were controlled by Rome and its administrative structure. Both the client Kings and the religious leaders had their control over Palestine. It may be explained that the imperial rule of Rome represented the State through the Herodian client kings, the vassal of the Empire[90] and the authority of Jewish leaders in Jerusalem represented the religion. In this backdrop, Luke's Gospel, by the references to the Roman history as well the Palestinian history exposes its complex rule and gives the impression that it caused the community to anticipate an alternative King, the Messiah. So, in order to understand the *Sitz im Leben* of the Lukan text, the political scenario of Palestine's complex rule referred to in Luke's Gospel may be viewed in relation to *i)* Roman history and, *ii)* Palestinian history.

Roman History

Luke 1:5a, in its historic reference to, "in the days of King Herod of Judea," depicts the social as well as political context of Jesus' time especially, the power dynamics in Greco-Roman Palestine. Both the introduction of King Herod and Emperor Augustus in 1:5 & 2:1 indicate the Romans' direct control over Judea. Herod was a Jew by religion, but at the same time a Roman citizen and a Hellenist, than obeying Torah, who gave much importance to the Roman Emperor Augustus,[91] known as Octavian. He brought to an end the broken tranquility of Roman Empire from war and unified the Empire with his mighty arm, known as *Pax Romana / Pax Augusta*. Herod embraced it and was ruling Palestine during 37-4 BCE. He burned alive the protesters who destroyed the golden eagle placed over the gate of the Temple.[92] At the end of his days, he divided his Kingdom to his sons. Josephus in his *The Antiquities of the Jews 146* says that Herod the Great, a vassal king, bequeathed his kingdom to his youngest son Antipas.[93] Later, in his final codicil of will, divided his kingdom to his three sons and his sister Salome: Philip to be the tetrarch of Gaulonitis, Trachonitis and Paneas; Antipas to be the tetrarch of Galilee and Berea; Archelaus, Judea and Salome to be the tetrarch Jamnia, Ashdod and Phasaelis.[94] This created a big commotion among the sons of Herod. Both Archelaeus and Antipas went to Rome separately to get the Kingdom as it was written in the former and later wills. Riots and revolts had occurred in Palestine due to the problem of attaining the Kingship. But the Emperor, for the sake of keeping control of the whole nation, gave half of the Kingdom to Archelaus and, the rest of the two quarters to Philip and Antipas respectively, instead of giving the whole Palestine to one person.[95]

Meanwhile, the Roman Emperor, Augustus Caesar demanded a temple to be built in his honour as his divinity was widely accepted.[96] R. M. Victor says, "Colonialism and imperialism are not only confined to the political arena, but also cover every other aspect of life… culturally and emotionally."[97] It may be the emperor's vision of attaining the super power in the society and state by being worshipped. However, he was controlling the power over the Herodian client Kings and the census in 2:1f echoes the super power of Rome over Palestine in the context of Jesus' birth. At that time, the province of Syria was under the governorship of P. Sulpicius Quirinius.[98] Augustus was succeeded by Emperor Tiberius. During his period, CE 14-37, John started his ministry, as it is introduced by Luke in 3:1. His rule was more tyrannical than the other emperors of Rome.[99]

Palestinian history

In relation to Palestinian history, as it has been noted previously in the Roman history, Luke, in 1:5 refers to the jurisdiction of King Herod over Judea. According to Matthew 2:1 & 15, Jesus was born during this period. In 23:6-12, Luke refers to his son, Herod Antipas, the tetrarch of Galilee during 4 BCE-CE 39 to whom Jesus was sent by Pontius Pilate, the fifth governor of the Roman province of Judea. It indicates the direct rule of Rome over Judea through the governors amidst the rule of tetrarchs.[100] Roman tribute was imposed on Judea. The governor was in charge of looking after that. During the period of Pontius Pilate, CE 26-37, the Judeans lived a life of political-economic-religious slavery.[101] It may be evident from 23:2, that Jesus was accused before Pilate as one who perverted their nation forbidding paying taxes to the Emperor.

Considering the role of high priests in the politics of Roman imperial rule, in spite of representing the religion and worshipping God, they obliged to the human Emperor. The priestly governance of high priests is referred to in 3:2. Annas and Caiaphas hold their offices during CE 6-15 and CE 18-36 respectively. But, the pity is that the high priests became puppets in the hands of Roman and Herodian client Kings and did everything in accordance to the orders of Rome for the sake of their survival.[102] In this state of oppressiveness by both religious leaders and the Roman rule[103] through the client Kings, Luke seems to portray Jesus as a charismatic leader, who is an alternative King to the Roman Super Power.

Charismatic Leadership of Jesus

Concerning charismatic leadership, scholars consider a person who might be a reformer but one who saves the people from their oppression.

M. Weber who has analyzed the religious phenomenon of charismatic leadership in ancient Israel and Judaism proposes that a prophet is one who appears in a society when it is in crisis of leadership and experienced a threat to the future hopes and aspirations, and articulated their concerns to provide confidence in their crisis.[104] According to Mol, a charismatic leader is not the one who renews the tradition through revolution, but one who appeals to the objectives of the people and protests against a corrupt or hypocritical regime.[105] Malina says, "Jesus movement was a conservative revival, aspiring not to the creation of a new order but to the restoration of Israel that Jesus eventually committed himself."[106] Theissen views Jesus as the founder of a renewal movement; and, Horsley as a reformer who founded it to reform within itself as an alternative to the oppressive structures in anticipation of political revolution by God Himself.[107] As, Weber, Mol and Malina view, Lukan portrayal of Jesus seems to be the King who appeared during the time of the Jewish crisis and a committed one for the restoration of them through revolution. D. L. Migliore articulates in short that the understanding of Jesus Christ arose out of the socio-political world of Luke in the context of suffering and hope.[108] In all these views, it is obvious that the socio-political world of Luke illuminates the life of Jesus as a reformer as well a Charismatic leader who founded a new movement in utter hopelessness.

During Jesus' time, four types of charismatic leadership existed against the Roman rule: 1) an insurrectionist; 2) a miracle worker; 3) an itinerant teacher-philosopher; and, 4) a seer who might be an astrologer, diviner and prophet who had announced the impending destiny of Roman power.[109] In this historical context, not only the juxtaposition of the leadership of Jesus with all these qualities of a charismatic leader, but the words and life of Jesus as well present him to be a charismatic leader, who was identified as the King of the Jews by the evangelists at the time of his death.

While Jesus, the King of the Jews is identified as a charismatic leader, it raises an issue whether Jesus was a King of a region or a wandering charismatic. In Luke 9:58, the words of Jesus, "Son of Man has nowhere to lay his head," depict him as a wandering charismatic. But, Jesus movement cannot be understood exclusively in terms of a wandering charismatic because local communities and settled groups of sympathizers of Jesus were there; probably, they may be the nucleus of later communities.[110] For instance, in 10:38ff, Mary and Martha; and in 8:2f, Jesus was supported materially by women. So, Jesus was not merely a wandering charismatic, but understood later as a King of the Jews in Palestine.

Another issue that arises here is the relationship between the religious and the socio-political reality of the Jesus movement. In other words, whether Jesus was a religious or a political leader? Concerning the socio-political reality and spiritual phenomena of Jesus movement, Theissen says, "Religion can be a social cement and an impulse towards renewal."[111] He may be right in a way. It depicts the role of religion in society. But, as it has been noted earlier, the high priests joined hands with the Roman Emperor and meshed up both religion and politics. So, the reformer had to establish theocracy in both religion and the political world during that time. Considering all these, it seems that the leadership of Jesus was as expected by Lukan community in its struggle. Further, it can be discerned from the major components of the Palestinian social system: socio-economic, socio- ecological, socio-political and socio-cultural factors of first century which signifies the struggle of the Lukan community in their livelihood.

Socio-Economic Factors

The Socio-economic factors during Jesus time, early Christianity and Luke's time are categorized as: social rootlessness; poverty and the oppression of double taxation. The social rootlessness was one of the striking socio-economic factors in Jesus movement parallel to all the renewal movements within Judaism during the first century. For instance, in 10:1ff, in the commissioning of seventy, they were reminded of the same rules given to the twelve apostles in 9:1ff.[112] According to Josephus, the fishermen of Lake Tiberias belonged to the class of those penniless sailors who had involved in a rebellion at the beginning of Jewish war.[113] 5:1ff implies this penniless state of Peter through his frustration. Even, the family of Jesus symbolizes insignificant people, who lived in difficult circumstances of a peasant class.

Historically, there are evidences that the Diaspora Jews served as mercenaries, slaves, fugitives or in search of a new basis for existence. They were used by the Herodian client Kings to found their new cities like: Caesarea, Sebaste, Sepphoris, Philippi, Phasaelis, Bathyra, Tiberias and so on. Numerous people lost their possessions by an earthquake at the Dead Sea during CE 31, and a great famine occurred between CE 46-48 and its devastating consequences.[114] W. D. Davies says that Palestine was in dire poverty during the first century despite the fact that Rome was doing well.[115] So, the have-nots endured the oppression of Rome.

Considering the poverty in Palestine, Jesus focused on the poor in his ministry which is evident in his Nazareth manifesto.[116] Although, the activities of the rich were accepted in 7:3ff; 8:3; 16:9 & 19:1ff, the criticism on riches in 6:24f raises an issue. H. Braun identifies it as a lack of principle in Jesus movement; whereas, Theissen addresses it as a consequence of the need of the produce[117] in view of the prevailing distributive tensions between the productive community and the consumer community from 10 BCE.[118] This scenario is viewed by D. E. Oakman as, "political character of ancient economics, redistribution, and debt."[119] According to Horsley and J. S. Hanson, the land and the produce of the poor peasants were controlled by the wealthy in abuse of their power.[120] As poverty increased, people in debt and land-loss became a cause for social unrest.

Moreover, double taxation became a burden, and caused resentment and violence[121] among the Palestinians. The state tax[122] as well as religious tax[123] led the debtors to take refuge with the freedom fighters to be released from their debt. Theissen interprets 16:1ff, relating it to this context that the remission of debt seems positive to avoid protest and losing the whole.[124] Double taxation resulted in more banditry since they wouldn't be able to pay the taxes. Jesus' fundamental question about the necessity of paying both state and religious taxes in Mt. 17:24ff &

Lk. 23:2 acknowledge this burden of Palestinians. Horsley and Hanson depict the peasants' revolt led by the bandit or the charismatic King against the Jewish and Roman overlords for the imposition of new ruling class in the social structures which caused to deteriorate their economic condition.[125] It is vivid in 22:52, where Jesus questions those who came to arrest him as, "Have you come out with swords and clubs as if I were a bandit?" Concerning the taxation, Crossan comments, "Roman Imperialism meant not just taxation of an economy already in place but the commercialization of the local economy for more taxes and revenues in the future."[126] In these economic systems and the burdens of the society, the Jewish people anticipated a leader or a King to rescue them from this economic situation of their society, which Crossan sees the thirst for Divine Justice.[127] It may be seen further from the socio-ecological factors in Palestine.

Socio-Ecological Factors

Socio-ecological factors are normally considered as the outcome of interaction between the human and nature. In the socio-political world of Luke it is related to the relationship between city and country; and its related class conflicts of the people. Archaeological evidence proves that the Sepphoris in Lower Galilee, the Roman urbanization, symbolizes the power of the city. Urbanization alienated the peasants from their land and these affected their survival. Conflict between city and country became visible in the speeches of Jesus. In 4:23-29 & 9:49f, the tension and social unrest between two groups are noticeable in the episodes concerning the determination of the boundaries. According to Green, it was due to the estrangement of the Galilean peasantry by their discrimination as rural and urban in the world of Luke.[128] It is evident in the utterances of Jesus in 13:33ff, rebuking Jerusalem with a bad status of killing the prophets by having his base in the country. These topographical or boundary conflicts seem to be a major factor in the first century CE and the same seems to be a continuation of its earlier periods. For instance, the Essenes and the prophetic movements centered in the wilderness; Zealots chose the hill-country as their hiding places; and, the Jesus movement was based in densely populated areas. According to Theissen, all these groups detached themselves from Jerusalem in diverging to the idea of a holy city.[129] The confrontation in the temple also reveals urban domination. For instance, the Essenes rejected the sacrificial worship of the temple; the Zealots murdered a large number of the temple aristocracy; and, Jesus prophesied that it would soon be destroyed.

Along with the tension between the country and the city there seems to be a Socio-ecological factor that afflicted the situation - the issue of lower class and the upper class conflict that prevailed in the world of Luke. According to Theissen, this conflict cannot be expressed in terms of lower class and the upper class issue because, Joseph of Arimathea, who buried the corpse of Jesus, belonged to the upper class.[130] But, we get evidence in 22:2 that Jesus movement establishes its success not in the city of Jerusalem where the upper class people lived and Jesus was executed, but in the countryside where the lower class people lived. The class resistance in Palestine thus continued on the basis of regional differences particularly between Judea/Jerusalem and Galilee. These factors were intertwined with the political issues and regional differences and perhaps were related to the Socio-political conflict between the rulers and the ruled.

Socio-Political Factors

Socio-political factors demonstrate the oppressive structures of administration in Palestine, by client rulers and the governors of Roman Empire as it has been already noted under the title, Roman imperial rule of Palestine during 1st century. In Roman rule by the Emperor and native Kings, there was a tension in terms of governance between theocracy and aristocracy.[131] According to Flemington, the political situation of John's time reflects the eagerness of the people throughout Palestine for God's intervention in favor of the well-being of Israel, during the power of Romans at the dawn of first century.[132] John the Baptist's words: "the wrath to come,"[133] the ax is lying at the root of the trees," "cut down and thrown into the fire,"[134] etc. point out the imminent Messianic age against the political factors in Palestine. The context of John's call for repentance and baptism in 3:1-18 was a prophetic appeal for people to turn away from their loyalty toward the political leaders and to join the Kingdom of God.

Subsequently, the tyrannical political situation is portrayed by Luke in 9:9 as John the Baptist's life became a precedent for it as he was being arrested and executed by the ruler Herod Antipas. The polemic accent is evident in the *Gospel of Thomas*:

Jesus said:

Why did you go out into the field?

To see a reed that is shaken by the wind?

And to see a man clothed in soft raiment?

[Lo, your] Kings and your great ones

are they who are clothed with soft raiment,

and they [shall] not be able to know the truth![135]

Along with this political scenario of hostility, Paul's call to abide by the governing authorities in Rom 13:1-7, depict that the world of Luke became suspicious of the state and the state became hostile to them.

In this hostile milieu, people's enthusiasm for God's intervention and apocalyptic vision might have accepted the movements accompanied by prophetic proclamations and promises. For instance, Theudas promised Jordan to be divided once again; another prophet promised the miracle at Jericho to be repeated upon the walls of Jerusalem; Jonathan promised miracles in the wilderness; a Samaritan prophet wanted to trace the missing temple vessels to Mount Gerizim; and, being a charismatic prophet, Jesus promised a new Temple,[136] which probably, might have annoyed the Roman government as well the Jewish authorities in view of rebellion and caused him to undergo brutality.[137] Akin to these resistance movements accompanied by prophetic proclamations and promises, Jesus might have been by proclaiming the sole rule of God, rejected earthly rulers; rebelled against the Romans through his words; and, with reservation emphasized his Messiahship, probably, by considering himself as a King.

In addition, while tracing the resistant movements and Kingship in the despotic political situation, Judas of Galilee, the founder of a movement, in all probability intended himself to be a King; succeeding him, at the outset of Jewish war, Menahem appeared in Jerusalem with royal dress as a King;[138] a slave, Simon claimed himself as a King across Jordan in Perea; and a shepherd, Athronges and his four brothers claimed as Kings in Judea who were executed by Rome as Kingly or royal pretenders.[139] Likewise, Jesus' proclamation of the Kingdom of God might have perhaps perceived and induced suspicion among the authorities pertaining to who the King would be. Along with these political factors, Socio-cultural factors also illustrate the longing of the world of Luke to have a Messianic King for a peaceful life.

Socio-Cultural Factors

Socio-cultural factors include values, norms, traditions, religions and philosophy which provide a society with self-awareness and identity. The Hellenistic impact had developed the structural growth of Palestine[140] and the upper class people were benefited more through the expansion of cities, education, theatres and gymnasiums. Whereas, the life of the poor peasants who were struggling to make their everyday livelihood were severely affected.

Along with this disparity among the upper class and lower class during the early first century CE, Jewish-Gentile conflicts started concerning the religious practices of Judaism. In Judaism, most of the Gentile proselytes were inducted either through imitating Jewish customs or by accepting the practice of circumcision. On the other hand, there were uncircumcised Gentiles, known as God-fearers who also attended the Synagogues without becoming proselytes.[141] In addition to that, in Luke, the hostility between Jews and the Gentiles are noteworthy. For instance, 4:16-30 portrays the rejection of Jesus at Nazareth by the Israelites when he extended the message of salvation to the Gentiles, rich and poor alike.[142] In 4:25-27, Luke portrays the Gentiles as more devout than the Jews by alluding to two Old Testament events: 1) widow of Zarephath, a Gentile who had cared the prophet Elijah,[143] and 2) the leprosy cleansed Naaman,[144] who was a Gentile and a military commander of a Gentile King.

However, it should be inferred that Jewish and Gentile hostility occurred due to the transformation of their culture and tradition. Neyrey cites a quip from Karris that "Jesus was killed because of the way he ate."[145] Although it is not the fact, the practice of Jesus eating with others during his life time raises an issue. Was it a deliberate act of Jesus eating across culture with the people who were classified as holy and as sinners? According to Luke, the practice of Jesus was a deliberate act. 7:34b points it out ironically with the words of Jesus as he was considered by the Jews as, "a glutton and a drunkard, a friend of tax collectors and sinners."

This hostile situation was an entrenched reality for a long time in the history of Palestine: In 167 BCE, the Seleucid King Antiochus Epiphanes IV with the aim of Hellenizing Palestine, prohibited the practices of Judaism and compelled the Jews to eat swine's flesh, and at the stake of death they refused; during the Babylonian captivity in 167-163 BCE, Jewish youth who were selected for the Babylonian King's service were given the food which defiled them; during the period of the Maccabean rising, when Judith went on her duty to beguile and slay Holofernes, refused to eat the food and wine which Holofernes offered to her; there are evidences in the Book of Esther that Esther abstained from the Royal table; and, in the book of Tobit, Tobit reports that when he was a captive in Nineveh, he did not eat the food of the Gentiles. However, during the 1st century CE, amidst this hostile situation there was evidence for table-fellowship between Jews and Gentiles. Dunn cites a Mishnaic passage, where the 'Gentile,' actually a Samaritan is present at a meal with Jews.[146]

Along with the issue of Jewish and Gentile hostility, the elite and non-elite outrage, and the issue of rich and poor also obstructed the table-fellowship. While interpreting the parable of the great dinner, found in 14:15-24, R. L. Bohrbaugh says,

> Elite Christians who participated in the socially inclusive Christian community risked being cut off from the prior social networks on which their positions depended. It is not simply 'worldly cares' or 'excessive materialism' that holds them back. It is nothing less than the network in which they have been embedded since birth. It is their friendships, their place of residence, their economic survival (and probably health as well), the well-being of their extended families and even the 'system' of the elite that is at stake. If becoming part of the Christian community provided a social haven for the poor, it occasioned a social disaster for the rich.[147]

In this milieu, Luke records the table-fellowship which was encouraged by Jesus: 1) dining with the Pharisees in 7:36-50; 11:37-44 & 14:1-4; 2) at Zacchaeus' house in 19:1-10; and 3) at Emmaus in 24:13-32 after his resurrection.

Lukan portrayal of table-fellowship raises another issue that whether the Lukan community turned aside the Mosaic Law. By observing the table-fellowship amidst hostility, Luke did not neglect the Law of Moses. For instance, he depicts pious Jews thus in 1:6, Zechariah and Elizabeth; in 2:22-39, Mary and Joseph; and in 2:25, Simeon and Anna, as being obedient to the law. In 10:25-28, he depicts it through Jesus' question, "what is written in the law? And Jesus' guidance to the lawyer was to follow it. It could be perceived then that Jesus respected the law but transcended it. The story of the rich ruler in 18:18-30, sheds light on it. While he claimed that he kept the commandments from his childhood and the matters related to Sabbath in 6:1-5, 6-11; 13:10-17 &14:1-6, the words of Jesus to distribute his wealth to the poor and follow him transcended the law. This transcendence along with the table-fellowship encouraged and challenged by Jesus probably points out to his leadership as a King in leading a community beyond its practice.

The challenge of Jesus and its outcome may be understood further through the interpretation of Malina and Neyrey. According to them, 'challenge-riposte' is a type of social communication, but at the same time, a channel of a culturally recognized reception. In the context of honour,[148] challenge-riposte becomes a social interaction at least in three phases: 1) challenge in terms of some action by the challenger; 2) perception of the message by both the individual to whom it is directed and the public at large; and 3) reaction of the receiving individual and the evaluation of the reaction on the part of the public. In this ideology of challenge, action, reception, and reaction it should be noted that the person who challenges is honoured by the public. As per the social patterns of 'honour contest' it must be perceived that only equals can play the part.[149] It is evident from the cultural settings of Luke that Jesus as a counterpart to the rulers of that time he transcended the law. For instance, the question of Pilate, "Are you the king of the Jews?" Besides, Jesus is portrayed by Luke from the beginning of the Gospel as, "He will be great, and will be called the Son of the Most High, and the Lord God will give him the throne of his ancestor David." In 1:32f; and, in the genealogy in 3:23-38 and perceived as an honourable person linked with royal and priestly group along with ascribed honour. But, at the same time it should be noted that the title, Son of Joseph, who was a carpenter seems contradictory. Perhaps, Luke presents Jesus as a rejected and a shameful one, yet the Kingly descent as the successor of King David enables him to face the challenges of his day. Further, the recent studies in Q also have reconstructed the Jesus movement as it had emerged in a context where it experienced conflict with Jewish codes and sensibilities.

Q and the Socio-Political World of Early Christianity

Q[150] concretizes the knowledge of differing social styles available to early Christians.[151] Social location of the Q people has been suggested as either Galilee or perhaps an adjacent area such as the Decapolis, and some of their activities are assumed in the context of the countryside.[152] According to B. L. Mack, "The tradents of Q were followers of Jesus who cultivated a critical stance toward social conventions by acting out their statements of independence and by forming a loose network of groups that met for mutual support."[153] It would be helpful for this research to view the socio-economic, socio-ecological, and socio-political factors related to the Q people as well as their view of charismatic leadership to understand the socio-political world of Luke since it influenced the composition of the Gospel.

Q and the Socio-Economic Factors

The economic condition of the Q people was horrific. They became poor. The drought during 25-24 BCE caused a famine and the decrease of seed grain in subsequent years affected the Q people economically. It increased the debt of the people and this might have been one of the contributing causes for the revolt in CE 70.[154] It gives the image of a poverty-stricken state of the people during that time. The use of the terms πτωχός and ἐργάτης serve a positive function in Q's rhetoric, and implies a critical view of the society and their vision of promoting the Kingdom through Jesus movement. 6:20b-21 = Mt. 5:3 & 6 identifies the disciples as πτωχός and, the term ἐργάτης used in the mission speech mentioned in 10:2 & 7 connotes the dispossessed day labourer rather than the peasant to denote their poverty. In the Son of Man saying in 9:58 = Mt. 8:20, albeit the term, πτωχός is not used, it seems to be an extolled homelessness and an idealization of poverty, which is probably a counterbalance to a context of penniless or failing culture. Correspondingly, 6:30 = Mt. 5:42, "Give to everyone who begs from you; and if anyone takes away your goods, do not ask for them again" is perhaps a response to predatory lending practices and the chronic problem of indebtedness of that time.[155] Even the Q beatitudes in 6:20-23 = Mt. 5:3-6 articulate the blessing upon a group afflicted socially and economically by poverty, hunger, distress and persecution.[156] Jesus' words in Luke 6:20 & 24 and its parallel present hope for the peasants and at the same time warning to the powerful rich. In general, poverty and hopelessness made the people to see Jesus as the hope of life as well, the one who is with them in their affliction. Further, the prevailing socio-ecological factors of the

Q people may give evidence to the early Christianity's longing for and view of Jesus as King.

Q and the Socio-Ecological Factors

The fundamental social division in Palestine was between the various sectors as: rulers and ruled; taxers and taxed; and, city/court/temple and, town/village. As well, the fundamental structural opposition of the governing communities was obvious in Palestine along with their past regional differences, particularly between Judea/ Jerusalem and Galilee. Amidst these conflicts and opposition, Jesus' words about the Kingdom points out the growth of his movement in ecological pictures. For instance, 13:18-21 = Mt. 13:31f portrays the rapid growth of mustard and the amplification of leaven; in 12:1 = Mt. 16:6, the portrayal of a warning concerning the yeast of the Pharisees in relation to their hypocritical activities against the Q people; 10:2f = Mt. 10:16 in the image of plentiful harvest and scarcity of labourers, who are depicted as lambs amidst wolves;[157] 12:2-12 = Mt. 10:26-33 exhorts Q people to confess courageously at the time of persecution; 12:22-31 = Mt. 6:25-34 addresses the people not to worry about the necessities of life comparable to lilies; In 11:44 = Mt. 23:27, Pharisees are named as unmarked graves which Matthew writes as whitewashed tombs; 11:37-54 = Mt. 15:1-9 condemns the activities of the Pharisees of their tithing of mint, rue and herbs of all kinds; love to be greeted in the market places; to have seat of honour in the synagogue; washing of vessels' outside instead of inside etc, amid their exploitation of marginalized people. In all these evidences, it is obvious that all the eco-related expressions highlight the suffering context of the early Christianity. Further, it could be observed regarding the socio-political factors from the Q passages.

Q and the Socio-Political Factors

13:28-35 = Mt. 8:11f; 19:30; 20:16 & 23:37-39 the passages concerning: the partakers of the Kingdom of God; the warning of Jesus' death by Herod; Jerusalem as a city that kills the prophets; and the parable of the great dinner in 14:16-24 = Mt. 22:1-14 signify the socio-political antagonism of the Jewish rulers of Jerusalem, Jesus and the Q people. Even the addressed woes toward the Pharisees in 11:44 = Mt. 23:27 & 11:37-54 = Mt 15:1-9 show their role and actions in preventing people from entering the Kingdom of God in opposition to Jesus' Kingship and his movement. The renewal of the people of Israel by indicating the mission discourse in 10: 2-16 = Mt. 9:37f; 10:7-16, 40; 11:20-24, a deliberate, organized effort in preaching and healing among Galilean villages and towns, the curses against the unresponsive Galilean towns of Chorazin and Bethsaida, and the references to the close by cities of Tyre and Sidon seem to be Jesus' programmatic declaration of justice for the twelve tribes of Israel. As well in 3:8-9 = Mt. 3:9-10, the inadequacy of physical descent due to their hypocrisy; 7:1-10 = Mt. 8:5-13, 7:31-35 = Mt. 11:16-19; 10:12-15 = Mt. 11:20-24; & 11:31-32 = Mt. 12:41-42, comparison between the faith-filled Gentiles and non-believing Jews; and, 13:22-30 = Mt. 7:13-14; 22-23; 8:11-12; 19:30; 20:16; 25:10-12; 25:41, the rejection of Israel and the acceptance of the far-off Gentiles in the Kingdom depict the hostile situation. In this context of hostility, how did the Q people view the leadership of Jesus?

Q and the Charismatic Leadership

The event of baptism, subsequent contest with Satan, and signs of overcoming the powers of evil by mighty works denote Jesus' power as well as his summon to the people for political repentance. The utterances of Jesus to deny the earthly families and joining in the coming God's Kingdom explicitly show Jesus' charismatic leadership.[158] Q's position obviously goes further in depicting Jesus as a messianic King. 14:27 = Mt. 10:38 refers to taking up the cross, and 22:28-30 = Mt. 20:28 shows service is the requirement in Jesus' ministry or Kingdom. The beatitudes in 6:20-22 = Mt. 5:3-6 depict Jesus' vision concerning the Q community:

> Blessed are you who are poor, for yours is the Kingdom of God. Blessed are you who are hungry now, for you will be filled. Blessed are you who

weep now, for you will laugh. Blessed are you when people hate you, and
when they exclude you, revile you, and defame you on account of the
Son of Man. Rejoice in that day and leap for joy, for surely your reward
is great in heaven.

Boring argues that this beatitude is pronounced to those who endure
hatred, insult, and ostracization, and refers to the later period of
early Christianity rather than that of Jesus.[159] His argument could be
accepted in the light of Lukan composition of the Gospel in a later
period, but the words of Jesus refer to the Q people inclusive of
both who suffered during Jesus' time as well later. The anticipation
of a Messianic King was prevalent even before Jesus' arrival, which
according to Guignebert is 'the impulse behind Jesus of Nazareth born
in Galilee's career should have been the anticipation of the Messianic
Kingdom.'[160] So, it is clear that the Q people considered Jesus as a
Charismatic leader as well the anticipated Messianic King who is with
them in their affliction. Above and beyond, Lukan special material also
seems to prove Jesus' Kingship through his benevolence towards the
socially ostracized.

Lukan Special Material and the Socio-Cultural and Political Factors

Through the special material, Luke portrays Jesus as a King who
reforms the evil in the society as well as an alternative King. While
focusing on pious individuals like: priest Zechariah, cousins Elizabeth
and Mary, sisters Mary and Martha, Cleopas and his companion, et al.,
he gives evidence for Jesus' deep concern over the social outcasts such
as: immoral women in 7:36ff, widow of Nain, Zacchaeus in 19:8ff, the
robber in 23:39ff, and, the parables illustrative of gracious attitude,
i.e., the prodigal son, the two debtors and the publican. Particularly,
concerning the portraits of woman, he mentions thirteen women. It
shows how Jesus broke the cultural barriers in the cause of uplifting
women who were ostracized, and Gentiles, in addition to his approach
to have table-fellowship with them. Even though there are scholarly
disputes concerning the empowerment of women in Luke's Gospel,
it is obvious that to a prime part, Luke in his special materials by

marking these events in the lives of the outcast, banished, and destitute women along with the act of repentance and the acceptance of them by Grace, depicts Jesus as a Messianic King.

In addition, in the special Lukan material, the coming of Jesus of Nazareth is considered as the beginning of a new order in Luke. The use of the terms, Gospel/ good news and, the Kingdom of God should be understood in terms of its *Sitz im leben*. In 1 Sam. 31:8-10, to bring good news denotes bringing good news of a victory in the battle. The term, gospel in the first century was used in connection with Emperor worship. On the birthday of a Roman Emperor, who was considered as a divine being, he was expected to bring good news or benefits, especially the gift of peace, which would persevere throughout his reign.[161] In this milieu, the use of this term with the definite article, the gospel by Luke denotes the one good news against the many benefits of a lesser kind. It can further be seen by the birth of Jesus during the reign of Caesar Augustus in contrast to him as the prince of peace, the Anointed one, the Messianic ideal King.

Summary

In this investigation of surveying the use of the title, King in various social, historical, political and biblical milieu, it is identified that Luke seems to have taken the idea of the King which had prevailed in history. Jesus as King obtained its meaning from diverse cultural, social, historical and political contexts: in Hellenism as well in West Asian countries, King was known as divine, above human, a shepherd, and the one who sustains the life of the subjects as a benefactor; in Egypt, an incarnation of the deity as the son of god; in Mesopotamia, a divine institution; in ancient Sumer, a descendant from heaven; in Israel, chosen by God and, in the Roman imperial history, considered as god and worshipped.

In Israel's royal history during the Old Testament times, particularly from the pre- exilic period, Yahweh was referred to as the King and His supremacy was accepted albeit human King was ruling the country. In their distress in exile and later, the Israelites cried for the providence of Yahweh. In their agony, they were comforted with the promises of Messianic Kingship in relation to the restoration of the Davidic monarchy. The priest-king ideology of the Messiah was deeply rooted in the Intertestamental Period. The development of the Old Testament concept of Messianic King is found in the intertestamental literature and the titles of Messiah culminated as Son of Man and Servant King.

The expectation of the messianic prophecies of the Old Testament and the understanding of them during the Intertestamental period derived their meaning in the New Testament Christocentric understanding. Particularly Luke in his composition of the Gospel portrays the words and deeds of historical Jesus as the fulfillment of Old Testament messianic prophecies in Him and recognized by the early Christians after His resurrection.

The socio-political world of Luke discloses the complex politics of Roman imperial rule through the Herodian client Kings and Jewish leaders in Judea during the time of historical Jesus, Luke, as well the early Christians. Both the Roman and Palestinian histories of the 1st century reflect the *Sitz im leben* of Luke's Gospel. The Roman rule, known as *Pax Romana/Augusta* indicates the tyrannical rule of Emperor Augustus. Under the Herodians, the Jews lived a life of slavery. However, the religious leaders under the subjugation of Rome obliged the emperor than God. In this oppressive state, Jesus, the Charismatic leader is presented by Luke as the Messianic King who seems to be an alternative King to the Roman Super power.

The longing for an alternative King by the Lukan community is traced from the socio-political world of Luke in its *Sitz im leben*: the socio-economic, ecological, political cultural factors. Social rootlessness, poverty, debt, over-population, burden of double taxation, conflict in determination of boundaries, class struggles, and regional differences are the socio-economic and ecological factors that caused the afflicted people to anticipate a redeemer King. John's call for baptism indicates the messianic age and invites the people to join in the new movement in anticipation of the imminent messianic Kingdom. The arrest of John the Baptist and his execution reveal the tyrannical politics of that time. Culturally, by the expansion of cities, facilities for education, establishment of theaters and gymnasiums, improved the life of the upper classes while the peasants struggled for their living. Impact of other religions and philosophies affected further the culture of the Jewish people. The elite and non elite outrage, rich and poor, Jew and Gentile discrimination obstructed table-fellowship. In this hostile context, Luke portrays Jesus as the one who challenges it as a Davidic descendant along with the ascribed honour and acquired honour by his act of encouraging table-fellowship.

Recent studies in Q have concretized further the context of Lukan community's suffering. While the famine and earthquake during the middle of 1st century CE affected the Q people, it increased debt and caused a revolt. The use of the terms πτωχός and ἐργάτης provide Q's rhetoric, and implies a critical view of the society and their vision in promoting an alternate Kingdom through Jesus movement. The eco related expressions of Jesus, as well as Q passages concerning the partakers of the Kingdom, warning of Jesus' death by Herod, warning to the religious leaders by Jesus highlight the suffering context of early Christians. The beatitudes uttered by Jesus in relation to the Q community depict Jesus as a Messianic King along with his Messianic programme.

Lukan special materials indicate Jesus' deep concern for social outcasts and the empowerment of women in society. His parables illustrate his gracious attitude along with acts of repentance. The use of the terms, 'gospel' had profound meaning in the Lukan Socio-Political world in relation to the Roman Emperor's birthday; and, 'good news,' indicated proclamation of victory in the battle. In the next chapter, Luke's composition of the infancy narrative in the Gospel will be explored introducing Jesus' Kingship at his birth in the context of anticipating an alternative King.

Endnotes

[1] Social unrest existed in Palestine during the first century CE. [J. B. Green, *New Testament Theology: Theology of the Gospel of Luke* (Cambridge: University Press, 1995), 12f.]; B. M. Metzger describes the oppressive political scenario of that time. [B. M. Metzger, *The New Testament. Its Background, Growth, and Content*, 1965, 2nd ed. (Nashville: Abingdon Press, 1983), 109.]; Gospels reflect the conflict in Temple power during the first century CE.

[2] Literally means the rule of God.

[3] U. Luz, "βασιλεία," *Exegetical Dictionary of the New Testament*, vol 1, Ἀαρων-Ἑνώχ, ed. by Horst Balz and Gerhard Schneider (Edinburgh: T & T Clark, 1980), 201.

[4] H. G. Liddell and R. Scott, *A Greek-English Lexicon*, vol I α-κώψ, revised ed. (Oxford: Clarendon Press, 1925), 309; Kleinknecht, "βασιλεύς in the Greek world," *Theological Dictionary of the New Testament*, vol 1, Α-Γ, ed. by G. Kittel (Grand Rapids: Wm. B. Eerdmans, 1964), 564.

[5] C. SpicQ, "βασιλεία, βασιλειος, βασιλεύς etc." *Theological Lexicon of the New Testament*, vol 1, ἀγα-ἐλπ, tr. and ed. by J. D. Ernest (USA: Hendrickson, 1994), 256.

[6] Generally used by the Western writers as "Orient."

[7] Kleinknecht, "βασιλεύς in the Greek world"..., 565.

[8] W. Whiston A.M. (tr), *The Works of Josephus: Complete and Unabridged* (Peabody: Hendrickson, 1987), 261.

[9] *Ibid.*, 261f.

[10] Seybold, "The Word Group mlk." *Theological Dictionary of the Old Testament*, vol VIII, מֹר-לִכֹד, ed. by J. Botterweck, H. Tinggren, and H. Fabry, tr. by D. W. Stott (Grand Rapids: William B. Eerdmans, 1997), 354.

[11] For instance, Lk. 1:5, the King Herod; Lk. 22:25, Kings of the Gentiles, *passim.*

[12] Lk. 19:38; 23:2, 3, *passim.*

[13] P. Lampe, "βασίλειος" *Exegetical Dictionary of the New Testament*, vol 1, Ἀαρων-Ἑνώχ, ed. by H. Balz and G. Schneider (Edinburgh: T & T Clark Ltd, 1980), 206.

[14] The Western writers use it as "the Ancient Near Eastern."

[15] Twentieth-century research has established the following: 1) King, the title of a ruling deity primarily belongs to heaven. As an extension of the divine order, human ruler, who is appointed by God as mediator, to be

in humble dependence towards God and face his subjects and enemies in power; 2) the King, as a shepherd, mother and father as it is his royal righteousness has to nourish the weak, cherishes his flock and defends the widow and orphan so that the society and nature can thrive; and 3) through the festivals and royal ceremonies, the divine relationship to the King was renewed by reinstating him. [J. Eaton, "Kingship," *A Dictionary of Biblical Interpretation*, ed. by R. J. Coggins and J. L. Houlden (London: SCM Press, 1990), 379.]; T. N. D. Mettinger distinguishes the divine Kingship from the sacral Kingship. According to him, the former indicates the idea of a King as a divine descendant and made as an object of a cult, whereas, the latter indicates the King chosen by God. [T. N. D. Mettinger, *King and Messiah: The Civil and Sacral Legitimation of the Israelite Kings* (CWK: Gleerup, 1976), 14.]

[16] Ringgren, "מֶלֶךְ" *Theological Dictionary of the Old Testament*, vol VIII, מר-לכד, ed. by J. Botterweck, H. Tinggren, and H. Fabry, tr. by D. W. Scott (Grand Rapids: William B. Eerdmans, 1997), 349f; J. Becker, *Messianic Expectations in the Old Testament*, tr. by D. E. Green (Philadelphia: Fortress Press, 1980), 39.

[17] It is noted in Assyrian court poetry. [A. Laato, *A Star is Rising: The Historical Development of the Old Testament Royal Ideology and the Rise of the Jewish Messianic Expectations* (Atlanta: Scholar Press, 1997), 13-22.]

[18] H. Ringgren, *The Messiah in the Old Testament* (London: SCM Press, 1961), 20.

[19] Ringgren, "מֶלֶךְ"..., 351.

[20] D. J. Muthunayagom, *The Relationship between Election and Israel's attitude towards the nations in the book of Isaiah* (Delhi, ISPCK, 2000), 248.

[21] Laato, *A Star is Rising...*, 29.

[22] Ex. 15:18; 1 Sam. 8:6f; 12:12, *passim.*

[23] Jer. 10:7, 10; Ps. 24, *passim.*

[24] J. K. Wiles, "Wisdom and Kingship in Israel," *Asia Journal of Theology* 1/1 (April 1987): 55.

[25] "...they have rejected me from being King over them." [1 Sam. 8:7.]

[26] J. J. M. Roberts, "The Enthronement of Yhwh and David: The Abiding Theological Significance of the Kingship Language of the Psalms," *The Catholic Biblical Quarterly* 64/4 (October 2002): 676.

[27] Von Rad, "מֶלֶךְ and מלכות in the OT," *Theological Dictionary of the New Testament*, vol 1, A-Γ, ed. by G. Kittel (Grand Rapids: Wm. B. Eerdmans, 1964), 569.

[28] Laato, *A Star is Rising...*, 51.

[29] K. Koch, *From Amos to Jesus: Biblical Eschatology and Its Social and Political Implications*, tr. by J. Gomes (Delhi: ISPCK, 1999), 25.

[30] Isa. 40-55.

[31] 1 Sam. 8 & 12. Cf. Deut 17:14f.

[32] 1 Ch. 28:5; 29:23. [Seybold, "The Word Group mlk"..., 370.

[33] Laato, *A Star is Rising...*, 3; J. J. Collins, "Messiah, Jewish," *The New Interpreters Dictionary of the Bible*, vol 4, Me-R, ed. by K. D. Sakenfeld (Nashville: Abingdon Press, 2009), 59.

[34] Laato, *A Star is Rising...*, 4.

[35] J. R. J. S. Raj, *The "Anointed Ones" in the Qumran Literature* (Delhi: ISPCK, 2005), 98; Is 41:21; 43:15; 44:6; 52:7 Ob 21; Ezek 17:22, 24; 34:23ff; Hagg 2:23; Zech 6:9ff; 9:9f, *passim*. [T. N. Swanson, "The Kingship of God in Intertestamental Literature," *Bangalore Theological Forum* 12/1 (January-June, 1980): 2.]

[36] Laato, *A Star is Rising...*, 176; The name of Cyrus mentioned in Isa. 45:1 is not approved directly by scholars either as a Messiah or a Davidic King: For instance, James D. Smart explains it as an intrusion; Bernard Anderson says that the description of new Exodus is fashioned after the Exodus; G. Jones portrays him as the anti-type of Abraham; J. McKenzie says that he got a place in the history of salvation; R. Clifford says that he is a typical King who rebuilt the temple as Yahweh's unwitting instrument; W. Holladay says that the term מָשִׁיחַ used here refers to a King who belongs to a foreign empire as God's agent and not the Messiah; A. Bentzen says that it is the portrayal of the universalism of royal ideology in the Cyrus oracle by Second Isaiah but, the 'Ebed Yahweh' is the true Messiah; G. A. F. Knight argues that Cyrus being a "pagan King" never be a Messiah; H. Barstad says that he, a Gentile Persian King, as Yahweh's anointed-one symbolizes the agent of restoration; Robert says that none of the thirty-nine usages of מָשִׁיחַ in the Old Testament originally referred to an anticipated Messianic future figure. In line with that Isa. 45:1 doesn't fit to the definition of messianism; E. J. Young proposes that Cyrus might be a type of Messianic Servant of the Lord. [R. Heskett, *Messianism within the Scriptural Scroll of Isaiah* (New York: T&T Clark, 2007), 15-28.]; Quite the reverse, Laato, Hanson, Pomkala and Becker speculated that Second Isaiah viewed Cyrus as Messiah [*Ibid.*, 33.] whereas, Heskett argues that Messiah is not a King fulfilling a temporal role but with an eschatological function fulfills the promises given to David. [*Ibid.*, 36]. According to Laato,

exilic messianic ideology was influenced by Babylonian royal ideology and the Judean royal ideology by the reign of Josiah. It was reinterpreted at the beginning of the Persian period to refer simultaneously to Cyrus on behalf of Israel. [Laato, *A Star is Rising...*, 180]. However, the concept of the King's charisma and loyalty to Yhwh might have made the author to address Cyrus as an ideal servant, Messiah as in 2 Kings 22-23, Jeremiah 22-23 and Ezekiel 17-19 Josiah is depicted as a model of a righteous King. [*Ibid.*, 174].

[37] R. E. Brown, *An Introduction to New Testament Christology* (London: Geoffrey Chapman, 1994), 156ff.

[38] Isa. 9:6, 7; 11:1-5; 32:1; Micah 5:1-4; Jeremiah 23:5f; Ezekiel 17:22ff; 34:23f; 37:24f & Zechariah 9:9ff.

[39] C. Guignebert, *The Jewish World in the time of Jesus* (New York: University Books, 1959), 253.

[40] Pseudepigrapha is a collection of manuscripts which covers c.400 years, from 200 BCE – CE 200. But, in this research the pre Christian literature, which speak about the Messianic King only looked into.

[41] S. H. Levey, *The Messiah: an Aramaic Interpretation, the Messianic Exegesis of the Targum* (New York: Hebrew Union College Press, 1974), xvii.

[42] D. S. Russell, *The Method and Message of Jewish Apocalyptic 200BC-AD 100* (London: SCM Press, 1964), 308.

[43] *Ibid.*, 309.

[44] G. W. E. Nickelsburg, "Disserning the Structure(s) of the Enochic Book of Parables," in *Enoch and the Messiah Son of Man*, ed. by G. Boccaccini (Grand Rapids: Wm. B. Eerdmans, 2007), 23.

[45] R. H. Charles, *The Apocrypha and Pseudepigrapha of the Old Testament,* vol II (Oxford: Clarendon Press, 1913), 217.

[46] R. M. Victor, *Colonial Education and Class Formation in Early Judaism: A Postcolonial Reading* (London: T & T Clark, 2010), 2.

[47] A. A. Orlov, "Roles and Titles of the Seventh Antediluvian Hero in the Parables of Enoch: A Departure from the Traditional Pattern?" in *Enoch and the Messiah Son of Man*, ed. by G. Boccaccini (Grand Rapids: Wm. B. Eerdmans, 2007): 132.

[48] L. W. Walck, "The Son of Man in the Parables of Enoch and the Gospels," in *Enoch and the Messiah Son of Man*, ed. by G. Boccaccini (Grand Rapids: Wm. B. Eerdmans, 2007), 301.

[49] S. Chiala, "The Son of Man: The Evolution of an Expression," in *Enoch and the Messiah Son of Man*, ed. by G. Boccaccini (Grand Rapids: Wm. B. Eerdmans, 2007), 1260.

[50] M. McNamara, *Intertestamental Literature* (Wilmington: Michael Glazier, 1983), 70.

[51] Russell, *The Method and Message of Jewish Apocalyptic...*, 331f.

[52] *Ibid.*, 332.

[53] *Ibid.*, 336.

[54] Levey, *The Messiah: an Aramaic Interpretation ...*, 63.

[55] *Ibid.*

[56] Pss. Sol 17f; J. H. Charlesworth, (ed.), *The Old Testament Pseudepigrapha*, vol 2 (New York: Doubleday & Co, 1985), xxxif.

[57] Heskett, *Messianism within the Scriptural Scroll of Isaiah...*, 286f.

[58] G. L. Davenport, "The 'Anointed of the Lord' in Psalms of Solomon 17," in *Ideal* Figures *in Ancient Judaism: Profiles and Paradigms*, ed. By J. J. Collins and G.W.E. Nickelsburg (Michigan: Scholars Press, 1980), 78.

[59] Charles, *The Apocrypha and Pseudepigrapha...*, 649.

[60] Swanson, "The Kingship of God in Intertestamental Literature"..., 13f.

[61] J. H. Charlesworth, *The Old Testament Pseudepigrapha and the New Testament* (Cambridge: University Press, 1985), 116.

[62] J. H. Charlesworth, *The Old Testament Pseudepigrapha,* vol. 1 (London: Darton, Longman &Todd, 1983), 794.

[63] Charlesworth, *The Old Testament Pseudepigrapha and the New Testament...*, 115.

[64] F. J. Murphy, *The Structure and Meaning of Second Baruch* (Atlanta: Scholars Press, 1985), 66.

[65] Charlesworth, *The Old Testament Pseudepigrapha and the New Testament...*, 114.

[66] *Ibid.*, 116.

[67] D. S. Russell, *Between the Testaments* (London: SCM Press, 1960), 129.

[68] *Ibid.*, 116f.

[69] *Ibid.*, 117.

[70] Russell, *Between the Testaments...*, 115.

[71] Laato, *A Star is Rising...*, 289-299; Fabry, "Qumran," *Theological Dictionary of the Old Testament*, vol VIII, *ed.* by J. Botterweck, H. Tinggren, and H. Fabry, tr. by

D. W. Scott (Grand Rapids: William B. Eerdmans, 1997), 374f;S. E. Porter, *The Messiah in the Old and New Testament* (Grand Rapids: William B. Eerdmans, 2007), 6.

[72] A. Hultgard, "The Ideal 'Levite', The Davidic Messiah and the Saviour Priest in the Testaments of the Twelve Patriarchs," in *Ideal Figures in Ancient Judaism: Profiles and Paradigms, ed. by* J. J. Collins and G. W. E. Nickelsburg, (Michigan: Scholars Press, 1980), 93.

[73] Charlesworth, *The Old Testament Pseudepigrapha and the New Testament...*, 116.

[74] Becker, *Messianic Expectations...*, 14.

[75] J. Klausner, *The Messianic Idea in Israel: From the Beginning to the Completion of the Misnah,* tr. by W. F. Stinespring (London: George Allen & Unwin, 1956), 9.

[76] Becker, *Messianic Expectations...*, 33.

[77] E. F. Scott, *The Kingdom and the Messiah* (Edinburgh: T & T Clark, 1911), 29.

[78] Levey, *The Messiah: an Aramaic Interpretation ...*, 2-11 & 21-27.

[79] T. F. Best, "The Sociological Study of the New Testament: Promise and Peril of a New Discipline," *Scottish Journal of Theology* 36 (1983): 181.

[80] C. A. Briggs, *Messianic Prophecy* (Edinburg: T & T Clark, 1886), 498.

[81] R. W. L. Moberly, "The Christ of the Old and New Testaments," in *The Cambridge Companion to Jesus*, ed. by M Bockmuehl (Cambridge: University Press, 2001), 190.

[82] C. W. Hedrick, "Introduction: The Tyranny of the Synoptic Jesus," in *The Historical Jesus and the Rejected Gospels, Semeia* 44 (Atlanta: Scholars Press, 1988), 2.

[83] M. E. Boring, "The Historical-Critical Method's "Criteria of Authenticity": The Beatitudes in Q and Thomas as a Test Case," in *The Historical Jesus and the Rejected Gospels, Semeia* 44 (Atlanta: Scholars Press, 1988), 12-15.

[84] R. A. Horsley, "Q and Jesus: Assumptions, Approaches, and Analyses," in *Early Christianity, Q and Jesus, Semeia* 55 (Atlanta: Scholars Press, 1991), 177.

[85] A. Von Harnack's idealistic abstraction viewed Jesus as a Jew of his time and culture. Both R. Bultmann and M. Dibelius emphasized the *Sitz-im-Leben* of the tradition as the clue to understand the primitive Christianity. Dibelius viewed functional settings as: preaching, teaching, worship and Bultmann distinguished "Palestinian" and "Hellenistic" settings. A. Deissmann proposed that the social and linguistic background of the New Testament writings was based on non-literary documents. In America, Shirley Jackson Case

proposed that Christian origins be studied as a social process rather than as a literary or institutional history. By the mid-1970^s, biblical scholars began to examine the social process by which the Christian movement originated by employing methods derived from the social sciences. In Germany, G. Theissen and in America, A. Malherbe used sociological method in biblical studies. It was followed by J. Gager and others. [H. C. Kee, *Christian Origins in Sociological Perspective* (London: SCM Press, 1980), 14-18.]

[86] Considering the authorship of Luke's Gospel, Luke is generally accepted according to the tradition and 2nd century evidences like, Muratorian Canon, anti-Marcionite Prologue to Luke, the writings of Irenaeus, Clement of Alexandria, Origen and Tertullian [D. Guthrie, *New Testament Introduction, 1961*, 4th ed. (Illinois: Intervarsity Press, 1990), 114.]; as well, Hobart attributes the authorship of the Gospel to Luke, who is referred to as "the beloved physician" in Col. 4:14; Phlm. 24; 2 Tim. 4:11, due to the similarity in his language and style of Greek physicians [Luke's description of illness with medical precision than the other Synoptists is to be noted: in 4:38, Peter's mother-in-law suffers from a 'high' fever; in 5:12, a person affected by leprosy is said to be 'covered with leprosy'; and in Lk. 8:43, Luke omits the lines that the woman suffering from haemorrhage had spent her savings on doctors and was not cured.]; Zahn, Harnack, Moffatt, Höpfl-Gut, Meinertz, Alberts, Michaelis, Wikenhauser, Geldenhuys, Feine-Behm, and others agree to it. [W. G. Kümmel, *Introduction to the New Testament* (London: SCM Press, 1966), 103f; Guthrie, *New Testament Introduction...*, 118.]; in addition, H. J. Cadbury's argument authenticates the authorship of Luke, not being of an apostle but as a companion of Paul, by counting the use of first person plural "we" by the author in Acts 16:10-17; 20:5-15; 21:1-18 & 27:1-28:16 with the data concerning the associates of Paul during his imprisonment in Col. 4:10-12; Phlm. 23f & 2 Tim. 4:9-12 [Kümmel, *Introduction to the New Testament...*, 103; Guthrie, *New Testament Introduction...*, 116.]; further, it is important to note that by and large Lukan authorship is maintained by many scholars, such as: F. F Bruce, C. S. C. Williams, W. Michaelis, Bo Reicke, F. V. Filson, M. Dibelius, R. M. Grant, B. Gärtner, W. L. Knox, R. R. Williams, E. M. Blaiklock, W. Grundmann, I. H. Marshall, et al. But, W. G. Kummel, Conzelmann, Haenchen, Marxen, Veilhauer, Klein, Evans, O'Neill and E. Schweizer refuted Lukan authorship, due to the disagreement of it with Paul's letters [*Ibid.*, 125.], albeit there are remarkable affinity with Paul's theology in relation to universalism, emphasis upon faith, God's love for sinners, Gospel of joy, etc. [Kümmel, *Introduction to the New Testament...*, 104]; However, the author's statement that he was not an eyewitness and had received information from other "eyewitnesses and ministers of the

word" proves his access to earlier narratives and his period was later than Jesus' time [Lk. 1:1-4; Guthrie, *New Testament Introduction...*, 113.] appends support to the discussion that the author might be Paul's associate.

[87] Harnack, Höpfl-Gut, Meinertz, Schäfer, Albertz, Cerfaux-Cambier, Sahlin, Koh, Hastings, A. J. Mattill, and Geldernhuys had established the date of the Gospel as it was written during the beginning of the sixties, just before the end of Paul's trial; I. H. Marshall proposed the date just before CE 70; J. A. T. Robinson argues for a date before the fall of Jerusalem, because no history of war is mentioned in Luke [J. A. T. Robinson, *Redating the New Testament* (London: SCM Press, 1976), 13; Guthrie, *New Testament Introduction...*, 130f.]; whereas, Kümmel raises the issue on the basis of Lk. 1:1ff that it is too early for the existence of many Gospel writings in the sixties and suggests a probable period between CE 70 and 90. i.e., after the fall of Jerusalem, and argues that Lk. 21:20, 24; cf. Mk. 13:14ff, the prophecy concerning "the desolating sacrilege," appears to have been the prophecies *ex eventu* of the destruction of Jerusalem. W. G. Kümmel supports his argument of the prophecies *ex eventu* through the prophecy about the destruction of the city mentioned in 19:43f, in comparison to the reports given about Titus' march upon Jerusalem [Kümmel, *Introduction to the New Testament...*, 105; Guthrie, *New Testament Introduction...*, 130f.)]; G. Theissen identifies the event of *desolating sacrilege* during CE 39-40 under the reign of Gaius Caligula [G. Theissen, *The Gospels in Context*, tr. by L. M. Maloney (Edinburgh: T&T Clark, 1992), 157.] Dodd, Creed, T. W. Manson, J. A. Fitzmyer, et al. date it after CE 70 [Robinson, *Redating the New Testament...*, 29; Guthrie, *New Testament Introduction....*, 128f.]; but, J. Knox, J. C. O'Neill dated the Gospel between CE115 and 130 by arguing against the early use of Marcion and Justin in their writings that they might have used the special source of Luke [*Ibid.*, 126f.]; it may be questionable. However, to the issue of pre-war and postwar composition, it is possible to date it as a postwar composition for two reasons: 1) although, the purpose of writing the Gospel is historical and at the same time also theological. Green uses the phrase, Luke the theologian, implies that the third gospel is not only a historical book but also it is written as a theological gospel [Green, *New Testament Theology...*, xi.].

[88] Concerning the place of composition, scholars Michel and Klijn have conjectured Caesarea; along with the reference in anti-Marcionite Prologue; Jerome and T. W. Manson view that it was in Achaea; Koh says Decapolis; and Michaelis, Geldenhuys, Hastings and others suggest Rome. But for Kümmel none of these conjectures are conclusive suggestions to be adduced. He accepts the view that Luke's Gospel might have been written

outside Palestine [Kümmel, *Introduction to the New Testament*..., 106; Guthrie, *New Testament Introduction*..., 108f.]; though Kümmel's proposal seems to be a fair one, the place of composition cannot be dealt alone because of its complex issue related to the question, *to whom* it was written? F. Gerald Downing refers to Loveday Alexander's view that Theophilus might be the real name of a person and impossible to be an imaginary one because it was a favourite name among Hellenistic Jews. Besides, Downing suggests that either Theophilus being a patron, or a friend with a Roman official status, it is very clear that he was a sympathizer of the Christian community and likely to be a member of that community [F. G. Downing, "Theophilus's First Reading of Luke-Acts," in *Luke's Literary Achievement: Collected Essays*, ed. by C. M. Tuckett, (Sheffield: Academic Press, 1995), 91, citing L. Alexander, *The Preface to Luke's Gospel* (Cambridge: University Press, 1993), 73ff.]; the addressee's title κράτιστε means *most excellent* may perhaps indicate the position of his social rank [Guthrie, *New Testament Introduction*..., 108.] , and considered as the one who had become a Christian or about to be [I. I. D. Plessis, "Once More: The Purpose of Luke's Prologue (Lk. I 1-4)," *Novum Testamentum* 16/4 (October 1974): 269.]; But, if the name is considered as *a coined one*, it indicates that the Gospel was primarily designed for all people because the meaning of the name characterizes any 'lover of God' [Guthrie, *New Testament Introduction*..., 109.]; O'Toole has the same view of *a coined one* and argues that since Luke's Gospel addresses Christian world at large, it might have been written from the Pauline community [O'Toole, "Luke's Position on Politics and Society..."..., 2.].

[89] According to Esler, "Luke has shaped the Gospel traditions at his disposal in response to social and political pressures experienced by his community." [P. F. Esler, *Community and Gospel in Luke-Acts: The Social and Political Motivations of Lucan Theology* (Cambridge: University Press, 1987), 2.]; while aiming the interrelationships between Lukan theology and the social and political moves upon Lukan community, he identifies the image of the flock in Luke's Gospel (Lk. 12:32) as fragile, small Christian community [Esler, *Community and Gospel*..., 26.]; it might have perhaps comprised of both Jews and Gentiles (Lk. 2:31-32; 4:25-27; 13:29; 14:15-24 & 24:47) inclusive of rich, poor, the crippled, the blind, the lame (Lk. 14:21), and guests (Lk. 14: 15ff); according to T. W. Mansion, the original guests represent righteous Jews; the first of the new guests represent the religious lower classes, such as publicans and sinners; and the second group of new guests, who came from beyond the city boundaries, stands for Gentiles [Esler, *Community and Gospel*..., 16 &34.] including some Romans, who had been associated with synagogues before accepting Christianity. Gager interprets this Lukan

community as a movement among the economically and socially deprived ones in Roman Empire [D. J. Harington, "Sociological Concepts and the Early Church: A Decade of Research." *Theological Studies* 47/1 (March 1980): 184.]; concerning the socially deprived ones, J. D. Crossan refers to G. Alfoldy's Book, *The Social History of Rome* says that in the Roman Empire the poor and impoverished sections of the rural population, particularly, the peasants who could not attain their means of support and the privileged status of a Roman citizen belong to the oppressed social strata and not the *slaves* who were fed by their masters [J. D. Crossan, *The Birth of Christianity: Discovering what Happened in the Years Immediately after the Execution of Jesus* (Edinburgh: T&T Clark, 1998), 178.]; and, T. Parsons identifies the community as a non-privileged group who remains outside the prestigious structure of the society and Mol as the marginal group which remains on the edge of the society [Kee, *Christian Origins...*, 55; J. H. Elliott, "Social-Scientific Criticism of the New Testament: More on Methods and Models," in *Social-Scientific Criticism of the New Testament And its Social world, Semeia* 35 (Decatur: Scholars Press, 1986), 11]; Due to scanty source material for the sociological study of the Jesus movement, Theissen finds data through the process of inference: a) Constructive conclusions; b) Analytical conclusions; and, c) Comparative conclusions [G. Theissen, *Sociology of Early Palestinian Christianity*, tr. by John Bowden (Philadelphia: Fortress Press, 1978), 1-3.] sees this community as Jesus movement in analogues to its contemporary movements. According to him, 'it was a renewal movement founded by Jesus within Judaism as a response to the social phenomenon of Palestine crisis like other renewal movements within Judaism in the first century CE' [*ibid.*, 1.] B. J. Malina defines a social movement organization as "a complex, or formal, organization which identifies its goals with the preferences of a social movement or a counter-movement and attempts to implement those goals." [B. J. Malina, "Normative Dissonance and Christian Origins," in *Social-Scientific Criticism of the New Testament and its Social world, Semeia* 35 (Decatur: Scholars Press, 1986), 35.] In that line, Jesus movement may be understood as a millenarian movement, which expected the change of the prevailing rampant evil to a new state of salvation by God [Esler, *Community and Gospel...*, 49f], where, Jesus was a charismatic prophet. [Harington, "Sociological Concepts..." ..., 184.]

[90] Yong-Sung Ahn, *The Reign of God and Rome in Luke's Passion Narrative: An East Asian Global Perspective* (Boston: Brill, 2006), 52.

[91] Emperor of Rome during 27 BCE-CE 14.

[92] P. Fredriksen, *Jesus of Nazareth, King of the Jews* (New York: Alfred A. Knof, 2000), 166.

[93] Whiston, *The Works of Josephus...*, 460.

[94] *The Antiquities of the Jews* 188; Whiston, *The Works of Josephus...*, 463f; H. K. Bond, *Pontius Pilate in History and Interpretation* (Cambridge: University Press, 1998), 1.

[95] Whiston, *The Works of Josephus...*, 464-473.

[96] W. D. Davies, *Invitation to the New Testament* (London: Longman & Todd, 1967), 14f.

[97] Victor, *Colonial Education and Class Formation in Early Judaism...*, 18.

[98] J. A. Fitzmyer, *The Gospel According to Luke I-IX* (New York: Doubleday & Company, 1986), 175.

[99] R. B. Edwards, "Rome," *Dictionary of Jesus and the Gospels*, ed. by J. B. Green and S. McKnight (Illinois: Inter Varsity Press, 1992), 710.

[100] R. A. Horsley, *Jesus and Empire* (Minneapolis: Fortress Press, 2003), 41.

[101] Horsley, *Jesus and Empire* ..., 47.

[102] Bond, *Pontius Pilate* ..., 18.

[103] It will be dealt further in section *e) Socio-political Factors.*

[104] Kee, *Christian Origins...*, 27, 54f, citing M. Weber, *Sociology of Religion* (Methuen, 1965), 60ff.

[105] *Ibid.*, 56, citing H. J. Mol, *Identity and the Sacred* (Macmillan, 1964), 45.

[106] B. J. Malina, *The Social world of Jesus and the Gospels* (London: Routledge, 1996), 131.

[107] D. S. D. Toit, "Redefining Jesus: Current Trends in Jesus Research," in *Jesus, Mark and Q: The Teaching of Jesus and its Earliest Records*, ed. by M. Labahn and A. Schmidt (England: Sheffield Academic Press, 2001), 122.

[108] D. L. Migliore, "Christology in Context: The Doctrinal and Contextual Tasks of Christology Today," *Interpretation* 49/3 (July, 1995): 242f.

[109] Toit, Redefining Jesus..., 57-72.

[110] The term 'community' may be misleading because there was no separate division in Judaism at that time. These groups remained within the framework of Judaism and had no intention to found a new 'church.' [Theissen, *Sociology of Early Palestinian Christianity...*, 17.]

[111] *Ibid.*, 2; Here we should apprehend the reality of religion, as it plays its role in social change, often in its structure as an institution it becomes an oppressive one.

[112] Theissen, *Sociology of Early Palestinian Christianity...*, 33ff., Social rootlessness: Theissen connects this to the have-nots of that time. He

says the Qumran community, the resistance fighters, prophetic movements within Judaism and emigrants, new settlers, robbers, beggars etc., belongs to this category of social rootlessness.

[113] *Ibid.*, 34, citing Josephus, *Vita* 12.

[114] Theissen, *Sociology of Early Palestinian Christianity...*, 35-40, city of Tiberias was founded by Antipas in CE 19 with the work of the people who had no means to live. Cf. *Antt.* 18:2.3, 37; In Mark 13:8 earthquakes and famines are depicted as signs of the present; Many natural catastrophes during the first century BCE were confirmed by Josephus: a drought, a hurricane, an earthquake, epidemics, and a famine. There is evidence for a great famine under the domain of Claudius about CE 46/7. Cf. *Antt.*20.2.5 &51ff; Acts. 11:28.

[115] Davies, *Invitation to the New Testament...*, 18.

[116] Lk. 4:18.

[117] Theissen, *Sociology of Early Palestinian Christianity...*, 38.

[118] *Ibid.*, 42.

[119] D. E. Oakman, "The Countryside in Luke-Acts," in *The Social world of Luke-Acts: Models for Interpretation,* ed. by J. H. Neyrey (Peabody: Hendrickson, 1993), 163.

[120] R. A. Horsley and J. S. Hanson, *"Bandits, Prophets, and Messiahs* (London: Harper & Row, 1985), 2.

[121] Lk. 20:9ff, the parable of the wicked tenants.

[122] Lk. 23:1ff; State tax has a number of various forms: 1) land tax; 2) tribute or head tax; 3) Levies at crossroads; etc. [A. Storkey, *Jesus and Politics: Confronting the Powers* (Grand Rapids: Baker Academic, 2005), 215.]

[123] Tithe. In Lk. 18:12, it is depicted that the priestly aristocracy justified their taxation on ideological and religious grounds. Temple tax includes the categories of: Corban, tithe, and annual tax. [Storkey, *Jesus and Politics...*, 216.]

[124] Theissen, *Sociology of Early Palestinian Christianity...*, 42-44.

[125] Horsley and Hanson, *"Bandits, Prophets, and Messiahs ...*, 50.

[126] Crossan, *The Birth of Christianity...*, 182.

[127] *Ibid.*

[128] Green, *New Testament Theology...*, 12f.

[129] Theissen, *Sociology of Early Palestinian Christianity...*, 48-50.

[130] Theissen, *Sociology of Early Palestinian Christianity...*, 54-57; Lk. 23: 50ff.

[131] G. Theissen, *The Social Setting of Pauline Christianity*, ed. and tr. by J. H. Schutz (Edinburgh: T & T Clark, 1982), 29.

[132] W. F. Flemington, *The New Testament Doctrine of Baptism* (London: S.P.C.K., 1948), 17f.

[133] Lk. 3:7.

[134] Lk. 3:9.

[135] Gerd Theissen, *The Gospels in Context: Social and Political History in the Synoptic Tradition,* tr. by L. M. Maloney (Edinburg: T&T Clark, 1992), 42, citing *Gos. Thom. 78.*

[136] Mk. 14:57.

[137] Theissen, *Sociology of Early Palestinian Christianity...*, 60, citing *Antt.* 20.5.1, 97ff; *Antt.* 20.8.6, &167ff; *BJ* 7.9.1, & 438, cf. *Antt.* 20.8.6, & 167f; *Antt.* 18.4.1, & 5ff.

[138] *Ibid.*, 61, citing *Antt.* 17.10.5, && 271f; *BJ* 2.17.8f. & 434, 444.

[139] H. K. Bond, *Caiaphas: Friend of Rome and Judge of Jesus?* (Westminister: John Knox Press, 2004), 27; J. J. Collins, "Messiah, Jewish"..., 65 citing Josephus, *Ant.* 17.271-285.

[140] V. J. John, *The Ecological Vision of Jesus: Nature in the Parables of Mark* (Thiruvalla: CSS, 2002), 143.

[141] Lk. 7:1-10; 23:47; Esler, *Community and Gospel...*, 36; Davies, *Invitation to the New Testament...*, 38; C. A. Evans, "Context, family and formation," in *The Cambridge Companion to Jesus,* ed. by M. Bockmuehl (Cambridge: University Press, 2001), 11.

[142] *Ibid.*, 56.

[143] Cf. 1Kgs. 17:8-16.

[144] 2 Kgs. 5: 1-14.

[145] J. H. Neyrey, "Ceremonies in Luke-Acts: The Case of Meals and Table Fellowship," in *The Social world of Luke-Acts: Models for Interpretation,* ed. by J. H. Neyrey (Peabody: Hendrickson, 1993), 361, citing R. J. Karris, *Luke: Artist and Theologian* (New York: Paulist Press, 1985), 70.

[146] 2 Macc. 6f; Dan. 1:3-16; Judith 10:5-12: 19; Esther 4:17; & Tobit 1:11. [Esler, *Community and Gospel...*, 80-83.]

[147] R. L. Rohrbaugh, "The Pre-industrial city in Luke-Acts: Urban Social Relations," in *The Social world of Luke-Acts: Models for Interpretation,* ed. by J. H. Neyrey (Peabody: Hendrickson, 1993), 146.

[148] Honour can be achieved either as ascribed or acquired: ascribed honour is received passively by one through birth, family connections, or endowment by notable persons of power; and, acquired honour is achieved actively by the opposite way, i.e., through one's efforts or at the expense of social contest of challenge and riposte. [B. J. Malina and J. H. Neyrey, "Honour and Shame in Luke-Acts: Pivotal Values of the Mediterranean World," in *The Social world of Luke-Acts: Models for Interpretation,* ed. by J. H. Neyrey (Peabody: Hendrickson, 1993), 27f.]

[149] *Ibid.,* 27-30.

[150] A common source of both Matthew and Luke referred to as Quelle (Q). "T.W. Manson gives a useful list of Lukan passages upon which V. Harnack, Streeter and Bussmann agree. They are: Lk. 3:7-9; 4:1-13; 6:20-23, 27-33, 35-44, 46-49; 7:1-10, 18-20, 22-35; 9:57-60; 10:2-16, 21-24; 11:9-13, 29-35, 39, 41, 42, 44, 46-52; 12:2-10, 22-31, 33, 34, 39, 40, 42-46, 51, 53, 58, 59; 13:18-21, 24, 28, 29, 34, 35; 14:26, 27, 34, 35, 16:13, 16-18; 17:1, 3, 4, 6, 23, 24, 26, 27, 33-35, 37." [R. H. Fuller, *A Critical Introduction to the New Testament* (Great Britain: Duckworth, 1966), 72f.]

[151] J. S. Kloppenborg and L. E. Vaage, "Early Christianity, Q and Jesus: The Sayings Gospel and Method in the Study of Christian Origins," in *Early Christianity, Q and Jesus, Semeia* 55 (Atlanta: Scholars Press, 1991), 9f.

[152] J. S. Kloppenborg, "Literary Convention, Self-Evidence and the Social History of the Q People," in *Early Christianity, Q and Jesus,* Semeia 55 (Atlanta: Scholars Press, 1991), 96.

[153] B. L. Mack, "Q and the Gospel of Mark: Revising Christian Origins," in *Early Christianity, Q and Jesus,* Semeia 55 (Atlanta: Scholars Press, 1991), 16; Q 12:11-12.

[154] J. S. Kloppenborg, "Literary Convention, …"…, 87.

[155] *Ibid.,* 88f.

[156] Horsley, "Q and Jesus…"…, 184 citing J. S. Kloppenborg, *The Formation of Q: Trajectories in Ancient Wisdom* Collections (Philadelphia: Fortress Press, 1987), 188.

[157] Wolves refer to hostile rulers. cf. Ezek. 22:27 & Zeph. 3:3.

[158] Kee, *Christian Origins…,* 135.

[159] Boring, "The Historical-Critical Method's…"…, 30.

[160] Guignebert, *The Jewish World in the time of Jesus…,* 260.

[161] Davies, *Invitation to the New Testament…,* 147f.

Chapter - 2

Kingship Motif
in the Infancy Narrative

Subsequent to the survey of the use of the title King in various social, historical, political and biblical milieu, and the status of the Socio-political world of Luke, this chapter proceeds to locate how Luke has picked up the ideas of Kingship from the *Sitz im leben* of the Lukan community around its history to introduce the ideal image of Kingship in Jesus in juxtaposition to the oppressive rule of Roman Emperor in the composition of the Infancy Narrative. The notions of Kingship will be examined here through the episodes of the Infancy Narrative in the light of Fitzmyer's observation that the Kingship motif of Jesus occurs in the Lukan Passion Narrative without a real significance in the rest of the Gospel except only with a reference in the Infancy Narrative.[1] A profound eye on the Christological implications, especially, the motif of Kingship in the composition of Luke's Gospel from the beginning of the Infancy Narrative may thus facilitate one to find the author's skill and intention in writing the Gospel coherently.

In order to explore the political overtone of the Kingship motif in the Infancy Narrative of Luke in relation to the composition of the entire Gospel, the following questions will be addressed: Does the Infancy Narrative of Luke differ from Matthew's? If so, do Lukan

additions and transpositions of Matthew make any emphasis on
Jesus' Kingship? Does the reference to the 'historic present'[2] signify
imperialism? Does the Davidic descent of Jesus portray Jesus as a King?
Do the courtly languages used in the Infancy Narrative portray Jesus'
birth as an alternative King of the Roman empire? Do the Canticles,
the special material of Luke depict Jesus as an anticipated King?
etc., These questions will be dealt with in six sections: 1) Correlation
between the Infancy Narratives of Luke and Matthew, in which the
artistic compositional style of Luke in introducing Jesus as a King in
a covert manner will be sought; 2) the historic present which signifies
imperialism and juxtaposes the birth of Jesus as a King against the
Roman emperor will be viewed; 3) The Davidic Descent, in which
how Luke portrays Jesus as a King in the Old Testament promise
fulfillment will be looked into; 4) Lukan usage of Courtly languages
that comes out of the imperial culture which reflects the Kingly aspects
in the 1st century CE; 5) political overtones of the reversal of power
and reordering of position seen in the Canticles; and, 6) Jesus in the
Temple at the age of twelve, which depicts both his Davidic descent
and his Messianic identity. All these elements in the Infancy Narrative
of Luke seem to expose Jesus as an ideal Messianic/Davidic King in
its context either covertly or overtly.

Correlation between the Infancy Narratives of Luke and Matthew

Among the four evangelists, only Luke and Matthew include the Infancy
Narrative in their respective Gospels. Both Mark and John directly
introduce Jesus by his ministry without giving any importance to his
birth details. Even though Luke and Matthew give the details of the
birth of Jesus, along with similarities there are differences in: style;
events; people involved; etc., Luke seems to juxtapose the Kingship of
Jesus by his birth against Augustus',[3] the Roman Emperor and using
the courtly term, gospel in the annunciation to the shepherds who were
uncared. Whereas, Matthew explicitly introduces Jesus as the King of

the Jews through the conversation of Magi and Herod, the Palestinian King under the Roman Emperor, along with the depiction of the Old Testament fulfillment. Although, Luke maintains secrecy motif[4] in his introduction of Jesus as a King in juxtaposition to Augustus, both of them introduce Jesus as a Davidic King either explicitly or secretly through their Infancy Narratives. In looking at the sources of composing the Infancy Narrative, it is obvious that since Mark doesn't have the Infancy Narrative, some of the common materials reflect Q along with their own respective special materials, L and M.

Q Material

A careful study of the Q materials in both the Gospels' Infancy Narratives reveals that there are certain similarities in them. The similarities in the occurrences are: a) Mary and Joseph are engaged but not yet come together to live;[5] b) Joseph's Davidic descent;[6] c) angelic announcement regarding the birth of the child;[7] d) the conception of Mary by the Holy Spirit;[8] e) the angelic announcement of Jesus as the child's name;[9] f) angelic declaration of Jesus as the Saviour;[10] g) the birth of the child after the parents lived together;[11] h) the birth at Bethlehem;[12] i) historic present of the birth to the reign of Herod the Great;[13] j) the child's brought up at Nazareth.[14] Amidst the similarities, the historical reliability of the Infancy Narratives in both Luke and Matthew are questionable due to occurrences of the supernatural elements of angelic appearances, virgin birth, etc., However, along with the common materials, although both of them seem to have a common perspective in writing the Infancy Narrative, the criss-cross of their individual materials at significant points indicate the independent motif of their respective Infancy Narratives.

L Material

The peculiar Lukan materials: the story of Elizabeth, Zechariah, and the birth of John the Baptist; the census that caused Joseph to come to Bethlehem; the scenario of the shepherds; Jesus in the Temple at the age of twelve; and the four canticles, which are the major additions along with the Q materials. The L materials resemble some of the Old Testament events and characters. Scholars view that Luke might have consulted the LXX while composing his Gospel. Brown, P. Winter and N. Turner identify the peculiarity of Luke's Infancy Narrative in its highly Semitizised style and Semitizised Greek influenced by the vocabulary and style of the LXX.[15] C. W. Jung, along with J. Drury, O'Fearghail, Fitzmyer, Goulder, and Ravens say that Luke consulted LXX in composing the Infancy Narrative; and argue in line with Brown that Luke imitated the style of LXX to associate the Old Testament events to the Infancy Narrative.[16] In addition to these views of scholars, it is perceptible that in the linking of the Old Testament happenings in the Infancy Narrative the author reveals his own theological motif in composing the Gospel in relation to the birth of Jesus. This is done not only introducing him as the Saviour but also as a King in line with the promise and fulfillment of the Davidic Kingdom.

M Material

Along with Q materials, Matthew adds his special materials concerning the star, the Magi, Herod's plot against Jesus, the massacre of the children in Bethlehem, the flight to Egypt and special genealogy.[17] These are however not used by Luke but indicate Jesus as the King of the Jews at the outset overtly.

Compositional Style of the Lukan Infancy Narrative

Along with the observations of additions and transpositions from Matthew's, the Infancy Narrative of Luke might be reasonably understood as an introduction to both the Gospel of Luke and the biography of Jesus. But, scholars differ in their opinions: Audet, Minear, Songer and Brown consider the Infancy Narrative as a true introduction to some of the main themes of the Gospel;[18] Fitzmyer observes that it resonates with many of the motifs orchestrated both in the Gospel and Acts;[19] Conzelmann, Oliver, Tatum, and Voss find that it diverges to the main thought of Luke/Acts;[20] and, Hendrickx says that it does not belong to the core of the Gospel but it might be a Lukan attempt to elicit Jesus' early days against the primitive preaching of Jesus' death and resurrection.[21] On the other hand, M. Kähler, K. L. Schmidt, M. Dibelius, R. Bultmann, W. Bussmann, V. Taylor and J. Jeremias agree that the earlier parts of the gospels are the extended introductions of the Passion Narrative.[22] Their speculations are though acceptable this research, which seeks the Kingship motif in Lukan composition, speculates further that the intention of the author in composing the Infancy Narrative is to introduce the early life of Jesus as the introduction to his Gospel.

The use of common materials along with their own special materials in the Gospels of both Luke and Matthew, show their particular interest in composing their respective Infancy Narratives. In Luke's Gospel, around one-third seems to be his own special material. The angelic imagination and poetical style of Luke can't be reconciled with the narrative of Matthew. Concerning the Kingship of Jesus, Matthew openly declares Jesus as King through the portrayals of: the search of the Magi with the title, "the child who has been born King of the Jews;"[23] the reigning Herod's fear of losing his throne; the adoration of the Magi; and the offering of royal gifts. While Matthew presents Jesus as the King of the Jews in the Infancy Narrative, Lukan presentation of Jesus in the Infancy Narrative is interpreted by C. R. Erdman in terms of "the ideal Man, and the story is full of human interest."[24] However, this is not acceptable fully because Luke seems to be more artistic in his composition by maintaining the secrecy motif in revealing the Kingship of Jesus, instead of openly declaring as Matthew did, by using the canticles and the angelic annunciation in connection with the anticipation and fulfillment of Messianic prophecies and themes of the Old Testament.

The compositional style of both the Gospels show the respective authors' own interests in writing the Infancy Narrative not as a historical record but as one with their own theological motifs. This is obvious in their interpretation of the Old Testament incidents in association with the birth of Jesus. For instance, Luke's description of Zechariah and Elizabeth resembles the Old Testament portrayal of Abraham and Sarah.[25] Mary's song of praise resembles Hannah's prayer in 1 Sam 2:1-10. According to Fitzmyer, the association of Old Testament events is aimed at introducing the child as the agent of salvation.[26] According to M. Coleridge, the Lukan Infancy Narrative exposes the Davidic Messiah by means of promise and fulfillment; as well as, praise and proclamation.[27] Concerning the Old Testament influence on the composition of the Infancy Narratives of Luke, C. T. Ruddick notices the parallels in the three canticles which refer back to the patriarchs, particularly the references to Jacob in 1:54; 1:67 & 2:32.[28] In this connection of the Old Testament influence concerning the prophecy-fulfillment theme, Sheeley sees in it the legitimation of the authority and identity of Jesus.[29] Even though Ruddick sees only the references to the patriarchs, as Fitzmyer, Coleridge, and Sheeley see, Luke presents Jesus as the Saviour and the Davidic Messiah which is vivid in the recognition of the city of David as Bethlehem in 2:4&10f.

In all probability, although Fitzmyer identified 1:33 as the only direct reference to Lukan account of Jesus' Kingship in the Infancy Narrative, the nuances of Jesus' Kingship in the composition of the Infancy Narrative, such as the usage of historic present, reference to the Davidic descent, the use of courtly languages, political overtones of reversal of power and reordering of a privileged position, etc., seem to portray the Lukan motif of Kingship. The implicit motif of Jesus as a King in Luke's Gospel seems to have effectively and emphatically catalyzed the character of Jesus from the time of his birth as a King in order to reveal it in the Passion Narrative.

The Historic Present: Significance of Imperialism

The historic present: "in the days of King Herod of Judea;"[30] "in those days a decree went out from Emperor Augustus… while Quirinius was governor of Syria;"[31] and, "in the fifteenth year of the reign of Emperor of Tiberius, when Pontius Pilate was governor of Judea, and Herod was ruler of Galilee and his brother Philip ruler of the region of Ituraea and Trachonitis, and Lysanias ruler of Abilene, during the high priesthood of Annas and Caiaphas, the word of God came to John son of Zechariah in the wilderness,"[32] draw the attention of the social setting in a particular period of political tension in Rome. The reference to the fifteenth year of Tiberius Caesar is fairly calculated as CE 29 by the death of Augustus in CE14 as it is mentioned in 3:1. Pontius Pilate was the Governor of Judea, while Herod was the Tetrarch of Galilee, and his brother Philip and Lysanias' rule are seen as true as per history.[33] According to P. Richardson, Matthew and Luke are convinced of the Intertestamental period expectation of the Messianic King and they have woven their accounts of Jesus' birth accordingly as Jesus is the Messiah and portrayed him in conflict with Herod the King.[34] Richardson's speculation might be right but concerning the historic present in Luke it indicates Jesus' conflict not only with Herod, but also with Emperor Augustus which is implicit throughout the Gospel.

On the other hand, "a decree went out from Emperor Augustus… while Quirinius was governor of Syria,"[35] and "during the high priesthood of Annas and Caiaphas,"[36] have created difference of opinion among the scholars about the historical value of Lukan writings. Dealing with this issue of historicity, almost everyone agrees that as a Hellenistic historian, Luke does not write the actual event but roots the biblical event in history.[37] Along with this view of Luke's historical perspective, the historic present of the decree from the Emperor Augustus for a worldwide census is perceived as Luke's intentional composition to juxtapose Jesus during the reign of Emperor Augustus.

Decree from Emperor Augustus

Ἐν ταῖς ἡμέραις ἐκείναις in 2:1 literally means 'in those days,' but the reference to an edict implies an imperial action of the Roman Senate.[38] The reference to a historical event in this and the following verses, concerning a decree from the Emperor Augustus[39] and a worldwide census at the time of Jesus' birth during the time of Quirinius, the governor of Syria, raise a lot of issues about its historical genuineness.

Although it is known from the Egyptian papyri that the census was common in the East and from Fitzmyer's description that during the times 28 BCE, 8 BCE, and CE 14 Augustus conducted enrollments of Roman citizens in his empire which was known as *census populi*,[40] the dating of it becomes problematic. W. Manson calculates a fourteen year cycle of census from the imperial Egypt in CE 20 and proposes that a similar one might have taken place in Syria during CE 6.[41] As per the Roman history, Publius Sulpicius Quirinius was made the legate of Syria and the Procurator of Judaea in CE 6 after the deposition of Archelaus, the son of Herod the Great. However, the census of Quirinius in CE 6 and the historic present of Luke,[42] disagree with Matthew's account because King Herod was alive during the time of Jesus' birth.[43] So, the reference to census in Luke is inaccurate. According to Peter Richardson, census was possible only after Archelaus' exile. He refers to *Ant.*18:26, which dates Quirinius' census to CE 6, i.e., "the thirty-seventh year after Actium," and suggests that Luke possibly backdated the census of Quirinius and included Joseph and Mary's trip to Bethlehem in that milieu.[44]

Besides, the reference to first[45] census during the governorship of Quirinius indicates several censuses under Quirinius and leads to the understanding that no Roman census apart from Rome had been held in Judea before CE 6-7.[46] But, in the Old Testament, there was a precedent of King David's census in Israel and Judah.[47] So, the discrepancy in the historic present indicates that Luke might have been influenced not only by Roman history but also by Jewish history of the Old Testament. It may be further understood from his reference to the city of David and the Temple in 2:1-40.

Moreover, the census of 'everyone to his own city'[48] covers Judeans and all the people in the Roman Empire including Roman citizens and non-Roman inhabitants of the provinces, such as Syria. But, the evidence of *Protevangelium of James* 17:1 limits the enrollment only to the inhabitants of Bethlehem.[49] It is possible because, as a native of Bethlehem, Joseph might have gone with Mary. However, amidst all the historical and topographical problems, the intention of the author here seems to show Bethlehem as the native place of Jesus instead of Nazareth.

Another possibility of referring to the census of Quirinius, which had provoked the rebellion of Judas, a half-century later, culminated with the Jewish revolt against Rome in CE 70.[50] It seems that Luke deliberately associates the birth of Jesus with the rise of the Zealot movement, in which the leader, Judas the Galilean became prominent and lost his life in his patriotic attempt. In this political context, Luke might have possibly tried to expose Jesus as a non promoter of revolt by showing the obedient Galilean parents to the Roman census. The patriotic intention is evident in the angelic annunciation in Luke 2:11 against the Roman rule.

There is an additional possibility that Luke might have been influenced by the reference to the census mentioned in Ps. 87:6[51] and associates it theologically with the birth of Jesus, the messianic King. Ps. 87 describes the people of various nations coming to Jerusalem, gaining knowledge of the Lord and registering as citizens of Zion. Although LXX reads it as, "The Lord will recount it in the inscription of the peoples and of the princes who were born in her," the *Quinta* Greek version attested by Eusebius in the *Commentary on the Psalms* reads, "In the census of the peoples, this one will be born there." LXX speaks of the birth of the Princes and the Aramaic version of the psalm reads it as the rearing of a King.[52] So, Luke in his composition of the Gospel might have regarded the Psalm as a prophecy of the future birth of the messianic King by recounting Jesus' birth during the rule of Caesar Augustus in juxtaposition to him through a census.

Emperor Augustus and the Birth of Jesus

As a unique significance, Luke declares Jesus' birth during the time of Caesar Augustus, who was the Roman Emperor between 27 BCE and CE 14. His mightiness was known throughout his Kingdom and he has hailed as saviour and god in the eastern Mediterranean world. An inscription at Halicarnassus addresses him as the saviour of the whole world.[53] Mainly, a lengthy period of Augusts' rule was regarded as an era of peace, the *Pax Augusta*. In worship of him, the Roman senate had consented to found an altar of *Pax Augusta*, the so-called *Ara pacis augustae* in the campus Martius. As a monument it was rebuilt and exists till today at Rome. As it is seen in Priene inscription 40-42, every year, his birthday was celebrated on 23rd September as the beginning of good news for the world since he had pacified the world.[54] In this backdrop of the historical *Pax Augusta*, Luke records *Pax Christi* in the Infancy Narrative as a Saviour King, as it was anticipated to fulfill the hopes of the people which the Roman King Augustus could not.

Further, at the time of Jesus' birth, instead of human proclamation Luke portrays the heavenly host's involvement in announcing the good news. Luke juxtaposes the Priene inscription's message of Augustus' birthday as the good news for the world, with the angelic announcement of Jesus' birth as, "Do not be afraid; for see-I am bringing you good news of great joy for all the people: to you is born this day in the city of David, a Saviour, who is the Messiah, the Lord."[55] It indicates the motif of Luke in composing the Infancy Narrative along with depicting Jesus' messianic Kingship.

Consequently, it raises a question: does Luke artfully write this to depict the political scenario? It is very well obvious that Luke in the backdrop of the political scenario introduces Jesus as the Messianic King. It may be understood from the scholars' opinions. Brown says that it can hardly be accidental but depicts an implicit challenge to the imperial propaganda of Rome by claiming the real peace of the world by Jesus,[56] the messianic King. According to J. B. Green, because Luke's presentation of Jesus in 2:11 &14, as the Saviour, the Lord in whom peace comes to the world is in the context of the explicit reference to Emperor Augustus in 2:1 who was known as the divine saviour who brought peace to the world.[57] S. Kim says that in the context of Rome, while it was so sensitive to the rise of a new ruler, Luke deliberately contrasts Jesus to Augustus by declaring Jesus as the Lord and Saviour who brings peace on earth.[58] However, the reference to Caesar Augustus in his oppressive rule, therefore, exposes the birth

of Jesus, a messianic King in juxtaposition to the peace and security
of Augustus' dominion.

Priesthood of Annas and Caiaphas

"During the high priesthood of Annas and Caiaphas" raises another
historical issue that whether single priesthood was administered by
both of them simultaneously and if so, did both belong to the same
period? Acts 4:6 also reads in the same manner of confusion along
with other two: Annas the high priest, Caiaphas, John, and Alexander,
and all who were of the high-priestly family. The reference to Annas
and Caiaphas might have been from Luke's special source L. Caiaphas
was the acting high priest during the time,[59] dated CE 18-36, and
Annas, preceded him in the high priesthood, who was his father-in-
law, dated CE 6-15.[60] According to H. K. Bond, from the narrative it
seems that Luke is not much interested in mentioning either of them
as historical persons or powerful figures with respect.[61] But according
to Fitzmyer it is to date the ministry of John and followed by Jesus
within the Palestinian history. The reference to the fifteenth year of
the reign of Emperor Tiberius is dated CE 28 and the governorship
of Pontius Pilate in Judea, which is dated during CE 26 – CE 36.[62]
The anchoring of the episode in Roman history as well as in the
Palestinian history is vivid here in Lukan composition of the Gospel
through the historic present.

John the Baptist and Jesus

The artistic composition of Luke in connection with John and Jesus
is manifested not only at the beginning of their ministry like in
Matthew and Mark, but also in the birth narratives: the annunciations
of conceptions;[63] followed by their birth and, naming.[64] Although Luke
has paralleled the traditions of both the birth of John and Jesus into
an artful symmetry, the attention is focused on Jesus,[65] and it is known
as step-parallelism.[66] Whether it is a step-parallelism or not, it is clear
that Luke distinguishes both John and Jesus by birth along with the
focus of their forthcoming ministry as well their nature of birth. John

is portrayed as a great human person previous to Jesus, who prepares the way for him. He was filled with the Holy Spirit from his mother's womb. But Jesus is a divine person begotten by the Holy Spirit and considered as the one who will rule over the house of Israel. In this, Luke's emphasis on Jesus' Kingship is very clear from the portrayal of the child Jesus, in the episode of the angel Gabriel's annunciation to Mary as written in 1:32f,

> He will be great, and will be called the Son of the Most High, and the Lord God will give to him the throne of his ancestor David. He will reign over the house of Jacob forever, and of his Kingdom there will be no end.

The pre-Lukan tradition exposes John the Baptist and Jesus as the two Messiahs hailing one from Aaron and another from David. John the Baptist resembles Elijah, on the basis of Deut. 18:18, the prophet. It is vivid in 1:17, the angelic declaration about John that with the spirit and power of Elijah he prepares the way for the coming one. Here it is vivid that Luke associates John the Baptist and Elijah in the preparation of way for the Messiah according to the Old Testament and Apocryphal texts: Mal. 4:5f; and, Sirach 48:10.[67] Indeed, Luke portrays him as a reincarnation of Elijah who appeared in the desert and uttered thunders of rebuke, shook the nation, stirred the conscience of the people and acknowledged Jesus even before birth as the anticipated Messianic King.

Davidic Descent

The Davidic descent of Jesus in Luke also raises the issue of its historical value. Jesus' birth was foretold and located not only in the house of David and in the city of David but also labelled him as a Davidic.[68] However, scholars differ in their views concerning this due to the difficulty in tracing the family tree after several hundreds of years. But Brown expounds the genealogy in an aesthetic way thus,

> The Christian community believed that Jesus had fulfilled Israel's hopes; prominent among those hopes was the expectation of a Messiah, and so the traditional title "Messiah" was given to Jesus;

but in Jewish thought the Messiah was pictured as having Davidic descent; consequently Jesus was described as "son of David"; and eventually a Davidic genealogy was fashioned for him.[69]

In opposition to this view of a historicized *theologoumenon*, Cullmann, Hahn, Jeremias, Michaelis, and Stauffer put forward it as a historical one.[70] But, it is a difficult process to identify the historical lineage. Amidst this difficulty, there are some evidences that hint at the Davidic ancestry and the Israelite tribe's lineage,[71] which have survived at the time of Jesus as well as later. However, from Luke's depiction of Jesus as the Davidic Messiah as it is seen in the episode of virgin birth, in the usage of the phrase, the city of David and, in the Davidic pedigree referred to in the angelic annunciation, it is feasible to admit that it had survived as a fulfillment of the Palestinian pre-Christian messianic expectations of the Magna Charta of Davidic monarchy.

The Magna Charta of Davidic Monarchy and the Lineage of David

In 1:32, Luke, through the mouth of the angel Gabriel establishes the fulfillment of the Magna Charta[72] of Davidic monarchy promised in 2 Sam. 7:11-16. According to Luke, the child of Mary is the Davidic King, who brings joy to the house of Jacob. Among the Infancy Narrative writers, only Luke brings the connection to the Magna Charta of the Davidic monarchy. Though Matthew directly names Jesus as the King of the Jews through the inquiry of the Magi, he doesn't make any reference to the Magna Charta of the Davidic monarchy. The Lukan special material evidences Lukan motif of exposing Jesus as the Davidic, Messianic King by depicting both Joseph and Mary in the lineage of David.

When we look back to the history of Zerubbabel[73] in 505 BCE, Zerubbabel, as a Davidid had served as a Persian governor when the royal house of David had no power in Palestine. Later, at the time of Maccabeans and Hasmonians in 2nd century BCE, along with the monarchical hopes, the high priest was anointed as a messiah and became the political leader in Judah.[74] The use of the title, King by the Hasmonean high priests revived the expectation and restoration of the Davidic Kingdom as it is portrayed in Psalm 2:7 concerning the coronation of the King and in Ps. 89:29 about the lineage of Davidic King. Further, the Jewish literature in the late first century BCE, *Psalms of Solomon* 17:23[21] refers to the title, Son of David for the expected King who destroys the unrighteous rulers and gathers the holy people by purging Jerusalem. The Qumran text, 4Q *Florilegium* 1:10-13 interprets the Davidic dynasty referred to in 2 Sam. 7:11-14 as 'my son' and the 'shoot of David,' who would be on David's throne to save Israel as prophesied in Amos 9:11. Another biblical commentary, 4Q Psalm 2:7 interprets Isa. 11:1-3 to refer to the Davidic branch to whom God will give a throne of glory.[75]

Contemporaneous to Jesus' time and later also there are references: *Shemoneh Esreh or Eighteen Benedictions* during the end of the first century CE was a standard Jewish prayer for the re-establishment of the throne of David. IV Ezra 12:32, an apocalypse written after the fall of Jerusalem anticipated the Messiah, who shall spring from the seed of David.[76] Further, there is evidence that the grandsons of Jude and the brother of Jesus were accused in front of the Emperor Domitian during the 80[s] as politically dangerous since they were descended from David.[77] Thus the trajectory indicates that the Christians of Jewish descent acknowledged Jesus as the Messiah, a Davidid.

Moreover, during the time of Jesus, his adversaries hadn't raised any objection against his Davidic descent. But, Mark 12:35-37 is often adduced as an evidence for the relinquishment of Davidic origins by Jesus himself:

> How can the scribes say that the Messiah is the son of David? David himself, by the Holy Spirit, declared, 'The Lord said to my Lord ... David himself calls him Lord; so how can he be his son?'

The *prima facie* seems to be that Jesus is denying his Davidic descent.[78] But, how does this discrepancy arise, while all the three evangelists understood Jesus as a Davidid. The reference may probably be to underline Jesus' pre existent state. It may be comprehensible from the writing of Apostle Paul, ca. 58, who was a zealous Jew seeking valid reason to refute the followers of Jesus, after his conviction of Jesus writes in Rom. 1:3, "the gospel concerning his Son, who was descended from David according to the flesh and was declared to be the Son of God ..."

In spite of all these arguments, since, Joseph was considered from the house of David, the legal Davidic descent of Jesus is assured[79] from both the genealogies of Matthew and Luke. But Mary, according to Luke 1:36 is a kinswoman of Elizabeth, in the line of the daughters of Aaron.[80] This indicates that Mary too was of Levitic descent. Plummer argues that Luke points out the relationship of Mary and Elizabeth, which Wicliff identified as cousin, and continued as kinswoman, which gives a definite meaning that Jesus was from both Levi and Judah. Further, he states that the Levites marry from other tribes also. So, Elizabeth, descended from Aaron, might be related to the one who descended from David.[81] However, both Mary and Joseph's Davidic lineage is asserted by Syr.sin 2:4, 5 where, instead of singular pronoun referring to Joseph plural is used: 'because both of them were of the house of David.'[82] Yet, there may arise a question as to how Joseph could be counted as the father of Jesus on the basis of virgin birth recounted in Luke 1:32ff? The genealogy of Jesus as given in Luke 3:23-38 and in Matthew 1:1-17 state that Jesus is the son of Joseph albeit Matthew adds Mary's husband. Along with all these interpretations, the Davidic lineage can be understood further in the concept of virgin birth.

Virgin Birth

Lukan Infancy Narrative gives more emphasis to the virginal conception of Mary, the so called mystery of Christian faith, in giving birth to Jesus as referred to in Isa. 7:14. In Luke 1:27, Mary is twice referred to as a virgin, which P. Chakkalakal says that the double reference in the same verse indicates her virginal state before conceiving Jesus,[83] and 1:31 echoes Isa. 7:14, regarding the prophecy of conception, giving birth and naming the child. 1:34f describes the conception as Mary had no relations with a man but through the intervention of the Holy Spirit, the power from the Most High. It indicates the omnipotence of theocracy than human effort. The Lukan perception of the child may be understood from the title he uses for the child. In v. 32, he uses υἱος ὑψίστου and in v. 35, υἱος θεοῦ. As it has been noted in the 1st chapter, the Egyptian understanding of the King' divinity seems to be emphasized here along with the understanding of the divinity of the Roman Emperor as the son of god.

Though the concept of virgin birth, conceivably, might have been from Q source, both the evangelists differ in stating the event. Luke begins it with the annunciation to Mary whereas in Matthew it is told to Joseph when he had planned to dismiss her quietly. But, Luke as his own special material prudently puts forward the information of virgin birth through the question of Mary in v. 34, "How can this be, since I am a virgin."

However, the statement, 'from a woman betrothed to a man' has raised the issue of whether she articulates a vow of perpetual virginity[84] or a confusion of her in the conception of a child prior to her marriage.[85] G. B. Caird argues that even though the belief of virgin birth is indicated in 1:34 and 3:23, the Infancy Narrative depicts the account of birth as an ordinary human birth.[86] To Brown, Jesus is considered as the supposed son of Joseph as it is implied in 3:23.[87] Leaney argues that this mystery occurs because Luke might have combined two quite incompatible traditions[88] and it may be a reference to Deut. 22:23, a virgin betrothed to a man should not have any other relationship and bear a child, to prove Mary's perfectness.[89] This tradition seems to have developed among the 1st century Christians in three stages: 1) On the basis of similar cases in the Old Testament; 2) In reference to Deut. 22:23 and the view of the action of Holy Spirit in the conception of Isaac, Samson and Samuel; and 3) On the fulfillment of scripture, Jesus was born of a virgin.[90] Streeter and Harnack see the idea of conception without a human father as an interpolation of the evangelist.[91] However, it is generally accepted that Joseph is the father of Jesus from the time of Jesus till today amidst the scientific problem of conception. For instance, in Luke 2:5, Mary is spoken of Joseph's wife; and in 2:48b Mary tells Jesus, "…your father and I have been searching for you…"

Nevertheless, the conception of Mary through the power of the Holy Spirit mentioned in 1:35 reflects the Jewish expectations in terms of the Davidic Messiah as it is described in Isaiah 11:1-2 that the Spirit of the Lord is upon the Davidic branch; the term, holy is significant in Isaiah 4:2f with a future Davidic shoot; and the phrase, Son of God parallels to Son of the Most High which echoes God's description of the Davidic ruler as his Son in 2 Sam. 7:14 and Ps. 2:7.

The City of David

The reference to the city of David in the Old Testament indicates the fortress of Zion, which was formerly the stronghold of the Jebusites, as it is referred to in 2 Sam. 5:7, 9 & 1 Chron. 11:5, 7. According to Luke 2:4, Joseph went to the city of David, called Bethlehem in Judea from Nazareth in Galilee. Bethlehem is around six miles away from Jerusalem and it was known as the town/city of David and a shepherd-country. According to 1 Sam. 16:11; 17:12ff & 58, David was a Bethlehemite, hailed from the family of a shepherd Jesse, and tending the flocks. In the Infancy Narrative, Luke has associated the shepherds to both the birth of Jesus and Bethlehem, the city of David.

In this context, Ragg points out that the shepherds were the first devotees of the Shepherd King, Jesus.[92] The annunciation of Jesus' birth by the angels to the shepherds recorded in 2:8-14, according to R. Bultmann, seems to have been to the 'representatives of an ideal humanity.'[93] In 2 Sam. 5:2, shepherd is considered as a political or a military leader. M. Ford sees the introduction of shepherds in the Infancy Narrative as it parallels the imagery in Micah 4, a military setting; and, the Infancy Narrative includes the nationalistic overtone of the words στρατιά and σωτὴρ, Χριστὸς and κύριος. Moreover, he points out that the Maccabees and the Zealots recruited the shepherds.[94] But, in Jesus' time, shepherds were considered as dishonest and outside the

Law. Particularly, in Luke, they represent the group of sinners, poor and the outcasts whom Jesus has come to save. Even though in the Infancy Narrative, there is no hint about this, the Lukan poor shepherds are linked very closely with Bethlehem, the city of David.

Besides, Luke's reference in 2:8, to the shepherds pasturing their flock in the region of Bethlehem may perhaps reflect the Migdal Eder, the tower of the flock mentioned in Micah 4:8 and 5:1f. Concerning Gen. 35:21, the Targum Pseudo-Jonathan reads, "The Tower of the Flock, the place from which it will happen that the King Messiah will be revealed at the end of days."[95] The birth of Jesus in Bethlehem might possibly be derived from Micah's use of the ruler from Bethlehem.[96] In 2:4 &11f, Luke calls Bethlehem the city of David which resembles Micah's "the mountain of the house of the Lord."[97] In line with this, the response of the shepherds in 2:15, "Let us go over to Bethlehem and see the event that has taken place," indicates the relationship between Bethlehem, the city of David and the birth of the Messianic King.

Angelic Annunciation

The angelic appearances and their prophecies, and their declarations raise a lot of issues among scholars about their historical accuracies. But, it seems that Luke uses them as tools in composing his Gospel to establish his motif of Jesus' Kingship at the time of his birth itself. Especially, the Davidic theme is prevalent in the angelic annunciation of Jesus' birth. In the first century Jewish and Jewish-Christian circles, Messianic hope continued to retain the promise of David's line. So, that might possibly be spoken of Jesus in the natural way.

Brown sees the angelic words of Gabriel, as recorded in Luke 1:32f, as an interpretation of 2 Sam. 7:8-16, the promise of the prophet Nathan to David.[98] According to Ford, the annunciation reveals a messianic figure in accordance with the Jewish messianic expectation.[99] Above and beyond, there are parallels to the annunciation to Mary in the Old Testament: in Gen. 17:15ff, Abraham is promised a child;

in Judg. 13:2ff, Manoah' wife is announced of her conception etc., indicate the prophetical and saving nature of the child.

However, when comparing the annunciation of the birth of Jesus as an anticipated Davidic Messiah with Acts 1:6 concerning the enquiry of the disciples to the risen Jesus, "Lord, is this time when you will restore the Kingdom to Israel?" it implies the longing of the community, and discloses the political intention of restoring the Kingdom to Israel. So, it is vivid that Look uses angelic annunciation episodes as one of the tools to establish his motif of Jesus' Kingship in his composition of the Gospel.

Along with the angelic annunciation, the words of the multitude of heavenly host[100] reflect Isaiah 9:6 & 11:1, that the child is an heir to the throne of David, being called: Wonderful Counsellor, Mighty God, Everlasting Father, and Prince of Peace. Further, some of these words seem to be used as the courtly language of the imperial culture.

Courtly Language

In addition to the terms βασιλεύς and βασιλεία, which are already dealt with in the 1ˢᵗ chapter, the words εὐαγγέλιον, σωτήρ, εἰρήνη and χαῖρε, addressed by Thompson as "Luke's deliverance vocabulary,"[101] are some of the technical terms of Hellenistic thought derived from the courtly language of the imperial culture. In that Hellenistic milieu, Jesus' birth was announced by using these terms and he was presented as the Saviour through whom peace and new order would come to the world.[102] To know the intention of the author, we need to see the meaning and usage of the terms during those days.

Gospel

During the first century, the term εὐαγγέλιον was used in association with the Emperor worship. The Roman Emperor was considered as a divine being and on his birthday, he was expected to bring the gospel, i.e., good news or benefits, especially the gift of peace, which would persevere throughout his reign. According to Creed, the terms, εὐαγγελίζομαι and σωτήρ used in angelic annunciation in 2:10 agree to the language of the Priene inscription concerning the birthday of Augustus.[103] A. Stöger says that the angelic annunciation is well constructed to recall the inscription at Priene, in which Augustus was portrayed as a saviour, who ends all feuds; and his birth as an emperor-god was a message of joy for the world at the dawn of a new era.[104]

In this context of Roman rule, the use of this term depicts the prevalent anticipation of the people for a new ideal King to bring a new order in the society. The early Christians used the term with the definite article, the Gospel along with the arrival of Jesus. It denotes the momentous good news against many benefits[105] and is used to introduce the ideal King, the prince of peace, the Anointed one, the Messianic King Jesus in contrast to the reign of Caesar Augustus. It seems that Luke deliberately sets the birth of Jesus against the reign of Emperor Caesar Augustus. The Christocentric understanding of the Messianic King could be evidenced in Acts 17:7 by the words of the 1st century Christians that "there is another King named Jesus" than Caesar.

In the Old Testament, although, the noun Gospel doesn't occur, the verb form, to bring good news occurs in several places. For instance, in 1 Kings 1:42, it is used in the sense of bringing good news that David had made Solomon the King; in Jeremiah 20:15, it denotes the birth of a son; in 1 Sam. 31:8-10, it is used to denote the good news of a victory in battle etc., The use of the verb form in the Old Testament contains the idea of joy, associated with the idea of victory in battle and of a celebration or in connection with a sanctuary. Isa. 40:1-5 & 52:7-10 elucidates that the people of Israel in the Babylonian exile were longing to be back in Jerusalem, hoping God's victory over their foes after the proclamation of the good news by a messenger, an evangelist. In line with that, the term gospel in relation to Jesus implies a decisive victory over God's enemies, the foes of Israel; and, Jesus of Nazareth may have been thus set over against Caesar and acknowledged as the inaugurator of a new epoch.

Saviour

The word, σωτήρ is one of the technical terms of Hellenistic thought derived from the courtly language of the imperial cults.[106] According to M. Borg and J. D. Crossan, as per the Roman imperial theology, the emperor was called as the Lord, Saviour, and the one who had brought peace on earth.[107] The term σωτήρ in the backdrop of the Roman emperor worship implies three characteristics: 1) restoration of the societal order by the rulers; 2) physical and external healing of ills by Soter Asklepios; and, 3) redemption through the mystery deities.[108] With the impact of these implications, by using the term σωτήρ, Luke seems to present his vision of salvation through the life and teachings of Jesus: empowering the disadvantaged, seeking the lost, reconciling persons across social divisions, calling people to repentance, healing the sick, forgiving sins, and initiating people into the community of God's people. For instance, these are found in 4:18ff, the declaration of the Isaianic paradigm of salvation in Jesus' Nazareth Manifesto; in 18:9ff, the parable of the tax collector; in 19:9, Jesus' words to Zacchaeus, "Today salvation has come to this house"; the immediate pronouncement of salvation to the penitent thief; etc., With the vision of salvation to the people, unlike Matthew, ascribing to the new born child, the title saviour in 2:11 shows Luke's theological and Christological intention. It may be pointing to the fulfillment of God's plan as well.

Σωτήρ ὅς ἐστιν χριστὸς κύριος in 2:11 without any article can be understood as anointed Lord by considering χριστός as an adjective.[109] The usage of Χριστὸν κύριου in 2:26 is being considered as the original reading by Winter and others.[110] Creed says that it is possibly an error at some stage of translation from the Aramaic.[111] Leaney argues that it is an intentional use of Luke. If the words are considered in apposition they seem to be a double title as Luke uses in Acts 2:36 with conjunction, κύριον καὶ Χριστὸν. The literal translation, anointed Lord is hard to use as a title but, the title with two nominatives in close juxtaposition occurred in Hellenistic environment.[112] Leaney's argument of the phrase σωτήρ ὅς ἐστιν χριστὸς κύριος as the intentional use of Luke in the backdrop of Hellenistic understanding of the title is acceptable. But, the use of the term, σωτήρ to the χριστὸς κύριος indicates the post-resurrection understanding of the Christocentric Kingship of Jesus in the Hellenistic milieu, which occurs in Acts 2:36ff, instead of the name Jesus albeit the grammatical usage is queried.

Peace

Emperor Augustus was acknowledged as the divine saviour who brought peace to the world by ending war in his jurisdiction.[113] In that milieu, in Luke, Jesus is presented as the Saviour through whom peace comes to the world. It raises the issue: Does Luke create an alternative model for an empire in juxtaposing the *pax Romana*, the so-called peace of Rome by sword? The oracle of the prophet Zechariah, in chapter 9, depicts an alternative King who is "humble and riding on a donkey"[114] in the context of judgment on Israel's enemies, which depicts the scenario of war and victory.[115] In Luke, parallel to the *Gloria in Excelsis*[116] in which the heavenly host proclaims peace on earth at the time of Jesus' birth, in the procession of Jesus' Jerusalem entry[117] people praise him as, "Peace in heaven and glory in the highest heaven." Brown comments on it as the angels of heaven recognized peace at the beginning of Jesus' life whereas the disciples recognized peace at the close of his life.[118] According to Leaney, Glory in the highest represents an enactment of a new covenant depending upon the King's arrival and acceptance.[119] Brown's speculation might be acceptable because, the intention of Luke is vivid in its composition in Jesus as the alternative King who brings peace to the people. By the words of the people at the close of Jesus' life, at the triumphal entry, Luke declares Jesus as the King.

The term, εἰρήνη has redactional emphasis and significance of salvation in Luke.[120] Isa. 52:7 implies peace that the Messiah brings and in Isa 9:6, the prophet says that he is the prince of peace. In 1:79, Luke sees peace as a gift of God for salvation. In 2:30, the messianic vision of Simeon's words would be seen through the background of Judaism at the time of Jesus. Luke's reference to Simeon seems to reflect *Psalms of Solomon* 17:50, a first-century source, "Blessed are they who will exist in those days to see the good fortune of Israel which God will bring to pass."[121] Simeon's reference to departure in peace echoes the hope for peace in the re-establishment by the Messianic King in the line of King David. Thus through the heavenly chorus and the words of Simeon, it seems that Luke intends the peace through the alternative King for the happiness of the people.

The first century view of peace by the terms: Hebrew *Shalom* and the Greek εἰρήνη are: co-existence, absence of conflict, not longing for others' destruction, reconciliation, peace within oneself, etc.,[122] It is described by C. P. Lyngdoh along with F. Bovon as, "harmonious condition of people whose life is characterized by security, wholeness, well-being, prosperity, and living in fellowship with God."[123] On the whole, by using the term εἰρήνη in the courtly language of the imperial culture, Luke associates the birth of Jesus with a renowned Roman emperor to portray Jesus as the real King who brings peace and salvation to the entire world, the *Pax Christi* instead of *Pax Romana*.

Rejoice

Concerning the term χαῖρε in 1:28, the Kingship element of Jesus reflects the LXX background of Zech. 9:9.[124] This angelic salutation to Mary may be an interpolation from 1:42. Luke redacts it with a pun on the Greek words χαῖρε and κεχαριτωμένη.[125] The term, χαῖρε means hail, and at the same time a Semite would say peace to thee. But Creed refers to Gressmann who suggests that χαῖρε may be a literal translation of the term, הדי which means, rejoice, and translates the angelic salutation to Mary as, 'Rejoice, thou blessed one…'[126] If it is taken as rejoice, then the term denotes the good news of the King's victory to the nation after a war. It is vivid in the words of Simeon, in 2:25, as the one who was waiting for the consolation of Israel.[127] Simeon seems to be the one who recognizes Jesus as the promised bearer of messianic peace, salvation, and light which give joy. Brown agrees that rejoice is the literal meaning of the verb χαίρειν, whereas as an imperative it serves as a normal salutation: hail as it is used in Mt. 27:29; 28:9; 2 Cor. 13:11; James 1:1 & 2 Jn. 10.[128] Lyonnet prefers rejoice and argues that if Luke wanted the angel to give Mary an ordinary greeting in 1:28, he would have used εἰρήνη reflecting the Hebrew *shalom*, which is the Semitic custom, as he does in 10:5 and 24:36.[129] While considering its usage in the Septuagint, among the eighty occurrences of χαίρειν, about a quarter refers to the joy of divine saving act, announcement or promise. For instance, Ex. 4:31 depicts the joy of God's visitation to his people in their affliction in Egypt; Isa. 66:10 portrays God's promise of deliverance from exile that they will rejoice when they love Zion etc.

In LXX, χαῖρε is addressed to the Daughter of Zion, or to the land of Israel, or to the children of Zion.[130] Among those, Zech. 9:9, "Rejoice greatly, O Daughter Zion!... Lo, your King comes to you..." was familiar to early Christians and is cited in Matt. 21:5 and John 12:14-15. However, Luke 1:28-30, Gabriel's greetings to Mary resembles Zephaniah 3:14-17, a song of joy. Brown argues that if Luke uses χαῖρε to mean rejoicing at messianic salvation, he could have used the verb, εὐφραίνω which is used in Isaiah 54:1 in the context of a conception after barrenness or in Zech. 2:14-15 in a Daughter of Zion passage.[131] Brown's argument stands valid while isolating 1:28 from the context of Lukan Infancy Narrative. But, if we take the whole scenario of Infancy Narrative, for instance, in 2:30f, Simeon gives the reason for his gladness at the prospect of death. As it had been promised in Isaiah 40:5 that all flesh shall see the salvation of God, salvation is now personified in the Infant Jesus by Simeon in 2:30. Not only Simeon, but also in 1:47 & 69, Mary as well as Zechariah inferred salvation through their rejoicing. Further, it is vivid in Luke's use of special source L, which indicates his composition with this motif of Kingship through peculiar materials, such as *Magnificat, Benedictus,* and, *Nunc Dimittis,* with the political overtones of reversal and re-ordering of the situation.

Political Overtones of Reversal of Power and Reordering of Position

The episode of John's appearance with the historic present at the reign of King Herod depicts the political oppressive state. The frequent usage of the nouns saviour, salvation and redemption and the longing of the Lukan community to have a King to save them from the prevailing social unrest as manifested in the wordings of the Infancy Narrative seems to set the birth of Jesus in contrast to the contemporary political situations. Particularly, the Song of Mary, known as *Magnificat*,[132] the song of Zechariah, known as *Benedictus*;[133] and the Song of Simeon, known as the *Nunc Dimittis*,[134] communicate the reversal of positions: the powerful against the lowly as a socio-political reversal. J. B. Green vividly says that Jesus' proclamation of the Kingdom of God might have instigated a political threat as it is vibrant in the other episodes of Luke's narrative 'co-texts,'[135] which have more political overtones than the other Gospels.

Concerning the origin of the canticles, they might have been either composed by Luke or adapted by him from Jewish sources. A. V. Harnack, H. F. D. Sparks, N. Turner, M. D. Goulder, M. L. Sanderson and others say that these hymns were composed by Luke.[136] Whereas, Bornhäuser, H. Gunkel, E. Klostermann, P. Winter, S. Mowinckel, Spitta, P. Benoit and others say that these canticles were adapted by Luke from Jewish compositions:[137] particularly, the concept of salvation accomplished through the House of David and the catastrophic conditions during the alien persecution.

There are two common features in all the three canticles: 1) the introductory infinitive which denotes the purpose of action; and 2) the declaration of the salvation-event as fulfillment of God's promise.[138] Concerning the *Sitz im leben* of the canticles, the community seems to be the *anawim*, the poor, who may be defined as the lowly, sick, downtrodden, widows and orphans, who rely upon God.[139] In these canticles, Luke focuses upon the group who represent the piety of the *anawim*: Mary, the handmaid of the Lord; Zechariah, a Temple priest and his barren wife Elizabeth; and Simeon, a devout Jew. All these three canticles along with the Gloria in Excelsis[140] of the Lukan Infancy Narrative expose the same community and their longing in response to their diverse experiences of political oppression.

The Magnificat

The Magnificat, which is considered as a hymn of hope sung by the nation of Israel, of the Lukan Infancy Narrative resembles the hymn of Hannah in 1 Sam. 2:1-10. It shows not only the author's knowledge of the Jewish literature, but also, introduces Jesus as a Messianic King who liberates the people from their state of oppression. It portrays the evolution of Christocentric Kingship from Theocentric and human Kingship of Israel's history. Concerning the placing of it in Lukan composition, Leaney suggests that it should have been placed either after the annunciation or the birth of Jesus.[141] But, this song of joy's placement after the greeting of Elizabeth seems to be accurate in the art of Luke in exposing the context of the community's longing for redemption.

Elizabeth's greeting of Mary as, "Blessed are you among women, and blessed is the fruit of your womb" in 1:42 echoes the blessing promised to Israel in Deut. 28:4. Addressing her as "the mother of my Lord" in 1:43, it echoes Ps. 110:1 & 2 Sam. 24:21. 1:44, as the leaping of the child in womb created ecstasy in Mary to show the *Sitz im leben* of composing the song with an overwhelming joy in attaining the goal. According to Brown, the reference to the jumping of the child in the womb with gladness in vv. 41 & 44b indicates the advent of the messianic age and probably signifies the perception of the child as the Messiah by Elizabeth.[142] My lord in 1:43, in comparison to 2 Sam. 24:21 seems to be a juxtaposition to the King. The title κύριος applied to Jesus while growing in his mother's womb suggests that he is on a par with Yahweh and connotes him as a Christocentric King.

Besides, *Magnificat* resonates with the political milieu of those days and the community's joy at the arrival of the Messianic King. The words of the angel in 1:30ff, that the child will be given "the throne of his ancestor David," exposes Jesus as the anticipated Davidic King, the Messiah. W. Carter says that the throne of David is depicted by Luke in contrast to Rome's harsh and exploitative rule albeit they claimed it as a divinely sanctioned one.[143] A. Maclaren considers the words of the Magnificat as it depicts the anticipation of the appearance of the Messiah who was acknowledged as a warrior King in the Old Testament.[144] But there arises an issue of the canticle in which the past tense is used. According to Erdman, the use of past tense clandestinely describes the future events aimed at the coming of the Messianic King.[145] For instance, 1:52, "He has brought down the powerful from their thrones, and lifted up the lowly," confirms the vindication of Israel by conquering its enemies.

The salvation referred to in the *Magnificat* encompasses Mary and her people of Israel who are poor and oppressed. H. B. Beverly comments on Mary's canticle that she gave birth to a new reality of new social vision which is apocalyptic feature for transformation.[146] Mary's words of communal emphasis and her representation as a spokesperson on behalf of the poor and the oppressed in Israel are apparent. In v. 34, it is not Mary's own distress she is revealing in her query to the angel, "How can this be, since I am a virgin?" or "do not know a man," signifies her thirst to know how the conception will take place unnaturally. Matthew in 1:19 writes about her distress, "Her husband Joseph, being a righteous man and unwilling to expose her to public disgrace, planned to dismiss her quietly," whereas, Luke's omission of this signifies that he does not want to focus on Mary's distress separately in this context, which seems to be his intention in depicting the political overtone than her personal problem. Mary, by her submission as a servant in 1:38, is identified as a faithful and obedient representative of God in his work of redemption.

In addition to God's mighty act of salvation to the community, dethronement of the powerful and the upliftment of the lowly are portrayed as a Socio-political reversal in 1:51-55. This social reversal underlines the deliverance of the marginalized people.[147] The hungry are filled and the rich are sent away empty in 1:53. This resembles the beatitude addressed to the poor in 6:20 and the woe directed toward the rich in 6:24. The poverty and hunger of the oppressed indicate the physical realities faced by the early Christians, the Galileans who became the nucleus of the post-resurrection church. In v. 54, the verb, μνησθῆναι, 1st aorist passive infinitive, is the infinitive of result[148] related to a purpose indicating the future proceedings: "He has helped his servant Israel in remembrance of his mercy." According to Isaiah 41:8, it was the promise given to the Israelites. The translation for μνησθῆναι in NRSV, "in remembrance" literally means, in order to be remembered or in order to be kept in mind. It is akin to Ps. 98:3, where the theocratic Kingship is elevated in revealing his victory to Israel in the days to come. In 1:55, "according to the promise he made to our ancestors, to Abraham and to his descendants forever," it is evident that it is the victory achieved in the Magnificat as the result of ancient promise referred to in Mic. 7:20. On the whole, by the canticle of Magnificat, Luke depicts not only the social salvation to Israel by the Messianic King but also Jesus is revealed as the anticipated Messianic King by the words of Mary.

The Benedictus

The *Sitz im leben* of *Benedictus* is also out of the ecstasy of Zechariah after begetting a son in his old age according to the promise of God which explains the redemption of Israel. It seems to be a hymn in anticipation of the Messiah rather than the forerunner. The historic associations are recounted here in terms of the covenant of God with Abraham[149] concerning the national deliverance as an age of peace. In Lukan context, this is conceivably the hope of deliverance from Rome. It reminds one the salvific act of God in human history.

The phrases in this canticle, such as: looked favourably, in the house of David, raised up a mighty saviour for us, peace, and prophet of the Most High, seem to explicate the Messianic idea as it prevailed in the Old Testament. The concept of the saviour referred to in 1:68f arises from the house of David and implies the Messianic ideology. Ἐποίησεν λύτρωσιν literally means 'made redemption' and denotes the redemption from the enemies as it is noted in vv. 71&74. The redemption indicated in the Benedictus is determinative for the present age, than the past event.[150] In addition to that, the syntax, τῷ λαῷ αὐτοῦ the article with nouns governing genitive[151] lays emphasis on the characteristic quality, which again points out the Old Testament promise of redemption to his own people. It could be seen explicitly, in 1:74f, where Zechariah predicts the complete control of enemies under the Messianic King.

Concerning 'raised up a mighty saviour for us,' in v. 69, the phrase, κέρας σωτηρίας literally means a horn of salvation, but NRSV reads it as mighty saviour. Horn in West Asian countries is a symbol of power and strength.[152] In the Old Testament, the metaphor 'erect horn' depicts the image of an ox or a bull standing alert in its strength and symbolizes a victorious warrior's helmet; and, the verb ἐγείρω is commonly used in the view of God raising judges, priests, prophets and Kings, which fits with the Jewish expectation of a triumphant Messiah, a King from the House of David.[153] The phrase, 'horn of salvation' may not directly mean Messiah. But the following phrase, in 1:69, 'in the house of his servant David,' introduces the Messianic implication and it denotes the Messianic King. Hence, the adaptation of this hymn from the Jewish literature indicates that Luke intends these phrases to denote the Messianic King.

Besides, "Rescued from the hand of our enemies" in 1:74, cf. v. 71, reminds the expectation of the restoration referred to in Jer. 30:7f. Lyngdoh sees this phrase as salvation from forgiveness of sins.[154] But, it is not possible to think in that line because the context of Infancy Narrative as well the entire Gospel reveals the political scenario. Mangatt suggests that it is the salvation in terms of the national-political messianic expectations of Israel.[155] Along with the indication of national-political salvation, the term, enemies referred to in it indicates, probably the political enemies, the Romans.

Moreover, 1:78f, the conclusion of the Benedictus seems to recapitulate the motifs of the hymn.' Ἀνατολή, the dawn or rising sun, is used as a metaphor for Messiah and his redemption.[156] The Greek phrase ἀνατολή ἐξ ὕψους refers to the Messiah from the Most High, probably, sent from the Most High as in the LXX of *Testament of Judah* 24:4, which renders the meaning, the sprout of the God Most High. In Zech. 3:8 & 6:12, it is used as the Davidic branch or shoot, a metaphor to refer to the Messiah.[157] As well, "To give light to those who sit in darkness and in the shadow of death...into the way of peace," in v.79, depicts the prophecy of Isa. 9:1ff, where the Prince of Peace is referred to the redemption of the desolated region of Galilee, Zebulun and Naphtali of the Northern Kingdom ravaged and depopulated by Assyria. The same is referred to in Mt. 4:12-17 as a fulfillment of the prophecy, by the beginning of Jesus' ministry. On the whole, it seems that Luke composes the canticle of *Benedictus* to fit in the Infancy Narrative of the Gospel along with the motif of Jesus' Messianic Kingship. Similar to this *Benedictus*, the anticipation of redemption is portrayed in Simeon's *Nunc Dimittis*.

Nunc Dimittis

The overwhelming joy of Simeon in his attainment of seeing the anticipated Messiah is introduced by Luke in the canticle, *Nunc Dimittis* known also as the song of nativity. Simeon an old priest, who anticipated the consolation of Israel, received the child in his arms and with ecstasy praised God by the canticle, which is called, *Nunc Dimittis*. Luke depicts this scenario as the fulfillment of the Messianic expectation in Jesus, which is stated in v. 26 as, "revealed to him by the Holy Spirit that he would not see death before he had seen the Lord's Messiah." It proves further that Luke composes his Gospel to highlight the motif of Jesus' Kingship.

Σωτήριον in v. 30 denotes victory in a battle.[158] But in the backdrop of the promises made to the Israelites, it means deliverance from the oppressors. In line with that in this canticle, redemption is portrayed as concerning not only Israel but extended to the entire world with universal emphasis. The salvation and universalism of the *Nunc Dimittis* resemble Isa. 40:5; 42:6; 46:13; 49:6 & 52:9-10, as well thus taken from other biblical and early Jewish literature, such as Ps. 98:3; Baruch 4:24;[159] Dead Sea Scrolls, IQM 1:5; CD 20:20, 34.[160] Yet, these themes are later realized in the ministry and person of Jesus,[161] which will be discussed in the next chapter. The theme salvation by the child is already introduced by Luke in 1:47 as Mary identified Jesus as saviour, and also by Zechariah in 1:69, 71 &77. These titles might have been given to him in the early tradition with the hope of deliverance from political oppression.[162] The prophecy of Simeon to Mary after blessing the child, "This child is destined for the falling and the rising of many in Israel,...so that the inner thoughts of many will be revealed-and a sword will pierce your own soul too"[163] defines the child's mission in his Kingly role. After *Nunc Dimittis*, in 2:36-38, Luke also adds the character of a prophetess, Anna who is over one hundred years old.[164] She spoke about the child, as it was anticipated by all people in terms of the redemption of Israel. This brief episode also recites the fulfillment of the Messianic expectation in Jesus.

The Gloria in Excelsis

Along with the three canticles, the angelic hymn, one of the special materials of Luke throws more light on the Kingship of Jesus. It is a well-composed hymn in combination of different traditions. In the context of Luke, it is a hymnic confession, which proclaims God's grace on earth and broadens the meaning of what the angel said to the shepherds.[165] The word εἰρήνη in this hymn indicates the achievement of God in the birth of the child, which could be understood from the Hebrew word *shalom* which portrays not only the absence of war but also the whole social order of well-being and prosperity, security and harmony under a King.[166] *Shalom* is normally used as a victory in a well-conducted war.[167] So, this angelic hymn, by declaring peace, depicts the fulfillment of the promises in the Old Testament among the longings of the oppressed Lukan community through the Messianic King.

This hymn has resemblances to the shouts of people at the triumphal entry in which Luke openly declares Jesus as King.[168] Both the hymns agree in the usage of the phrase, δόξα ἐν ὑψίστοις. But, they differ slightly in 2:14, where the angels sing ἐπί γῆς εἰρήνη and in 19:38, the people sing ἐν οὐρανῷ εἰρήνη. It may be the skill of the author to indicate the Kingship of Jesus: the former may be heavenly angels' pronouncement of peace on earth which was the longing of the people and the latter, at the time of the triumphal entry of Jesus the people perhaps realized the fulfillment of the Old Testament promise and had sung peace in heaven.

In addition, the syntax, ἐν ἀνθρώποις εὐδοκίας the genitive of quality[169] emphasizes God's chosen ones. In the backdrop of Roman imperialism, particularly in the prevalence of *pax Romana*, the declaration of peace to the longing elects indicates the author's skillful introduction of the Messianic Kingship through his secrecy motif. The acclamation in the first line and the motivation in the second line parallel the cry of victory in the Book of Revelation.[170] However, the appearance of the heavenly army in the Infancy Narrative seems to be a militant one. The placement of this hymn by Luke after the proclamation of a single angel concerning the birth of Jesus made the shepherds recognize Jesus as who he was.[171] On the whole, it is obvious that by all these canticles Luke exposes the chord of Jesus' Christocentric, Messianic Kingship. It denotes Luke's skill in the composition of the Infancy Narrative as an introduction to the entire Gospel to introduce his motif of Jesus' Kingship.

Jesus in the Temple at the Age of Twelve

Luke composes the Gospel with a special interest in the Temple, which is vivid through the frequent use of the two Greek words: ἱερόν and ναός. Particularly in the Infancy Narrative, there are six references to them. The important incidents in the Temple were: the birth of John the forerunner of Jesus is revealed in the Temple; the infant Jesus was taken to the Temple; Simeon welcomed the infant Jesus as the Messiah in the Temple; and, at the age of twelve he was found having deliberations with the Temple leaders. Considering this event, Jesus in the Temple at the Age of Twelve, Luke might have intended to portray it as the peak of piety as it takes place in the Temple and Luke's deliberate attempt in relating Jesus to the Temple throughout his life and action from his birth onwards.

The account of Jesus in the Temple at the age of twelve in 2:41-52 breaks the silence of Jesus' hidden years in the Gospel and the same is narrated in distinction to the other apocryphal gospel's miracle stories of his boyhood.[172] Luke uses this account as a literary device[173] to his composition of the Infancy Narrative in order to reshape the story to fit it into his context along with his theological perspective.[174] This is well noticeable in his redaction of this independent account of the Infancy Narrative in relation to the themes of the virgin birth and the sonship of God. In 2:48f, while Mary says that Joseph is the Father of Jesus, Jesus responds to her that he is in his father's house. At the very first glance, it may be a dualism, but to Luke, it is the place where he solves the issue of Davidic descent of Jesus' virgin birth through the words of Jesus' mother Mary that Joseph is the human father of Jesus; and, simultaneously maintains that Jesus is the Son of God through the words of Jesus.

At the age of twelve, a Jewish boy is considered as a son of the law.[175] In this account, Jesus is depicted as a genius in his boyhood in view of the fact that the people and his parents were impressed and astonished by his listening and interrogation.[176] Jonge in reference to 1 Enoch 49:3, points out that it is one of the expectations of the Messiah that "he will be endowed with wisdom."[177] In 2:46, Luke says that he was sitting among the teachers in his childhood. While comparing the usage of the title, 'teacher' in other places of his Gospel, 13 times Luke refers to Jesus as a teacher, which is not in others. It seems that Luke portrays his authority and identity from his early stage. In all this, it is comprehensible that by this account Luke portrays the authority and the Messianic identity of Jesus along with his piety and obedience to his parents.

Summary

The Infancy Narrative of Luke's Gospel serves as the introduction to the entire Gospel in its composition, as well as the biography of Jesus in introducing Jesus to the world as the Messianic King. This Luke does in accordance with the fulfillment of the Old Testament foresights against the unjust human Kingship. The historic present; reference to the Davidic descent; the usage of courtly languages; the canticles describing the political overtones of the reversal of power and the re-ordering of a privileged position in the socio-political world of Luke; and the presentation of Jesus at the age of twelve in the Temple, in the Infancy Narrative expose the artful composition of Luke, in introducing Jesus either overtly or covertly, as an alternative King to Roman Emperor.

Concerning Jesus' birth both in Matthew and Luke, Matthew introduces overtly Jesus as the King of the Jews; whereas, our study has shown that Luke maintains the secrecy motif in juxtaposing the birth of Jesus against the Roman Emperor Augustus. Luke's special materials resemble Old Testament events and characters through which Luke introduces Jesus as the Saviour as well as the King in line with the promise of the Davidic Kingdom. By including the historic present which signifies the imperialism of Roman and Palestinian history, Luke's composition seems to contrast the birth of Jesus during the reign of Emperor Augustus, known throughout his Kingdom as saviour and god. It may be Luke's portrayal of *Pax Christi* in the backdrop of *Pax Augusta* to fulfill the anticipation of the people which the Roman King Augustus could not. In addition, the angelic announcement of the good news regarding the birth of Jesus is noted in juxtaposition to Augustus' birthday. Hence, in his compositional style, it is vivid that Luke juxtaposes Jesus' birth with the Roman Emperor and history. As well, the reference to the period of the high priesthood of Annas and Caiaphas though inaccurate, it exposes the *Sitz im leben* of the Gospel during the Jewish leaders' rule in Palestine. In addition, from the composition of John the Baptist and Jesus at the beginning, it is noticeable that Luke intends not only to date the ministry of John but also portrays him as the one who resembles Elijah as the one who prepared the way for Jesus, the anticipated Messianic King along with the birth of Jesus in the Palestinian history.

Besides, the Davidic descent of Jesus gets more emphasis in the Infancy Narrative through the allusion to the Magna Charta of Davidic monarchy; the episodes of virginal conception of Mary; association of the birth of Jesus to Bethlehem, the city of David; the annunciation of the angels; the account of Jesus in the Temple at the age of twelve; and, the reference to the census at the time of Jesus' birth in associating Mary and Joseph, the residents of Nazareth to Bethlehem in the town of David in accordance with the scripture.

The words εὐαγγέλιον, σωτήρ, εἰρήνη and χαῖρε, which are some of the technical terms of Hellenistic thought derived from the courtly language of the imperial culture indicate Jesus as the Christocentric King of a new epoch as an alternative King to Caesar Augustus. The canticles of *Magnificat, Benedictus,* and *Nunc Dimittis* communicate the reversal of positions of the community during the political oppression.

All these events and facts, in contrast to Fitzmyer's view that in only one place in the Lukan Infancy Narrative the Kingship theme gets its prominence and also to the views of other scholars that the Kingship motif is less in Luke, denotes the skill of Luke's composition of the Infancy Narrative with the motif of Jesus' Kingship. Along with these findings, we will be exploring in the next chapter, how Luke exposes Jesus' Kingship by narrating the ministry and teachings of Jesus through his journey around Galilee and Jerusalem.

Endnotes

[1] Lk. 1:33, Gabriel spoke to Mary that "He will reign over the house of Jacob forever, and of his Kingdom there will be no end." [J. A. Fitzmyer, The Gospel According to Luke I-IX, vol. 1 (New York: Doubleday, 1979), 216.]

[2] The reference to the Kings and rulers in history is made use of by Luke in his theological composition of the Gospel. Those references to history referred to by the author are known as, with the phraseology, 'historic present.' It should

be noted that it is different from the grammatical usage of the 'historical present,' which denotes the use of present tense to refer to the past events. It indicates an event as it has taken place immediately after a point of time already given. It is common to the New Testament authors. The evangelist Mark uses it frequently but Luke seldom uses it. [F. Blass and A. Debrunner, A Greek Grammar of the New Testament and other Early Christian Literature, tr. by R. W. Funk (Chicago: University Press, 1961), 167.]

[3] Augustus was the title given by the Roman Senate to Octavian in 27 B. C.

[4] As Wrede points out the messianic secret in Mark, in Luke, it is obvious that Luke maintains the secret of Jesus' Kingship in his composition. He discloses it during the triumphal entry of Jesus and declares him as the King during the trial and death narratives.

[5] Mt. 1:18 & Lk. 1:27, 34.

[6] Mt. 1: 16, 20 & Lk. 1:27, 32; 2:4.

[7] Mt. 1:20-23 & Lk. 1:30-35. There is a subtle difference in both: in Matthew, angel speaks to Joseph; and in Luke, to Mary.

[8] Mt. 1:19f, 23, 25 & Lk. 1:34f.

[9] Mt. 1:21 & Lk. 1:31.

[10] Mt. 1:21 & Lk. 2:11.

[11] Mt. 1:24-25 & Lk. 2:5-6.

[12] Mt. 2:1 & Lk. 2:4-6.

[13] Mt. 2:1 & Lk. 1:5.

[14] Mt. 2:23 & Lk. 2:39.

[15] R. E. Brown, The Death of The Messiah: From Gethsemane to Grave, vol. I (New York: Doubleday, 1994), 65; A. M. Salazar, "Questions about St. Luke's Sources," Novum Testamentum 2/3-4 (October, 1958): 316.

[16] C. W. Jung, The Original Language of the Lukan Infancy Narrative (London: T&T Clark International, 2004), 213; According to Jung, Luke might have used written Greek source/sources in the composition of the Infancy Narrative in imitation of LXX. He deduces it from the heavily Septuagintalized Greek of the Infancy Narrative. [Ibid., 215.]

[17] Mt. 1:1-17. Cf. Lk. 3:23-38. (It is to be noticed that Luke has placed the genealogy after the Infancy Narrative.)

[18] R. E. Brown, The Birth of the Messiah: A Commentary on the Infancy Narratives in Matthew and Luke (London: Geoffrey Chapman, 1977), 242; P. Minear, by seeing the similarity of style in the birth narratives and the rest of Luke-Acts, proposes that Luke chapters 1 & 2 are integral to the total work. [C. H. Talbert, Literary

Pattern, Theological Themes, and the Genre of Luke-Acts (Montana: Scholars Press, 1974), 2]

[19] Fitzmyer, *The Gospel According to Luke I-IX...*, 163.

[20] Brown, *The Birth of the Messiah...*, 241f; M. A. Powell, "Toward a Narrative-Critical Understanding of Luke," Interpretation 48/4 (October, 1994): 342.

[21] H. Hendrickx, *The Infancy Narratives*, 1975, revised ed. (London: Geoffrey Chapman, 1984), 2.

[22] J. A. Fitzmyer, *The Gospel According to Luke X-XXIV*, vol. 2 (New York: Doubleday, 1986), 1360.

[23] Mt. 2:2.

[24] C. R. Erdman, *The Gospel of Luke* (Philadelphia: The Westminster Press, 1925), 31.

[25] Brown, *The Birth of the Messiah...*, 36.

[26] Fitzmyer, *The Gospel According to Luke I-IX...*, 309.

[27] M. Coleridge, *The Birth of the Lukan Narrative: Narrative as Christology in Luke 1-2* (England: Sheffield Academic Press, 1993), 227.

[28] R. Laurentin, *Structure et Théologie de Luc I-II*, Paris 1957, 64ff, cited by C. T. Ruddick, "Birth Narratives in Genesis and Luke" in Novum Testamentum 12/4 (October, 1970): 343.

[29] S. M. Sheeley, *Narrative Asides in Luke-Acts* (Sheffield: Academic Press, 1992), 144.

[30] Lk. 1:5.

[31] Lk. 2:1f.

[32] Lk. 3:1f.

[33] H. K. Bond, *Caiaphas: Friend of Rome and Judge of Jesus?* (Westminister: John Knox Press, 2004), 111; amidst the difficulty of dating Jesus' birth and death, Richardson comes to the conclusion that he was born in 7 BCE, before the death of Herod and died in 33 CE. [P. Richardson, Herod: King of the Jews and Friend of the Romans (Edinburgh: T&T Clark, 1996), 296.]; Herod's dominion included Samaria, Galilee, a great deal of Peraea, and Coele-Syria. [A. Plummer, Critical and Exegetical Commentary on the Gospel according to St. Luke, 5th ed. (Edinburgh: T&T Clark, 1922), 8.]; after the death of Herod the Great in 4 BCE, the territory under his rule was divided to his sons: Archelaus; Herod Antipas; and Philip. Since Archelaeus was exiled, his tetrarchy became a Roman territory. [Fitzmyer, The Gospel According to Luke I-IX..., 401.]; Pontius Pilate was the Procurator of Judaea between CE 26-36; Herod Antipas reigned during 4 BCE to CE39; Lysanias, the Tetrarch of Abilene, succeeded his father Ptolemaeus as the lord of a principality with its capital at Chalcis in 40 BCE [A. R. C. Leaney,

A Commentary on the Gospel according to St. Luke (London: Adam & Charles Black, 1958), 48.]; Herod, (Lk 1:5), Βασιλέω" τη"'Ιουδαία" reigned Palestine from 37 BCE till 4 BCE, known as Herod the Great, and obtained the title, 'King of the Jews' from the Senate. He was an Idumaean by birth and a Jew by religion. The massacre of the innocents recorded by Matthew would be in the last years of his reign. [L. Ragg, St Luke (W.C.: Methuen & Co, 1922), 8; the time of his death is, however, narrowed down by the reference to the census under Quirinius the Governor in Luke 2:1-2 [Fitzmyer, The Gospel According to Luke I-IX..., 321f].

[34] Mt. 2:1 & Lk. 1:5; Richardson, Herod: King of the Jews..., 295f.

[35] Lk. 2:1f.

[36] Lk. 3:2.

[37] According to Hendrickx, 1:1-4 points out that Luke intends to write a history, which is a religious historiography, biblically presented in relation to the ancient biblical stories. i.e., the events were interpreted as a fulfillment of the Old Testament and it can't be viewed as a modern history [Hendrickx, The Infancy Narratives..., 54.]; F. G. Downing identifies Luke's historiography as an apologetic which emerged out of the Greco-Roman world in which the audience Theophilus lived and could understand the content of the tradition [F. G. Downing, "Theophilus's First Reading of Luke-Acts," in Luke's Literary Achievement: Collected Essays, ed. by C. M. Tuckett (Sheffield: Academic Press, 1995), 100.]; Dhal and Fitzmyer view Lukan history as not an interpretation of the past events but as a recount of Jesus' story in ancient Hellenistic history [Fitzmyer, The Gospel According to Luke I-IX..., 15f.]; C. K. Barrett sees Luke not as a modern scientific Historian, but as one of the biblical writers, who is a "historian of the Hellenistic age" [C. K. Barrett, Luke the Historian in Recent Study (London: The Epworth Press, 1961), 9f.]; a "historian out of theological and ecclesiastical environment" in which he lived [Fitzmyer, The Gospel According to Luke I-IX..., 15.]; narrates a redemptive history [Barrett, Luke the Historian..., 39.]; I. I. D. Plessis says that the purpose of the author was not to draw important lessons from history, but to give a "true report of God acting in history" [I. I. D. Plessis, "Once More: The Purpose of Luke's Prologue (Lk. I 1-4)," Novum Testamentum 16/4 (October, 1974): 271.]; According to Conzelmann, in the Lukan writings the Kerygma has been historicized in terms of "salvation history;" Fitzmyer agrees with Conzelmann's threefold division of Lukan salvation-history in the discussion of the Lukan historical perspective, particularly the three periods: the period of Israel (from creation to John the Baptist); the period of Jesus (from the beginning of his ministry to his ascension); [Lk. 16:16 an example of Lukan demarcation of two periods: Israel and Jesus] and the period of the Church under Stress (from ascension to the Parousia). Likewise, Luke has historicized the Christ-event, casting "salvation"

as something that happened in the past (in the period of Jesus) [Fitzmyer, The Gospel According to Luke I-IX..., 18.]; Haenchen and others accept this view, whereas, W. G. Kummel, U. Luck et al. do not. [Ibid., 19.]; Brown says that the problem of historicity in the Infancy Narrative could be solved by considering it as "vehicles of the evangelist's theology and Christology"[Brown, The Birth of the Messiah..., 26.]; Fitzmyer sees it as, "Lukan historical perspective roots the Christ-event in human history, not just for the sake of historicizing it, but to present it as inaugurating a new era in human existence" [Fitzmyer, The Gospel According to Luke (I-IX).., 145.]; According to K. Rajayyan, Lukan history may be defined as an Abuse of History because history is used/misused with certain purposes of ignorance, prejudice or motivation of the historian due to the influences of interested parties in the reconstruction of events [K. Rajayyan, History in Theory and Method: A Study in Historiography (Madurai: Ratna Pub, 2006), 50.]; and, P. F. Esler sees Luke's Gospel as the author appropriates Hellenistic prose style and historiographical techniques to indicate his sensitivity to the wider cultural context and synchronizes the birth of Jesus with imperial Rome [P. F. Esler, Community and Gospel in Luke-Acts: The Social and Political Motivations of Lucan Theology (Cambridge: University Press, 1987), 58f.].

[38] Luke uses the expression "edicts of Caesar" in Acts 17:7.

[39] Augustus is a Greek transliteration of the Latin title, Σεβαστός. F. F. Bruce, I. H. Marshall, J. A. Fitzmyer, and C. J. Hemer agree to this. This is the only occurrence of the word, Augustus in the New Testament. R. L. B. Morris raises the issue that when the Lukan community, Greek audience, who were not familiar with the Latin meaning, why did Luke use this Latin transliteration? And he advocates that in Luke's Gospel, Augustus was at the very centre of the 'infancy narrative.' Further, he points out Fitzmyer's view that its primary purpose was 'to make Christological affirmations about Jesus at the outset of his earthly existence.' [F. F. Bruce, The Acts of the Apostles (London, 1951), 436; I. H. Marshall, The Gospel of Luke (Grand Rapids, 1978), 98; Fitzmyer, The Gospel According to Luke I-IX..., 399 & 446; and, C. J. Hemer, The Book of Acts in the Setting of Hellenistic History (Tübingen, 1989), 107, cited by R. L. B. Morris, "Why ΑΥΓΟΥΣΤΟΣ? A Note to Luke 2:1," New Testament Studies 38/1 (January, 1992): 142f.]

[40] Fitzmyer, The Gospel According to Luke I-IX..., 400.

[41] W. Manson, The Gospel of Luke (New York: Harper and Brothers, 1930), 16; Ragg, St Luke..., 1922), 26f; J. M. Creed, The Gospel According to St. Luke: The Greek Text with Introduction, Notes, and Indices (London: Macmillan and Co., 1930), 28.

[42] Lk. 1:5 & Mt. 2:1ff.

[43] Matt. 2:16.

[44] Richardson, *Herod: King of the Jews...*, 300.

[45] Lk. 2:2.

[46] Brown, *The Birth of the Messiah...*, 395.

[47] 2 Sam. 24; 1 & 1 Chr. 21.

[48] Lk. 2:3.

[49] Brown, *The Birth of the Messiah...*, 395f.

[50] Acts 5:37; Josephus speaks of this census as an innovation which was hated and led to the rising of the Zealots under Judas of Galilee; Creed, The Gospel According to St. Luke..., 28; Brown, The Birth of the Messiah..., 416.

[51] "The Lord records, as he registers the peoples, 'This one was born there.'" (Ps. 87:6).

[52] Brown, *The Birth of the Messiah...*, 417f.

[53] Fitzmyer, *The Gospel According to Luke I-IX...*, 394.

[54] The inscription at Priene in Asia Minor is dated, 9 BCE; A. Stöger, *The Gospel According to St. Luke*, vol. I (London: Burns & Oates, 1969), 40.

[55] Lk. 2:10f.

[56] Brown, *The Birth of the Messiah...*, 415f.

[57] Joel B. Green, *New Testament Theology: Theology of the Gospel of Luke* (Cambridge: University Press, 1995), 7f.

[58] S. Kim, *Christ and Caesar* (Grand Rapids: William B. Eerdmans, 2008), 80f.

[59] Mt 26:3, 57 & Jn 11:49.

[60] Jn 18:13; Leaney, *A Commentary on the Gospel...*, 48.

[61] Bond, Caiaphas: *Friend of Rome...*, 111f;

[62] Fitzmyer, *The Gospel According to Luke I-IX...*, 176f.

[63] Lk. 1:5-25 & 1:26-45.

[64] Lk. 1:57-66, 80; 2:1-12, 15-27 & 34-40.

[65] G. Stanton, *The Gospels and Jesus* (New York: Oxford University Press, 1989), 99.

[66] K. A. Kuhn, "The Point of the Step-Parallelism in Luke 1-2," New Testament Studies 47/1 (January 2001): 38.

[67] Brown, *The Birth of the Messiah...*, 276f; Erdman, The Gospel of Luke..., 21; There are three kinds of proposals regarding the association of Elijah with Jesus (4:25-27; 9:8, 19, 30, etc) and John the Baptist (1:17, 76, etc.,): 1) Luke never identifies Elijah with John; 2) Luke intends to refer only to Jesus despite there are references to John; and, 3) Both John and Jesus are compared to Elijah.

[R. J. Miller, "Elijah, John and Jesus in the Gospel of Luke," New Testament Studies 34/4 (October, 1988): 611.]

[68] Lk. 1:26f, 69 & 2:11; the term, Davidid is used to refer to the person who comes in the lineage of David.

[69] Brown, *The Birth of the Messiah...*, 505.

[70] Ibid.

[71] For instance, Paul twice insists on his Benjaminite descent (Rom. 11:1 & Phil. 3:5).

[72] It is discussed in Chapter I: 1. d.

[73] Son of Shealtiel, governor, at the time of rebuilding the Temple (post-exilic period). [J. L. McKenzie, Dictionary of the Bible (Bangalore: ATC, 1983), 952.]

[74] Brown, *The Birth of the Messiah...*, 310.

[75] Ibid., 505f; Fitzmyer, *The Gospel According to Luke I-IX...*, 310ff.

[76] Brown, *The Birth of the Messiah...*, 506.

[77] Information gleaned from Hegesippus. [Ibid., 507.]

[78] Ibid., 509.

[79] Hendrickx, *The Infancy Narratives...*, 71; Brown, *The Birth of the Messiah...*, 396.

[80] Lk. 1:5.

[81] Plummer, Critical and Exegetical Commentary..., 25.

[82] Creed, *The Gospel According to St. Luke...*, 16; Brown, The Birth of the Messiah..., 396.

[83] P. Chakkalakal, "Women's Discipleship and Leadership in Jesus' Movement: An Indian/Asian Feminist Biblical-Theological Reconstruction," in Bible and Hermeneutics, ed. by C. J. D. Joy (Tiruvalla: C.S.S., 2010), 77.

[84] It is a Roman Catholic interpretation. But it is questioned by a lot of scholars concerning the anachronism of the idea of "a vow of perpetual virginity" during the 1st century. M. Villanueva, O. Graber, M. Zerwick, L. Laurentin, and C. P. Ceroke are prominent in raising this issue. [Landry, "Narrative Logic in the Annunciation..."..., 65.

[85] P. Gaechter, J. B. Bauer, and C. J. Jellouscheck are prominent in questioning this issue. [Ibid.]

[86] G. B. Caird, *The Gospel of St. Luke* (New York: Seabury, 1963), 30.

[87] Brown, *The Birth of the Messiah...*, 299-301.

[88] 1) Son of Joseph and 2) Son not by a man but by the power of Spirit.

[89] Leaney, *A Commentary on the Gospel...*, 20.

[90] R. Leaney, "The Birth Narratives in St Luke and St Matthew," New Testament Studies 8/2 (January, 1962): 166.

[91] Creed, *The Gospel According to St. Luke...*, 13.

[92] Ragg, St Luke..., 29; In John 10, Jesus declares himself as the Good Shepherd.

[93] Fitzmyer, The Gospel According to Luke I-IX..., 395.

[94] J. M. Ford, "Zealotism and the Lukan Infancy Narratives," Novum Testamentum 18/4 (October, 1976): 289.

[95] Brown, *The Birth of the Messiah...*, 423.

[96] It can be evidenced from Jn. 7:42, where, the people of Jerusalem say, "Has not the Scripture said that the Messiah is descended from David and comes from Bethlehem, the village where David was?" It may probably a reference to Micah 5:1f and Matthew uses it in 2:5f as a fulfillment of the Old Testament prophecy.

[97] Cf. Micah 4.

[98] Brown, *The Birth of the Messiah...*, 310.

[99] Ford, "Zealotism and the Lukan Infancy Narratives"..., 284.

[100] Lk. 1:32-35 & 2:10-14.

[101] G. H. P. Thompson, *The Gospel According to Luke* (Oxford: Clarendon Press, 1972), 28f.

[102] Lk. 2:11, 14.

[103] Creed, *The Gospel According to St. Luke...*, 34.

[104] Stöger, *The Gospel According to St. Luke...*, 45.

[105] W. D. Davies, *Invitation to the New Testament* (London: Longman & Todd, 1967), 147f.

[106] H. Flender, *St Luke Theologian of Redemptive History*, Trans. by Reginald and Fuller (London: S.P.C.K, 1967), 58.

[107] M. Borg and J. D. Crossan, *The Last Week: What the Gospels really teach about Jesus' Final Days in Jerusalem* (London: SPCK, 2008), 150.

[108] Green, *New Testament Theology...*, 136; Manson, The Gospel of Luke..., 18.

[109] Creed, *The Gospel According to St. Luke...*, 35; R. C. Nevius, "Kyrios and Iesous in St. Luke," Anglican Theological Review 48/1 (January, 1966): 76; κύριο" is used in Luke for Jesus in other occasions also. Lk. 2:11; 7:13, 19; 10:1, 39, 41; 11:39, 12:42; 13:15; 17:5, 6; 18:6; 19:8, 22:61 & 24:34.

[110] Brown, *The Birth of the Messiah...*, 403.

[111] Creed, *The Gospel According to St. Luke...*, 35.

[112] Leaney, *A Commentary on the Gospel...*, 95f.

[113] Green, *New Testament Theology...*, 7f.

[114] Zech. 9:9.

[115] Zech. 9:1-16.

[116] Great hymn of the nativity, named in Latin version, the Gloria in Excelsis. [Erdman, The Gospel of Luke..., 33.]

[117] Lk. 2:13f; cf. 19:38.

[118] Brown, *The Birth of the Messiah...*, 427.

[119] Leaney, *A Commentary on the Gospel...*, 96.

[120] W. M. Swartley, "Politics or Peace (Eirene) in Luke's Gospel" in *Political Issues in Luke-Acts,* ed. by R. J. Cassidy and P. J. Scharper (New York: Orbis Books, 1983), 3; R. J. Karris, What are they saying about Luke and Acts?: A Theology of the Faithful God (New York: Paulist Press, 1979), 25-30.

[121] Brown, *The Birth of the Messiah...*, 457.

[122] W. Klassen, "'A Child of Peace' (Luke 10.6) in First Century Context," New Testament Studies 27/4 (July, 1981): 489.

[123] C. P. Lyngdoh, "'God Visiting His People' in the Lucan Texts, Part II," Indian Journal of Spirituality 18/3 (July-September, 2005): 300.

[124] Leaney, *A Commentary on the Gospel...*, 82; Luke particularly uses the verb χαῖρε in the episode of the triumphal entry which was not used by the other Gospel writers. [Luke 19:37].

[125] Creed, *The Gospel According to St. Luke...*, 17.

[126] Ibid.

[127] The idea of the consolation of Israel is referred in Isa. 40.

[128] Brown, *The Birth of the Messiah...*, 321.

[129] Ibid., 322.

[130] Isa. 52:1f; 56:7; Mic.4:8, 13; Jer. 4:31; 6:23; 8:19-22; Zeph. 3:14-20; Zech. 2:10; 9:9; Joel. 2:21-23.

[131] *Ibid.,* 324.

[132] Lk. 1:46-55.

[133] Lk. 1:67-79.

[134] Lk. 2:28-32.

[135] 'Co-text' means the sentences and larger textual units surrounding the text and relating to it so as to constrain its interpretation. [Green, New Testament Theology..., 1f.]

[136] D. Jones, "The Background and Character of the Lukan Psalms," The Journal of Theological Studies 19/1 (April, 1968): 19.

[137] Brown, The Birth of the Messiah..., 350; Jones, "The Background and Character of the Lukan Psalms"..., 19.

[138] Brown, *The Birth of the Messiah...,* 27.

[139] Ibid., 351.

[140] Lk. 2:13-14.

[141] Leaney, *A Commentary on the Gospel...,* 23.

[142] Brown, *The Birth of the Messiah...,* 341f.

[143] W. Carter, *The Roman Empire and the New Testament* (Nashville: Abingdon Press, 2006), 98.

[144] A. Maclaren, *St. Luke* (Grand Rapids: Wm. B. Eerdmans, 1932), 22.

[145] Erdman, *The Gospel of Luke...,* 27.

[146] H. B. Beverly, "An Exposition of Luke 1:39-45," Interpretation 30/4 (October, 1976): 397.

[147] M. A. Beavis, "Expecting Nothing in Return," Interpretation XLVIII/4 (October, 1994): 363.

[148] Blass and Debrunner, *A Greek Grammar of the New Testament...,* 197f.

[149] Lk. 1:72f.

[150] W. Carter, "Zechariah and Benedictus (Luke 1, 68-79) Preaching what He Preaches," Biblica 69/2 (Fasc., 1988): 245.

[151] Blass and Debrunner, *A Greek Grammar of the New Testament...,* 135.

[152] Lyngdoh, "'God Visiting His People' in the Lucan Texts, Part I"..., 148.

[153] Brown, The Birth of the Messiah..., 371.

[154] Lyngdoh, "'God Visiting His People' in the Lucan Texts, Part II"..., 292.

[155] Mangatt, "The Gospel of Salvation"..., 62.

[156] Creed, The Gospel According to St. Luke..., 27; Cf. Mal. 4:2; Lyngdoh, "'God Visiting His People' in the Lucan Texts, Part II"..., 297.

[157] Brown, *The Birth of the Messiah...,* 373f.

[158] Jones, "The Background and Character of the Lukan Psalms"..., 40.

[159] Baruch 4:24, where promise is stated, "The neighbours of Zion...will shortly see the salvation of God come to you with great glory." The references to Dead Sea Scrolls also speak of the salvation of the people.

[160] Brown, *The Birth of the Messiah...,* 458f.

[161] Lk. 4:18-21 and 7:22.

[162] Plummer, *Critical and Exegetical Commentary...*, 32.

[163] Lk. 2:34b-35.

[164] J. K. Elliott, "Anna's Age (Luke 2:36-37)," Novum Testamentum 30/2 (April, 1988): 100.

[165] B. Olsson, "The Canticle of the Heavenly Host (Luke 2:14) in History and Culture," New Testament Studies 50/2 (April, 2004): 155f.

[166] J. Nolland, *Word Biblical Commentary,* vol. 35: Luke 1:1-9:20 (Dallas: Word Books, 1998), 108.

[167] Ford, "Zealotism and the Lukan Infancy Narratives"..., 288.

[168] Lk. 19:38.

[169] Lk. 2:14; Blass and Debrunner, A Greek Grammar of the New Testament..., 91f.

[170] Olsson, "The Canticle of the Heavenly Host ..."...,157.

[171] M. L. Moore-Keish, " Luke 2:1-14," Interpretation 60/4 (October, 2006): 444.

[172] C. Stuhlmueller, "The Gospel According to Luke," The Jerome Biblical Commentary, Vol II, ed. by R. E. Brown, Joseph A. Fitzmyer and Roland E. Murphy (Bangalore: TPI, 1968), 125.

[173] B. V. Iersel, "The Finding of Jesus in the Temple," Novum Testamentum 3/3 (October, 1959): 172.

[174] J. F. Jensen, "An Exposition of Luke 2:41-52," Interpretation 30/4 (October, 1976): 401.

[175] H. J. D. Jonge, "Sonship, Wisdom, Infancy: Luke II. 41-51a," New Testament Studies 24/3 (April, 1978): 319.

[176] Lk. 2:46-48.

[177] H. J. D. Jonge, "Sonship, Wisdom, Infancy..."..., 348.

Chapter - 3

Kingship Motif in the Life and Teachings of Jesus

A careful study of the motif of Jesus' Kingship in Luke's Infancy Narrative reveals that Kingship elements are found either explicitly or implicitly in it and that serves as an introduction to both the Gospel and the biography of Jesus. In continuation with that investigation, in this chapter as the next stage, the life and teachings of Jesus recorded between the Infancy Narrative and Passion Narrative are explored to find out the motif of Jesus' Kingship along with the question, does Luke expose any anti-imperial teachings in the actions of Jesus against the Roman rule? In order to study the Roman political oppressive situation in Palestine and the portrayal of the alternative Messianic King in the topographical structure of Jesus' ministry and Journey section in Luke, which is peculiar to his composition along with Q and L in addition to the triple tradition sources, the inquiry of how Luke, the artist[1] and theologian has woven the life and teachings of Jesus including some of the themes, events, the miracles and parables in his composition of the Gospel and how he skillfully exposes Jesus openly as the King at the final stage of his entry into Jerusalem in a procession along with a lot of followers are dealt with.

Besides, in the geographical composition of the journey toward Jerusalem, particularly the threefold topographic ministries of Jesus: in Galilee;[2] Samaria;[3] and, Judea,[4] the Lukan significance will be explored as whether it has any theological importance in his composition of the Gospel in line with the motif of Jesus' Kingship. Because, in 4:16-30, Jesus' ministry at Nazareth symbolically stands for Israel and Jerusalem is placed in contrast to Capernaum, the gentile world where he was accepted; 8:1-3 seems to be a new section in the Travel Narrative and it shows the inclusion of women in Jesus' ministry as witnesses in Galilee; in 23:5, the accusation of Jesus points out to his earlier ministry in this geographical structure, "He stirs up the people by teaching throughout all Judea, from Galilee where he began even to this place." In 4:44 and 7:17, Judea is referred to as the area of Jesus' ministry; and, in 7:17 Jesus' reputation spreads throughout the entire Judea, and to all the surrounding countries, and people flock to him from every village in Galilee, Judea, Jerusalem, Tyre and Sidon;[5] Jerusalem is portrayed as the hub of the Christ-event. In general, not only the places, but also the activities and teachings in each place seem to have theological implications, particularly the motif of Kingship which is alternative to the emperor is apparent. To analyze that, let us study in this chapter the text 3:1-21:38 in two sections: A) Grounding of Jesus and the Galilean ministry;[6] and, B) Travel Narrative: The Journey from Galilee to Jerusalem, which includes the last few days of Jesus in Jerusalem.[7]

GROUNDING OF JESUS' MISSION AND THE GALILEAN MINISTRY

Luke the evangelist seems to have well structured his Gospel in writing the biography of Jesus. After the Infancy Narrative, before composing the ministry of Jesus in Galilee, Samaria and Judea, he gives the details of Jesus' preparation for ministry, which is acknowledged in this research as Grounding of Jesus' Mission.

Grounding of Jesus' Mission and its Socio-Political Context

Luke furnishes details of Jesus' grounding of mission in 3:1-4:13, also known as "inauguration narrative,"[8] and includes in it the proclamation of John the Baptist; Jesus' baptism; genealogy of Jesus; and, the temptation of Jesus. These events not only give the details about Jesus' preparation but also, the socio-political context of Jesus' mission.

Baptism: Political Oppressive Context of Palestine

In 3:1f, Luke grounds the ministry of John the Baptist in the historical milieu of Roman rule in Palestine along with the references to the historic present of the reign of Emperor Tiberius; the governor, Pontius Pilate; rulers, Herod, and Philip; and, the high priests, Annas and Caiaphas. John is presented as the one who was thought to be the Messiah[9] by his valiant speech pleading for repentance and baptism. John's proclamation of the baptism of repentance gives the picture of people joining the new community.[10] Oepke states it as, "an initiatory rite for gathering the Messianic Community."[11] If baptism of repentance leads one to a new community, it raises the issue, whether the concept and act of baptism had any political impact during the 1st century BCE.

The political oppression during John the Baptist's time is elicited by scholars in varied forms. According to Flemington, people throughout Palestine were longing for God's intervention for the well-being of Israel due to Roman power in the first century.[12] The oppressive state of Roman rule is vivid in B. M. Metzger's words. He explains the situation as:

> What made John's ministry so thrilling to every Jewish heart was the strong messianic hope present in his message. He declared that nothing less than the Day of Jehovah was at hand and that at long last God would vindicate his people and deliver them from oppression. Referring to the coming Judgment in terms which Palestinian peasants could comprehend, John compared the coming of the Messiah to a farmer using a winnowing fork to separate the wheat from the chaff he would burn with unquenchable fire (Lk. 3:17f)...John had to tell his hearers that the nation as a whole was utterly unprepared

for the Messiah. It was for this reason, and not merely for the sake of inculcating general ethical standards, that John called the nation at large- every class and every individual- to repentance as the indispensable preparation for participating in the blessings of the new epoch. As an outward symbol of an inward change, he baptized in the Jordan all who received his message with faith.[13]

It should be noted that although the Pharisees and the Sadducees opposed each other, people came forward from both the groups to be baptized by John. By addressing them as the brood of vipers, John indicated their turn-coat attitude toward the Roman rule in its theology while remaining in Judaism; and, condemned their self esteem and pride for being the chosen people that their Abrahamic ancestry secured their relationship with God.[14] John's baptism seems to be an act of rededication to God on the part of the Israelites, who had lost their privileges and relationship by the sin of worshipping the Roman Emperor. This was also the opportunity further to be integrated again in the community of true Israel.

In this socio-political context, Jesus accepts John's baptism, which not only depicts Jesus' mode of entrance to the messianic work,[15] but also reveals Jesus as the Son of God. In depicting this, like Mark, Luke seems to keep the Messianic secrecy in not revealing Jesus as the Son of God as yet. The voice therefore from heaven is heard by Jesus himself and not by the audience,[16] whereas, in Matthew and John the declaration was to the audience.[17] In addition to the redactional device of secrecy motif, as it has been discussed in the previous chapter, perhaps, Luke may juxtapose this title Son of God which is used for the Emperor to Jesus to establish the Kingship of Jesus in his composition.

Besides, both John and Jesus are depicted with an anti-temple behaviour, which seems to be a revolutionary act in the context of political oppression. The Temple ideology however consisted in forgiveness of sins through sacrifice; whereas, John practiced the baptism of repentance by denying the temple's role in forgiveness and approaching God. As well, during his ministry later, Jesus forgave sins through his action and pronouncement[18] which caused the conflict with the leaders who in their murmuring queried: who is he to forgive sins? And in which authority he does these? For instance, in 5:17-26, Luke proclaims the identity and authority of Jesus as the Son of God to forgive sins in response to their question.

Nevertheless, in this event of baptism and proclamation of John, Luke portrays the roles of both John and Jesus distinctively. There is no question of John's Messiahship, since, in 3:16-17 through the words of John, Luke explains that John is not the one but the coming one is the Messiah. Luke presents John's ministry as the fulfillment of the prophecy of Isaiah,[19] in preparing the way of the Lord. Jesus is focused sharply, and his superiority is maintained as it is in the Infancy Narrative. It is further seen in the Q passage 7:28 = Mt. 11:11a, "among those born of women no one is greater than John..." Although it is considered as a later addition by scholars,[20] Luke seems to be exposing the superiority of Jesus from the beginning. As C. Guignebert points out, the expectation in the Jewish apocalyptic writings was that, the Messiah comes along with the precursor Elijah, and he establishes the Messianic Kingdom by overthrowing the wicked,[21] as it is written by the prophet Malachi in 4:5. Thus in the event of John's Baptism, Luke portrays the political oppressive context of Palestine as well as the Messianic Kingship of Jesus through the roles of both John and Jesus. The political oppressive nature of the event could be further seen in the episode of the arrest of John in 3:19f.

Arrest of John: Tyranny of Herod

All the Synoptic Gospels have a commonality in relating the episode of John's arrest as per the triple tradition material.[22] Thus all the three evangelists give the same reason for his arrest John condemned the tetrarch for marrying Herodias, the wife of his brother.[23] As it has been seen in chapter I: 2. a, the clash between the sons of Herod the Great in attaining the rule in Palestine might have caused this situation of Herod Antipas in occupying his father's Kingdom by marrying the wife of his brother,[24] another tetrarch and his cruelty on John due to his condemnation of the human King Herod for his misconduct by the commandment of the theocratic King.

However, the issue arises due to Lukan placement of this event in between John's baptism and the baptism of Jesus. Matthew places it in the context of Herod's inquiry about Jesus' authority due to his miraculous activity and observing whether Jesus as the risen John. Mark and Luke[25] place it as the inquiry of Herod after the sending out of apostles for the ministry. While Luke records that Herod wanted to see Jesus, both Matthew and Mark seem to portray it as Herod was scared of Jesus' fame. But the transposition of Luke, in 3:19f, obviously, portrays: John's preaching was against the oppressive Roman rule in the context of baptism where the question of Messiahship was aroused; the good news of John concerning the coming one, Jesus; introducing Jesus as he started his vocation during the time of Herod's atrocity by accepting John's baptism; and, the heavenly declaration of Jesus as the Son of God. So, the insertion of Herod's tyranny of John's imprisonment in between the baptismal episode clearly indicates the motif of Luke in composing his Gospel with the intention of portraying Jesus as the Messianic King in juxtaposition to the human king, who himself wanted to see Jesus. Eventually, the genealogy of Jesus in Luke also portrays Jesus as King.

Genealogy of Jesus: Messianic/Davidic Kingship and Son of God

Matthew places the genealogy of Jesus at the outset of his Gospel[26] along with the emphasis on Jesus' Messiahship through Davidic lineage; whereas, Luke places it after the baptism of Jesus.[27] Though the genealogy follows Q material, both the evangelists add their own special materials to emphasize each one's purpose. In that way Luke stresses at the end that Jesus is the Son of God through Davidic lineage along with Adam. Within the immediate social and political context of Jesus' baptism, along with the focus on his lineage of Adam and David, the political/emperor's title Son of God depicts the scenario of the creation of the world order; fall of humanity; the united Davidic

Kingdom; and, the fulfillment of the messianic prophecy in Jesus in accomplishing the anticipation of the Lukan community.

The Temptation of Jesus: Submission to Rome or God?

The temptation of Jesus in 4:1-13[28] shows the spirit-led life of Jesus after his baptism in Jordan. It nuances the effect of his baptism as a mode of entrance into the Kingly messianic work. In this event, all the three temptations in the Q source point to the fact that the authority of Jesus was tested. The first and the last, show that it was the temptation to gratify bodily appetites, and to seek prestige by unlawful means.[29] Besides, the last further indicates that the devil wanted to test him whether he is the Son of God. The second one is the temptation to seize power, to test whether he is a power-monger to become a King. According to W. Carter, both Matthew and Luke's reference to the devil as the one having power over the world and world's empires symbolize the Roman throne which is under the control of the devil.[30] K. Yamazaki-Ransom says, in Luke, "Satan is depicted as the ruler of the worldly political system, which is roughly equivalent to the Roman Empire."[31] In addition to these scholars' views, it is obvious in this episode that Satan expected Jesus' submission to the ruler of the earthly Kingdom. This is the reason why the event contains the elements of prostration before Satan who has the power and authority to bestow Kingdoms, and to worship him.[32] Here, the tension between theocracy and human Kingship can be seen in Jesus' answer to worship God rather than the devil, which denotes God's supremacy as the ultimate source of authority.

From the historical point of view, during his reign from 30 to 14 BCE Octavius Augustus introduced the divinization of the Emperor and his worship which had unparalleled political effect on the empire.[33] Besides, there was precedence in attaining power with enthusiasm by Alexander the Great, the Caesars, and others.[34] In that context, the response of Jesus, "worship the Lord your God," indicates the rule of God against the Roman imperial theology as the fundamental confession of Israel, to be sustained against all temptations and dangers. So, it is very clear that the scenario of the temptation to seize power, in the political context of Roman rule in Judea, indicates that the Roman Empire expected Jesus to be submissive to the human Kingship of Rome rather than God.

Amidst this tension between theocracy and human Kingship, is an issue of whether Jesus becomes another political King against the Roman imperialism. Z. Mattam says that the test upon the pinnacle of the Temple shows the devil's scheme of changing God's plan of establishing Jesus as the Messiah by protecting him in the hands of angels.[35] According to J. B. Fuliga, Satan tested Jesus whether he could avail of the Father's security forces as the political leaders of Israel had security forces. But Jesus proved that he was an apolitical Messiah.[36] This argument however cannot be accepted in toto. The first part of his argument might be taken as an outlook of this story. But, the latter part that Jesus proved as a non-political Messiah is questionable. J. Jeremias sees this event in line with Luke 22:31f,[37] as a test to prove Jesus as the political Messiah.[38] Storkey gives another reason to depict it as a political temptation on the pinnacle of the Temple. It is said that the Temple was rebuilt by Herod the Great and the golden eagle was erected at the front door to appease Rome against the Jewish God. It annoyed the Jews.[39] So, in connection with the Temple theology it seems to be a nationalistic test against the imperial theology to prove Jesus as the political as well as the priestly Messiah. Also, from Josephus' history of Judea during the time of Herod concerning the erection of the golden eagle and its controversy,[40] it is obvious that Luke wanted to show Jesus as not a power-monger but as a Messianic King in juxtaposition to Rome in its theology and rule. Even the use of the title Son of God seems to be plain when it is taken as an independent one; but when it is related to the second test with the indication of the Kingdom, it shows the skill of the author in composing this with the intention of depicting the Kingship of Jesus, apparently a pun on the title, Son of God in aiming to show an alternative King.

Galilean Ministry of Jesus

After grounding Jesus' mission in 4:14-9:49, Luke describes the beginning of Jesus' ministry at Nazareth along with the manifesto of his mission, rejection and ministry throughout the region of Galilee. Most of the miracles recorded in the Gospel of Luke fall in this area along with his teachings and only a few occur in the Travel Narrative. The events of anointing of Jesus by a sinful woman, transfiguration, etc., are also significant in the composition of the Galilean ministry.

Nazareth Manifesto and the Rejection of Jesus: Messianic Kingship

The inaugural incident of the Nazareth manifesto[41] with a few changes from Mark, Luke adds the themes of fulfillment, universality of the gospel, prophetic role of Jesus and His rejection as already foretold by Simeon in 2:29-35. It may be the Lukan description of Jesus' programmatic mission. In other words, Luke, at the outset of Jesus' ministry itself, introduces him as the messianic King.

The Spirit associated life of Jesus gets importance in the composition of Luke's Gospel: his birth was by the Spirit;[42] the Spirit descended at the time of Baptism;[43] Jesus was led by the Spirit to the wilderness;[44] Jesus' declaration that the Spirit was upon him;[45] transfiguration;[46] and at the close, the risen Jesus dispenses the Spirit to his disciples.[47] At the outset of Jesus' mission, i.e., during the baptism, the Spirit descended on Jesus and, at the end during the ascension, he was carried up into heaven. However, by the Spirit associated life of Jesus, Luke not only relates the fulfillment of Scripture with Jesus' life as portrayed in his Jubilee proclamation at Nazareth but also at the anointing of Jesus with messianic Kingly programme.

It is to be noted that the declaration of the fulfillment of the Old Testament prophecies in the Nazareth Manifesto depicts the dawn of the new age by the arrival of Jesus:[48] good news to the poor; release to the captives; recovery of sight to the blind; let the oppressed free; and, the proclamation of the year of the Lord. Luke writes it as Jesus read it from one place, "He stood up to read, and the scroll of the prophet Isaiah was given to him. He unrolled the scroll and found the place where it was written…"[49] But, this kingly messianic programme of Jesus is not only from Isa. 61:1f, but also from Ps. 146:6-8; Isa. 35:5; 53:5& 58:6. There are additions and deletions: "to bind up the broken-hearted; to proclaim…the day of vengeance of our God"[50] are deleted; at the same time Luke adds, "to let the oppressed go free" from Isa. 58:6. In this context D. Carr says, that there is a possibility that these words had been changed already in the scroll given to Jesus.[51] But, there is another possibility to think that Luke in his composition deletes the intolerant words of 'bind up' and 'vengeance,' which directly points to the worldly Kingship[52] of invasion and courteously adds freeing the oppressed, which is Jesus' Kingly Messianic act.

D. Hamm describes the manifesto as an "eye-opening revelation" through the images from Isaiah.[53] However, J. D. G. Dunn argues that since Jesus quoted it from Isa. 61:1-2, he accepted himself as a prophet rather than as the Messiah. Dunn's view is not acceptable because at Nazareth, Jesus announces his Kingly programme of Messianic mission. W. H. Brownlee identifies Jesus as a priestly Messiah. E. E. Ellis and J. M. Casciaro regard 61:1-2 to be messianic.[54] W. Carter says that Luke depicts Jesus as the one who offers social vision and challenges the elite-dominated Rome by citing Isaiah 61.[55] Carter's view is correct because the historical context of 1st century CE Palestine as it has been noted already indicates the need of Jesus' programme of challenging mission along with the vision of the society. 4Q521,2 + 4.ii.1-13 of the Dead Sea Scrolls has parallel to this text:

> …Messiah …For the Lord seeks the pious and calls the righteous by name. Over the humble his spirit hovers, and he renews the faithful in his strength. For he will honor the pious upon the th[ro] ne of the eternal Kingdom, setting prisoners free, opening the eyes of the blind, raising up those who are bo[wed down]. And for [ev] er(?) I (?) shall hold fast [to] the [ho]peful and pious […]…shall not be delayed […] and the Lord shall do glorious things which have not been done, just as he said. For he will heal the critically wounded, he shall revive the dead, he shall proclaim good news to the afflicted, he shall…[…the…], he shall lead the […], and the hungry he shall enrich(?).[56]

In addition, 11Q Melch explicitly links the jubilee legislation of Leviticus 25 with Isa. 61:1-3. Perhaps this might be a backdrop to Jesus' use of Isaiah 61 in 7:22 = Mt. 11:5; cf. Lk. 4:16-30.[57] I. H. Marshall points out that the anointing in 4:18 is apparently a prophetic but he emphasizes that anointing is much more related to the appointments of priests and kings.[58] On the whole, according to Luke, the Spirit-led life of Jesus had the implication of his Messianic Kingship which is accounted for in 4:18f, "The Spirit of the Lord is upon me, because he has anointed me...to proclaim the year of the Lord's favour."

Considering the prophetic role of Jesus in the Gospel, Luke portrays Jesus as the one who expected his death as a prophet. He establishes it through the conversation of the two on the way to Emmaus with the risen Jesus, "The things about Jesus of Nazareth, who was a prophet mighty in deed and word before God and all the people,"[59] and, through the words of Jesus himself as well as by his audience. Besides, Luke establishes Jesus' prophetic role through his performances of miracles in relation to his Messianic Kingship:[60] in 4:23-27, Jesus' words denote him as a prophet as well on a par with Elijah and Elisha; and, in 7:16, after raising the son of the widow at Nain,[61] through the words of Jesus' audience, Luke depicts Jesus as, "A great prophet has risen among us!" to the inquiry of John's disciples, with the response of Jesus that the miracles performed by him are symbolic of the arrival of the anticipated messianic King who would transform the tyranny into tranquility.[62] The backdrop may be understood from John 20:30f, as not all the miracles of Jesus are recorded, but a small number of them are recorded to believe that Jesus is the Messiah, the Son of God. So, it is evident that the prophetic role of Jesus is considered by the evangelists Luke and John as the Messiah, the Son of God.

Moreover, the reference to the prophets in the manifesto reflects the universality of Jesus' mission plan. C. Crockett says that the reference to the Old Testament prophets in this Nazareth episode has no proleptic function of Jewish-Gentile relation, rather reconciliation to live and eat together in the new age, which Luke develops in his Gospel.[63] Evans says that the Elijah/Elisha references allude to the concept of Election of the Gentiles.[64] It caused the rejection of the Messianic King by the Jews. Goudoever rightly points out that the wrath of the people and the rejection of Jesus are in opposition to the universality of Jesus' mission.[65] O. Betz also says that the miracles referred to in the Nazareth pericope is his programme of ministry, but without tolerating it they rejected his Messiahship.[66] However, in the Nazareth event, the marginalized, gentiles and neglected groups get attention and identity in Jesus' Kingship; particularly, women and widows. Besides, this event depicts Jesus not only as the prophet but also as one who challenges the Roman Empire with his Messianic programme as the one who seems to be the Messianic King reversing the conditions of the people who live on the periphery.

Miracles: Kingly Messianic Authority over Satanic Forces

While portraying the life of Jesus like the other evangelists, Luke introduces him as a miracle-worker. The miracles of Jesus contain the acts of exorcism, accounts of healing, performances of revivification and nature miracles.[67] The following miracles are included by Luke in his Gospel: the man with an unclean spirit;[68] the healing of Simon's mother-in-law and many people;[69] cleansing of a leper;[70] the healing of a paralytic;[71] the man with the withered hand;[72] ministering to a great multitude;[73] healing of a centurion's servant;[74] raising of the widow's son at Nain;[75] the calming of a Storm;[76] the healing of the Gerasene demoniac;[77] raising of Jairus' daughter; the healing of the woman who touched Jesus' garment;[78] the feeding of the five thousand;[79] the healing of a boy with an unclean spirit;[80] the healing of a crippled woman on the Sabbath;[81] the healing of the man with dropsy;[82] the cleansing of ten lepers;[83] and the healing of a blind beggar near Jericho.[84] Totally, Luke has 20 miracle stories and 3 summaries; whereas Matthew has 19 stories and 4 summaries; as well, Mark has 18 stories and 4 summaries. Among these, Luke has used 12 of Mark's miracle stories and, 8 of his own and Q.

The placement of four miracles immediately after the rejection of Jesus at Nazareth strengthens Jesus' Messianic mission, reveals

Luke's intention to portray Jesus' Messianic authority and power as a Messianic King in healing and giving life to his people. 4:18-22, his pronouncement of his activity; and, 4:23-27, his justification of his miracles are seen to be his programmatic mission. The healing of the Gerasene demoniac in 8:26-39 reveals the power of Jesus over Rome and the destruction of its oppressive structure. The context of the miracle of feeding the five thousand is an event where the crowd followed an alternative Galilean Zealot[85] due to the shaky position of Herod in need of a powerful King. It is vivid in Jn. 6:15 from the realization of Jesus that, "...they were about to come and take him by force to make him King..."

Besides, Luke introduces the core of Jesus' teaching before healing; and the miracle stories focus on Jesus' might. It shows Luke's art of balancing both Jesus' teaching and miraculous act. Achtemeier says that the validating power of Jesus is typically found in Lukan composition of the miracles.[86] For instance, in 4:35, Jesus silenced the demon possessed person by his command, "Be silent and come out of him." In sequence, Jesus' teaching and miraculous acts along with his might validate Jesus as the Messiah.

By hearing what Jesus had done to the centurion's servant and the son of the widow at Nain mentioned in 7:1-17, John the Baptist queried, in the subsequent verses, as to whether Jesus is the anticipated Messiah. It should be noted that the context as well as the importance of Jesus is different in Matthew 11-2-6, where, in the context of missionary activity of disciples John queries it.

In addition to that, the miracles of Jesus become a deep-rooted faith for his disciples to follow him. The power of healing, exorcisms and defying dehumanizing structures manifest the ministry of Jesus;[87] convey the reality of God's Kingly rule;[88] and, explicate, the presence of the in-breaking Kingdom of God.[89] It may be viewed that Jesus' miraculous power transforms the human being into a new world of human existence.[90] In Lukan composition, the calling of Peter, James and John are only after the miraculous catch of fish, whereas, in Mark it was after Jesus' proclamation.[91] The episode of calling of Levi in Luke is also placed after a miracle event.[92] So, it may be understood that in Luke the disciples were rooted in faith by the miracles; they followed Jesus; and, their calling and obedience led people for a new life/rule.

In exorcism, as Wrede points out the Markan messianic secrecy, while following the Markan frame work and source, Luke seems to follow the messianic secrecy motif. In 4:31-37, Jesus rebukes the man with the unclean spirit, not to declare his messianic title, by saying, "Be silent." It is vivid in the following pericope of healing at Simon's house.[93] After healing Simon's mother-in-law, he healed many. Though it is a triple tradition source, Luke goes beyond in adding the shouts of demons which came out of people, "You are the Son of God!" as the disclosure of the Messianic King. Jesus rebukes them but does not allow them to speak. Luke gives the reason that "they knew that he was the Messiah,"[94] which is typically Lukan addition and implies that he wanted to show Jesus as the Messianic King who has authority over the Satanic forces. Besides, in the healing of the Gerasene Demoniac,[95] the demon haunted person addresses Jesus thus: "What have you to do with me, Jesus, Son of the Most High God? I beg you do not torment me." In general, while following Mark, Luke skillfully depicts the scenario of casting out the demon by Jesus with his Messianic authority. His command to go back home indicates the restoration and acceptance of the unchained person at home and society.

Social Acceptance of the Marginalized through Miracles

The intention of Jesus in healing the disabled may be identified in the sociological context. Leprosy healed by Jesus resisted the purity regulations followed on the basis of Lev 13:45f, which affected human life.[96] By touching the unclean,[97] Jesus wanted not only to cure the person but also extended his concern for the affected and pointed out the hard-hearted behavior of the society towards the people who were affected by leprosy. On the one hand, it explains the physical healing of the leprosy-affected and on the other hand, in 17:11-19, the faith of the Samaritan shows the breaking of boundary tension between the Jews and the Samaritans,[98] which is seen in Jn. 4:20, in the conversation of the Samaritan women with Jesus concerning the worship place of the Jews in Jerusalem and the Samaritans on Mount Gerizim.[99]

Likewise, the defilement due to menstruation was reversed by Jesus through the act of healing the woman who touched his garment.[100] Stanton comments on it thus: "Many of the healings and exorcisms of Jesus were an indication of his full acceptance of those who were socially and religiously marginalized."[101] The miracles of Jesus, among the socially and religiously ostracized, symbolically explain the intention of Jesus in reforming the evils of the nation to bring new life to the people, which are evidenced in the reversal of the old rigid laws on purity regulations. For instance, the command of King David in 2 Sam. 5:8 against the blind and the lame is reversed by Jesus' Kingly act in the Temple as it is recorded in Mt. 21:14.

The miracle, Healing the crippled woman in 13:10-17,[102] depicts how the powerless woman for the past 18 years was made straight to stand up.[103] In other words, she was restored into her position. L. M. Maloney and E. J. Smith explain that, straighten up depicts liberation from the oppressive state, i.e., deformed by patriarchy.[104] The words of Jesus that she must be set free from the bonds of Satan, redefines the Sabbath as the celebration of freedom from slavery and darkness.[105] The words used in v. 11, 'having a spirit of illness' and v. 16, 'whom Satan bound for eighteen years' point out her oppressive state. The way Jesus performed it by calling her over, declaring her cure and laying his hands on her[106] has given acceptance to her in the society.

Concerning the healing on the Sabbath, the discussion between the Synagogue leader and Jesus gives two alternative interpretations:[107] 1) violation of Sabbath by breaking the Mosaic Law; and, 2) fulfillment of the Sabbath.[108] Through riddles[109] Jesus challenges the conventional thinking of Sabbath which Luke portrays in 14:3, 5, "Is it lawful to heal on the Sabbath or not?... Which one of you should have a son or an ox fall into a well, and would not immediately pull him out on a Sabbath day?" The healing of the man with dropsy along with the riddle conform the lawyers and silence the Pharisees.[110] However, Jesus' reinterpretation of the Sabbath and his performance depict his Messianic Kingly act.

The verb ἀνορθόω used in the healing of the crippled woman by Luke elucidates the crippled woman's restoration, as it is found in Davidic contexts in LXX, particularly to refer to the establishment of David's throne.[111] It indicates that Luke refers to Jesus as the King who restores the Kingdom by reversing the oppressive state.' Ἀνορθόω inclusively refers to the restoration of Israel in Amos 9:11. O'Toole associates ἀνορθόω with ἀνακύπτω and ἐπαίρω used in 21:28 to denote stand erect and lift up,[112] where redemption is expected. "Now when these things begin to take place, stand up and raise your heads because your redemption is drawing near," and the preceding verse, "Then they will see 'the Son of Man coming in a cloud' with power and great glory." It may be a puzzle, whether the Kingship of Jesus is to be understood as a present reality or an eschatological hope. However, as the usage of the verb ἀνορθόω in Davidic contexts indicates it is obvious why Luke portrays Jesus as a Davidic King who restores the life of the people during his life on earth.

Ancient Miracle Stories and Luke's: A Brief Comparison

There were Jewish miracle-workers who lived at the time of Jesus. In the Old Testament, miracles were associated with the prophets: Moses, Elijah, and Elisha. During Paul's ministry, there were references to the exorcists in Acts 19:11-17. Yet, there is no information about the Jewish miracle-workers' healing of the deaf, dumb, and lame. In 11:19 = Mt. 12:27, Jesus himself refers to other exorcists who could cast out demons. In CE c.180, Celsus attributed the miracles of Jesus to magical power.[113] Morton Smith designates Jesus as a magician.[114] According to Achtemeier, in Luke's narration of miracle stories, there are indications for a magical view of Jesus. He points out the difference between the Hellenistic magicians and Jesus as he openly performs the miracle, whereas the former did it in secret.[115] In Luke, although Luke has some influences of Hellenistic magic acts, his composition of the Gospel emphasizes the miracles during Jesus' ministry along with his birth narratives in a programmatic way that is vivid in the deliberations of John the Baptist's disciples and Jesus.

The miracles recorded in the Synoptic Gospels vary in their focus. In Luke, the prophetic role of Jesus is presented in performing the miracles as the one who came from God; in Matthew, the fulfillment of the prophecies are depicted; and, in Mark, the authority of Jesus along with his emotions of anger, pity, and compassion are exposed.[116] Although E. P. Sanders and Becker view Jesus as a prophet, Sanders considers Jesus as an exorcist too, which is not a characteristic feature of a prophet albeit it manifests God's Kingly rule; and, Becker compares Jesus to the sign prophets by the eschatological proclamation.[117] In recent decades, since the miracle stories are found in ancient writings, the scholars wonder whether Jesus has performed miracles at all as recorded in the Gospels.

Jesus' Performance of Miracles: Resistance of Exploitation

On the basis of 4:18-21, it is considered that Luke depicts Jesus as the one who performed miracles by the power of the Spirit. But, according to Max Turner, Luke relates the Spirit with the Jewish idea of "the Spirit of Prophecy," as the source of inspiration for Jesus' authoritative speech but the source of miracles to δύναμις, that is, "the reality which carries the actual potency of the spirit world into our world."[118] It is vivid in Luke's exorcism and healing episodes that he never associates them with the Spirit but to miraculous power. But, Stanton points out that both Jesus' followers and foes alike accepted Jesus' healing powers during his life time, albeit there were disputes on whose authority and whose power with which Jesus performed them.[119]

Besides, Stanton states that a few scholars in recent decades view many of the healed diseases and disabilities as psychosomatic.[120] In that vein, J. P. Meier argues that in modern times, an educated person cannot accept the possibility of miracles.[121] Meier's argument may perhaps be based on the 21st century enactment of miracles on stages by preachers, tele-evangelists and crusaders. Crossan sees God at work in Jesus in the miracles of Jesus and, according to him the miracles of Jesus point to the resistance of discrimination, exploitation, and oppression.[122] Meir's cynical view is not acceptable because the literary texts of the evangelists claim the events of the miracles, which we consider as the major documents for reconstructing Jesus' life. At the same time, Crossan's view of Jesus' miracles as resistance to discrimination, exploitation, and oppression seems to be derived from the Kingly attitude of Jesus, for the welfare of the downtrodden people in resistance to the prevailing injustice. However, it is obvious that the miracles described by Luke expose Jesus as King, who was anticipated as the Messiah. Stanton, by referring to Twelftree, says that exorcisms, a form of healing, denote the arrival of God's Kingly rule.[123] According to J. Moltmann, the response of Jesus to the disciples of John the Baptist,[124] though seems to be an indirect answer, it indicates the signs of the Messianic age, and the miracles authenticate Jesus.[125] In 11:20, Jesus' words are evident of it: "If it is by the finger of God that I cast out demons, then the Kingdom of God has come to you."[126]

Choosing the Disciples: Exposition of Jesus' Kingship

Luke logically sets the choosing of the twelve in adapting the Markan source. The twelve disciples of Jesus were called[127] and commissioned by him to proclaim the Kingdom of God.[128] At the outset of the travel account, in 9:59-62 = Mt. 8:19-22, the expected characteristics of discipleship are explained by Jesus not to look back on the world and relations. The radical nature of this discipleship seems to depict the urgency of Jesus' mission. In the same chapter, 9:23, Luke states, "If any want to become my followers, let them deny themselves and take up their cross daily and follow me." It seems that it is like the call for soldiers to get ready for war by means of absolute detachment from property and family. The risk of life in the mission of the seventy is portrayed in 10:3 as, "lamb into the midst of wolves." Kingsbury says that perhaps, Jesus might have had the intention of invading the Kingdom by changing the hard-hearted Jews who supported the Roman Empire.[129] But, in the composition of Luke, invasion for establishing the Kingdom is not endorsed. As noted in the miracles, it is for messianic restoration. Their calling is meant for catching people for a new life. Even though they proved themselves to be double-minded, finally, the risen Jesus entrusted them with the responsibility of proclaiming repentance and forgiveness of sin throughout the world.

In 5:27-32,[130] when Levi was called to be a disciple, he had arranged a great feast in his house. A large number of tax collectors and others partook in the feast along with Jesus. Seeing that, the Pharisees murmured that Jesus was with the tax collectors and sinners. The response of Jesus, particularly, the Lukan addition to the other Synoptics, εἰς μετάνοιαν illustrates the purpose of Jesus' calling of disciples. The term μετάνοια means to change one's mind; to repent; and, repent and turn away from something.[131] Here, the act of repentance toward a changed attitude, we see in Zacchaeus. At the end of the Gospel, in 24:47, Luke adds the term, μετάνοιαν to Markan material that the Lord commissioned his disciples to proclaim repentance and forgiveness of sins. F. W. Danker defines μετάνοια as a revolution of the mind in political decision to renounce the political devices that lead to exploit and oppress the poor and the outsider.[132] Presumably, the scenario of Levi's call, as a disciple along with the Lukan additional input of repentance, implies the Kingship attitude of Jesus.

Concerning the call and commission of the disciples, Danker comments,

> Delegation-of Responsibility... Because Jesus was anxious to broaden his messianic political base beyond the boundaries set by people of far less vision, he prepared not only the Twelve for the apostolate but also the Seventy. This double dispatch displayed political sagacity. The apostolate of the Twelve has not been especially notorious for creative advancement of the Lord's mission....With the seventy as back-up, Jesus guaranteed that the Mission would succeed... to maintain the momentum of the New Age.[133]

The number twelve may be a symbolic one. But as Deut. 30:1-10 and Ezek. 37:15-28 speak about God's future reign which envisaged the ingathering of the scattered people of Israel and the reconstitution of the twelve tribes by casting out Israel's enemies it takes on a significant meaning here.[134] The presence of the twelve disciples symbolizes the restoration or the re-establishment of Israel as it was in the days of David and Solomon.[135] This significant choice of the number twelve has been interpreted by Stanton as, "the nucleus of the 'true' or 'restored' twelve tribes of Israel which he sought to establish."[136] Jesus' words of the Q saying is comprehensible concerning this: 22:29f, "I confer on you, just as my Father has conferred on me, a Kingdom, so that you may eat and drink at my table in my Kingdom, and you will sit on thrones judging the twelve tribes of Israel."[137] In this unique farewell discourse, an eschatological, future rule over Israel is revealed.[138] So, in choosing the disciples and commissioning those to proclaim the good news to repentance and forgiveness of sins Luke exposes the Kingship of Jesus as he himself stated to the disciples with authority that the Father has conferred on him the Kingdom.

Role of Women: Kingly Vision of Changing the Society

In 8:2ff, Luke states that women were with Jesus in addition to the twelve disciples. Luke's Gospel is traditionally known as the women's gospel and until three decades back, it was considered as the one which gave much importance to women in Jesus' ministry than any other synoptic Gospels. It is obvious that by accompanying women, Jesus reversed the traditional society of his time, which did not allow women to partake in public activities. M. A. Thomas finds it as more than a revolutionary act.[139] But, Maloney and Smith see it as problematic for many women today since it contains a significant number of texts negative of women.[140] E. S. Fiorenza says that Luke weakens the leadership of women in the movement of Jesus.[141] According to M. R. D'Angelo, Luke limits the role of women by not giving them a chance even to speak and with apologetic motive distances women in Jesus' ministry.[142] According to B. E. Reid, women are only beneficiaries of Jesus' mission, and he joins with J. Schaberg in accusing Luke that women were not treated on par with men. Particularly no women disciples are mentioned in Luke, except for Elizabeth, Mary and Anna in connection with Jesus' birth.[143]

In spite of all these views, it is evident in 8:3b, that women like Mary Magdalene, Joanna, Chuza, Susanna and many others provided them with their resources. In 10:38ff, Mary the sister of Lazarus is praised by Jesus as the one who chose the better part since she sat at the feet of him. One cannot expect Luke to be a 20th century author to promote the gender equality since he lived in a patriarchal society. The parables of Jesus are concerned with woman: woman hiding the yeast in dough;[144] woman searching the lost coin;[145] and, the widow who confronts an unjust judge in pursuit of justice[146] depict the transformation of the divine reign among and by women. So much so women become the metaphor for the Kingdom. According to T. K. Seim, Luke even attributes a positive function to women.[147] However, in general, Luke skillfully composes his Gospel along with the accompaniment of women in Jesus' Messianic mission as their role and positions are recognized in a reversal of the tradition.

Poor and Rich: Egalitarian Outlook of Jesus' Kingship

Jesus' message concerning the poor seems to be the message of salvation, as it is stated in Mary's song as the reversal of fortunes.[148] Blessing to the poor is one of the central messages of Jesus in Luke.[149] It can be understood as bringing a blessing to the poor who are exploited and woe to the rich who are satisfied.[150] Due to taxation, redistribution, debt, and oppressive economic realities as it has been noted in the first chapter, the poor had become poorer at that time. Luke alone adds in his beatitudes a series of woes, as their significance is widespread throughout the Gospel.[151] The rich are condemned. The following passages confirm it: 6:20-26; 12:15-21; 14:12-14, 15-24; 16:19-25 & 19:1-9.

At the outset of Jesus' ministry, by reading from Isaiah 61:1f, in the Nazareth manifesto Jesus reveals the focus of his ministry, particularly to the downtrodden by means of his Kingly character of the Messiah. It is not only to the downtrodden, but also to the people other than the Jews by ethnicity and faith.[152] According to F. Pereira, the poor in Isaiah 61f, refers to the ones who turn to God in trust seeking help and Salvation.[153] Sheeley comments on the message and ministry of Jesus as, "He transcends the exclusivism of the Jewish people to minister to Samaritans and Gentiles. He eats with tax collectors and sinners, claiming that they have more need of his message of salvation than those who are righteous."[154] It is vivid further in 10:37, where the Samaritan is appreciated more than the priest and Levite; and, in 17:16ff, the Samaritan who was cured from leprosy is appreciated by Jesus more than the Jews. In 7:29f, while, the Pharisees and lawyers rejected the messages of both Jesus and John, in acceptance of the repented, the roles of tax collectors and sinners have been reversed. It indicates that Luke envisioned a world with one human community that comprised of both the poor and the rich. However, in this inclusive act Jesus promised a radical social reversal to the poor to be free and fruitful and may be counted as justice to the people.

In that vision, the people who were marginalized and sick partake in the table-fellowship with Jesus.[155] In the parable of the banquet in 14:16-24, God's Kingdom is indicated as belonging to the poor. M. A. Beavis considers the context of Jesus' message as, "the reversal of socio-cultural expectations underlining the message of deliverance for the marginalized people."[156] In 18:18ff, to follow Jesus meant the criterion was given to the ruler to renounce of all one's possessions. It was expected of the disciples too in their calling.[157] These events seem to point to the Kingdom movement of Jesus towards the downtrodden for their betterment. In all these, Jesus assures a complete reversal of economic power in the new era.

Conflicts: Issues of Authority and its Associations with King Jesus

The theme, conflict between Jesus and various Jewish groups form the core of all the four Gospels from the beginning of Jesus' ministry until his arrest and trial. Sheeley, who has studied the Narrative Asides in Luke-Acts, finds conflict as one of the major themes in Luke's Gospel to understand its plot.[158] Abernathy sees conflict as a structural theme in Luke.[159] Eric Franklin points out that a series of Lukan conflict dialogues between the scribes, Pharisees and Jesus are found in

Mk. 2:1-3:6.[160] Kingsbury agrees with Franklin and says that like the other Gospels, Luke portrays the conflict between Jesus and Israel, particularly with the religious authorities.[161] Although, the conflict scenario is indisputable, the reason for the emergence of conflict between Jesus and the Jewish religious authorities need to be traced out. The pertinent question in this regard is: Was it due to the authority of Jesus revealed in his performances of miracle and message?

D. Hill says that Jesus provoked hostility in refusing to perform miracles among his own people. Besides, the hope of resurrection in the message of Jesus irritated the Sadducees and they had conflict over that.[162] M. A. Powell says that in Luke Jesus is presented as the initiator of a new age whereas the leaders are depicted as the custodians of the old age.[163] But in history, they were the custodians of the law and prophets. So, they rejected the good news of the Kingdom and had conflict with Jesus who fulfilled the law and prophesies. When we study 5:29-32 and its parallel to triple tradition,[164] the object of the scribes and Pharisees seem to fall not only on Jesus but also on his disciples. In 15:2, the L material represents the determined hostility of a closed mind than a genuine complaint. By adding the ideology of μετάνοια to Q parable: the Lost Sheep[165] and L parables: the Lost coin and the Lost Son, Luke narrows down the gap between the Pharisees, Scribes and Jesus. The reason for the conflict may be because of their blindness. On some occasions, Jesus warned his opponents against their inner blindness, and pointed out their hardening of heart. For instance, in 12:56, Jesus says, "You hypocrites! You know how to interpret the appearance of earth and sky, but why do you not know how to interpret the present time?"

In 7:36-50; 11:37-54 & 14:1-24, it seems that Luke takes a mediatory position between hostility and hospitality by showing that Jesus dined with the Pharisees. But, Jesus' conflict with the Pharisees runs throughout the Gospel. Even in the procession of Jesus toward Jerusalem, Luke depicts that some Pharisees opposed the multitude's acclamation, which is mentioned in 19:37-39.[166] In general, the conflicts and hostility become more severe. Even at the meal in 11:37-54, Jesus passes strictures against the Pharisees and in 12:1 warning against their hypocrisy. Throughout the Travel Narrative, in Luke's composition, mutual antagonism is explicit.[167]

In the Gospel of Luke, as Tyson identifies, the conflict between Jesus and the Jewish authorities may be seen in three major sections: anticipation of conflict;[168] early conflicts;[169] and, climatic conflict.[170] In the anticipation of conflict, from the Infancy Narrative, the language of conflict is not a dominant one,[171] but in the early conflicts, after the two programmatic narratives: 1) the temptation narrative, which expresses the nature of Jesus' conflict on the non-human level and 2) narrative of Jesus in Nazareth, which expresses the nature of Jesus' conflict on the human level. In this programmatic narratives, Luke not only describes the ministry of Jesus in Galilee and the trip to Jerusalem but also, includes healings, exorcisms, and teaching, particularly most of the teachings in the form of verbal combat, where the Pharisees constitute a major group of opponents.[172] There are about sixteen conflict dialogues in which Pharisees play a distinct role: 5:17-26; 5:29-32; 5:33-35; 6:1-5; 6:6-11; 7:29-30; 7:36-50; 11:37-41; 11:42-54; 12:1; 13:31-33; 14:1-6; 15:1-2; 16:14-15; 17:20-21; 18:9-14. Among them, 11:42-54; 12:1; 16:14-15; 18:9-14 characterize Jesus' criticism of Pharisees and their associates. The issues of conflict in these passages may be reduced into three categories: 1) the authority to forgive sins; 2) purity regulations; and, 3) Sabbath observance.[173] In the climatic conflict, conflict in the Temple, the episodes in 19:28-21:4 happen to be the pinnacle. The temple teaching of Jesus seems to be intentionally used by Luke in developing the theme of conflict and fabricating the tone of the opposition.[174] It may be seen in 20:19 as it is stated that the scribes and the chief priests immediately wanted to lay hands on him when they realized that the parable was told against them. The focus of antagonism is noticeable in this parable of the wicked tenants as well in the temple conflicts.

In Luke's narration, the authority shown by Jesus in the temple becomes the hub of this conflict. At the outset of Jesus' ministry itself in Galilee, that Jesus depicted as having the power of the

Spirit;[175] authority in words,[176] authority in performing miracles and forgiving sins.[177] Although the audience responded to his authority with amazement,[178] the authority of Jesus becomes an issue of hostility.[179] In general, Jesus' association with the outcasts, the message of salvation and the reversal of oppression with authority seem to irritate the Jewish authorities resulting in Jesus' death.

Tax Collectors and Sinners: Restoration into King Jesus' Fellowship

The tax collectors, as quislings, in collaboration with Rome and dishonest customs officers preyed on the populace by charging too much.[180] The tax collectors and the prostitutes were considered as wicked, who sinned willfully and heinously, never repented, and betrayed God by disobeying the law and oppressed the weak, the lowly, the destitute, and the needy. As traitors they betrayed God, the redeemer and law-giver.[181] Even though they betrayed God, Jesus as a Messianic King forgave their sins and accepted them into his fellowship.

Jesus seems to be a preacher of repentance who favoured penitential response. However, Stanton disagrees, as he compares Jesus to John and says that Jesus was not a repentance-minded reformer like John the Baptist.[182] In fact, Crossan considers Jesus as a prophet of Jewish restoration who admitted the wicked into his community without demanding any restitution or obligation to the law. Further, he argues that if Jesus accepted unrepentant sinners, he repudiated not only the Law of God and Judaism but the moral basis of almost all religious life, secular law, and human decency.[183] As Crossan understands it is vivid in Luke that the acceptance of Jesus naturally made them to change their attitudes along with repentance. For instance, the special material of Luke, the story of Zacchaeus in chapter 19 articulates the repentance and the change in Zacchaeus' attitude and life. Luke focuses the act of repentance on Jesus' mission and seen in 5:32 and, in chapters 15; 18; 19 & 23. And the emphasis of Jesus' mission is seen even after the resurrection, in 24:47, where the Lord commissions his disciples to proclaim repentance and forgiveness of sins.

Concerning the parable of the Lost Sheep in chapter 15, Matthew emphasizes the idea of the shepherd who goes after the lost in search of it;[184] whereas, in Luke, the lost must decide to come back by repentance. Luke omits the term ζητεῖ of Matthew but adds the term μετανοίας. While reading both the texts one may get this view. But, the *Sitz im leben* of them are different: in Matthew, the parable loses its original historical setting and it becomes a hortatory material and stands amidst isolated sayings, concerning the support of the least and the discipline of the erring, which are the Markan collection recorded in Mk. 9:33-50. But, Luke seems to have preserved the original situation. Matthew's parable of the Lost Sheep is addressed to Jesus' disciples as the leaders of the community to exercise faithful shepherdship towards the apostates. In Luke, the parable is the response to the opponents: the Pharisees and the Scribes' grumbling about Jesus' ministry toward sinners.

Besides, Luke's addition of repentance places more emphasis on the Kingship of the shepherd. Beyond the act of searching, the act of repentance changes not only the lost, but also leads towards the welfare of the community or Kingdom. In fact, comparison of the usage of the term μετάνοια in the Synoptics, reveals that Luke uses it significantly than the other two evangelists: Lukan Jesus uses it 8 times; Matthean Jesus 4 times and Markan Jesus only once. The story of Zacchaeus in chapter 19 which deals with the act of repentance is explained by R. White as a "vindication story," as Jesus vindicates Zacchaeus' name in public[185] and as a "quest story," by R. C. Tannehill to mark the end of its quest for the Son of Man.[186] Beyond their views, in Luke's story of Zacchaeus[187] it is evident that when the tax collector repents his attitude is transformed. He gives back to the poor. It benefits not only Zacchaeus, but also the oppressed community by taxation. Sanders sees the Lukan portrayal of Jesus here in this episode as a reformer.[188] Possibly, he might have mistaken the idea of Luke in this regard because of Lukan term, Jesus as a Saviour.[189] Reformer means, one who changes the structure, but Saviour in the Roman context, as it has been noted, the Emperor who gives life to the people.

The Anointing of Jesus by a Sinful Woman: Kingly Act of Jesus' Forgiveness

In Matthew, Mark and John[190] the scene is set in Bethany during the Passover time while John places it before the triumphal entry as an anointed King. Whereas, in Lk.7:36-50 it is set in Galilee in Jesus' earlier ministry and not in the Passion Narratives but as a preparation of Jesus' mission preceded by the rejection of John the Baptist.[191] Perhaps, it might be that this event is taken from another source because, the place is not mentioned; and Simon is considered a Pharisee here instead as a leper as he is identified by both Matthew and Mark.[192] However, as per the triple tradition, the event took place at a table-fellowship.[193] Matthew, Mark and John join hands in describing it as an act of 'anointing for burial.' However, Luke emphasizes that it was for the forgiveness of sin.[194] This may be due to the purposeful placing of the event in the Gospel. Mark's anointing event in the Passion Narrative indicates the preparation for Jesus' death and burial; whereas, Luke with the confidence of resurrection as a past happening, places the event to suit his theological context and reshapes it to indicate the opposition of the Pharisees.[195]

The unknown woman in Matthew and Mark, named Mary in John is acknowledged by Luke as a sinful woman. She is portrayed as, 'a sinner in the city' who washes Jesus' feet, wipes it with her hair, kisses it and anoints him with the oil from the alabaster flask when Jesus was reclining at the table. A woman's unbound hair public in the ancient Mediterranean world symbolized many things such as:

> Sexually suggestive act; an expression of religious devotion; a hairstyle for unmarried girls; a sign of mourning; a symbolic expression of distress or proleptic grief in the face of impending danger..., a hairstyle associated with conjury, a means of presenting oneself in a natural state in religious initiations, and a precaution against carrying demons or foreign objects into the waters of baptism.[196]

As Cosgrove says, the context of 7:38 reveals it as not sexually provocative or other acts, but as a gesture of expressing grief and gratefulness which led her towards God's forgiveness.

Moreover, in Matthew and Mark the act of anointing is done over the head; whereas, Luke and John describe it on the feet. D. A. S. Ravens says that the repeated use of feet in Luke seems to be accidental and might be his literary style in line with Isa. 52:7 that points out the context of preaching.[197] According to Davies and Allison, 'probably in well-to-do circles, at feasts it was a customary act. So, the woman affectionately anoints Jesus as a part of celebration.'[198] The words of Luke and John that she poured it over the feet may lead us to think in line with Davies and Allison. But, their view is contentious because, if it was so, was it applicable to only one person in the feast to be anointed? If so, who anoints whom, the owner or the guest or vice versa or even the guests with one another? etc. However, the issue at stake is, do both the descriptions of the anointing 'over the head' and 'on the feet' imply the same meaning of messianic concept? Anointing the head is regarded as a mark of Kingship, which, Mann interprets as 'a sign of royal and priestly dignity.'[199] But Barrett points out that John's interest lies in the anointing, as a means of expressing the royal dignity of Jesus, in preparation for his triumphal entry into Jerusalem,[200] than not so much within the limits of Jewish thoughts and customs.[201] Although Luke doesn't mention anything except forgiveness of sins, John's use of feet gives room for us to establish that the terms feet or head do not make any difference in the messianic implication and both signify the messianic character of Jesus. In addition to that, as per Luke, the one who anoints Jesus is a sinful woman and not a prophet. Therefore Luke avoids saying the act of anointing over the head and but as an act of forgiveness, he emphasizes the role of the Messianic King in accepting sinners into his fellowship.

Peter's Declaration and Transfiguration: Kingly Messianic Disclosure of Jesus

Peter's response, "The Messiah, of God," to the question of Jesus, "What do you say that I am?" discloses the Messiahship of Jesus.[202] Like Mark, Luke narrates the incident briefly than Matthew.[203] But, here again in 9:21, Luke maintains his messianic secrecy through the words of Jesus, 'not to tell anyone.' As Jeremias says, the confession of Peter demarcates the teaching of Jesus as a public proclamation from this personal portrayal concerning the passion and triumph. It is an 'esoteric self-revelation' of Jesus.[204] However, at the close of Jesus' Galilean ministry, Jesus foretold his messianic suffering, death and resurrection. It is further focused in the scenario of transfiguration.[205] The conversation among Jesus, Moses and Elijah in their glory is portrayed by Luke as about Jesus' "departure, which he was about to accomplish at Jerusalem,"[206] which is not in Mark and Matthew. It once again depicts the skill of Luke in composing the Gospel from the Infancy Narrative, step by step, focusing on Jesus' death as the Messianic King. Further, it is developed in 9:35, where Luke again portrays the revelation of Jesus as the Son of God. Here, it should be noted that it is declared to the three disciples of Jesus: Peter, John and James, who were with him in the mount of transfiguration. While the title was revealed only to Jesus at his baptism, here as a messianic title implying an alternative King it is disclosed to others. It might be getting its culmination in the next section, i.e., the Travel Narrative of Luke.

TRAVEL NARRATIVE: THE JOURNEY FROM GALILEE TO JERUSALEM

The Travel Narrative, 9:51-19:48 is peculiar to Lukan composition. In 9:51, "When the days drew near for him to be taken up, he set his face to go to Jerusalem," Luke introduces his theological impetus for Jesus' journey.[207] In other words, Luke programmatically composes the Travel Narrative to introduce Jesus as the alternative King, at the final stage of his journey, as he enters Jerusalem. This journey peculiar to Luke, is furnished with about a dozen parables, a few healings, and short episodes of relative features.[208] Thus, long sections within the journey reports Jesus' presence in Samaria,[209] which is theological in nature than historical[210] since it emphasizes the Kingship motif of Jesus.

Basically, as in Mark's Gospel, Luke structures this Travel Narrative as only one journey of Jesus toward Jerusalem and differs from John's Gospel in its structure of three journeys. In this section, rejection at

Samaria, parables, table-fellowship, triumphal entry, concept of the Kingdom of God, etc., get more importance as it seems that through these things, Lukan redaction brings out Jesus' Kingship to the climax.

Rejection at Samaria: Lukan Personification of a Benefactor King

In 9:51-56, at the outset of the Travel Narrative, Luke depicts the rejection of Jesus in a Samaritan village as he was rejected at Nazareth in the beginning of Galilean ministry. In v. 53, Luke shows the cause of rejection as they were ready to go to the Temple.[211] It seems that the Temple controversy is cryptically stated here. Jesus goes on his way towards Jerusalem in spite of opposition.[212] By sending messengers to prepare the way for him, Luke depicts his anticipation as he would be accepted in a non Jewish country. Due to his non acceptance in Samaria, in v. 58,[213] Jesus explained that he has no place to lay his head.

The incident of rejection at the Samaritan village doesn't make any difference in Jesus' attitude towards the Samaritans. To the angry attempt of his disciples, to request heavenly fire to come down and consume an inhospitable Samaritan village, Jesus says no. In fact, Luke points out that he rebuked them. Subsequently, in 17:12-19, in the healing of ten lepers, when the healed Samaritan comes to give thanks Jesus approves the Samaritan with an exclamatory remark over against the nine Jews.[214] On the other hand, the Samaritan's thankfulness to Jesus in the Greco-Roman context indicates Jesus as the Great Benefactor.[215] Besides, the parable of the Good Samaritan is Jesus' response to the lawyer who asked, "Who is my neighbour?" In that parable Jesus appreciates the character of the Samaritan.

Parables and Aphorisms

The parables of Jesus, drawn out from the daily life of Palestine, might have emerged from a double historical context: 1) the original context of his utterances; and, 2) subsequent written form as they survived in the primitive church with modifications. Even translating the Galilean Aramaic of Jesus into Greek some alterations might have occurred in the meaning. While commenting on the parabler, Sanders says that 'by the sayings and parables of Jesus, he is assumed as a teacher or a difficult riddling teacher, whose meaning is not clear.'[216] R.W. Funk and Stanton presume him to be a wisdom teacher. Crossan considers him as a Jewish Cynic.[217] It should be noted that Jesus used the parabolic stories often as weapons against critics and foes in offering forgiveness.

The Hebrew word, מָשָׁל and its Greek equivalent, παραβολή mean parable, proverb, prophetic figurative discourse, similitude, etc.,[218] J. W. Sider considers every parable as an analogy.[219] Parables in the Gospels are used in different contexts as well in different types. For instance, in: 4:23, a proverb, 'Doctor, cure yourself!'; 6:39, 'Can a blind person guide a blind person? Will not both fall into a pit?' 14:7ff, general advice with regard to proper behavior at a feast; etc., and aphorisms, pithy and arresting sayings in the form of admonitions, for instance, 12:33bf = Mt 6:19-21; 13:23f = Mt 7:13f & 12:58f = Mt 5:25f.

Although Law undergirds all the parables, the components of parables are sorted out as: the Temple; the Land; the Economy; and, the People. Many parables in Palestine evoked out of these components. In course of time, however, the Temple became a central issue in Palestinian Jewish thought and life as well as the Land, a promised one.[220] In the society where Jesus lived, the religious observance of the Temple, the peasant life on the land, the stratified economy, and, the communal lives of the people seemed to be the major social settings. In the words of B. H. Young, "…the parables of Jesus are intimately related to the religious heritage, culture, language, agricultural life and social concerns of the Jewish people during the Second Temple Period."[221]In addition, the parables of Jesus are Kingdom trajectories in Roman occupied Palestine, particularly in Galilee.

Many times, a parable is often understood as an image that tells a fictional story, and as a consequence a suitable response either implicit or explicit from the audience is elicited.[222] There is another group of parables, identified as riddles[223] and by that one understood Jesus as a sage, who was capable of answering intricate questions.

The parables are also understood as: similitude, narrative parable, and allegory. Similitude is an extended comparison which refers to a familiar everyday scene in the form of a simile; narrative parable is a metaphor that offers a direct comparison; and an allegory in the narrative has a significance of its own.[224] Generally, parables may be classified as: 1) true parables; 2) story parables; and, 3) illustrations. True parable is an illustration from day to day life of the audience mostly used in the present tense, for instance: 7:31f, children playing in the marketplace; 15:8-10, a woman losing a coin in her house; etc. Story parable is an analogy, which doesn't rely on any obvious truth or generally accepted custom but refers to a particular event that occurred in the past, normally an experience of a person to convey the truth, for instance: 16:1-9, the story of the rich man whose manager had wasted his possessions; 18:1-8, the repeated plea of a widow to the judge; etc., Illustration is an example story that focuses directly on the character and the conduct of an individual, for instance: 10:30-37, the parable of the Good Samaritan; 12:16-21, the rich fool; 16:19-31, the rich man and Lazarus; 18:9-14, the Pharisee and the tax collector etc.

The parables from the Old Testament seem to be a strong precedence for the use of Jesus' parables. Jesus might be the first Jewish Teacher who used parables to instruct the people. In comparing the parables of Jesus and those of rabbis of the later first century, the parables of Jesus contain some Scriptural images and deal with new truths and themes, whereas the latter illustrate or expound scripture[225] but do not deal with any new truths or themes like: the Kingdom of God; love, grace, and mercy of God; the rule of the Son of God and so on. In Luke, particularly the parables of Lukan special material indicate Jesus' Kingly attitudes against the socio-political tyranny.

L Parables: Jesus' Kingly Aspect against the Socio-Political Tyranny

Luke uses more parables of Jesus to reveal Jesus' teaching than the other Synoptics: Luke, twenty nine; Matthew, twenty-one; and Mark, only six. Particularly, Luke uses his own special L parables in his composition of the Gospel to denote the intention and character of

Jesus along with the motif of his Kingship. They are: i) 10:25-37, the Good Samaritan; ii) 11:5-8, friend at midnight; iii) 12:13-21,the rich fool; iv) 13:6-9, the barren fig tree; v) 14:7-14, a lesson to guests and a host; vi) 15:8-10, the lost coin; vii) 15:11-32, the lost son; viii) 16:1-13, the dishonest Steward; ix) 16:19-31, the rich man and Lazarus; x) 17:3-10, Unprofitable Servants; xi) 18:1-8, the widow and the judge; and, xii) 18:9-14, the Pharisee and the tax collector. Luke, obviously, seems to have added these parables with a special purpose to describe a particular structure of either political rule or social relationship.

The Parable of the Good Samaritan: Boundary Breaking Aspect of Kingship

The parable of the Good Samaritan stated in 10:25-37 as an illustration, focuses directly on the character and the conduct of an individual but at the same time describes the social relationship between Jews and Samaritans. The intention of the parable seems to be to counter ethnic controversy. In the conversation between Jesus and the lawyer, the question of the lawyer might have arisen from Lev. 19:33f, where the Israelites were commanded to consider the alien who resides with them as a citizen among them. However, a distance in relationship was to be maintained.[226] As well, according to Deut. 15:1ff, it was instructed that from the alien, the debt if any must be exacted in the seventh year, whereas, from the Israelites it should not be. In this understanding, the lawyer might have raised this question as to who is his neighbour.[227] To reverse this understanding of distancing the alien, Jesus might have told this parable. According to M. Gourgues, it is "a reversal of roles" with the model of neighbourly love.[228] It indicates loving one's neighbour in responding to the need of others by breaking the boundaries. Schottroff considers it as a radical interpretation of the Torah in respect of loving one's neighbor.[229] As a reversal of practice, and a radical interpretation of the Mosaic Law, it seems, Jesus wanted to change the attitude of the Jewish people by appreciating the act of a Samaritan as he modifies or reverses the Law in the Sermon on the Mount, written by Matthew in 5:17-48. On the whole, this parable exhibits the establishment of social relationship as the reversal of the entrenched concepts and practices of distancing others.

The episode stated in this parable is geographically located on the road from Jerusalem to Jericho, the residential area of many priests and the road is used by both the priests and Levites to travel to and fro the Temple. The religious leaders: the priest and the Levite are explicitly portrayed in an unusual way. The priest and the Levite had obeyed the Mosaic Law concerning the corpse-defilement given in Lev. 21:1ff and Num. 19:11ff. But, amid the Jewish religious structure, this parable contrasts the act of Samaritan against the priest and the Levite. It must be noted that the Samaritan is juxtaposed to the Jewish Priest and Levite in the milieu of continual attacks and exclusions regarding the Temple on Mount Gerizim and the Temple in Jerusalem,[230] which is already indicated at the outset of the Travel Narrative by Luke in 9:52f, that the Samaritan village refused hospitality to Jesus and his disciples because they were going to the Temple. Besides, it can be evidenced from the dialogue of Jesus with the Samaritan woman which is found in the fourth Gospel.[231] It shows the new aspect of Jesus to change a society with good leadership. Although it is an entrenched issue among both Jews and Samaritans, and a difficult matter to handle, his Kingly nature is explicit through his teaching as well as by his action that he wanted to transcend geographical and social boundaries.

The Parable of the Friend at Midnight: Reciprocal Care

The parable of friendship in Luke 11:5-8, shows God's answer to the persistent prayers of his people in juxtaposition to the unwilling friend to help. Luke uses the friendship theme more than any other New Testament author and it runs throughout the Gospel from the beginning. Luke's prologue highlights the friendship theme by the use of the name, Θεόφιλος and it seems to reflect the Hellenistic concepts of friendship. Luke uses it in terms of various categories among equals and those of unequal status: in 7:6, refers to centurion's subordinates; in 7:34, refers to the patron and the beneficiaries; in

11:5-8, refers to reciprocal friendship between two people; in 12:4, refers to the leader and the fan; in 12-14, refers to the teacher and the appealed; in 14:10-12, refers to the host and the guest; and in 15:6 & 21:16, refers to the social equals.

Lukan emphasis of friendship is identified in the inflected use of the word, φίλος as it is applied twice in accusative case, once in vocative case, and once in nominative case. Lately, scholars have taken note of the rhetorical *topos* of friendship in the parable. It reflects God's character that he is a reliable friend who remains loyal to the reciprocity of friendship.[232] It is not simply sharing the ideas or feelings, but the "real sharing of life,"[233] and the solidarity of friends in providing shelter at night and demand solidarity beyond the limits of decency. In general, the usage of friendship by Jesus depicts that he is a leader who wants to teach his fans not to show any disparity among them. His Kingly attitude of leading his flock is implied in it by being friendly with everyone and caring for each one with equality.

The Parable of the Rich Fool: Kingly Warning against Apathy of Others

The rich fool in 12:13-21 as an illustration, is pronounced by Jesus in the context of a fan who appealed to him to settle his problem of sharing his family inheritance. The key statement: "Take care! Be on your guard against all kinds of greed; for ones' life does not consist in the abundance of possessions," is the thrust of Jesus' message in this parable. It depicts the action of the wealthy as unconcerned about anyone except himself as well as Jesus' note on the reversal of action.[234] Concerning the wealth and economy, Jesus' outlook is clear here in opposing the rich in amassing more and more by marginalizing the poor. According to Schottroff, this parable's viewpoint is shaped by the suffering of the enslaved and impoverished people.[235] On the whole, this parable clearly explains the socio-economic context of Jesus' time as it has been noted in the 1st chapter. Jesus, with his Kingly attitude condemns this attitude of marginalizing the people.

The Barren Fig Tree: Kingly Call for Repentance and Awareness

The parable of the barren fig tree in 13:6-9, as a story parable, deals with repentance and refers to a particular event that occurred in the past. The context of the whole chapter may be taken as a unit explaining the progress of the Kingdom in view of the rejection of Jesus by the Jews.[236] But, the immediate context of this parable is the historical and political context referred to in 13:1-5. Pilate, the Roman prefect in Judea from CE 26 to CE 36 along with great many brutal and oppressive acts, murdered a group of Galileans within the precincts of the Temple and mingled their blood with the blood of the sacrificial animals, which was a deliberate religious provocation to the Jewish people. Those who were killed in this brutal act were regarded by the Roman authorities as politically dangerous to them. Moreover, Pilate was marching his troops into Jerusalem and used the Temple money to build an aqueduct. This past historical event of oppression is used by Jesus as a recollection along with the collapse of a tower at the Siloam pool, which might have fallen due to the aqueduct that Pilate built. Instead of reacting to Pilate's bloody deed with a condemnation of Rome, Jesus regards them as consequences of the guilt of the Jewish people against defiling themselves as it is mentioned in Lev 18:24f. Here, the key statement precedes the parable: vv. 3 & 5, "...unless you repent, you will all perish as they did." The call to repentance is given through the parable of the barren fig tree. At the same time, the gardener's plea shows his gracious mind in giving some more time to change one's attitude as well, marking the political and Kingly attitude of Jesus in conscientizing the people.

The Lost Sheep, the Lost Coin & the Lost Son: Joy of Jesus' Kingship

The parables of Lost Sheep in 15:3-7 = Mt. 18:12-14, Lost Coin in 15:8-10, and Lost Son in 15:11-32 are the trilogy in Luke 15th chapter which deal with the repentance of sinners and falls under the classification of true parables as illustrations drawn from the day to day life of the audience. As it has been noted earlier in this chapter, Luke introduces Jesus ministry along with the cry of John the Baptist for repentance and Baptism, as an act of rededication to the Israelites, who lost their privileges by the sin of worshipping the Roman Emperor. This was again a call to be integrated in the community of true Israel.

In this trilogy, Luke accentuates the need for repentance. The immediate context of this trilogy mentioned in 15:1-2, is the accusation of the Pharisees and Scribes that Jesus eats with sinners and tax-collectors. In this context of Pharisaic polemical attack, these parables seem to be a defense of Jesus' association with the lost.[237] The sinners here as Luke points out are those who obeyed the Roman Emperor in deviating the Law and theocracy; and the tax collectors who are the employees of the Roman government. It is obvious that Luke intended by these parables to explain Jesus' invitation to sinners and tax collectors and dining with them to retrieve the lost sheep. Danker says that this trilogy broadens the divine political base by including such people in the New Age.[238] There seems to be a possible perception of the Lukan motif indicating Jesus' Kingship in these parables.

Concerning the parable of the Lost Sheep, Jeremias says that the Q parable was though addressed to the Pharisees, the Scribes, or the Crowd, later it was related by the primitive church to the disciples of Jesus.[239] Jeremias' speculation may be related to Matthew's outlook. Luke introduces this parable at the Pharisees' grumbling, whereas in Matthew,[240] the audiences are not Jesus' opponents but his disciples as the leaders of the community, to exercise faithful shepherdship towards the apostates. It could be also seen in the use of the terms for the lost one: Matthew says that the one as τὸ πλανώμεον, whereas Luke says it as τὸ ἀπολωλὸς. i.e., in Matthew the shepherd goes in search of the one who went astray but in Luke, it is the lost one. Besides, Luke's addition of the term, μετάνοια in the key statement of this parable emphasizes more on the Kingship of the shepherd in going beyond the act of searching and rejoicing with the act of repentance which maintains the welfare of the community along with the lost one's change of mind and turning away from the sinful act.

In the parable of lost coin the woman probably had lost a coin from her *thali*,[241] the symbol of marriage as in a wedding ring, implying the betrothal covenant of her life. Reid opposes this view saying that it is an imaginative interpretation based on modern nomadic Bedouin women and not of the first century Jewish woman.[242] But, a coin in a decorative bridal headdress or a necklace is considered a valuable part of woman's dowry. Derrett calculates it as her possession of wealth which might be ten days wages capable of sustaining 10 days of life.[243] According to Carr, it was a day's wage.[244] However, although it might be a coin of less value, here Luke gives the value of life to it, as much as losing the symbol of a covenantal life and indicates the woman's distress in losing it. The value of it could be calculated from the joy of her with the neighbours when she finds it, i.e., her life is restored. It is apparent that Jesus, as an alternative Messianic King joyfully restores the lost in making them valuable in the Kingdom.

The parable of the lost son exposes the broken family of the father by the loss of a member in his family. Schottroff says, the feast arranged by the father symbolizes a Messianic feast of rejuvenating Israel and the nations.[245] According to Jill Robbins, the Messianic feast of the parable of the lost son depicts the economic status of a restorative movement structures, and the entire confession illustrates the self-recovery of a greater restoration.[246] According to Jeremias, the parable of the lost son is an apologetic one that portrays God's abounding love with no barriers.[247] According to C. E. Carlston, while generally, Lukan moral emphasis on repentance is an accepted fact, theologically, Luke's interest seems to focus on the father's love for the penitent sinner.[248] Although, it reflects the father's love, as seen by Jeremias and Carlston, in Lukan composition, as Robbins points out, the theme of repentance indicates the grater restoration of a family at a micro level as well as all humanity at a macro level along with the bliss of the Messianic Kingdom.

Besides, as pointed out at the close of the parable, the self-righteousness of the elder son makes him a sinner. As per the Jewish practice, the elder son has to receive two-thirds of the father's wealth.[249]

Beyond that legacy, now the younger son is accepted again even after he squandered his share. The father's invitation to the elder brother to join the banquet and his refusal shows Luke's design of the reversal of outsider and insider on the basis of one's repentance of attitudes. On the whole, these three parables, while they intend the same thing, each one is valuable in itself in restoring the welfare of the community of pointing to the act of restoration of the lost and the marginalized in the Kingdom through Jesus' movement.

The Dishonest Steward: Grace to the Least

The parable of the dishonest steward in 16:1-13, a story parable, is a radical scrutiny of the money economy, which depicts the reduction of debt. Since the steward doesn't follow the Law, he is called as the dishonest steward. But, the word οἰκονόμος connotes the trustworthy as well a hard working person.[250] The reduction of debt seems positive to avoid protest and losing the whole.[251] It may be further evidenced as his precaution in contrast to the rich fool in 12:13ff and his action at the reduction of money in contrast to the rich man in 16:19ff.[252] J. S. Ukpong in his essay, "The Parable of the Shrewd Manager," in line with liberation theology depicts debtors as small farmers and the manager as poor who has no rights and the rich man as one who recognizes the farmer's need and accepts the forgiveness of debts on their behalf.[253] While it was not rare to harass the debtors for their due, sometimes in the social history of Palestine, it resulted in more banditry because they would not be able to pay the taxes.[254] But, according to Schottroff, since the quantities mentioned in the parable are more, there is less possibility to consider it as debts of the consumers or tenants or farmers. Rather, it might be the case of dealers with a future contract, which J. S. Kloppenborg also has the same view as large farmers or businessmen as Luke intends.[255]

Moreover, the three fold power structure: master, steward and tenants, provides a relationship system. The meaning of the parable needs to be elicited from the context of other parables of Jesus in the context of forgiveness of sins. As in the parable of the prodigal son, the welcoming of the lost son caused the elder son to complain against him as unjust; the parable of the hired labourers ends with the complaints about the unjust payment of the master; the parable of the great feast and wedding feast, the invited lost the enjoyment but others enjoyed it. In line with all these parables, the parable of the dishonest steward, hints at the subversion of traditional values, while Grace to the least is asserted.[256] The master's praise of the treacherous steward in verse 8, refers to Jesus as the one who praised the cheater because of the forgiveness of debts to build up a community.

From a socio-historical perspective, it might be two different social systems of that era: the social order of the world[257] and of the community who are the people of light.[258] The injustice of the steward, which is the key element of this parable, is changed by his act of forgiveness as it is considered as justice, and becomes "an expression of totally unexpected grace," that made him trustworthy as an heir of the Kingdom.[259] V.9 indicates the imminence of the Kingdom. This parable induces the community to act quickly, decisively, and wisely as the treacherous manager and at the same time challenges the conventional view of wealth as a sign of divine blessing.[260] So, it may be a invitation to leave the Satanic rule and follow God.

D. Landry and B. May point out that Kloppenborg who agrees with B. Malina opines that the master's social codes of honour and shame are challenged by the steward's incompetent responsibility, since honour is counted more than wealth.[261] According to Beavis, the identity of the steward as per the Greco-Roman culture, is a slave and says that a slave is normally sold rather than dismissed. But citing W. O. E. Oesterley, she says that dismissal of a slave is worse than selling. i.e., the slave is left without home, occupation, and food which lead to the danger of loneliness and dying in starvation.[262] To avoid the impending danger, the steward restored his honour by his shrewd action of slashing the profits. The misappropriation of funds may be understood along with the act of the younger son's squandering of his inheritance, where it was not expected of return of his inheritance and with Luke's concern for the redemption of a sinner, which depicts the character of Lukan King, Jesus. It may also be viewed as a feature of theocracy and its continuation in Christocracy.

Since the master is referred to as Κύριος and in v 9, its application to the disciples of Jesus to make use of the dishonest wealth to attain the eternal homes, Jeremias doubts whether this is the original meaning of the parable, because, v. 10, in the form of a proverb in vv. 11-12 is applied to mammon and the everlasting riches. According to him, it is not an example of the steward, but a dreadful warning,[263] because the key statement of the parable in v. 13, "No slave can serve two masters; for a slave will either hate the one and love the other, or be devoted to the one and despise the other," shows, a sharp contrast between the service of God and the service of mammon. In light of the Roman Emperor's Rule in the first century Palestine, indicating the rule of an alternative King Jesus, Luke might have made this contrast between Christocracy/ Theocracy and the Human Kingship.

The Rich Man and Lazarus: Reversal of Economic Exploitation

The parable of the rich man and Lazarus in 16:19-31, an illustration, points out the character of the rich man who was only concerned about himself and not of others. He might be a Sadducee, who doesn't believe in the resurrection of the dead and the judgment of God.[264] On the other hand, the reversal in the economic exploitation is to be noted in this parable of Jesus. The placement of it in continuation to the ridicule of the Pharisees, who are attributed the title, lovers of money;[265] and, after the parable of the dishonest steward, seems to be a critical view of economic exploitation. The fate of the poor and the rich are shown in contrast. The social history reveals the situation in Judea before 66 CE and seems to stem out of it. The Jewish upper class was excessively wealthy and they extended credit to small farmers to acquire their land, and enslaved them since they could not repay the money borrowed from the wealthy.[266] Luke by this parable brings out the eschatological idea of the reversal of social order in defying conventional thinking and equating poverty with eternal reward; wealth with eternal suffering; and, demands the repentance of the rich to change their attitude in the earthly life. This parable has two motifs: 1) reversal of fortune after death; and, 2) the message for the living.[267] The rich man was condemned of his misuse of wealth as well juxtaposed of his luxury with the poor man's painful starvation. The reversal of roles is to be understood as an awareness of the "drastic revision of values" in the emergence of the Kingdom.[268] According to Prabhu, it is "Jesus' uncompromising stand against riches" and the "commitment to the poor."[269] Prabhu may be right but it might also be added that Jesus stood against the inhuman rich. Above all, this parable reveals that it is not only a reversal of fortunes, but also the establishment of justice and righteousness of the Messianic King.

Unprofitable Servants: Roman Oppression

In the parable of the unprofitable servants in 17:7-10 told to his disciples, after the two sayings of hindrance to the little ones and faith to the amount of a mustard seed, Jesus says about a slave and a master as a model in working for the welfare of the community. It is special Lukan material. In history, during the expansion of Rome, slavery prevailed in Palestine as people became prisoners of war. It became a daily experience of many enslaved Jewish people. Besides, the humiliation of a slave becomes an image for self-surrender.[270] The key statement of the pericope is, "...when you have done all that you were ordered to do, say, we are worthless slaves; we have done only what we ought to have done!"[271] It is obvious that Jesus used the prevailing imagery of a slave in Palestine to point out their ministry along with his Kingship, that it has no reputation, fame or reward but they are expected to do what they are commanded.

The Widow and the Judge: Anticipation for Deliverance

The parable of the widow and the unjust judge in 18:1-8, a story parable, illustrates God's answer to the persistent prayer of people in their situation of isolation and cruelty. In this Lukan material, though the widow's demand is for justice against her opponent, Luke deals it as a parable of prayer.[272] Although, the parable of the widow and the unjust Judge contrasts the parable of the Friend at Night, both seem to be the intention of Luke in assuring hope to the disciples that God will deliver them from the impending tribulation and injustice by his rule.

The Pharisee and the Tax Collector: Call for Repentance

The parable of the Pharisee and the Tax collector in 18:9-14, an illustration, reveals the Jewish religious practice negatively. It might be out of the impact of anti-pharisaic texts that emerged after the destruction of the Temple in 1st century CE.[273] It is a condemnation of the Pharisee with a call for repentance.[274] The parable compares the character of both the Pharisee and the tax collector: the Pharisee boasts himself of how he strictly observed the Law; whereas, the tax collector humbles himself even standing far off and longs for God's mercy. Here, Luke explicitly shows his reversal idea in stating that the tax collector was justified and gives the moral that boasting of oneself destroys the fellowship with God and others whereas, humility leads to community life.

In general, the thrust of L parables lies on the concept of reversal of economy, wealth, social systems, religious practices, exclusivism, and the attitudes with the intention of restoration, repentance, transcending geographical and social boundaries, reciprocity, humility, persistent and hopeful prayer and self surrender, that speak of the Messianic Kingly aspect of Jesus in uniting people and doing good for the people in building the community life over against the socio-political situation of that time.

Parables Common in Q and Triple Tradition

As the motif of Jesus' Kingship has been noted in the special material of Lukan parables, it has to be further looked at in terms of the composition of some other parables which belong to Q and triple tradition.

Parable of the Sower: Warning against the Fear of Roman Authority

In the triple tradition parable of the sower in 8:4-8 & 11-15 in the
Galilean ministry section,[275] Luke emphasizes the warning against
people's hardening of the heart. The *Sitz im leben* of the parable may
be helpful in understanding the meaning of the parable. Although
Jesus began his ministry in the synagogues, he condemned the ritual
of Sabbath and Jewish exclusivism. Because of this he was opposed by
his own people.[276] Besides, the inability of his disciples to understand
him and his teaching also made him to a state of great disappointment.
The seed which fell on the way, rocky place and among the thorns
indicate the backdrop of the people and their inability to receive the
word of God. In the interpretation of the parable in 8:11-15,[277] while
Matthew and Mark say about tribulation and persecution in which
the hearers fall away from their belief, Luke says, temptation in 8:13.
This seems to indicate the Lukan mind that the people are afraid of
Roman authority and tempted to be attached with the rulers than the
message of Jesus.

Parable of the Mustard Seed: Invisible Growth of Jesus' Community

In the triple tradition parable of the mustard seed in 13:18f,[278] Luke
follows Mark and indicates the phenomenal growth of the Kingdom,
that was originally taken from the Old Testament imagery given in
Dan. 4:11f; Ezek. 17:23 & 31:6. It may be seen as the extensive
growth; and, the Q material in 13:20f,[279] the parable of the yeast as
the intensive growth, which Luke in line with Matthew indicates as
invisible growth.[280] D. H. V. Daalen says that the ingredient in the
Kingdom of God is Jesus, the King, who is the leaven.[281] In other
words, the phenomenal growth of the Messianic Kingdom both visibly
and invisibly is well portrayed along with the parables of the mustard
seed as well as the yeast.

Parable of the Tenants: Challenge to Political Leadership

The triple tradition parable of the tenants in 20:9-19,[282] an allegory,[283]
is placed after the question of Jesus' authority. In this parable, Jesus

personifies himself as the Son. Mark and Luke say that the owner of the vineyard will destroy the evil tenants, whereas Matthew, in 21:40f, states that the response of the audience of the parable that the evil tenants will be killed. It depicts that the people never like the evil of the leaders. According to V. J. John, it is, "a clear challenge to the political leadership."[284] It is obvious that the high priests and the leaders who were in collaboration with Rome were possibly considered to be the opponents, and it seems to be a warning to point out their corruption. Jesus' view of himself as the beloved son of the owner of the vineyard, whom they have killed, seems to be his prophecy and the reference to the scribes and priests, who feared the people to lay hands on him, shows the situation of Jesus' fans around him who wanted a social-political change in Palestine.

Parable of the Pounds: Jesus' Kingship against Exploitative Kingship

The parable of the Pounds in 19:11-27 and its parallel in Matthew 25:14-30,[285] seem to be at variance with each other. Feuillet, L. Fonck, N. Geldenhuys, P. Joüon, J. Knabenbauer, A. Plummer, P. Schanz, J. M. Vosté, T. Zahn et al. say that they are independent of each other. But, Fitzmyer maintains that they have a common root but written in two forms, since there are common materials as well as parallelism in them.[286] Of course, though they seem to be different, they have common materials. Luke modifies and places this parable at the close of the Travel Narrative and immediately after the incident in the house of Zacchaeus.

Predominantly, in addition to Matthew Luke introduces the new idea of the King who goes away to receive a Kingdom. Historically, it resembles Archelaus who travelled to Rome in order to obtain his reign. Despite the opposition and delegation of Jews as well as Samaritans after he went to Rome, he attained Kingship and destroyed his enemies. The words King, Kingdom or rule appear five times in vv. 11, 12, 14, 15 & 27 which are not of Matthew and, contrary to it the servants are rewarded with authority over cities in Luke.[287] Generally, the noble man is considered as Jesus and his departure and return mean his death and Parousia.[288] Against this allegorical interpretation, Richardson says that the elements of the story bear Archelaus as the nobleman since the details are historically close to him. But, he was made only an *ethnarch* and did not receive the Kingdom.[289] Besides, historically in 6 CE, Archelaus was deposed by Augustus on account of his outrageous administration and unbearable tyranny[290] and was banished to Vienne in Gaul.[291] It raises the issue, why does Luke historicize details of a long-deposed ruler? It might perhaps show the reason for the composition of Luke in juxtaposing the Messianic King Jesus against the Herodian family.

This parable in relation to the economic and political scenario of exploitative Kingship, further, points out Luke's juxtaposition of Jesus against Archelaus or in other words, the impending Christocracy and the cruel human Kingship.[292] Jerusalem is mentioned twice and there is no delay in the noble man's return as a King. Receiving the Kingdom is a present event and not an eschatological one. The King exercises his power over the cities under his control which shows the political aspect of the parable. Besides, it points out that the people who do in accordance with the King will be honoured. Since it is placed after the event of Zacchaeus, it seems to be a juxtaposition of Jesus' Kingship of saving a sinner's life against the worldly Roman authorized Jewish King. By and large, it should be noted that in continuation of this parable, Luke narrates the triumphal entry of Jesus where he reveals him as a King through the voice of the people, which so far he maintains in secrecy motif throughout the Gospel.

The intention of the parable seems to be to correct the Jewish anticipation of the appearance of the Kingdom as it is mentioned in 19:11. By the placement of this parable in the above said context, it is identified as a Kingship parable.[293] Jeremias says that the context of this parable in both the Gospels is Parousia and written so in order to refute the false expectations of the imminent Kingdom.[294] This is contentious because the citizens referred to in this parable stand for Israel and according to Goudoever, might be Essenes, since the

Messianic movement started with them.[295] However, it seems to be a warning to the hostile leaders who hesitated to accept Jesus as the King, shown by Luke corresponding to 19:11 and the subsequent entry story.

The Parable of the Great Banquet: Kingly Character of Jesus

The Q parable of the great Banquet in 14:15-24,[296] depicted as the final unit in the dinner episode, although appears as a separate literary unit located in the middle of the Lukan Travel Narrative, proves itself as a sophisticated composition and evidences itself in its thematic and rhetorical coherence, which differs from Matthew. In Luke, v. 15, begins this parable with the statement of a man who was sitting along with Jesus in the feast, "Blessed is anyone who will eat bread in the kingdom of God." It depicts the aim of this parable in Lukan composition. Matthew's context of the parable is the marriage of the King's son, whereas Luke simply states as a man's banquet, which seems to be Luke's secrecy motif of Jesus' Kingship. Matthew says that the King's servant was killed and the King angrily burned their city and destroyed the murderers by his troops in retaliation. Likewise, after inviting the poor, the one who doesn't have the wedding garment also is cast into darkness. Luke intentionally omits[297] those things and presents his key statement of the parable in v. 24, "For I tell you, none of those who were invited will taste my dinner" and explains why the poor, the crippled, the blind, and the lame will partake in his feast. This seems to be his reversal motif of Jesus' Kingship against the practice of hospitality among the upper classes throughout the Mediterranean world, including Israel. According to Thatcher, it symbolizes a brokerless Kingdom which illustrates Jesus' vision of the egalitarian Kingdom.[298] This parable indicates that the homeless, the beggars, and the handicapped are admitted in the houses of the well-to-do, instead of the people of the same class. Besides, it exposes the practice of Jesus in bringing up the marginalized and explicates his Messianic Kingly character.

Reed Shaken by the Wind: Comparison of John and Herod by Jesus

The riddle of Jesus from the Q material seems to be a contrast to John the Baptist against a royal person.[299] After the messengers from John the Baptist had gone away, Jesus addressed the crowd asking, "What did you go out into the wilderness to look at: A reed shaken by the wind? What then did you go out to see? Someone dressed in soft robes? Look, those who put on fine clothing and live in luxury are in royal palaces. What then did you go out to see? A prophet?"[300] Both the series of questions along with riddles parallel each other. If we take the first one, "a reed shaken by the wind alone," naturally one may be tended to think of the reed common in the Jordan desert and on the bank of Gennesaret or the vanishing of John's words and deeds. But, the following parallel riddle, "Someone dressed in soft robes?" which refers to a person and contrasting the former with something in the desert, indicates its reference to Herod Antipas through his "emblematic interpretation."[301] Historically, a reed appears as an emblem in the first coins of Herod Antipas, reflecting his political programme. Jesus refers to him as a wavering person, who was addressed by him in another place as fox.[302] He was criticized by John the Baptist, an ascetic who put on the archaic, simple dress, regarding his marriage with Herodias. Besides, Antipas survived a further crisis during CE 36 due to renouncing his Nabatean wife which caused the boundary conflict with the hostile neighbour.[303] However, it seems that Jesus juxtaposes John the Baptist, the messianic herald and prophet with the Roman client King, Herod Antipas in the context of people's wavering mind in moving towards the power and authority instead of following the Messianic call of John.

Table-fellowship: Vision of the Christocentric King Jesus

At the close of his Galilean ministry, Jesus provided food for the multitude.[304] Parallel to it, at the close of his ministry in Jerusalem Luke portrays the Farewell Meal.[305] Not only Jesus is depicted as a host, but also as a guest during his journey and the stay in Jerusalem.[306] Luke presents some events about Jesus' table-fellowship with sinners and tax collectors in 5:27-32; 7:36-50; 19:1-11 and with a Pharisee in 11:37-52, which nuance anticipated the Messiah, as indicated in the Infancy Narrative. He is the one who liberates Israel not only from physical repressions such as hunger, sickness etc., but also, from political and social oppression.

Because of the act of table-fellowship, the Pharisees grumbled and were filled with fury discuss. They discussed what they should do with Jesus.[307] The words of Jesus in 7:34 indicate that he was rejected as "a glutton and a drunkard, a friend of tax collectors and sinners." At a banquet in a Pharisee's house, Jesus' criticism of the Pharisees created hostility.[308] It seems that Jesus' table-fellowship invites the sinners to repentance. It is through which Jesus challenges the "Pharisaic mode of life." For instance, in 19:1-10, the repentance of Zacchaeus and in 15:11-32, the repentance of the younger son explicates the change of life in relation to the table-fellowships. The key word lost, used by Luke in both these events has a prehistory in the Old Testament, concerning the liberation of Israel under theocracy.[309]

The sinners in Luke are dishonest and those who rejected the law. Jesus' intimate table-fellowship with them in the Jewish context signifies friendship, intimacy and communion. G. Mangatt says that sharing of food denotes sharing of life.[310] In line with that Jesus gives the reality of life to those who lost it by their sin. In Jesus' activity, the dinner table becomes the place where bodies meet; particularly, where people from various backgrounds dine together regardless of sex or social status. Jesus' table-fellowship forms a new way of life along with the vision and an articulation of love and service to the outcasts and the marginalized in the Socio-Political world of Luke, where it was exclusively practised among one's own community. According to Crossan, the rhetorical strategy behind Jesus' activity depicts the symbolic relationship between the bodies of individuals and the larger body politic, i.e., body to society as microcosm to macrocosm.[311] By extending the table companionship to tax collectors and sinners, Jesus established his prophetic action and his proclamation of the Kingly rule of God in praxis. Rayanna explains this practice of Jesus as, the "translation of Jesus' messianic message and mission into action."[312] In general, the table-fellowship of Jesus with all kinds of people seems to be a shadow of his view of the Kingdom as he taught through the parables.

Kingdom of God: Anti-imperial Connotation of Luke

Generally, a Kingdom is understood both in geographical and functional sense[313] in relation to the sovereignty of a King. The phrase, Kingdom of God is not seen in the Jewish Scriptures, but many biblical passages speak of the Kingship of God, who chose Israel and reigns over them.[314] Jesus' proclamation of the Kingdom of God is a shift from the Old Testament concept of Kingdom of David or the Kingdom of Israel.[315] While the word, Kingdom designates primarily a place or region where subjects live under the protection of a King, in the Old Testament, the Semitic term doesn't imply a particular place,[316] but God as King to the entire cosmos.

In the Synoptic Gospels, Kingdom of God becomes central to Jesus' preaching. Through the parables, Jesus compares the Kingdom by using metaphors, which are instructive.[317] In Luke's Gospel, it seems to imply an anti-imperial movement against the secular Kingdom of that time along with the anticipation of a King, Messiah. Jesus' declaration of the Kingdom by forgiveness of debts or sins along with his goal of restoring Israel and his words and actions against the Temple establishment, similar to the covenanters of Qumran, seems to imply a political move.

Many a scholar has wondered whether ἡ βασιλεία τοῦ θεοῦ in the Synoptic tradition can be translated as God's Kingship or God's Kingdom. In Lukan usage, the verbs: to enter; to inherit; and to be in, point to God's Kingly rule as it is exercised among people, albeit it is not limited to geographical boundaries. It raises the following issues: whether it means the earthly Kingdom or the other worldly. In other words, is it in political or religious sense? If it is the earthly Kingdom, how will Jesus reinstate the throne of David as it is stated in 1:32f? Is it for the whole world or only to the people of Israel? and so on.

Practically, two centuries ago, Gilbert said that Jesus' message of the Kingdom of God reveals "the divine rule in the hearts of men," which is not political but ethical and spiritual. By the act of repentance one can enter the Kingdom, where Jesus is the King.[318] Schweitzer opposed his view of ethical Kingdom and proposed the eschatological Kingdom[319] and drew the attention to its imminence in Jesus' words and termed it as, consequent eschatology. C. H. Dodd opposed this consequent eschatology with the idea of the already arrived Kingdom by the words and deeds of Jesus, and termed it as, the realized eschatology. Jeremias synthesized both and pointed out the process of realization in Jesus' teachings and termed it as, the progressive eschatology. J. M. Robinson summarized all these as Jesus proclaimed it to the present age in concern to the imminent future.[320] And, W. G. Morrice proposed the phraseology, the inaugurated eschatology.[321] Crossan, on the basis of 17:20-24, termed it as permanent eschatology than the two divergent concepts: prophetic eschatology against apocalyptic eschatology that prevailed during the time of Jesus.[322] According to Millar Burrows, Jesus' idea of God's Kingdom is the universal sovereignty of God combined with the eschatological idea of the Kingdom as the coming age mentioned in the rabbinic literature.[323] But, G. E. Ladd says, "God's Kingdom is present in Jesus in a new and unique way."[324] In spite of all these deliberations of the New Testament scholars about the Kingdom of God idea from the teachings and actions of Jesus we need to look at the texts of Luke, what he intends in his composition.

The Lukan view of the Kingdom of God includes the following concepts: King, reign, Davidic lineage of Jesus, Christ, seated on a throne, Lord, Son of God, and Son of Man. Besides, in Matthew's Gospel, John the Baptist is the Kingdom-preacher,[325] whereas, in Luke's Gospel, John the Baptist is the one who introduces Jesus as the Kingdom-preacher.[326] So, Luke emphasizes the role of Jesus as the Kingdom preacher and omitted Matthew 3:2 in this regard to identify Jesus as the one in whom Isaiah's words[327] were fulfilled, which seems to have more importance in Luke's design of Jesus' programmatic mission.

Besides, the fulfillment of God's will and plan is apparent in the Lukan usage of both the future and the present state of the Kingdom ideology: 11:2 = Mt. 6:10, "Your Kingdom come" in the Lord's Prayer and 13:29= Mt. 8:11-12, "...People will come from east and west, from north and south, and will eat in the Kingdom of God," denote the future hope. 11:20 = Mt. 12:28, "But if it is by the finger of God that I cast out demons, then the Kingdom of God has come to you;" 17:21, "Kingdom of God is among you" and 6:20 = Mt. 5:3-6, "Blessed are...poor for yours is the Kingdom of God," denote the present reality.

As it is God's plan and will, Luke presents Jesus as the saviour who proclaims salvation.[328] H. Riedlinger argues that Jesus' Kingship can't be approached from an anthropocentric or cosmocentric point of view. It should begin with theology and ontology because his Kingship is neither from human plan or will, nor the consequence of historical or physical power but it is God's will.[329] It is debatable however, on the basis of Luke's Gospel. The Kingship of Jesus could be understood through his action as per the will of God in saving human beings. O. Cullmann identifies Lukan Christology not as mythology or metaphysics but in terms of Salvation history,[330] and therefore, Jesus' Kingship must be understood from a functional Christology.[331] E. F. Scott says that the Kingdom had begun to manifest through the life and teachings of Jesus.[332] A. Ritchl sees the Kingdom of God as human society initiated and organized through the action of love.[333] "Son of Man came to seek out and save the lost," the key statement of the episode of Zacchaeus, clearly states Luke's idea of seeing Jesus' saving act in order to gather people in the Kingdom of God.

In general, while the Synoptic Gospels focus on the idea of the Kingdom of God,[334] either as βασιλεία τοῦ θεοῦ or βασιλεία τῶν οὐρανων or βασιλεία τοῦ πατρός as central to Jesus' preaching, Luke particularly, implies Jesus' Kingship. This seems to have a new understanding, for instance, as it has been noted in the Infancy Narrative, in 1:32f where the angel Gabriel spoke to Mary that Jesus will be given the throne of David and he will rule the house of

Jacob but that Kingdom will never end. Besides, the nuances of Jesus' Kingship are prevalent in Jesus' preaching, particularly in his parables. The presence of the Kingdom is accentuated based on geopolitical issues through his words, person and action: his parabolic teachings: miracles; hospitality to the outsiders to be insiders; table-fellowship with all kinds of people; forgiveness to the sinners; his Kingly entry into Jerusalem; the cleansing of the Temple; in the compassion of a Samaritan; the faith of a blind man; and, the repentance of sinners. Abraham sees the act of repentance and forgiveness in the message of the Kingdom preacher as, "The message of the Kingdom involves repentance as well as the fruits of repentance, the world of forgiveness and the life of discipleship."[335] In general, Luke emphasizes the Kingship of Jesus in the Kingdom ideology and depicts Jesus as a Messianic King in line with David.

On the other hand, in Luke, Jesus' proclamation of the Kingdom of God seems to be political because it was a threat to the priestly and Roman authorities who wanted to keep the country in a sound position. While considering the threat to the authorities, Shillington identifies the phrase, Kingdom of God in Roman-occupied Jewish Palestine as a highly charged phrase.[336] Tomson sees its political meaning from the 1st century CE rabbinic prayers which include the petition for the downfall of the Roman Empire, considered as the Kingdom of evil.[337] Besides, Borg and Crossan say that 90% of Jesus' audiences were rural peasants and familiar to the phrase as political as well as religious metaphor in their existence under the Kingdoms of the Herods, and Rome.[338] Along with the observations of Shillington, Tomson, Borg and Crossan, the tone of an anti-imperial movement against the secular Kingdom is noticeable in Jesus' teachings: such as: in 6:20 "Blessed are you who are poor, for yours is the Kingdom of God," in 9:62 "No one who puts a hand to the plow and looks back is fit for the Kingdom of God;" in 10:9 "The Kingdom of God has come near to you;" in 11:20 "The Kingdom of God has come to you," in 17:21 "The Kingdom of God is among you," in 13:18ff, the depiction of the invisible growth of the Kingdom through the metaphors of mustard seed and yeast; in 14:15ff, the parable of the Great Dinner that the poor, the crippled, the blind and the lame will enter rather than the invited ones; and in 18:29, the need of self negation to enter the Kingdom of God, which W. F. Flemington sees as, "the sum and culmination of human progress"[339] and Crossan recognizes in its context as, "empowering to life and action in reversal of the world's understanding."[340] Along with them it may be said that the Kingdom interest group is focused on the destitute and the dispossessed groups in the peasant society, which longed for deliverance from Roman imperialism.

However, the proclamation of the Kingdom of God in Luke's Gospel indicates the arrival of it incognito along with the implementation of healing, forgiveness and restoration of Israel by Jesus' words and action. It may possibly reveal the secret of Jesus' Kingship. According to Johnson, Jesus related several parables dealing with a King and Kingdom of God which illuminate the Kingship of Jesus in restoring the life of the people.[341] According to Daalen, the parables referring to the Kingdom of God indicate that the Kingdom or the King has arrived incognito.[342] Luz suggests that in Luke's Gospel, the Kingdom of God is historically present in Jesus.[343] According to Bond, the Kingdom of God idea although exhibits religious language, Jesus' message had a clear political implication and a nationalistic dimension.[344] According to Paget, the idea of the Kingdom of God in Jewish context of political Kingdom is an alternative one.[345] On the whole, in Luke's Gospel, the anti-imperial movement against the secular Kingdom of that time is very clear in Jesus' demonstration of the Kingdom and Kingship by forgiveness of debts or sins along with his goal of restoring Israel by his saving act.

Davidic Lineage: Blind Man's Recognition of Jesus' Kingship

The healing of a blind man is a triple tradition episode.[346] While both Matthew and Mark depict the event outside Jericho, Luke depicts it as happening while Jesus approached Jericho, which seems to be an accurate record of that event in Luke. Concerning the blind man's enquiry of the commotion, he was informed that Jesus of Nazareth is passing by. But the blind man recognized Jesus as Υἱὲ Δαυίδ.

Although all the three synoptic Gospels say this, here it indicates that he already knew Jesus as the Messianic King in the lineage of David, who is capable of healing his blindness.

Luke expounds Jesus' Davidic pedigree from the beginning, as it has been noted in the Infancy Narrative as in the genealogy. The blind man at Jericho recognizes Jesus as the Son of David,[347] which could be considered as the fulfillment of the Old Testament prophecy.[348] Parsons comments that the composition of Luke in portrayal of Jesus follows the line of the Davidic King as he does it through the lens of the Davidic covenant and its associated messianic expectations.[349] Though, it may be the Lukan style of pointing out the Davidic lineage, on the other hand, it could be understood as Luke emphasizes the fact that even the blind people realize the presence of the anticipated Davidic King amidst them in the life and teachings of Jesus. It shows the artistic composition of Luke along with the fulfillment idea of Davidic dynasty through the Messianic/Davidic King Jesus.

Temple: A Place of Economic Control of the State

Unlike the compositions of other evangelists, Luke begins and ends his Gospel in Jerusalem at the Temple: in 1:9, Zechariah offers incense in the Jerusalem Temple and at the close, in 24:53, Luke tells about the eleven disciples and their companions who remain blessing God in the Jerusalem Temple. The Infancy Narrative portrays the infant Jesus journeying toward Jerusalem twice along with his parents.[350] Particularly, the event of the twelve year old Jesus' stay and deliberations with the Temple teachers astounding all foreshadows his Temple teaching ministry in 19:47. Besides, his words in 2:49 that he has to be in his Father's house parallels 19:45f, where he cites the Temple as God's house.

As per history, Roman Emperors tried to make the Temple a worship place for them. Therefore, Augustus declared himself as the son of god and made the cult of the living emperor. Though, his successor Tiberius discouraged it, Calilgula as the Emperor during CE 37 - CE 41 after Tiberius, demanded the emperor to be worshipped on par with other religious deities. In turn his statue had to be set up in the temples including the Jerusalem Temple,[351] which was the locus of the Jewish cult and the divine dwelling place.[352] The Temple, under the stewardship of the chief priests, was not found by Jesus as a house of prayer, as it should be. Malina and Neyrey see the oppressive political structure of the Jerusalem Temple as the controlling center of the Jewish social identity, social classifications, and social boundaries as the holy people of God.[353] Hengel depicts the Temple as 'the seat of political and religious authority of the nation.[354] In the past, after Herod's son Archelaus was removed in 6 CE, the Roman Emperor began to rule it with his governors. The Temple became the central economic and political institution and its authorities became intermediaries of the imperial domain.[355] The imperial rule was legitimized and the subjects were controlled through the Temple.[356] The Temple was centered upon the social and economic system and had economic power over "taxes, tithes, sacrifices and offerings." It was maintained by the priestly and aristocratic elite,[357] where the people were victimized.

Temples as the locus of socio-economic reality was not rare in ancient societies. In Egyptian temples, for example, a banking system was in operation, engaged in lending and recovering in trade.[358] N. Q. Hamilton points out the socio-economic system of the Kingly control of finance in Hellenistic times as it was prevalent in every chief town. For instance, he referred to Josephus, who calls the bank in the capital of Roman Galilee as Βασιλικὴν τράπεζαν. Nevertheless, the economic centre of Jerusalem Temple was addressed by Hamilton as "the royal bank of Judea."[359] In 2 Macc 3:10f, there is a reference to the deposits of widows, orphans and the rich. Its previous verses indicate the Temple in Jerusalem as the treasury. So, in cleansing the Temple, Jesus suspends the banking operation[360] which was entirely different from the action of the Zealots and Sicarii who by violence and, the Essenes as well as the prophetic movement's withdrawal of it.[361] Muthuraj refers to Elliott when Jesus condemns "self-aggrandizement and exploitation" without justice and mercy, and their system organized not of prayer.[362] This manifested in the words of Jesus in 19:46, "'My house shall be a house of prayer;' but you have made it a den of robbers." Jesus' confrontation in the Temple shows that he was against the prevailing economic practices. His message was critical of the temple and its role of administration system in collaboration with Rome, like the Essenes, who rejected the legitimacy of the temple and priesthood. Besides, as it has been noted earlier, the Jerusalem authorities were poignant to both John the Baptist and Jesus who had an anti-temple activity in their manner of forgiving sins which was an important role of the temple by means of sacrifice.

Likewise, in Luke, Jerusalem is the center of opposition to Jesus. Even in the Temptation scenario, Luke places the Temple temptation as the last one, which perhaps suggests that the power of evil reaches its climax in the Temple.[363] Cleansing the Temple thus became one of the major factors that created hostility among the authorities of the Temple. Though, the evangelists portrayed it as Messianic, scholars view it as both religious and political. Matera, Houlden, E. Rivikin, Wilson, Winter, Hengel and Sanders explore the truth behind Jesus' mission, as it would have had a threat to the life of the priestly and Roman authorities who sought to keep the country in a stable condition.[364] It must be noted that it reveals not only their religious authority but also, their control over the people against Roman authority. It is vivid in the words of Caiaphas,' as John writes in 11:50, "It is better for you to have one man die for the people than to have the whole nation destroyed."

Moreover, in the teachings of Jesus, divergent views of the temple and Jerusalem are present. For instance, in 13:34f, Jerusalem is depicted as the city that kills the prophets; and, in 19:41-44 Jesus weeps over the city.[365] Sanders along with other historical Jesus scholars of the third Quest say that Jesus was crucified due to his attack on the Jerusalem Temple which caused him a prophetic threat and declared him to be the King implicitly.[366] According to Conzelmann the goal of Jesus' journey toward the Temple was to attain Kingship, but not to invade the Empire, albeit it claims the supremacy of the Kingdom of God over the world.[367] Along with these scholarly speculations of Jesus' Kingship, it is vivid that Davidic Lordship is replaced by the title King in the triumphal entry. The event of triumphal entry procession is possibly, an indication to the deprived that the anticipated King has arrived to restructure the social order.

However, Luke is very mild and short in describing Jesus' action in the Temple. With regard to the act of cleansing the temple event, Luke narrates, "Then he entered the temple and began to drive out those who were selling things there."[368] Whereas both Mark and Matthew ruthlessly narrate that he drove out even the buyers by overturning the chairs.[369] Although, this event is portrayed at the beginning of Jesus' ministry in John 2:13-17, he also narrates it with severity that Jesus drove them out by making a whip of cords. Though in Luke, it is a mild and short narration, it shows the composition of Luke in narrating the event well fitting to his motif of Kingship of Jesus. By the temple act, Luke portrays it as the center of his messianic activity, as it is evident in 19:45: in his arrival at the temple; and in his teaching in the temple everyday as it is recorded in 19:47& 21:37; and 19:47f. Luke's presentation shows his authority over the temple as Israel's Messiah threatening the authority of the religious leaders among the people, which is further evident in their questioning of his authority in 20:1-8.

Triumphal Entry and Cleansing the Temple: Declaration of Jesus' Kingship

Throughout his Gospel Luke gives more importance not only to the Temple but also to the city of Jerusalem. Even the angel's words to Mary in 1:32f that the child born to her will be given the throne of David and reign over the house of Jacob denotes his Kingship in Jerusalem. It is obvious that Jerusalem is portrayed as the city of David as well as the city of destiny for Jesus. Mattill says that Jesus entered the city along with his fans in either CE 30 or less probably CE 33. He would have either wished to take his message to the capital of Judea due to his "Galilean crisis," the rejection mentioned in 10:13-15 = Mt. 11:20-24; or, believed it as God's will;[370] or turned his face toward Jerusalem in expecting death as mentioned in 9:51.[371] Conzelmann says that Jesus did not enter the city, but the Temple which indicates the "royal manner of the Entry."[372] But, M. Dibelius takes a mediatory position and says that the messianic entrance and his action in the temple according to his own plan depict that he knew himself as the Chosen One while he entered the city.[373] While Conzelmann and Dibellius say, though Jesus cleansed the Temple, Mattill's view gives more emphasis to Jesus' according to the compositional style of Luke's Gospel. As it has been noted in the previous section, Jesus had a negative view of both Temple and the city. So, by Luke's introduction of Jesus as King through the voices of the people in the procession, both the Temple and the city signify the Messianic Rule.

Colt can be considered as a vehicle of a King. In addition to F. M. Cross, who points out the Old Testament references: 2 Sam 13:29 &1 Kgs 1:33 to the use of mule by princes and Kings, G. M. A. Hanfmann points out that donkey is a royal animal in West Asia.[374] There are precedents as well as prophecies concerning the triumphal arrival of a ruler or military hero: in 1 Kgs 1:32-40, David commands the priest Zadok, the prophet Nathan and Benaiah to bring Solomon riding on David's mule down to Gihon and anoint him as King in his throne; in Zech. 9:9, considered as a messianic prophecy, the King is anticipated "riding on a donkey, on a colt, the foal of a donkey"; 1 Macc. 13:43-48, after capturing Gazara, Simon Maccabee expelled its dwellers, "entered it with hymns and praise and removed all uncleanness from it"; in 2 Macc. 4:21-22, Antiochus marched toward Jerusalem "with a blaze of torches and with shouts" against the hostile King Apollonius when he was away; in Josephus' *Antiquities of the Jews* 11.325-329 & 340-345, Alexander the Great went to Jerusalem in a procession with the priests and with the multitude of citizens;[375] in *Antiquities of the Jews* 17.195 & 205, Archelaus after his father's death as a King came by bands and with their commanders.[376] In this context, D. C. Allison says that the Greco-Roman texts mention: Attalus of Pergamum entering Athens; Anthony entering Ephesus; Aemilius Paulus' triumph in Rome; and Gaius entering Rome.[377] 1 Maccabees 13:49-53, like Mt. 21:8, refers to palm branches to celebrate the victory of Simon over the enemies. It was constituted to celebrate every year.

Storkey says that spreading cloaks on the road indicates his Kingship and the sign of honour[378] which has precedents, like the King Jehu referred to in 2 Kings 9:13. These precedents of entries illustrate the military triumphs, anointing of a King, public celebration, cultic activity, etc., In line with these, Jesus' entry should be noted that Jesus neither a military conqueror on a warhorse nor a pilgrim's approach of holy place by foot, but as a King riding on a donkey.

According to Luke, as it was determined[379] and, in accordance with the fulfillment of the prophecy of Zechariah in Zech 9:9, Jesus enters as a King in triumph,[380] riding on a colt and hailed by the crowd, "Blessed is the King, who comes in the name of the Lord! Peace in heaven, and glory in the highest heaven!" Among the Synoptics, only Luke introduced Jesus as a "King." Blessed is the King, who comes in the name of the Lord, is an allusion to Ps. 118:26. Ὁ ἐρχόμενος is the title of the pilgrim coming to the Temple. He now receives a new meaning on the basis of 7:19, where the question of John's disciples resembles the same phrase, and now identified explicitly as a King. According to Fitzmyer, Luke's ascription of the title "King" makes the entry of Jesus explicitly royal as well as alludes to the angel's words to Mary in 1:32 that her son will sit on the throne of David.[381] Jesus enters the city of David's throne, immediately goes to the Temple, not to look around as in Mark 11:11, but to purge it as in Mal. 3:1ff, with an act of authority. Mark uses the title, Son of David, Matthew sees him as the prophet Jesus from Nazareth of Galilee,[382] but Luke as King.

The Kingly aspect of Jesus is exposed thorough his power, authority in speech and action, revolution, and in his feelings of anger. Joel Marcus points out God's entry into the Temple with Kingly power through Ps. 68:24f, "Your solemn processions are seen, O! God, the processions of my God, my King, into the sanctuary - the singers in front, the musicians last, between them girls playing tambourines..."[383] J. M. Garland says that Luke depicts the King with kingly attributes of one who can weep, show anger and react against the temple's activities.[384] According to Brandon, Jesus attacked the "sacerdotal hierarchy" operated by the Roman Government by his revolutionary act of cleansing the Temple along with the motive of religious establishment.[385] Besides, the verb, ἐκβάλλω indicates casting out of demons in Jesus' exorcism. Here, the usage of the same verb by Luke in 19:45 implies Jesus as Priestly King as he drives out the demonic control of the Temple in its political, economic, social and religious power.

The act of Jesus as well depicts his act of restoration. Neill Q. Hamilton sees it to be an execution of Kingly prerogative,[386] which R. H. Hiers sees as the significance of restoration along with the anticipated Kingdom.[387] There are precedents of cleansing and restoration: in 2 Kgs. 18:4-12, when Hezekiah became King he purified the Temple; in 2 Kgs. 22:3-23:25, King Josiah sanitized Jerusalem Temple from idols, vessels used of idols and idolatrous priests; and in 1 Macc. 4:36-60 & 2 Macc. 10:1-9, Judas Maccabees and his brothers cleansed and dedicated the Temple signaling the attained independence of the Jewish state. Prophets also anticipated the messianic age with the restoration of the Temple: in Ezek. 37:26-28, the prophet Ezekiel visualizes the restored Temple as the locus of Israel; in Tobit 14:5-7, with the restoration of Israel, the rebuilding of the Temple is expressed in the words of Tobit;[388] prophets Haggai and Zechariah also anticipated the messianic era along with the reconstruction of the Temple; and, Malachi promised the blessing while keeping God's statutes in the Temple. So, it is evident that the reform and the renewal of the Temple were associated with the new age of the Messianic King. Whether Jesus had these prophecies and preceding history in his mind is a question. But, it is vivid that Luke introduces Jesus as King who entered Jerusalem triumphally on a colt along with the unanticipated, instant procession and by which he discloses the secrecy motif along with the messianic act of cleansing the Temple.

The procession of Jesus seems to be political. Jesus was not riding a horse as a nationalistic messiah based on the tradition of Zachariah 9:9.[389] But, it was a political demonstration in accordance with the Prophet Zechariah's words in 9:9 that the King who comes to Jerusalem is humble, and riding on a colt which Matthew explicitly quotes in 21:4f.

Zechariah's prophecy further states in 9:9f, that riding on a donkey, he will banish war, cut off chariots, war horses and bows. By declaring peace to the nations he becomes the King of peace. Although Jesus' procession was intentionally a counter to Pilate's procession, it is more a juxtaposition of his message concerning the Kingdom of God with the Kingdom of Caesar.[390] It may be evidenced from Luke as he states in 13:35, "You will not see me until... you say, 'Blessed is he who comes in the name of the Lord.'" In 19:37f, the disciples of Jesus see him as King, which Hamm identifies as nonpolitical in nature whose sovereignty is evidenced in his healing.[391] However, Hamm's view may not be acceptable being out of the Lukan composition. However, it is vivid that the entry is anti-imperial and political accompanied by action representing the people.

Besides, another question arises regarding the intensity of the procession. Borg and Crossan advocate that Jesus' entry from the east into Jerusalem is an anti-imperial one and it evoked great enthusiasm among people.[392] There was also from the west, on the opposite side of the city, Pontius Pilate, the Roman prefect of Idumea, Judea, and Samaria entering the city with another procession during the Passover.[393] The procession which followed Jesus is identified as a planned[394] peasant procession: down the Mount of Olives; riding on a donkey; with the ecstasy of his followers, who came from the peasant class in Galilee; belonging to the peasant village of Nazareth; and, centered his message about the Kingdom of God, journeyed toward Jerusalem. Another procession headed by Pontius Pilate like his predecessors and successors is identified by them as an imperial procession:[395] from the west, a column of imperial cavalry and soldiers who marched toward Jerusalem demonstrating Roman imperial power in the context of the Passover, a festival celebrated in remembrance of the liberation from Egypt by the Jewish people.[396] Pilate's procession exhibited the imperial power as well as Roman imperial theology as Rome was chosen by the gods; the Roman emperor was the son of god, who was "lord" and "saviour"; the one who brought "peace on earth" and so on.[397] So, to the Jewish subjects of Rome, Pilate's procession personified a rival social order as well, a rival theology; whereas, Jesus' procession seemed to counter that order.

On the other hand, it raises the issue why the Roman security was inactive during Jesus' entry at the time of Pilate's procession. B. Kinman notes, Pilate's procession took place five days earlier than Jesus' entry.[398] Pilate came to Jerusalem to ensure peace as well as to conduct trials. Further, the arrival of the governor enhanced the position of the rulers, merchants and the inhabitants.[399] However, Jesus arrived with his followers without any arms, but, rebuked by some of the Pharisees.[400] The response of Jesus to them in 19:40 was "If these were silent, the stones would shout out." It was a reference to a joyous acclamation.[401] But here, the anger of the Pharisees in trying to stop people from shouting seems to be their effort to please the governor that everything is under their control. And Jesus' refusal to it shows his anti-imperial stand as well as his motive. However, the Roman soldiers were unperturbed by the sort of procession led by Jesus.

In the act of temple cleansing, unlike other evangelists, Luke plainly mentions that Jesus "began to drive out those who were selling," and omits the references to buying, selling dove, money changers and forbiddance of carrying things through the Temple.[402] S. G. F. Brandon underlines the improbability Jesus' action on the basis of Markan account that no one opposed Jesus' action and its incredibility by the single person's act without the support of the crowd against the legitimate and necessary business.[403] Besides, the Temple police on duty to maintain peace and order did not arrest him. But, Bond points out that Jesus' action was a small incident in the temple and it didn't create any major disturbance; because, the temple court was as big as the size of twelve football stadia. So, only those surrounding him could notice what was going on.[404] It may have been a symbolic act. But Bond's argument can't be accepted as it is, because, in the procession of the triumphal entry itself, in 19:39, some of the Pharisees tried to stop the action of the crowd. Although the temple was big in size, it was noticed by every leader of the temple. Because, Luke in 19:47 says, that the leaders of the people, scribes and chief priests were waiting for a time to kill him. They were afraid of mutiny. So, they might not have used their security forces.

Some events in Luke however need clarity, For instance, while narrating the event in line with the Kingship motif, why does Luke omit the cursing of the fig tree? According to Kinman, Luke replaced the fig tree's fate with the prophetic words in 19:41ff, along with eschatological concerns.[405] It should be noticed that in the act of cleansing the Temple, Jesus neither opposed the Law nor the Temple cult nor the worshippers but opposed those who exploited the needy. Driving out the sellers in the temple was not simply a cleansing, but a symbolic destruction probably in line with the fig tree's fate as referred to in Mk. 11:20ff, which Luke omits, may be because he did not think of temple's destruction. Only he records it as a parable to denote the arrival of the Kingdom soon.[406] In contrast to the hope of people's immediate liberation, Jesus sees the danger that is approaching Jerusalem. However, by this anti-imperial, political event of peasant procession accompanied by action, Luke exposes Jesus as King with the voices of people, as the one who has authority even to drive out the demonic control of the Temple in its political, economic, social and religious power. It signifies restoration of the marginalized and the advent of the Messianic Rule.

Confrontation of Jesus: Christocentric Kingship

The texts 13:31-33, Lukan addition to the Q passage concerning the lament over Jerusalem;[407] 20:1-8, the triple tradition source episode of the authority of Jesus Questioned;[408] and, 20:9-19, the parable of the Vineyard and the Tenants, and the triple tradition material[409] indicate the impending danger of Jesus' death through various confrontations concerning his authority, might and Kingship.

In 13:31-33, the L material added by Luke as an introduction to Q material vv. 34-35, explains that on the way to Jerusalem Jesus condemns the evil of Jerusalem in killing the prophets. V. 33 clearly indicates through the words of Jesus that he meets his death in Jerusalem only. But, previous to that Luke puts forward that his life is in danger because of Herod the tetrarch in the words of Pharisees. In this conversation, Jesus speaks of Herod as a fox. It is necessary, in this research, to reason, why did Herod want to kill Jesus? And, why did Jesus name him a fox? Both, the questions need to be discussed together in order to see the purpose of Luke in adding this text along with the Q passage: Luke in the context of Baptism, in 3:19f, says that Herod put John the Baptist in prison. In 9:9, Herod who beheaded John wanted to see Jesus, due to his might and fame. According to J. A. Darr, it is a heightened scenario of Herod's eagerness to see Jesus.[410] Of course, it is a much heightened scenario by Luke because a king wanted to see his counterpart, who is followed by his fans. But, in 13:31, the report of the Pharisees indicates the reverse view of Herod on Jesus that he wanted to kill Jesus. By knowing his cunning attitudes and his evil schemes Jesus called Herod a fox. Because Herod had already tried to get his father's Kingdom by appealing to Caesar; marrying his brother's wife to attain his goal of the Kingdom; and had killed John for warning his evil; and, at this time, tried to kill Jesus. Besides, according to v. 32, Jesus' words of praxis, "Go and tell that fox for me, Listen, I am casting out demons and performing cures today and tomorrow, and on the third day I finish my work," indicate that he had to complete his Messianic work. In general, this conversation added by Luke portrays Jesus as the Messianic King.

Although, Luke places the episode at Jerusalem found in 20:1-8, the triple tradition material,[411] in between the event of cleansing the Temple and the Passion Narrative, its occurrence seems to be vague, as he says, "one of the days." Whereas, Mark indicates that it occurred on the next day of cleansing the Temple. It seems that Luke in his composition gives much importance to the thrust of the event, the confrontation of Jesus with the Jewish leaders concerning the tension between theocracy and human Kingship than the occasion. The chief priests and the scribes, who were authorized by the Roman emperor, asked, "Tell us, by what authority are you doing these things? Who is it who gave you this authority?" These questions indicate the issue of God's Kingship over against human Kingship. In addition, Jesus' response is tricky, "Did the baptism of John come from heaven, or was it of human origin?" and their confusion to answer it obviously indicates the dilemma of Jewish authorities due to the prevailing tension between theocracy and human Kingship.

In 20:9-19, the subsequent periscope from the triple tradition material,[412] concerning the parable of the Vineyard and the Tenants, a Christological[413] and an allegorical parable,[414] Jesus discloses and claims himself to be the Son sent by God. It resembles the Old Testament prophecy of the prophet Isaiah in 5:1ff[415] and indicates the impending danger to Jesus' life which is the divine plan. Jesus explains the plan of God and the performance of the people that though God sent his prophets, they did not accept them; but when the beloved son is sent, v. 14b, the tenants words, "This is the heir; let us kill him so that the inheritance may be ours," indicate when the Messianic King is sent, they tried to kill him, so that they could get the Kingdom for themselves. By relating this parable, Jesus discloses his Messianic Kingship, as it is time for him to face death at Jerusalem, as seen in the Passion Narrative.

Paying Taxes to Caesar: Question of Roman Sovereignty

It is said that the question of tribute money to Caesar[416] was asked by the spies of the chief priests and scribes; whereas Matthew says that the disciples of the Pharisees raised this question. But Mark says that some Pharisees and some Herodians asked the question. It shows that Luke leaves out the Pharisees in this issue. However, all the three evangelists raise the same question: "Is it lawful for us to pay taxes to the emperor, or not?" It indicates that the Roman Empire required tribute from the subdued Judea and collected it through local authorities. It was the Roman taxation that was burdensome on the Jews.[417] The oppressive state of the Roman Emperor could be gauged from Jesus' words concerning Kingship recorded in 22:25: "The kings of the Gentiles lord it over them; and those in authority over them are called benefactors." Carter points out that paying tax to Rome indicated the people's submission to Rome and elite's sovereignty. But at the same time, those who did not pay were considered as rebellious.[418] The emperor's power to subjugate people could be seen in connection with Matthew's other episode in 17:24-27. It is obvious that Jesus condemns the injustice of the Roman tax system. Jesus' inquiry, "From whom do kings of the earth take toll or tribute? From their children or from others?" And, Peter's response, "from others," indicates the injustice of the rulers. Carr comments that it was, "the unjust imperial practice of subjugating sovereign people and making them non-citizens in their own land and then making them bear a heavy tax burden in order that the emperor's own people may be let off the hook."[419]

The craftiness of the question depicts the intention of the leaders to break Jesus' relationship with the Zealots. To the Zealots, obeying the Roman Emperor was against the Law because according to the Law, Yahweh was the only God whom they should obey. A coin with Caesar's image, an idolatrous inscription, indicated Caesar as a divine Son of God.[420] Judas of Galilee condemned paying taxes to Rome because he considered it as the recognition of Roman sovereignty instead of God's.[421] Though, the Zealots revolted against the Roman rule over Israel during the days of Jesus,[422] Jesus did not associate himself with the Zealot movement which advocated the armed rebellion against the oppression. Rather, he criticized the Jewish leaders for their collaboration with Rome.[423] Besides, the claim of Caesar exposed that the land, people and the produce belonged to him. But by observing a *denarius*, and eliciting from them that the head and the title were emperor's, Jesus replied, "Then give to the emperor the things that are the emperor's, and to God the things that are God's." It discloses that Jesus nullified the payment of tribute on the basis of Lev. 25:23 that everything including the land belongs to God as the Zealots observed. But, Bruce opines that Jesus advocated non-resistance by this response.[424] D. T. Owen-Ball suggests that 'give to Caesar's what is his; denotes the civil obligation. However, the latter one 'to God what is God's' indicates one's entire being belongs to God.[425] This is what Paul in his letter to the Romans too points out the supreme authority of God.[426] Carter says that Jesus' words to give back to Caesar imply "literally a way of removing this illicit coin from Judea."[427] Despite these speculations, loyalty to theocracy is emphasized through this episode. In a way it is a condemnation of the rule of Caesar. The condemnation on secular Kingship is further explicit in the words of Jesus concerning the destruction of Jerusalem.

Desolating Sacrilege: Nationalistic Sense of Jesus, the Messianic King

The phrase "desolating sacrilege,"[428] in the prophetic words of Jesus is a key expression which denotes the persecution of Antiochus Epiphanes IV during 168-167 BCE. He ordered to erect idols in the altar of the Temple and sacrifice swine and other unclean animals.[429] It may be said that it was a transformation of the traditional altar into a pagan altar.[430] A parallel act was executed by Gaius Galigula during the years CE 39-40. He erected his statue in the Jerusalem Temple and profanely made himself as God. Though this incident happened about ten years after Jesus' death, according to Theissen, since the Gospels were written later, the handed over traditions adapted the new situations.[431] However, the nationalistic sense along with its own emphasis on faith and religion is explicit in Jesus' prophecy along with the condemnation of secular Kingship.

Summary

The Lukan composition of life and teachings of Jesus is placed in between the Infancy and the Passion Narrative using L and Q material in addition to the triple tradition exposes his skill in establishing the motif of Jesus' Kingship through a topographical structure of Jesus' journey. By thus recording the journey of Jesus' ministry as moving from Galilee toward Jerusalem through Samaria, Luke intends to establish his motif.

Jesus' grounding of the mission in 3:1-4:13: the proclamation of John the Baptist; Jesus' baptism; genealogy of Jesus; and, the temptation of Jesus not only give the details of Jesus' preparation for ministry but also, expose the historical, socio-political context of the Roman rule in Palestine. The call for repentance and baptism of John the Baptist which required the people to join the new Messianic community against the political oppression, the acceptance of Jesus as the mode of entrance to his Messianic work, and his declaration as the Son of God depict Lukan compositional skill in developing his kingship motif. The forgiveness of sins by repentance seems to be a revolutionary act in the backdrop of the Temple's role and ideology of forgiveness through sacrifice, which later Luke points out, became an issue of authority. In placing the Genealogy after the baptism of Jesus and his entry into messianic work, Luke depicts him as the Son of God, juxtaposing the emperor's title along with Davidic Kingship. In the temptation episode, the authority of Jesus is tested in juxtaposition to the supremacy of the Rule of God against the Roman imperial theology and Jesus is portrayed as one who refuses to be submissive to Rome.

In 4:14-9:49, Jesus' Galilean ministry, Luke includes the Nazareth manifesto which indicates Jesus' Messianic Kingship highlighting Jesus' programme of mission comprising the jubilee proclamation, deliverance of the oppressed, fulfillment of prophecy, universality of the Kingdom, and his rejection by the Jews. Most of the miracles with Jesus' authoritative teaching recorded by Luke in this section expose the resistance and reversal of discrimination, exploitation, political oppression, old rigid purity regulations, Sabbath observances and boundary issues. Luke refers to Jesus as King who restores the Kingdom and grants social acceptance by reversing the oppressive state. Like Mark, Luke maintains the Messianic secrecy not only in the event of baptism but also in exorcisms which again indicate his skill of maintaining Jesus' Kingship in suspense till the triumphal entry procession.

The twelve disciples symbolizing the twelve tribes and the seventy chosen to proclaim the Kingdom of God and preach repentance and forgiveness of sin throughout the world indicate his vision of extending his Kingship. The inclusion of women in Jesus' ministry along with the male disciples in the patriarchal society, blessing the poor and, woes to the rich point out the revolutionary and reversal act of King Jesus. By the theme of conflict, Luke portrays the hostility between the leaders. While the conflict with the Pharisees runs throughout the Gospel, Luke portrays Jesus' hospitality towards them by his Kingly act of table-fellowship. Through the act of repentance, Jesus expects the rich, leaders, tax collectors and sinners into his Kingly messianic community.

Anointing of Jesus by a sinful woman is transposed by Luke into the Galilean Ministry fitting to his context to emphasize the forgiveness of sin which is one of the major characteristics of Jesus' Kingship. And at the close of Galilean ministry, the Messianic secrecy is disclosed to the closer circle of disciples that Jesus is the anticipated Messianic King through the confession of Peter; through Jesus' foretelling of his Messianic suffering, death and resurrection; and, the event of transfiguration. It once again depicts the skill of Luke in composing the Gospel from the Infancy Narrative, step by step, focusing on Jesus' death as befitting a Messianic King leading toward its culmination in the Passion Narrative.

The Travel Narrative in 9:51-19:48 is peculiar to Lukan composition. It begins with the rejection of Jesus in a Samaritan village due to his travel plan toward Jerusalem. It parallels the Temple controversy as he was rejected at Nazareth due to the inclusion of Gentiles in his mission at the outset of the Galilean ministry. The parables of Jesus indicate his Kingly characteristics of forgiveness, love, grace and the values of the Kingdom of God. The L parables reveal the concept of reversal of factors - economy, wealth, social systems, religious practices, exclusivism, and attitudes, with the intention of restoration, repentance, forgiveness, transcending geographical and social boundaries, reciprocity, humility, persistent and hopeful prayer and self surrender. All these speak of the Kingly aspect of Jesus in uniting people and doing good to the people in building the community life against the socio-political situation of that time which was discriminative and divisive.

In the Parables common to Q and Triple Tradition, warning against the fear of Roman authority that was tempting the people against the message of Kingdom; the phenomenal growth of the Kingdom; challenge to the political leadership; juxtaposition of Jesus' Kingship of saving a sinner's life against destroying a sinner by Roman rule; Jesus' vision of egalitarian Kingdom in which the poor, crippled, blind, and lame are the partakers; and, warning given to people for their choice of leaders indicate the alternative Kingship of Jesus.

Throughout Jesus' journey and the stay in Jerusalem, Jesus is depicted as a host as well as a guest. Jesus' table-fellowship with sinners, tax collectors and with a Pharisee indicates the anticipated Messiah, who in praxis liberates Israel not only from physical repressions such as hunger, sickness, etc., but also from political and social oppression. Jesus compares the Kingdom by using the parables as metaphors and it connotes his Kingship. By depicting the healing of the blind man at Jericho, the Davidic pedigree in Lukan composition seems to indicate the fulfillment of Davidic dynasty through the Messianic/ Davidic King Jesus.

In his concern for cleansing the Temple, Jesus suspends their banking operation of Jerusalem Temple, the controlling center of the Jewish social identity, the seat of economic and political institution. The usage of the verb, ἐκβάλλω further indicates casting out the demonic control of the Temple in its political, economic, social and religious power. As it had a precedent and prophetic anticipation of the messianic age with the restoration of the Temple, the Temple act establishes Jesus as the King of new age according to Luke. The triumphal entry indicates the arrival of the anticipated King to lead the society to restructure the social order. By riding on a colt, spreading the clothes and being hailed by the crowd, Luke's ascription of the title "King" makes the entry of Jesus explicitly royal. Jesus' entry from the east into Jerusalem in the context of Pilate's entry during the Passover to maintain the imperial power as well as Roman imperial theology seems to be anti-imperial in action and evoked great enthusiasm among the people. Jesus' procession seems to be intentionally a counter move to Pilate's procession according to his message of the Kingdom of God in contrast to the Kingdom of Caesar.

Roman oppression of the Jews by burdensome taxation and the payment of tax to Rome indicate the people's submission to Rome and elite's sovereignty. But, God's supremacy is emphasized by Jesus. The phrase "desolating sacrilege," in the prophetic words of Jesus is a key expression of nationalistic sense, emphasising faith and religion.

On the whole, in the life and teachings of Jesus, Luke through a topographical structure of journey skillfully exposes the Kingship of Jesus. In this section along with the Infancy Narrative as an introduction to the Passion Narrative, Luke skillfully develops the motif of Jesus' Kingship in his composition to highlight Jesus as the alternative King to the Roman emperor in the Passion Narrative. Luke's portrayal of Jesus' Kingship in the Passion and Resurrection narratives will be explored in the next chapter.

Endnotes

[1] In addition to the title, artist, ascribed to the author by most of the New Testament scholars, C. H. Talbert sees Lukan design as an architectonic scheme. For instance: 1) There are significant correspondences between the content and events in Galilee and Jerusalem in Ch.9 and chs.22-23; and 2) Lk 4:16-8:56 falls into two parts: 4:16-7:17 and 7:18-8:56, which begin and end in similar ways and the same themes of Jesus' preaching and healing as fulfillments of Isaianic prophecies are dealt with.[C. H. Talbert, *Literary Pattern, Theological Themes, and the Genre of Luke-Acts* (Montana: Scholars Press, 1974), 26-39.]

[2] Lk. 4:14-9:50.

[3] Lk. 9:51-17:11.

[4] Lk. 17:11-21:38. Particularly in Jerusalem: 19:28-21:38.

[5] Lk. 5:17 & 6:17.

[6] Lk. 3:1-9:50.

[7] Lk. 9:51-21:38.

[8] R. Stronstad, *The Charismatic Theology of St. Luke* (Peabody: Hendrickson, 1984), 8.

[9] Lk. 3:15.

[10] P.J. Tomson, "Jesus and his Judaism," in *The Cambridge Companion to Jesus*, ed. by M. Bockmuehl (Cambridge: University Press, 2001), 30.

[11] Oepke, "βαπτω" in *Theological Dictionary of the New Testament*, ed. by G. Kittel (Grand Rapids: William. B. Eerdmans, 1964), 537.

[12] W. F. Flemington, *The New Testament Doctrine of Baptism* (London: S.P.C.K., 1948), 17f.

[13] B. M. Metzger, *The New Testament: Its Background, Growth, and Content, 1965*, 2nd ed. (Nashville: Abingdon Press, 1983), 109.

[14] Mt. 3:7. cf. Lk. 3:8.

[15] W. P. Weaver, *The Historical Jesus in the Twentieth Century 1900-1950* (Pennsylvania: Trinity Press International, 1999), 6f.

[16] Lk. 3:22 & Mk. 1:11.

[17] Mt. 3:17 & Jn. 1:34.

[18] M. Borg and J. D. Crossan, *The Last Week: What the Gospels Really Teach about Jesus' Final Days in Jerusalem* (London: SPCK, 2008), 21.

[19] Lk. 3:4-6.

[20] G. Stanton, *The Gospels and Jesus, 1989,* second edition (New York: Oxford University Press, 2002), 182.

[21] C. Guignebert, *The Jewish World in the time of Jesus* (New York: University Books, 1959), 135f.

[22] Mt. 14:3f; Mk. 6:17f; Lk. 3:19f, & 9:7-9.

[23] Herod Antipas divorced his wife, daughter of Aretas IV and married Herodias, wife of his brother Philip [P. Richardson, *Herod: King of the Jews and Friend of the Romans* (Edinburgh: T&T Clark, 1996), 307; Josephus in *the Antiquities of the Jews*, 18. 5, states the history of Herod's love for Herodias and his marriage with her [W. Whiston, A.M. (tr), *The Works of Josephus: Complete and Unabridged*, new updated edition (Peabody: Hendrickson, 2008), 484].

[24] Ex. 20:17.

[25] Lk. 9:7-9.

[26] Mt. 1:1-17.

[27] Lk. 3:23-38.

[28] Cf. Mt. 4:1-11 & Mk. 1:12f.

[29] M. C. Tenney, *New Testament Times* (London: Inter-varsity Press, 1965), 162.

[30] W. Carter, *The Roman Empire and the New Testament* (Nashville: Abingdon Press, 2006), 17.

[31] K.Yamazaki-Ransom, *The Roman Empire in Luke's Narrative* (New York: T&T Clark, 2010), 97.

[32] In addition, Theissen sees the historical evidence of these elements of mountain temptation in the person of Gaius Caligula. He speculates that Q source might have been formulated during the Gaius Caligula conflict during CE 40 regarding the worship of God or idols, particularly the statue of Emperor. [G. Theissen, *The Gospels in Context: Social and Political History in the Synoptic Tradition*, tr. by L. M. Maloney (Edinburgh: T&T Clark, 1992), 207f.]

[33] I. Lesbaupin, *Blessed are the Persecuted: Christian Life in the Roman Empire, A.D. 64-313*, tr. by R. R. Barr (New York: Orbis Books, 1987), 5.

[34] A. Storkey, *Jesus and Politics: Confronting the Powers* (Grand Rapids: Baker Academic, 2005), 77-79.

[35] Z. Mattam, "The Temptations of Christ. Lk 4:1-13," *Bible Bhashyam* 23/2 (June, 1997): 118.

[36] J. B. Fuliga, "The Temptations of Jesus: A Class Struggle," *The Asia Journal of Theology* 8/1 (1994): 183.

[37]"Simon, Simon, listen! Satan has demanded to sift all of you like wheat, but I have prayed for you that your faith may not fail..."

[38] J. Jeremias, *The Parables of Jesus,* revised edition (London: SCM Press, 1970), 123.

[39] Storkey, *Jesus and Politics...*, 76f.

[40] *The Antiquities of the Jews* 17:6. 2f, [W. Whiston, A.M. (tr), *The Works of Josephus: Complete and Unabridged,* new updated edition (Peabody: Hendrickson, 2008), 461].

[41] Lk. 4:16-30; cf. Mk. 6:1-6.

[42] Lk. 1:35.

[43] Lk. 3:22f.

[44] Lk. 4:1.

[45] Lk. 4:18 & 21.

[46] Lk. 9:34f.

[47] Lk. 24:49.

[48] Lk. 4:21.

[49] Lk. 4:16f.

[50] Isa. 61:1f.

[51] D. Carr, *Luke,* in Thiruvivilia Vilakam, ed, by K. Hironemus (Trichy: Arul Vaku Mantam, 2013), 72. (Tamil)

⁵² Cf. Jn. 6:15 &27.

⁵³ Isa. 49:6, cf. Lk. 2:32; Isa. 40:3-5, cf. Lk. 3:4ff; Isa. 61:1 & 29:18, cf. Lk. 7:22; D. Hamm, "Sight to the Blind: Vision as Metaphor in Luke," *Biblica* 67/4 (1986): 475.

⁵⁴ R. Heskett, *Messianism within the Scriptural Scroll of Isaiah* (New York: T&T Clark, 2007), 248.

⁵⁵ Carter, *The Roman Empire and the New Testament...*, 20.

⁵⁶ C. A. Evans, "The New Quest for Jesus and the New Research on the Dead Sea Scrolls," in *Jesus, Mark and Q: The Teaching of Jesus and its Earliest Records*, ed. by M. Labahn and A. Schmidt (England: Sheffield Academic Press, 2001), 170-172.

⁵⁷ *Ibid.,*, 173.

⁵⁸ I. H. Marshall, *New Testament Theology* (Illinois: InterVarsity Press, 2004), 146.

⁵⁹ Lk. 24:19.

⁶⁰ Cf. The prophetic role in Lk. 7:11-17, raising the widow's son at Nain by Jesus parallels to 1Kings 17:8-24, raising the son of the widow of Zarephath by Elijah; and, Lk. 5:12-16; 17:11-19, cleansing of Leprosy parallels to 2 Kings 5:1-19, the cleansing of Naaman, the Syrian.

⁶¹ Luke 7:16; According to J. G. Muthuraj, the widow at Nain was economically powerless. [J. G. Muthuraj, "Economic Scenarios of the NT Christianity: A Socio-Economic Reading of Luke-Acts," *Indian Journal of Theology* 38/1 (1996): 52.]

⁶² Lk. 7:18-23; cf. Isa. 29:18-20; 35:5-10 & 61:1; According to Joachim Jeremias, Jesus here takes up the prophetic images of messianic age. [Jeremias, *The Parables of Jesus...*, 115f.]

⁶³ L. C. Crockett, "Luke 4 25-27 and Jewish-Gentile Relations in Luke-Acts," *Journal of Biblical Literature* 88/2 (June, 1969): 177-183.

⁶⁴ C. A. Evans, "Luke's use of the Elijah/Elisha Narratives and the Ethic of Election," *Journal of Biblical Literature* 106/1 (March, 1987): 82.

⁶⁵ J. V. Goudoever, "The Place of Israel in Luke's Gospel," *Novum Testamentum* 8/2-4 (April-October, 1966): 113.

⁶⁶ O. Betz, "The Kerygma of Luke," *Interpretation* 79/2 (April, 1968): 137.

⁶⁷ Nature miracles: the incredible catch of fish in Lk. 5:1-11, cf. Jn. 21:1-14; stilling the storm in Lk. 8:22-25; Mt. 8:23-27 & Mk. 4:35-41 etc.,

⁶⁸ Lk. 4:31-37. cf. Mk. 1:21-28.

⁶⁹ Lk. 4:38-41. cf. Mk. 1:29-34 & Mt. 8:14-17.

[70] Lk. 5:12-16. cf. Mk. 1:40-45 & Mt. 8:1-4.

[71] Lk. 5:17-26. cf. Mk. 2:1-12 & Mt. 9:1-8.

[72] Lk. 6:6-11. cf. Mk. 3:1-6 & Mt. 12:9-14.

[73] Lk. 6:17-19. cf. Mt. 4:23-25.

[74] Lk. 7:1-10. cf. Mt. 8:5-13.

[75] Lk. 7:11-17.

[76] Lk. 8:22-25. cf. Mk. 4:35-41 & Mt. 8:23-27.

[77] Lk. 8:26-39. cf. Mk. 5:1-20 & Mt. 8:28-34.

[78] Lk. 8:40-54. cf. Mk. 5:21-43 & Mt. 9:18-26.

[79] Lk. 9:10-17. cf. Mk. 6:30-44 & Mt. 14:13-21.

[80] Lk. 9:37-43. cf. Mk. 9:14-27 & Mt. 17:14-18.

[81] Lk. 13:10-17.

[82] Lk. 14:1-6.

[83] Lk. 17:11-19.

[84] Lk. 18:35-43. cf. Mk. 10:46-52 & Mt. 20:29-34,

[85] Storkey, *Jesus and Politics*..., 86.

[86] P. J. Achtemeier, "The Lukan Perspective on the Miracles of Jesus: A Preliminary Sketch," *Journal of Biblical Literature* 94/4 (December, 1975): 552.

[87] P. B. Santram, "Jesus Christ and the Kingdom of God: A New Testament Perspective," *The Indian Journal of Theology* 29/2 (April–June, 1980): 87.

[88] Stanton, *The Gospels and Jesus*..., 219.

[89] J. B. Green, *The Theology of the Gospel of Luke* (Cambridge: University Press, 1995), 95.

[90] H. D. Betz, "The Cleansing of the Ten Lepers (Luke 17: 11-19)," *Journal of Biblical Literature* 90/3 (September, 1971): 324.

[91] Lk. 4:31-5:11; cf. Mk. 1:14ff.

[92] Lk. 5:27.

[93] Lk. 4:38-41; Mt. 8:14-17 & Mk. 1:29-34.

[94] Lk. 4:41.

[95] Lk. 8:26-39; Mt. 8:28-9:1 & Mk. 5:1-20.

[96] Lk. 5:12-16 & 17:11-19.

[97] Lk. 5:13.

[98] R. W. Roschke, "Healing in Luke, Madagascar, and Elsewhere," *Currents in Theology and Mission* 33/6 (December, 2006): 469.

[99] C. K. Barrett, *St. John* (London, SPCK, 1978), 238; Samaritans were neither Jews nor non-Jews. Samaritans used the Pentateuch as their Scripture. Like the Jews, they followed the Israelite biblical tradition. [R. Plummer, "Samaritanism - a Jewish Sect or an Independent Form of Yahwism?" in *Samaritans Past and Present: Current Studies,* ed. by M. Mor and F. V. Reiterer (Berlin: Walter de Gruyter GmbH & Co, 2010), 16f.]; the rivalry concerning the worship place is apparent in the conversation of Jesus with the Samaritan woman in John's Gospel. [Jn. 4:20.]

[100] Lk. 8:43-48; Mt. 9:18-26 & Mk. 5:21-43.

[101] Stanton, *The Gospels and Jesus...*, 238f.

[102] This event of healing the crippled woman is from the Travel Narrative. But, I group all the miracles together to see the intention of the author in describing them.

[103] M. D. Hamm, "The Freeing of the Bent Woman and the Restoration of Israel: Luke 13:10-17 as Narrative Theology," *Journal for the Study of the New Testament* 31 (October, 1987): 25.

[104] L. M. Maloney and E. J. Smith, "The Year of Luke: A Feminist Perspective," *Currents in Theology and Mission* 21/6 (December, 1994): 422.

[105] J. J. Kilgallen, "The Obligation to Heal (Luke 13, 10-17)," *Biblica* 82/3 (2001): 406.

[106] Lk. 13:12f.

[107] The healing of the dropsical man in 14:1-6 also raises the same issue of Sabbath.

[108] Hamm, "The Freeing of the Bent Woman...", 26.

[109] T. Thatcher, *Jesus the Riddler: The Power of Ambiguity in the Gospels* (Westminster: John Knox Press, 2006), 123.

[110] Lk. 14:1-6.

[111] 2 Sam. 7:13, 16, 26 & 1 Chr. 17:12, 14, 42; Hamm, "The Freeing of the Bent Woman...", 28.

[112] R. O'Toole, "Some Exegetical Reflections on Luke 13, 10-17," *Biblica* 73/1 (1992): 100.

[113] Stanton, *The Gospels and Jesus...*, 235.

[114] M. Smith, *Jesus the Magician* (London: Gollancz, 1978) cited by Ohler, "Jesus as a Prophet...", 131.

[115] Achtemeier gives the example of a story narrated by Apollonius of Tyana that he raised a girl via whispering a formula in secret. And he contrasts it with the Lukan story of raising the son of the widow at Nain

that Jesus performs openly as well made the bystanders to hear what he said. [Achtemeier, "The Lukan Perspective on the Miracles of Jesus...".…, 557.]

[116] Mt. 8:17 &10:7-8; Stanton, *The Gospels and Jesus...*, 233-236.

[117] M. Ohler, "Jesus as a Prophet: Remarks on Terminology," in *Jesus, Mark and Q: The Teaching of Jesus and its Earliest Records*, ed. by M. Labahn and A. Schmidt (England: Sheffield Academic Press, 2001), 131&139; Lk. 11:19-22 = Mt. 12:27-29; Stanton, *The Gospels and Jesus...*, 197.

[118] Max Turner, "The Spirit and the Power of Jesus' Miracles in the Lukan Conception," *Novum Testamentum* 33/2 (April, 1991): 124f.

[119] Lk. 11:14-23. Cf. Mt. 12: 22-32; Mk. 20-30; Stanton, *The Gospels and Jesus...*, 235.

[120] *Ibid.,,* 236.

[121] J. P. Meier, *A Mariginal Jew: Rethinking the Historical Jesus*, Vol. II (New York: Doubleday, 1994), 250.

[122] J. D. Crossan, *The Birth of Christianity: Discovering What Happened in the Years Immediately After the Execution of Jesus* (Edinburgh: T&T Clark, 1998), 304.

[123] Twelftree says that the exorcisms signify the Kingdom of God in operation (Twelftree, 1993, 170) referred to by Stanton, *The Gospels and Jesus...*, 238f.

[124] Lk 7:20-22.

[125] J. Moltmann, *The Crucified God: The Cross of Christ as the Foundation and Criticism of Christian Theology*, tr. by R. A. Wilson and J. Bowden (London: SCM Press, 1974), 98.

[126] Cf. Mt. 12:28.

[127] Lk. 6:12-16; Mt. 10:1-4 & Mk. 3:13-19a.

[128] Lk. 9:2.

[129] J. D. Kingsbury, *Conflict in Luke: Jesus, Authorities, Disciples* (Minneapolis: Fortress Press, 1991), 138f.

[130] Mk. 2:18-22 & Mt. 9:14-17.

[131] H. G. Liddell and R. Scott, *A Greek-English Lexicon* (Oxford: Clarendon Press, 1882), 950; W. Bauer, *A Greek-English Lexicon of the New Testament and other Early Christian Literature*, tr. by W. F. Arndt and F. W. Gingrich, 2nd revised ed. (Chicago: University Press, 1979), 513.

[132] F. W. Danker, "Politics of the New Age According to St. Luke," in *Currents in Theology and Mission* 12/6 (December 1985): 343.

[133] *Ibid.*, 344.

[134] H. K. Bond, *The Historical Jesus: A Guide for the Perplexed* (London: Continuum, 2012), 92.

[135] *Ibid.*, 93.

[136] Stanton, *The Gospels and Jesus...*, 201.

[137] Cf. Mt. 19:28.

[138] J. Jervell, *Luke and the People of God: A New Look at Luke-Acts* (Minneapolis: Augsburg, 1972), 76.

[139] M. A. Thomas, "Social Vision of Jesus," *Religion and Society* 39/2-3 (June-September, 1992): 56.

[140] Maloney and Smith, "The Year of Luke: A Feminist Perspective"..., 415.

[141] E. S. Fiorenza, "A Feminist Critical Interpretation for Liberation: Martha and Mary: Luke 10:38-42," *Religion & Intellectual* Life 3 (1986): 31, referred to by M. R. D'Angelo, "Women in Luke-Acts: A Redactional View," *Journal of Biblical Literature* 109/3 (Fall, 1990): 442.

[142] *Ibid.*, 452 & 460.

[143] B. E. Reid, "Luke: The Gospel for Women?" *Currents in Theology and Mission* 21/6 (December, 1994): 406-413.

[144] Lk. 13:20f.

[145] Lk. 15:8-10.

[146] Lk. 18:1-8.

[147] T. K. Seim, *Double Message: Patterns of Gender in Luke & Acts* (Nashville: Abingdon Press, 1994), 259.

[148] Lk. 1:46-55.

[149] M. V. Abraham, "Good News to the Poor in Luke's Gospel," *Bible Bhashyam* 14/1-2 (March–June, 1988): 68.

[150] Lk. 6:20-26.

[151] L. T. Johnson, *Sharing Possessions* (Grand Rapids: Wm. B. Eerdmans, 2011), 14.

[152] Lk. 4:25-27.

[153] "The materially poor or socially or religiously despised, oppressed and lowly, and thus lack all human or earthly resources...turn to God for help and liberation." F. Pereira, *Jesus, the Human and Humane Face of God: A Portrait of Jesus in Luke's Gospel* (Mumbai: St. Paul's, 2000), 92 & 102.

[154] Lk. 5:32. [S. M. Sheeley, *Narrative Asides in Luke-Acts* (Sheffield: Academic Press, 1992), 142]

[155] P. A. Sampathkumar, "The Rich and the poor in Luke-Acts," *Bible Bhashyam* 22/4 (December, 1996): 180.

[156] M. A. Beavis, "Expecting Nothing in Return," *Interpretation* 48/4 (October, 1994): 363.

[157] Lk. 5:11.

[158] Sheeley, *Narrative Asides in Luke-Acts...*, 140; not only narrative asides, but also the story itself the conflict manifests.

[159] D. Abernathy, "A Study on Lk 4, 16-30," *Bible Bhashyam* 27/3 (September, 2001): 229.

[160] E. Franklin, *Luke: Interpreter of Paul, Critic of Matthew* (Sheffield: Academic Press, 1994), 176.

[161] J. D. Kingsbury, "The Plot of Luke's Story of Jesus," *Interpretation* 48/4 (October, 1994): 369.

[162] D. Hill, "The Rejection of Jesus at Nazareth (Luke iv 16-30)," *Novum Testamentum* 13/3 (July, 1971): 170; Lk. 20:27-40.

[163] M. A. Powell, "The Religious Leaders in Luke: A Literary-Critical Study," *Journal of Biblical Literature* 109/1 (Spring, 1990): 101.

[164] Mt. 9:10-13 & Mk. 2:15-17.

[165] Mt. 18:10-14.

[166] J. T. Carroll, "Luke's Portrayal of the Pharisees," *The Catholic Biblical Quarterly* 50/4 (October, 1988): 604f.

[167] Lk. 14:1-6, 7-11, 12-14, 15-24; 15:1-32; 16:14-31; 17:20f; 18:9-14 & 19:37-39.

[168] Lk. 1:5-2:22.

[169] Lk. 4:1-19:27.

[170] Lk. 22:1-23:56; J. B. Tyson, "Conflict as a Literary Theme in the Gospel of Luke," in *New Synoptic Studies,* ed. by W. R. Farmer (Macon: Mercer University Press, 1983), 314-327; Sheeley, *Narrative Asides in Luke-Acts...*, 141.

[171] Tyson, "Conflict as a Literary Theme in the Gospel of Luke"..., 315.

[172] *Ibid.,* 316f.

[173] *Ibid.,* 318.

[174] *Ibid.,* 326.

[175] Lk. 4:14 & 18.

[176] Lk. 4: 32 & 36.

[177] Lk. 5:20-26.

[178] Lk. 4:32; 5:26; 8:25, 56 & 9:43.

[179] Lk. 5:21-24; 6:11; 7:49; 11:14-16 & 13:13-17.

[180] E. P. Sanders, *Jesus and Judaism* (London: SCM Press, 1985), 177f; It is to be noted here that Sanders later says that he is no longer confident of the view that the tax collectors are the quislings of the imperial power; E. P. Sanders, *The Historical Figure of Jesus* (London: Penguin Press, 1993), 229.

[181] *Ibid.*, 229; Crossan, *The Birth of Christianity...*, 338.

[182] Sanders, *The Historical Figure of Jesus...*, 232f.

[183] Sanders, *Jesus and Judaism...*, 203; Crossan, *The Birth of Christianity...*, 339f.

[184] Mt. 18:12f.

[185] R. O'Toole, *The Literary Form of Luke 19:1-10,"* *Journal of Biblical Literature* 110/1 (Spring, 1991): 108.

[186] *Ibid.*, 116.

[187] Luke depicts Zacchaeus negatively as short and rich as a tax collector and a sinner who longs for repentance. His physical size points out that he was socially marginalized. [M. C. Parsons, "'Short in Stature': Luke's Physical Description of Zacchaeus," *New Testament Studies* 47/1 (January, 2001): 57]; besides, the salvation of Zacchaeus seems to be one of the fulfillments of the anticipation of salvation in Jesus. [W. P. Loewe, "Towards an Interpretation of Lk. 19:1-10," *The Catholic Biblical Quarterly* 36/3 (July, 1974): 330.]

[188] Sanders, *The Historical Figure of Jesus...*, 236.

[189] Lk. 19:10.

[190] Mt. 26:6-13; Mk. 14:3-9 & Jn. 12:1-8.

[191] D. A. S. Ravens, "The Setting of Luke's Account of the Anointing: Luke 7. 2-8. 3," *New Testament Studies* 34/2 (April, 1988): 286-289.

[192] John also locates the place as Bethany, but concerning the host he mentions Lazarus instead of Simon.

[193] J. P. Mullen, *Dining with Pharisees* (Minnesota: Liturgical Press, 2004), 84.

[194] Ravens, "The Setting of Luke's Account of the Anointing...", 283f.

[195] Mullen, *Dining with Pharisees...*, 91.

[196] C. H. Cosgrove, "A Woman's Unbound Hair in the Greco-Roman World, with special Reference to the Story of the 'Sinful Woman' in Luke 7:36-50," *Journal of Biblical Literature* 124/4 (Winter, 2005): 691.

[197] Ravens, "The Setting of Luke's Account of the Anointing...", 285f.

[198] W. D. Davies and D. C. Allison, *Matthew: The International Critical Commentary*, vol. III (Edinburgh: T&T Clark, 1997), 445.

[199] R. T. France, *The Gospel of Mark* (Carlisle: The Paternoster Press, 2002), 552.

[200] Jn 12:12-16.

[201] Barrett, *St. John ...*, 409.

[202] Lk. 9:20f.

[203] E. F. Scott, *The Kingdom and the Messiah* (Edinburgh: T&T Clark, 1911), 160.

[204] Jeremias, *The Parables of Jesus...*, 219.

[205] Lk. 9:28-36.

[206] Lk. 9:31.

[207] J. A. Fitzmyer, *The Gospel According to Luke I-IX*, Vol. 1 (New York: Doubleday, 1979), 166.

[208] R. E. Brown, *The Death of The Messiah: From Gethsemane to Grave*, vol I (New York: Doubleday, 1994), 64.

[209] J. L. Price, "The Gospel According to Luke," *Studia Biblica* 7/2 (April, 1953): 206.

[210] A. J. Mattill, "The Jesus-Paul Parallels and the Purpose of Luke-Acts: H. H. Evans Reconsidered," *Novum Testamentum* 17/1 (January, 1975): 37.

[211] R. Bauckham, "The Scrupulous Priest and the Good Samaritan: Jesus' Parabolic Interpretation of the Law of Moses," *New Testament Studies* 44/4 (October, 1998): 487.

[212] Stanton, *The Gospels and Jesus...*, 91.

[213] Cf. Mt. 8:20.

[214] "Were not ten made clean? But the other nine, where are they? Was none of them found to return and give praise to God except this foreigner?" [Lk. 9:17ff.]

[215] Danker, "Politics of the New Age According to St. Luke"..., 342f.

[216] Sanders, *Jesus and Judaism...*, 4.

[217] Stanton, *The Gospels and Jesus...*, 228ff.

[218] F. Brown, S. R. Driver and C. A. Briggs, *Hebrew and English Lexicon of the Old Testament* (Oxford: Clarendon Press, 1952), 605.

[219] J. W. Sider, *Interpreting the Parables: A Hermeneutical Guide to Their Meaning* (Grand Rapids: Zondervan, 1995), 18.

[220] V. G. Shillington, *Jesus and His Parables: Interpreting the Parables of Jesus Today* (Edinburgh: T&T Clark, 1997), 9.

[221] B. H. Young, *Jesus and His Jewish Parables: Discovering the Roots of Jesus' Teaching* (New York: Paulist Press, 1989), 3.

[222] L. Schottroff, *The Parables of Jesus,* tr. by L. M. Maloney (Minneapolis: Fortress Press, 2006), 103.

[223] "A *riddle* is an interrogative statement that intentionally obscures its referent and asks the audience to name it." Riddle may be defined as an interactive metaphor; *metaphors* in the sense that they compare things from different mental categories of question and answer. [Thatcher, *Jesus the Riddler...*, 3 &11.]

[224] Stanton, *The Gospels and Jesus...*, 222ff.

[225] Stanton, *The Gospels and Jesus...*, 218; S. J. Kistemaker, *The Parables: Understanding the Stories Jesus Told* (Grand Rapids: Baker Books, 1980), 12.

[226] Lev. 20:1ff.

[227] Carr, *Luke...*, 178.

[228] M. Gourgues, "The Priest, The Levite, and The Samaritan Revisited: A Critical Note on Luke 10:31-35," *Journal of Biblical Literature* 117/4 (Winter, 1998): 713.

[229] Deut. 6:5 & Lev. 19:18; Schottroff, *The Parables of Jesus...*, 195.

[230] *Ibid.*, 135; Barrett, *St. John...*, 238.

[231] Jn. 4:7-42; v.9, "The Samaritan woman said to him, 'How is that you, a Jew, ask a drink of me, a woman of Samaria?' Where, John gives the remark in the bracket as, "Jews do not share things in common with Samaritans." In v. 40, he further says that, "...they asked him to stay with them; and he stayed there for two days."

[232] M. C. Parsons, *Luke: Storyteller, Interpreter, Evangelist* (Peabody: Hendrickson, 2007), 54ff.

[233] L. T. Johnson, "Making Connections: The Material Expression of Friendship in the New Testament," *Interpretation* 24 (April, 2004): 158.

[234] Parsons, *Luke: Storyteller...*, 120.

[235] Schottroff, *The Parables of Jesus...*, 195.

[236] R. J. Shirock, "The Growth of the Kingdom in Light of Israel's Rejection of Jesus: Structure and Theology in Luke 13:1-35," *Novum Testamentum* 35/1 (January, 1993): 16.

[237] J. T. Sanders, "Tradition and Redaction in Luke XV. 11-32," *New Testament Studies* 15/4 (July 1969): 438.

[238] Danker, "Politics of the New Age According to St. Luke"..., 339.

[239] Jeremias, *The Parables of Jesus*..., 11-39.

[240] Mt. 18:1.

[241] In the tribal culture of Tamilnadu, at Keezhnilavoor, a few old women have worn 10 silver coins in a string as wedding chain (*thali*), as in Palestine, as Barclay says, "The mark of a married woman was a head-dress made of ten silver coins linked together by a silver chain...the head-dress was almost equivalent of her wedding ring." [W. Barclay, *The Gospel of Luke* fifth impression (Edinburgh: St. Andrew's Press, 1960), 209; at Keezhnilavoor, I had the opportunity to see it during 1996 December.]

[242] Reid, "Beyond Petty Pursuits and Wearisome Widows"..., 288.

[243] J. D. M. Derrett, "Fresh Light on the Lost Sheep and the Lost Coin," *New Testament Studies* 26/1 (October, 1979): 40.

[244] Carr, *Luke*..., 247.

[245] Schottroff, *The Parables of Jesus*..., 195.

[246] J. Robbins, *Prodigal Son/Elder Brother* (Chicago: University Press, 1991), 24-39.

[247] Jeremias, *The Parables of Jesus*..., 131f.

[248] C. E. Carlston, "Reminiscence and Redaction in Luke 15:11-32," *Journal of Biblical Literature* 94/3 (September, 1975): 385.

[249] Carr, *Luke*..., 249.

[250] *Ibid.*, 253.

[251] G. Theissen, *Sociology of Early Palestinian Christianity*, tr. by John Bowden (Philadelphia: Fortress Press, 1978), 42-44.

[252] A. J. Mattill, *Luke and the Last Things* (Dillsboro: Western North Carolina Press, 1979), 37.

[253] Schottroff, *The Parables of Jesus*..., 163.

[254] Theissen, *Sociology of Early Palestinian Christianity*..., 44.

[255] Schottroff, *The Parables of Jesus*..., 159-161; J. S. Kloppenborg, "The Dishonoured Master Luke 16, 1-8a," *Biblica* 70/4 (1989): 486.

[256] W. Loader, "Jesus and the Rogue in Luke 16, 1-8A: The Parable of the Unjust Steward," *Revue Biblique* 96/4 (January, 1989): 528-531.

[257] Lk 16:8, 13f; lovers of wealth verses the lovers of God.

[258] Schottroff, *The Parables of Jesus*..., 161,

[259] L. J. Topel, "On the Injustice of the Unjust Steward: Lk 16:1-13," *The Catholic Biblical Quarterly* 37/2 (April, 1975), 227; H. Moxnes, *The Economy of the Kingdom* (Philadelphia: Fortress Press, 1988), 141.

[260] Thatcher, *Jesus the Riddler...*, 59.

[261] D. Landry and B. May, "Honor Restored: New Light on the Parable of the Prudent Steward (Luke 16:1-8a)," *Journal of Biblical Literature* 119/2 (Summer, 2000): 293; Kloppenborg, "The Dishonoured Master Luke 16, 1-8a"..., 494.

[262] Landry and May, "Honor Restored..."..., 295f.

[263] Jeremias, *The Parables of Jesus...*, 45ff.

[264] Carr, *Luke...*, 260f.

[265] Lk. 16:14.

[266] Schottroff, *The Parables of Jesus...*, 166f; Thatcher, *Jesus the Riddler...*, 59.

[267] R. Bauckham, "The Rich Man and Lazarus: The Parable and the Parallels," *New Testament Studies* 37/2 (April, 1991): 225.

[268] G. M. S. Prabhu, "Good News to the Poor the Social Implications of the Message of Jesus," *Bible Bhashyam* 4/3 (September, 1978): 199.

[269] Lk. 6:20-26; Prabhu, "Good News to the Poor..."..., 201.

[270] Schottroff, *The Parables of Jesus...*, 177-180.

[271] Lk. 7:10.

[272] Maloney and Smith, "The Year of Luke: A Feminist Perspective"..., 419.

[273] Schottroff, *The Parables of Jesus...*, 7f.

[274] W. O. Walker, "Jesus and Tax Collectors," *Journal of Biblical Literature* 97/2 (June, 1978): 229.

[275] Cf. Mk. 4:1-9; Mt. 13:1-9.

[276] Carr, *Luke...*, 126.

[277] Cf. Mk. 4:13-20 & Mt. 13:18-23.

[278] Cf. Mt. 13:31f & Mk. 4:30-32.

[279] Cf. Mt. 13:33.

[280] Kistemaker, *The Parables...*, 51.

[281] D. H. V. Daalen, *The Kingdom of God is Like This* (London: Epworth Press, 1976), 29.

[282] Cf. Mt. 21:33-46 & Mk. 12: 1-12.

[283] J. D. Crossan, "The Parable of the Wicked Husbandmen," *Journal of Biblical Literature* 90/4 (December, 1971): 453ff.

[284] V. J. John, *The Ecological Vision of Jesus: Nature in the Parables of Mark* (Thiruvalla: CSS, 2002), 157.

[285] Condensed version of the parable of the pounds is in Mk 13:34.

[286] Young, *Jesus and His Jewish Parables...*, 1989), 165.

[287] *Ibid.*, 166f.

[288] R. Maddox, *The Purpose of Luke-Acts* (Edinburgh: T&T Clark, 1985), 50.

[289] Richardson, *Herod: King of the Jews...*, 298ff.

[290] Guignebert, *The Jewish World in the time of Jesus* ..., 5.

[291] Richardson, *Herod: King of the Jews* ..., 300.

[292] Carr, *Luke...*, 292.

[293] Adelbert Denaux, "The Parable of the King-Judge (Lk 19, 12-28) and its Relation to the Entry Story (Lk 19, 29-44)," *Zeitschrift Für Die Neutestamentliche Wissenschaft* 93/1-2 (2002): 36.

[294] Jeremias, *The Parables of Jesus...*, 59-63.

[295] Goudoever, "The Place of Israel in Luke's Gospel"..., 120f.

[296] Mt. 22:1-10.

[297] W. G. Morrice and J. Jeremias say that Luke left Matthew's allegorization and sustained the original Q material. [W. G. Morrice, *Hidden Sayings of Jesus: Words Attributed to Jesus Outside the Four Gospels* (Great Britain: SPCK, 1997), 78; Jeremias, *The Parables of Jesus...*, 176.]; According to Crossan, the parables of Jesus seem to be repeated sometimes in identical words or sometimes with variations. The parables of the Great Supper and the Marriage of the King's son appear to be the same story, but vary to suit the occasion. [Crossan, *The Birth of Christianity...*, 91.]; Stanton says that the parables might have undergone adaptation and reinterpretation due to their transmission in the early church and in the use of them by the evangelists. [Stanton, *The Gospels and Jesus...*, 219.]

[298] Thatcher, *Jesus the Riddler...*, 130.

[299] Lk. 7:24-35; cf. Mt. 11:2-19.

[300] Lk. 7:24ff.

[301] Theissen, *The Gospels in Context...*, 26ff.

[302] Lk. 13:32.

[303] Theissen, *The Gospels in Context...*, 33-41.

[304] Lk. 9:10-17.

[305] Lk. 22:14-38.

[306] M. M. Ibita, "Dining with Jesus in the Third Gospel: Celebrating the Eucharist in the Third World," *East Asian Pastoral Review* 42/3 (2005): 255.

[307] Lk. 5:30; 6:11 & 15:1f.

[308] Lk. 11:39-54.

[309] Num. 27:17; Jer. 50:6; Ezek. 34:1-16; cf. Mt. 10:6 & 15:24.

[310] G. Mangatt, "Jesus' Option for Sinners," *Bible Bhashyam* 18/4 (December, 1992): 211.

[311] J. D. Crossan, *Jesus: A Revolutionary Biography* (San Francisco: Harper Collins, 1995), 77; Thatcher, *Jesus the Riddler...*, 129.

[312] G. Rayanna, *The Table-fellowship of Jesus (Luke 5.27-32)* (Guntur: St. Anthony's Shrine, 2009), 200.

[313] Luz, "βασιλεία"..., 201.

[314] H. K. Bond, *The Historical Jesus: A Guide for the Perplexed* (London: Continuum, 2012), 86.

[315] To survey this: in 1 Sam. 28:17 God gives the Kingdom to David; 2 Sam. 3:28, my Kingdom- belonging; 2 Sam. 5:12 cf. 1 Kings 2:12, his Kingdom (Shift comes in the Chronicler, who speaks of the Lord's Kingdom and the Lord's throne); 1 Chr. 17:14, my Kingdom; 1 Chr. 29:23, the throne of the Lord. In Daniel 4:3, 17 cf. Dan. 4: 34; 6:26, God himself is depicted as King over all of humanity; Ps. 22:28; 103:19; 145:11-13; Ob. 21; 1 Chr. 29:11- God's Kingdom using personal pronouns or equivalents; In Inter Testamental literature, the idea of the Kingdom of God becomes more explicit: Jub. 1:28 - God rules from Mount Zion, while in Pss. Sol. 17:3 exact phrase *Kingdom of God* and in T. Benj. 9:1 the synonymous phrase *Kingdom of the Lord* are used; Several passages in 1 Enoch God is depicted as King and as ruling the world; The Testament of Moses 10:1-3 anticipates the appearance of the Kingdom of God and the demise of the Devil; the Dead Sea Scrolls present ideas in the same manner: 1QM 6:6; 12:7; 1QH 11:i.4-7; 4QM;1QSb 4.25-26; 5.21. [C. A. Evans, "The New Quest for Jesus and the New Research on the Dead Sea Scrolls, in *Jesus, Mark and Q: The Teaching of Jesus and its Earliest Records*, ed. by M. Labahn and A. Schmidt, (England: Sheffield Academic Press, 2001), 166f.]

[316] cf. Ps. 145:11f; J. D. Crossan, *In Parables: The Challenge of the Historical Jesus* (California: Polebridge Press, 1992), 23.

[317] P. Ricoeur, "The "Kingdom" in the Parables of Jesus," *Anglican Theological Review* 63/2 (April, 1981): 166.

[318] Weaver, *The Historical Jesus in the Twentieth Century...*, 20.

[319] *Ibid.*, 29f.

[320] Crossan, *In Parables...*, 23f; Stanton, *The Gospels and Jesus...*, 225f.

[321] Morrice, *Hidden Sayings of Jesus...*, 103.

[322] Crossan, *In Parables...*, 25f.

[323] M. Burrows, "Thy Kingdom Come," *Journal of Biblical Literature* 74/1 (March, 1955): 8.

[324] G. E. Ladd, "The Kingdom of God – Reign or Realm?" *Journal of Biblical Literature* 81/3 (September, 1962): 237.

[325] Mt 3:2.

[326] Lk 4:43.

[327] Is 61:1ff.

[328] Lk 19:9f, Jesus proclaims the salvation at Zacchaeus house is found only in Luke.

[329] H. Riedlinger, "How Universal is Christ's Kingship?-A Bibliographical Study," *Concilium* 1/2 (January 1966): 58.

[330] L. Legrand, "Christological Issues in the New Testament," *The Indian Journal of Theology* 24/3&4 (July- December1975): 73.

[331] L. Chouinard, "Gospel Christology: A Study of Methodology," *Journal for the Study of the New Testament* 30 (1987): 32; O. M. Rao, "Jesus: Christ of the Atonement or Christ the New Man," *The Indian Journal of Theology* 24/3&4 (July-December1975): 162f.

[332] Scott, *The Kingdom and the Messiah...*, 150.

[333] Stanton, *The Gospels and Jesus...*, 205.

[334] Matthew uses the phrase, *Kingdom of heaven,* more frequently than other evangelists, thirty-eight times; Luke employs the phrase, Kingdom of God thirty-two times. Mark uses only fourteen times.

[335] Abraham, "Good News to the Poor in Luke's Gospel"..., 76.

[336] Shillington, *Jesus and His Parables...*, 1.

[337] Tomson, "Jesus and his Judaism"..., 31.

[338] Borg and Crossan, *The Last Week...*, 25.

[339] Flemington, *The New Testament Doctrine of Baptism...*, 17f.

[340] Crossan, *In Parables...*, 36.

[341] S. E. Johnson, "King Parables in the Synoptic Gospels," *Journal of Biblical Literature* 74/1 (March, 1955): 39.

[342] Daalen, *The Kingdom of God is Like This...*, 15.

[343] U. Luz, "βασιλεία," *Exegetical Dictionary of the New Testament*, Vol 1, Ἀαρων-Ἑνώχ, ed. by H. Balz and G. Schneider (Edinburgh: T & T Clark, 1980), 204.

[344] Bond, *The Historical Jesus...*, 92.

[345] J. C. Paget, "Quests for the Historical Jesus," in *The Cambridge Companion to Jesus*, ed. by M. Bockmuehl (Cambridge: University Press, 2001), 142.

[346] Lk. 18:35-43; Mt. 20:29-34; & Mk. 10:46-52.

[347] Lk. 18:38f.

[348] Z. Mattam, "The Cure of the Blind Man of Jericho (Lk 18:35-43): A Kerygmatic, Patristic and Theological Study," *Bible Bhashyam* 24/1 (March, 1998): 19.

[349] Parsons, *Luke: Storyteller...*, 152f.

[350] Lk. 2:22 & 42.

[351] H. Koester, *History, Culture, and Religion of the Hellenistic Age* (Philadelphia: Fortress Press, 1982), 369f; C. J. Roetzel, *The World that Shaped the New Testament* (Atlanta: John Knox Press, 1985), 18.

[352] S. P. Matthew, *Temple-Criticism in Mark's Gospel: The Economic Role of the Jerusalem Temple during the First Century CE* (Delhi: ISPCK, 1999), 1.

[353] J. H. *Elliott*, "Temple Versus Household in Luke-Acts: A Contrast in Social Institutions," in *The Social world of Luke-Acts: Models for Interpretation*, ed. by J. Neyrey (Peabody: Hendrickson, 1991), 221.

[354] M. Hengel, *Crucifixion* (Philadelphia: Fortress Press, 1977), 13.

[355] Borg and Crossan, *The Last Week...*, 15.

[356] V. J. John, "The Role of the State in Jesus' View: A Synoptic Perspective," *Bangalore Theological Forum* 34/1 (June, 2004): 10.

[357] Muthuraj, "Economic Scenarios of the NT Christianity...",..., 53.

[358] Matthew, *Temple-Criticism in Mark's* Gospel..., 3f.

[359] N. Q. Hamilton, "Temple Cleansing and Temple Bank," *Journal of Biblical Literature* 83/4 (December, 1964): 370.

[360] Hamilton, "Temple Cleansing and Temple Bank"..., 370; According to Patrick Mullen, Rome's policies and taxes created hostility among the Jews and led them toward a rebellion against Rome in the sixties. Due to that Rome destroyed the Temple, Jerusalem and many country side places during 70 CE. [Mullen, *Dining with Pharisees...*, 40f.]

[361] Matthew, *Temple-Criticism in Mark's Gospel...*, 75.

[362] Elliott, "Temple versus Household in Luke-Acts...."..., 221, referred to by Muthuraj, "Economic Scenarios of the NT Christianity...."..., 53.

[363] P. W. L. Walker, *Jesus and the Holy City: New Testament Perspectives on Jerusalem* (Grand Rapids: William B, Eerdmans, 1996), 69.

[364] J. L. Houlden, "Passion Narratives," *A Dictionary of Biblical Interpretation*, ed. by R. J. Coggins and J. L. Houlden (London: SCM Press, 1990), 516.

[365] According to G.N. Stanton, Jerusalem is not only depicted negatively as the place of rejection by Luke, but also depicted positively as the place of triumph. [Stanton, *The Gospels and Jesus...*, 96.]

[366] Sanders, *The Historical Figure of Jesus...*, 254-260; P. Balla, "What did Jesus think about his Approaching Death," in *Jesus, Mark and Q: The Teaching of Jesus and its Earliest Records*, ed. by M. Labahn and A. Schmidt (England: Sheffield Academic Press, 2001), 250f.

[367] H. Conzelmann, *The Theology of St. Luke*, tr. by G. Buswell (Philadelphia: Fortress Press, 1982), 189-199.

[368] Lk. 19:45.

[369] Mk. 11:15; Mt. 21:12.

[370] The divine necessity, δει represents the messianic motif as it has to be fulfilled. There are 18 occurrences of δει in Luke's Gospel.

[371] Mattill, "The Jesus-Paul Parallels and the Purpose of Luke-Acts...."..., 26.

[372] Conzelmann, *The Theology of Luke...*, 198.

[373] Weaver, *The Historical Jesus in the Twentieth Century...*, 152.

[374] G. M. A. Hanfmann, "The Donkey and the King," *Harvard Theological Review* 78/3-4 (January-April, 1985): 425.

[375] Whiston, A.M. (tr), *The Works of Josephus: Complete and Unabridged...*, 306f.

[376] *Ibid.*, 464f.

[377] D. C. Allison, "Jesus Christ," in *The New Interpreters Dictionary of the Bible I-Ma*, vol. 3, ed. by K. D. Sakenfeld (Nashville: Abingdon Press, 2008), 269.

[378] Storkey, *Jesus and Politics...*, 241.

[379] Lk. 22:22.

[380] Lk. 19:35-38

[381] Fitzmyer, *The Gospel According to Luke I-IX...*, 167f.

[382] Mt. 21:11; in 21:46, Matthew depicts that the authorities wanted to arrest him but they could not, because the crowd regarded him as a prophet.

[383] J. Marcus, "Entering into the Kingly Power of God," *Journal of Biblical Literature* 107/4 (December, 1988): 667.

[384] J. M. Garland, "Signs of Kingship," *The Expository Times* 100/5 (1989): 185f.

[385] S. G. F. Brandon, *Jesus and Zealots* (New York: Scribners, 1968), 342; W. R. Wilson, *The Execution of Jesus* (New York: Charles Scribner's Sons, 1970), 224.

[386] Hamilton, "Temple Cleansing and Temple Bank"..., 365.

[387] R. H. Hiers, "Purification of the Temple: Preparation for the Kingdom of God," *Journal of Biblical Literature* 90/1 (March, 1971): 86.

[388] Cf. *Jubilees* 1:28f; 1 *Enoch* 90:28f & *Sibylline Oracles* 5:414-33.

[389] J. F. Coakley, "Jesus' Messianic Entry into Jerusalem (John 12:12-19 par.)," *The Journal of Theological Studies* 46/2 (October, 1995): 461f.

[390] Borg and Crossan, *The Last Week*..., 4.

[391] Hamm, "Sight to the Blind..."..., 471.

[392] Borg and Crossan, *The Last Week*..., 88.

[393] The governor resided at the Roman head quarters in Caesarea which was about 60 miles away from Jerusalem. [S.G.F. Brandon, *The Trial of Jesus of Nazareth* (London: B.T. Batsford Ltd, 1968), 36.]; in the *Antiquities of the Jews* 18/55, it is stated that the entry of Pilate from Caesarea to Jerusalem along with his army is described by Josephus as Pilate's entry "in order to abolish the Jewish laws," and introduce Caesar's effigies there. [Whiston, *The Works of Josephus*..., 479f.]

[394] Jesus' command to his disciples 'to go to the next village and bring a young colt which will be there and has never been ridden,' imply the planning of Jesus.

[395] An imperial procession of Pilate had, "A visual panoply of imperial power: cavalry on horses, foot soldiers, leather armor, helmets, weapons, banners, golden eagles mounted on poles, sun glinting on metal and gold. Sounds: the marching of feet, the creaking of leather, the clinking of bridles, the beating of drums. The swirling of dust, the eyes of the silent onlookers, some curious, some awed, and some resentful." [Borg and Crossan, *The Last Week*..., 3.]

[396] *Ibid.*, 2; Ex 12:21-27; B. Kinman, "Pilate's Assize and the Timings of Jesus' Trial," *Tyndale Bulletin* 42/2 (1991): 283. ATLAS.

[397] Carter, *The Roman Empire and the New Testament*..., 7.

[398] Kinman, "Jesus' 'Triumphal Entry' in the Light of Pilate's"..., 442.

[399] *Ibid.*, 443.

[400] *Ibid.*, 448.

[401] B. R. Kinman, "'The Stones will Cry out' (Luke 19, 40) – Joy or Judgment?" *Biblica* 75/2 (1994): 235.

[402] Mk. 11:15f; Mt. 21:12 & Jn. 2:14; John adds the sale of cattle and sheep along with selling doves.

[403] S. G. F. Brandon, *The Trial of Jesus of Nazareth* (London: B.T. Batsford Ltd, 1968), 84.

[404] H. K. Bond, *Caiaphas: Friend of Rome and Judge of Jesus?* (Westminster: John Knox Press, 2004), 64f.

[405] B. Kinman, "Lukan Eschatology and the Missing Fig Tree," *Journal of Biblical Literature* 113/4 (winter, 1994): 678.

[406] Lk. 21:29-33.

[407] Mt. 23:37-39.

[408] Mt. 21:23-27 & Mk. 11:27-33.

[409] Mt. 21:33-46 & Mk. 12:1-12.

[410] J.A. Darr, *Herod the Fox* (Sheffield: Academic Press, 1998), 173.

[411] Mt. 21:23-27 & Mk. 11:27-33.

[412] Mt. 21:33-46 & Mk. 12:1-12.

[413] C.E. Carlston, *The Parables of the Triple Tradition* (Philadelphia: Fortress Press, 1975), 178f.

[414] Carr, *Luke...*, 305.

[415] J. Jeremias, *The Parables of Jesus,* revised ed. (London: SCM Press, 1970), 22.

[416] Lk. 20:20-26; Mt. 22:15-22 & Mk.12:13-17.

[417] Borg and Crossan, *The Last Week...*, 63.

[418] Carter, *The Roman Empire and the New Testament...*, 28.

[419] D. Carr, *Re-Reading the Bible with New Eyes* (Bangalore: UTC, 2008), 72.

[420] Borg and Crossan, *The Last Week...*, 63f.

[421] D. T. Owen-Ball, "Rabbinic Rhetoric and the Tribute Passage (Mt. 22:15-22; Mk. 12:13-17; Lk. 20:20-26)," *Novum Testamentum* 35/1 (January, 1993): 5.

[422] John, "The Role of the State in Jesus' View..."..., 1f.

[423] *Ibid.,* 13.

[424] John, "The Role of the State in Jesus' View..."..., 4.

[425] Owen-Ball, "Rabbinic Rhetoric and the Tribute Passage..."..., 13f.

[426] Rom. 13:11-7.

[427] Carter, *The Roman Empire and the New Testament...*, 29.

[428] Lk. 21:5-24.

[429] 1 Macc. 1:20-50.

[430] Theissen, *The Gospels in Context...*, 157.

[431] *Ibid.*, 157-165.

Chapter - 4

Kingship Motif in the Passion and Resurrection Narratives

In the investigation of Lukan Infancy Narrative and the life and teachings of Jesus in the last two chapters, it was found that the Kingship motif either overtly or covertly pervades those narratives. As the Lukan socio-political world was longing to have an alternative King against the oppressive Roman emperor, Jesus was portrayed as the King as well, his teachings were recorded to exhibit his Kingly character in accommodating everyone under his Kingship. In the final stage of investigating the motif of Kingship in the composition of Luke, the Passion and Resurrection Narratives[1] are examined in this chapter.

Scholars generally accept that the Passion Narrative exposes the kingship of Jesus. But this chapter goes a step further to show that not only the Passion Narrative exposes the kingship of Jesus but also as the culmination of the motif of Kingship from the previous sections of Luke's Gospel. However, Luke maintains Jesus' Kingship as a mystery until his trial and death. It may be regarded as the skill of the author in disclosing this in the Triumphal entry that too in the voice of the people as King. In the investigation of the motif of Jesus' Kingship in the Passion and Resurrection Narratives of Luke, the important concerns are: Who was Jesus? Why did he die on the Roman Cross? Who killed Jesus? Whether the accusations against Jesus during the trial and its portrayals reveal him as the King? Why was he mocked at by the bystanders? Why was he charged contemptuously? Why should he accept the shameful death? Was he a Crucified King? How was he understood after his resurrection? etc. These issues are studied in this chapter under the headings, the Passion Narrative and the Resurrection Narrative.

PASSION NARRATIVE

M. Kähler, K. L. Schmidt and M. Dibelius consider the Passion Narratives of the Gospels as, "the first part of the gospel tradition to attain the form of a continuous or connected narrative."[2] R. Bultmann, W. Bussmann, V. Taylor and J. Jeremias also hold the same view along with their own varying nuances.[3] Particularly, the Passion Narrative, the core of the Gospels, according to Nickelsburg, is "the key that unlocks the significance of Jesus of Nazareth, revealing Kingship in death and divinity in the determination to accept human mortality."[4]

J. D. Crossan sees the Passion Narrative as a "prophecy historicized" instead of a "history remembered," since he could not locate any detailed historical information regarding Jesus' crucifixion.[5] While most of the historical critical scholars and New Testament theologians consider the formation of the Passion Narrative in the liturgical context or in the celebration of the Eucharist[6] of the early church where the history of crucifixion and the death of Jesus was remembered, Crossan's suggestion seems to be partly acceptable because of the inclusion of the prophecies along with history. So it can't be simply deserted as not history remembered. However, in this research, it is not the purpose to investigate the historicity of the Passion Narrative but the composition of Lukan Passion Narrative in line with the motif of Jesus' Kingship.

From Jesus' arrest onwards, all the four canonical Gospels recount the events in the same order: interrogation by the Sanhedrin, Roman Trial, release of Barabbas, crucifixion, death and burial. But, in the portrayal of Jesus' death, each one had their own independent views and perspectives. The Gospel of Mark portrays Jesus' Messianic status; Matthew, Jesus as the one who faces death by his own fate and prediction; John, Jesus as the true Lamb of God who takes away the sin; and Luke, Jesus as the one who faces death in accordance with the Father's will.[7] It seems that according to their redactional purposes, each evangelist adds, transposes and omits certain materials. In particular, Luke adds his special material of Jesus' trial before Herod, which is peculiar to his Gospel, and presents a different account of charge before Pilate[8] and the Sanhedrin trial.

The additions and alterations of Luke is viewed by J. Blinzler, Bultmann, J. M. Creed, Dibelius, J. Ginegan, H. J. Holtzmann, G. Iber, H. C. Kee, H. Lietzmann, R. H. Lightfoot, A. Loisy, G. Schneider, Fitzmyer, et al. as, modifying Markan Passion Narrative, Luke added materials from "L", and redacted according to his own theological motif.[9] But, E. Osty, J. A. Bailey, and F. L. Cribbs see Luke's prior knowledge of early form of Johannine tradition.[10] Taylor suggests that Luke might have derived the Passion Narrative from "an earlier non-Markan source or sources."[11] In all these suggestions, Luke's modification and addition of Mark seem to be viable because John's Gospel is dated later than Luke and scholars are of the view that John might have used Luke. Concerning the use of earlier form of Johannine tradition, one can't definitely say that Luke knew it. Taylor's view is also in question due to the unavailability of earlier non-Markan source. However, Luke's additions and alterations of materials in the Passion Narrative seem to expose his intention of portraying Jesus as an alternative King to the Roman Emperor. In this exploration of the Passion Narrative, each episode in it can be studied from the scene from the betrayal of Judas, who is depicted by Luke as Satan, presumably, Rome led him to do so.

Satan's Involvement in Judas' Betrayal: Implication of Rome

Satan's involvement in the Passion Narrative is unique to Luke. In 22:3f, Luke says, "Then Satan entered into Judas called Iscariot, who was one of the twelve; he went away and conferred with the chief priests and officers of the temple police about how he might betray him to them." It is vivid that the religious leaders conspire to kill Jesus due to the fear of his popularity and Judas joined them as Luke has already indicated him as a traitor in 6:16. But, the Lukan phrase, Εἰσῆλθεν δὲ Σατανᾶς εἰς Ἰούδαν, seems to indicate his compositional skill in depicting the Roman Emperor's part in the conspiracy.

According to Liddell and Scott, the noun Σατανᾶς means adversary, opponent, the devil, and chief of the evil spirits.[12] Foerster, in his word study brings out that Σατανᾶς was understood from the Dead Sea Scrolls as the evil spirit; and in the Old Testament, in the book of Job, as one who has access to God; and later in the New Testament as he has access to God to accuse the disciples. But, in the temptation scenario Jesus overcomes the devil that had the power of this world. Moreover, Peter was addressed by Jesus as σατανᾶ as an appellative in the sense of an opponent. In 22:3, Jesus fight against Σατανᾶς.[13] It has to be considered whether Luke uses this noun to portray Jesus' opponent in the context of Lukan social world, the Roman emperor and Roman power with the imagery of Satan. It may be helpful to see it in comparison to John's usage of it in 13:2 & 27. John uses both terms, διάβολος[14] and Σατανᾶς respectively in these verses. In v. 2, "The devil had already put it into the heart of Judas..." and in v, 27, "Satan entered into him." By separating the same event into two and using two various nouns, it is vivid that John wanted to explain that the διάβολος induces him to work against the purpose of God and by using the term Σατανᾶς he indicates the act of Roman power on Judas. W. Carter, in relation to the temptation scenario of both Matthew and Luke's, says that the devil refers to as it has power over the world and world's empires symbolize the Roman throne which is under the control of the devil.[15] K. Yamazaki-Ransom says that in Luke, Satan is portrayed as the ruler of the worldly political system, which is corresponding to the Roman Empire.[16] According to Theissen, the expectation of Jesus' submission to the ruler of the earthly Kingdom matches to the prostration before Satan who has the power and authority to bestow Kingdoms, and to worship him.[17]

In line with the temptation scenario, it is obvious that in the socio-political world of Luke, the noun Σατανᾶς indicates the Roman Emperor.[18] However, after partaking in the Lord's Supper, Judas might have thought that only Roman power will last and Jesus' destiny is closer without having any opposing strength. So, his thought of survival under Roman power is indicated by John as Satan entered into Judas.

Matera describes Satan's entry into Judas and as a non human involvement in the passion.[19] Fitzmyer is of the view that the Romans are not responsible for Jesus' fate, instead a Satan-possessed disciple.[20] It is questionable because Fitzmyer's view might be due to the impact of the issue, who killed Jesus. But, when we look at it in line with Lukan composition, as it has been dealt already in the previous chapter regarding the temptation of Jesus in which Jesus could not be made submissive to Rome, in contrast to that the devil made Judas submissive to the Roman power. Besides, according to Luke, only after Jesus cleansed the Temple, they decided to kill him. As claiming the superiority of the Roman theology over the Temple, it may not be considered as either a non-human force or a Satan-possessed disciple, but the Roman power was against Jesus.

It may further be evidenced from the warning of Jesus to Peter in 22:31f, "Simon, Simon, listen! Satan has demanded to sift all of you like wheat, but I have prayed for you that your own faith may not fail…" Here, it is clear that the Roman power wanted to destabilize the Kingdom movement of Jesus along with his disciples. It is symbolic of Roman oppression and persecution. Money and temptations seem to symbolize the cheating pattern of Roman government against the Jewish expectation of deliverance through the Messiah. It is further explained by Luke during the arrest of Jesus in 22:53, "But this is your hour, and the power of darkness," to indicate the power of Roman rule.

During the last week of Jesus, the confrontation between the two Kingdoms continued.[21] Luke depicts Jesus as an opponent of the Roman Emperor. By and large, the usage of Satan instead of Rome is explained by S. Kim as, the Roman Empire is another embodiment of the reign of Satan, *Pax Augusta/Romana* was achieved through the military conquest and political suppression without any real peace.[22] But, he says, according to Luke, Jesus did not alter the political, economic, and social structures of that time for Israel's political freedom, economic prosperity, and social justice although he was critical of the evils of the Roman imperial system. Rather he formed a common good through the acts of exorcism, healing, forgiveness of sins, restoration of sinners, and relief to the poor.[23] In this, Kim might be thinking of a political counterpart like the secular Kings in view of the invasion. But, the fruit of Jesus' message and acts, as Kim interprets, the liberating act of Jesus which the people needed under a Kingly rule. This may be further seen in the event of his Last Supper.

Last Supper: a Farewell Discourse of a Royal Figure, Servant King

Like the other Synoptics, after the plot to kill Jesus, Luke narrates the event of the Feast of Unleavened Bread and identified it as Passover, which John views as the Last Supper.[24] Unlike Matthew and Mark, Luke's narration is longer and differs at many points. Luke parallels the deliverance of Israelites from the bondage of Egypt with Jesus' death as an act of salvation as it was foreshadowed in 9:28-36 at the event of transfiguration about his accomplishment in Jerusalem.[25] In 22:15f, which is peculiar to Luke alone, Jesus says, "I have eagerly desired to eat this Passover with you before I suffer; for I tell you, I will not eat it until it is fulfilled in the Kingdom of God." Matera expresses the view that Jesus is portrayed in this episode by Luke "as a prophetic and royal figure who delivers a Farewell Discourse to his chosen apostles," and considers Jesus as a royal figure since he confers on them his Kingdom.[26] While v. 30a describes the occurrence of the table-fellowship ἐν τῇ βασιλείᾳ of Jesus, v. 30b promises the position of the twelve disciples in that Kingdom with rich royal imagery of judging the twelve tribes of Israel.

The two references to the Kingdom[27] imply that death will not defeat Jesus. According to Scott, his death will effect the coming of God's Kingdom. Especially as it is a memorial stated by Luke, it is

the inauguration of a new covenant foreshadowing the banquet in
the Kingdom of God.[28] Luke's interpretation of the cup as a "new
covenant" reminds the promise of new life prophesied in Jer. 31:31 to
the house of Israel.[29] Moreover, Lukan supper as an institution as well
as Jesus' farewell discourse like several elements of the Old Testament
farewell discourses in which the hero determines his imminent death
and that follows,[30] indicates Luke's artistic composition along with his
motif of Jesus' Kingship in setting his final meal and farewell address
to his disciples in portraying his royal stature.

Moreover, this table-fellowship of Jesus with his disciples shows
his authority of prior knowledge as a prophet in pointing the house
for the meal as in the triumphal entry where he mentioned the colt.
In both events, Luke says that he sent two of his disciples and they
found as he said. In comparing the prophetic dealing of Jesus in both
these events it should be realized that Jesus' Kingship is disclosed in
both the events.

The Passover meal indicates the fulfillment of Jesus' Messianic
mission. According to J. B. Green, the Passover meal in Luke was a
necessity in accordance with the pre-determined purpose in line with
Lukan portrayal of Jesus' death as a matter of divine necessity.[31] Donald
Senior sees this as, "Death comes as no surprise for Jesus but as part
of his God-given mission, a fearful yet inevitable climax to a prophetic
destiny."[32] Besides, in 22:21-23, the prophecy of betrayal indicates Jesus'
knowledge of things related to his death. While sharing the supper,
in 22:19, against Matthew and Mark, Luke adds the words of Jesus
concerning the bread/body, "which is given for you" indicating the
vicarious aspect of his "body" in relation to his mercy and forgiveness.
It is a profound Christological revelation of Jesus in offering his body
for others. Fitzmyer sees here probably, a sacrificial nuance in it in
relation to the soteriological purpose in Luke.[33] Scott sees the meaning
of his death in the Passover meal.[34] The Passover meal indicates that
Jesus faces his death with the realization of Father's will in relation
to the saving act as he says in the prayer at the Mount of Olives.[35]

Along with the salvific significance of his death James Massey says, Jesus' self-giving act leads toward laying the foundation for a New Community.[36] However, it seems to be Lukan art of interpreting the fulfillment of the Davidic Kingdom in Jesus.

Luke's references to Βασιλεία in 22:30 implies Jesus as the King in line with the Old Testament understanding of Kingship in Israel under the ultimate authority of God against the Greco-Roman thought which was familiar to the contemporaries of Luke.[37] In 22:25, the use of the phrases, "King of the Gentiles," "lord it over,"[38] "those in authority" and "benefactors," indicate the pervasive power of Rome, but it is contrasted in Jesus' Kingship as he says in v 27 b, "But I am among you as one who serves." The titles saviour and benefactor are synonymous terms in the Hellenistic era used to denote "human deliverers-physicians, military commanders, and Kings."[39] Luke characterizes Jesus as the benefactor, which seems to be an antitype, the servant–benefactor since the title benefactor implies the tyranny of those who exercise oppressive power and authority.[40] In vv. 26-27, the concept of greatness in relation to Greco-Roman world is associated with monarchs and other benefactors. But, vv. 19f symbolizes Jesus' own life, who made the ultimate sacrifice and the service of the benefactor.[41] So, through an alternative model of ruling, Jesus grants the disciples to sit at his royal, eschatological table and a dominion by which they will exercise judgment, lordship and authority over Israel.

Noticeably, this event of the Lord's Supper seems to be a reversal motif of Luke in the context of the disciple's desire to be great and Jesus' response in humble service. Traditional roles of leadership and authority are interpreted into service by the servant benefactor King. Matera sees it as a "new meaning of discipleship" parallel to Mk. 10:41-45.[42] According to Scott, since Jesus claimed his Kingship through this royalty of service, Jesus the ideal King is supreme in true Kingly qualities, and suffers on behalf of others.[43] However, the event of the Last Supper and the event on the Mount Olives are sharper in Luke than in Mark/Matthew in portraying Jesus' royal stature.

Jesus' Prayer on the Mount of Olives and Violence

Jesus' prayer on the Mount of Olives[44] shows his strength in divine authority.[45] Instead of three times, in Matthew and Mark consecutively, Luke mentions the prayer only once emphatically. It seems that Luke intends to expose the difficult situation at the beginning as well at the end of prayer. In v. 40, Luke uses the phrase μὴ εἰσελθεῖν εἰς πειρασμόν, in addition to the triple tradition's use[46] at the end of prayer, indicating the tension of the disciples to the oppressive situation of Rome concerning their survival. This prayer of Jesus at the Mount of Olives indicates it is a Roman punishment albeit a divine plan. In vv. 43-44, Luke alone explains the angelic help to Jesus in his sorrow and distress albeit he omits the sorrow of Jesus regarding his death. But he portrays Jesus as the obedient Son of God in accepting the Father's will without portraying Jesus' agony as Mark and Matthew do. However, none of the emotional reactions are shown in Luke rather than Jesus urging his disciples to pray and his withdrawal from them for prayer.

In the Mount of Olives, passion leads to apostasy, whereas in the parable of the sower, in 8:5-15, temptation preludes apostasy. Although Luke mentions the disciples' siesta only once instead of three times as in Matthew and Mark, it seems that he implies the failure to pray led them to use the sword. But from the saying about the two swords in 22:35-38, which is a Lukan addition, Black suggests that Jesus follows the Hebrew tradition of holy war, although he was not a political Zealot but an apocalyptic Zealot.[47] It should be compared with the Q material in 12:51 = Mt. 10:34, where Luke alters Matthew's 'sword' as 'division.' So, it may possibly indicate the division between the Kingdom of God and Satan's or in other words, division between God's Kingdom and Roman rule. Sword normally implies violence. But in Luke, it differs in the contexts of both mission[48] and passion. In mission, the authority to overcome Satan is given, whereas in passion, security's need is marked. However, in the assault on the servant of the High Priest, Jesus stops his disciple by saying "No more of this," and cured the wounded. The healing of the servant is mentioned by Luke alone. While Mark is brief in stating this event of striking with the sword, Matthew says elaborately that Jesus said to the one who struck the ear of the slave of the high priest as, "Put your sword back into its place... Dou you think that I cannot appeal to my Father, and he will at once send me more than twelve legions of angels?"[49] It seems to reflect Jesus' temptation on the pinnacle of the temple in Q 4:10 = Mt. 4:6, as it has been noted in the previous chapter where Jesus refused it as he had no desire of a power-monger. Hence, in Luke, it is vivid that he omits Matthew's words and depicts him differently with his command as a King, "No more of this!" It clearly indicates Luke's composition of Jesus' Kingship with authority but at the same, as it has been noted earlier, it denotes his messianic act of forgiveness and healing of an opponent. Further Lukan art of depicting Jesus a King is also vivid in his interpretation of Jesus' betrayal and arrest by the ruling of "the power of darkness."

Betrayal and Arrest: The Power of Darkness

In 22:1-2, Luke begins the scene by introducing the impatience of the chief priests and the scribes to kill Jesus amidst their fear of people. Concerning the betrayal and arrest, although it is a shorter narrative than the other evangelists, Luke doesn't mention the reason why Judas kissed Jesus, but he points it out through Jesus' question, "Is it with a kiss that you are betraying the Son of Man?"[50] which portrays not only Jesus' authority over the whole scene[51] but also, implies Jesus' foreknowledge of Judas and his pretention as it was already mentioned by Jesus at the event of Last Supper. Brown terms it as "higher Christology."[52] However, we need to look at the various titles of Jesus used in this episode, which are recorded by the evangelists: Matthew and Mark, Master; Luke, Son of Man; and John, Jesus of Nazareth. Do these titles have any implications of messianic Kingship? Matthew and Mark's use of Master, Greek ῥαββι perhaps implies the earthly function of the Son of Man. John's use of Jesus of Nazareth shows an ordinary human being with Jesus' acceptance of ἐγώ ἐιμι, whereas, at the close of the episode in 18:11, the question of Jesus,

"Am I not to drink the cup that the Father has given me?" shows the acceptance of suffering and indicates his messianic function as a Son of Man. But, Luke straight away implies the messianic act through the title, Son of man.

In the scenario of arrest, Jesus' question to the chief priests, the officers of the temple police, and the elders who had come to seize him, "Have you come out with swords and clubs as if I were a bandit?"[53] indicates two things: 1) Jesus was considered by the authorities as an insurrectionist; and, 2) a negative question, which seems to be a literary device of Luke to prove it at the end. Moreover, Jesus' words in the following verse, "When I was with you day after day in the temple, you did not lay hands on me. But this is your hour, and the power of darkness!" indicates their effort of arresting Jesus due to the power and authority of Rome in considering him as an opponent King. It seems to be Luke's portrayal of their move for capturing a King with striking forces along with the crowd and Jesus' interpretation of it as the "power of darkness" while other evangelists depict it through Jesus' words as the fulfillment of the Scripture. So, Lukan emphasis on the Roman authority indicates Jesus as their political rival. The Roman terror and the issue of survival could further be seen in the context of Peter's denial.

Peter's Denial: Time of Tribulation and an Issue of Survival

Jesus warned about Peter's denial at the close of Lord's Supper.[54] This is a transposition of Luke against the Markan context of sayings about the immediate future of Jesus' disciples. Luke reverses the order of Mark: the arrest, trial, mockery and denial into arrest, denial, mockery and trial. 22:54-62 describes the event of Peter's denial in triple tradition. According to Fitzmyer, it is a redacted form of Mark 15:53f & 66-72, whereas K. H. Rengstorf, W. Grundmann, G. Klein, D. R. Catchpole, I. H. Marshall consider it as from L source.[55] It seems to be the modification of Luke from both Matthew and Mark by leaving out the curse of Peter while denying Jesus and portraying the incident in front of Jesus as he turns and looks while Peter denied the third time. Both Matthew and Mark depict that Peter moved from the presence of Jesus after the first denial and after the third time only Peter remembers what Jesus had foretold during the Last Supper. However, the staring of the servant girl, her declaration of Peter was with Jesus, and another two men's pointing of Peter as a Galilean indicate the political rivalry of Jesus' fans and the emperor's, and depict the terror of survival and the time of tribulation. In addition the Lukan special material between the prediction and Peter's denial, v. 31, points out that due to the inevitable state of annihilation, Jesus prayed for the disciples. Foerster points out it as Jesus' battle against Satan, the power of the world.[56] Luke depicts not only Jesus knew the issue of his disciple's survival but also the danger of their separation from Him by the oppression of Rome. As well, Luke's composition of depicting the mockery after the denial of Peter further exposes Jesus as an alternative King.

Mockery of Jesus: Indication of an Inferred King

In Mark, three different groups: the bystanders, priests and scribes mock at him; whereas, Luke has transposed it as the soldiers,[57] Herod,[58] rulers,[59] and a thief[60] who, according to Matera, symbolize the three strata of society: soldiers, rulers and criminals.[61] According to Luke, it seems that not only Romans, but with the intention of safeguarding their authority by Rome, the Jewish authorities too mock at Jesus. Conzelmann says, mockery is the last confirmation of Jesus' royal dignity.[62] In light of the method, *Anumana* proposed in Saiva Siddhantha, the scenario of the mockery of Jesus by soldiers, Herod, the rulers and a thief as "King," indicate that they have either seen or heard about the Kingly attitude of Jesus in his speech and actions earlier along with his Kingly authority. But, when they actually see a powerless, voiceless and suffering Jesus mocked as King, they possibly infer his Kingship and mock at him as per their prior knowledge. Hence, they confirm the prevailing notion of Jesus' Kingship.

Mockery by the Soldiers

By the mockery of soldiers, Luke portrays Jesus as a prophet. In 22:64, he says, "they also blindfolded him and kept asking him, 'Prophesy! Who is that struck you?' They kept heaping many other insults on him." The addition, "They kept heaping many other insults on him," in v 65 along with the triple tradition mockery of prophet indicates the soldiers' derision might have been from the popularity of Jesus, as a mighty prophet in deeds and words through his act of miracles, exorcism, teachings and expressions as it has been noted in the previous chapter. As per the tool of *anumana*, the mockery of the soldiers indicates the popularity of Jesus among the socio-political world of Luke as the messianic King who has the foreknowledge of the events.

In addition, Luke adds the mockery of the soldiers while Jesus was on the cross, "If you are the King of the Jews, save yourself!"[63] Instead of the bystanders' mockery as depicted by both Matthew and Mark, Luke mentions the soldiers. Their mockery indicates not only the helplessness of Jesus against the Roman power, but also the doubtful nature of the soldiers concerning Jesus' Kingship.

Mockery by the Rulers and Inscription

In 23:11, Luke by his special material states, "Even Herod with his soldiers treated him with contempt and mocked at him; then he put an elegant robe on him and sent him back to Pilate." It is one of the most significant passages to identify Jesus' Kingship. The Jewish King, Herod sarcastically made him a King by putting on him an elegant robe. In this mockery, although it is not explained, the robe of Jesus indicates him as a King who is a powerless opponent before Herod. In light of *anumana*, it is obvious that Herod did this since he had the image of Jesus as a King who was popular among the people.

In addition to Herod's mockery, in 23:35-38, Luke uses the term, ἄρχοντες, i.e., the rulers scoffed at Jesus while Matthew and Mark use the term, ἀρχιερεῖς, the temple priests. This modification of Luke as rulers seems to indicate that the temple priests mock at Jesus as rulers with the authority of Rome. They said, "He saved others; let him save himself if he is the Messiah of God, his Chosen One!"[64] Though the inability of saving himself is pointed by all the three Synoptics, in Luke, it gives meaning by his unselfish action immediately after the saving event of the repentant criminal. It is the place where again Jesus' Kingship is highlighted. However, in this derision, the Jewish rulers' anger on Jesus is explicit. Their hesitation to accept him as the anticipated Messianic King is vivid in their words and it seems that their words portray him as the Messianic King in accordance with *anumana*. Besides, by mentioning the mockers as the rulers only, Luke portrays their intolerance on Jesus' popularity and Messianic authority. Lukan addition of "Chosen One" which is already used by Luke in 9:35, the declaration of Jesus by the heavenly voice, again recalls his Messianic title.

Along with the derision on the cross by the soldiers, the inscription over the cross,[65] Ὁ βασιλεὺς τῶν Ἰουδαίων οὗτος declares Jesus as the King. These mockeries again in line with *anumana* indicate Jesus as the Messianic King as he was anticipated and considered so by the socio-political world of Luke. According to W. Horbury, not only the accusation but also the inscription over the cross portrays Jesus as: Who was he? And why did he die a shameful death on the cross?[66] Matera says that the inscription over the cross has a double function in itself by functioning as a tool to disclose the crucified Jesus as the King of the Jews and at the same time, a tool to instigate others to mock at Jesus.[67] According to P. Richardson, this title not only asserts Jesus' Lordship but also indicates his identification with the nation.[68] Theissen states that it reveals to the people that Jesus was executed as the King of the Jews, as the one who wanted to take hold of political power.[69] Creed comments that it is noted after, instead of before and as mockery, it formulates "a climax and a conclusion" that Jesus is the King of the Jews.[70] As Horbury, Matera, Richardson, Theissen, and Creed view the inscription over the cross, it portrays Jesus not as a mocking King of the Jews but as the real who was mocked by others. However, it is obvious that the mockeries in Lukan Passion

Narrative exhibit the skill of Lukan addition and transposition in his composition of his Gospel to establish the motif of Jesus' Kingship.

Mockery by the Criminal

In 23:39-43, we have the mockery of the criminal and the response of the repented one taken from L. The criminal's words, "Are you not the Messiah? Save yourself and us" seems to be in line with *anumana* as Luke portrays Jesus as the Messianic King. In composing the Passion Narrative along with this mockery, Luke concludes it with the addition of another criminal who rebukes the mocker as well attests Jesus as the Messianic King through his request to remember him in his Kingdom. On the whole, Luke's composition of mockery episodes seems to be confirming Jesus' Kingship as it was considered in the socio-political world of Luke. It could be further seen in the trial narrative.

Trial Narrative

While all the four Gospels record two trials of Jesus: the Sanhedrin trial and Pilate's, Luke narrates four trials including his own special material of Herod's trial and two trials of Pilate. J. Stalker classifies the trial before the Sanhedrin as ecclesiastical, and the trial before the Roman governor as civil.[71] But, for the sake of looking at the Kingship motif, it is dealt here in two sections: 1) Jewish trial, and 2) Roman trial.

Jewish Trial

The Jewish trial can be divided into two sections: i) Jesus before the Sanhedrin[72] and, ii) Jesus before Herod.[73]

Jesus before the Sanhedrin

Matthew and Mark record that the trial took place in the night and again the next morning.[74] But, Luke records that Jesus was arrested during the night and the trial took place only once, the next day. After the arrest, the whole night Jesus was under the custody of the soldiers and they were mocking him as a prophet. Next morning, they brought him to the council, the Sanhedrin at Jerusalem. As Stalker states it was an ecclesiological trial, presided over by the high priest who had authority over Judea. Like Mark, Luke doesn't mention the name of the high priest, but maintains that the whole council interrogated him. Matthew names the high priest as Caiaphas.[75] But, John mentions that Jesus was brought before Annas, the father-in-law of Caiaphas.[76] However, by mentioning the whole council, Luke is brief in his report about the Sanhedrin interrogation. He doesn't say anything about the false witnesses and the accusation of destroying the temple as in both Matthew and Mark.[77] Here, the question is why would Luke omit this temple issue? It appears, Luke avoids it not only to show Jesus' positive attitude towards the Temple but also to sharpen the messianic issue.

In this interrogation scenario of the triple tradition, there are subtle differences amidst similarity: in Matthew,[78] the high priest asks, "I put you under oath before the living God, tell us if you are the Messiah, the Son of God." Jesus responded to him, "You have said so." In Mark,[79] the high priest asks, "Are you the Messiah, the Son of the Blessed One?" Jesus responded to him, "I am." But, Luke[80] differs in presenting the interrogator who was not the high priest, but as the whole council asking Jesus, "If you are the Messiah, tell us." In addition, without affirming directly like both Matthew and Mark, Jesus responded to him, "If I tell you, you will not believe; and if I question you, you will not answer." This response of Jesus in Luke seems not only different than other Synoptics, but also shows, Luke's literary device in depicting Jesus as the King, Messiah.[81] However, their suspicion of Jesus' Messianic authority is confirmed by Jesus through his pessimistic answer which echoes 20:1-8, where the Jewish leaders become speechless in the context of challenging Jesus' authority. In John 10:24f, Jesus gives a similar response when the leaders want him to reveal whether he is the Messiah. But, the immediate context of John follows that Jesus exposes him as the Good Shepherd.

The Sanhedrin's question of his Messiahship, in a way, indicates the Jewish authorities' problem of identifying him as the King Messiah. It was probably not surprising that Jesus was not understood as the

Messianic King by the people during the trial and his death. But the early church and the evangelists realized it only after his resurrection.[82] Nevertheless, all the three Synoptics record Jesus' words, in continuation to his response regarding his eschatological position as, "But from now on the Son of Man will be seated at the right hand of the power of God."[83] In Matthew and Mark the high priest immediately stopped questioning and tore his robe and said it was blasphemy. But, in Luke, the council raised another pertinent Christological question, "Are you, then, the Son of God?"[84] It is from a special Lukan Source which seems to indicate Jesus as an alternative King. Even though it was related to the Jewish belief, it is comprehensible that the assembly doubted him as an alternative King with the political nuance through this question. These two Christological questions: "Are you the Messiah?" and, "Are you, then, the Son of God?"echo the angelic announcement to Mary in the Infancy Narrative, as in 1:32 & 35 concerning the birth of Jesus in the Davidic lineage and as Son of God; in 4:3 & 9 the recognition of Satan in the temptation event; in 3:22, the event of baptism; and, in 9:35 at the time of transfiguration. It again indicates the compositional skill of Luke from the beginning of the Gospel with the Kingship motif of Jesus. Matera says that in this, Jesus' royal character comes to a sharper focus.[85]

Besides, the response of Jesus to the question of his Sonship,[86] the peak issue in the trial of Jesus before the Sanhedrin, as per Luke, is σὺ εἶπας. On the basis of Greek, it indicates an affirmative answer. But its corresponding Aramaic word אֲמַרְתְּ by no means connotes a clear affirmation. It can be understood as; you say so, but not I.[87] It may be either a non-committal answer or an outright denial[88] because it connotes a false perception of Jesus as "divine man"[89] or as a national, political "King"[90] by using the title Son of God to him.[91] There are differences of opinion among scholars regarding this title. According to Green, Luke understands the suffering of Jesus as integral to Jesus' identity as Son of God.[92] According to Matera, Luke exposes the new position of Jesus' enthronement, and equates the title Son of God with Messiah.[93] However, it is apparent that through this issue of the title, along with its political nuance, the council brought him to Pilate to sentence him to death.

The political scene may be further understood from the right of Sanhedrin in sentencing one to death. According to Jn. 18:31, their words, "We are not permitted to put anyone to death" indicate their limitation of power in sentencing one to death. But, C. Guignebert points out from Juster's study on the 'Talmudic Texts with the New Testament,' that the Sanhedrin had the right to impose death penalty on Jews for religious offences.[94] In accordance with that, it seems that their intention was not only blaming him on religious offences but also accusing him as a revolutionary of Rome. S. G. F. Brandon says that Luke never mentions either the verdict of Sanhedrin or what they understood from the words of Jesus.[95] It could be perceived from their political accusations to the Roman governor in 23:2 & 5. Further, it may be understood from the other Jewish trial by Herod on the basis of Jesus' nationality.

Jesus before Herod

In 23:6-12, we find the special Lukan material Jesus standing before Herod. This indicates that Pilate sends Jesus to Herod and avoids judging Jesus by the accusation of the assembly at the cause of perverting the nation in forbiddance of paying taxes to the emperor. His claim of being the Messiah, a King stirring up people against the authorities by his teaching throughout Judea and Galilee comes to the fore.[96] According to Luke, since Jesus was a Galilean and Galilee was under Herod's jurisdiction, Pilate sends him to Herod. H. W. Hoehner says that Pilate had no obligation to send Jesus to Herod; rather it might be due to some diplomatic reason.[97] Talbert says that amidst the perplexity of Herod, Luke depicts the greatness of Jesus as one who performs signs, which is prophetic as well as Kingly in nature.[98] However, Luke portrays that Herod was glad to see Jesus for some sign from him. His longing to see Jesus reveals the royal secret of who sees whom. It seems that not as criminal but as equals they meet one another.

Another incident in 9:9 states that he was anxious to see Jesus. It may be out of fear regarding the talk of the resurrection of John the Baptist whom he beheaded, which implies the greatness of Jesus as a prophet. Moreover, in 13:31-33, Luke notes the warning of Pharisees regarding the opposition of Jesus from Herod Antipas,[99] who wanted to kill Jesus. It is noteworthy to see that Jesus was challenging Herod that he can't do anything because his death will be in accordance with the will of God. That is, as it was predetermined, he will be killed only in Jerusalem. Through Jesus' challenge, Luke portrays him as one who had authority to confront a King. The possibility is that only equals can do it. So it implies Jesus' Kingship.

The opposition of Herod previously to Jesus' ministry in Galilee is evident in the withdrawal of Jesus from Galilee when he heard the news of John the Baptist's death. According to Richardson, the withdrawal of Jesus from Galilee is to be safe away in the political dilemma.[100] Besides, the woe sayings in the travel narrative on Chorazin and Bethsaida mentioned in the Q passages 10:13 = Mt. 11:21; and, Capernaum in 10:15 = Mt. 11:23 evidence Jesus' withdrawal of ministry from Galilee, particularly, from the tetrarch Philip's and Antipas' territories. The withdrawal of Jesus raises the issue as to whether it was due to any political crisis. Luke says that these unrepentant cities had seen Jesus' mighty works and got sufficient time to repent but they do not. John 6:15 exposes that the people wanted to make Jesus as King in Philip's region, which is presumed as the time during the rivalry among Herod's children when Philip was the tetrarch and Antipas went to Rome seeking the crown.

In addition, Herod, being a Jew and a client King, promoted Rome since he ruled under Rome's grace.[101] Pontius Pilate was the governor of the Roman province of Judea at the time of Jesus' trial. It is the way the direct rule of Rome over Judea through the governors amidst the rule of tetrarchs, the client kings.[102] It is vivid in 20:20-26 that the Herodians attempted to trap Jesus on the issue of paying tax to Rome in order to hand him over to the governor. Roman tribute was imposed on Judea.

Considering the trial of Herod, it ends with the mockery of Jesus' Kingship. But, the trial indicates Jesus' acceptance of him as the messianic King through his silence. In all the dealings of Herod with Jesus it seems that Jesus was considered by Herod as his counterpart and so he sent him back to Pilate, the governor of Judea by mocking him as a King.

Roman Trial

Pilate's presence in Jerusalem at the time of the trial of Jesus was due to his official tour and not a coincidence.[103] On this occasion, two trial sessions before Pilate are recorded by Luke, while the other evangelists[104] record only one. The first session precedes the trial by Herod as recorded in 23:2-5, as it has been already seen that Jesus was accused due to political expediency: 1) he perverts the nation; 2) forbids the Jews to pay taxes to Caesar; and, 3) he calls himself the Messiah, the King. It is to be noted in line with Fitzmyer that except Luke no other evangelist gives the details of accusations, by which Luke presents Jesus as a political figure through the details of real political character.[105] According to Brandon, all these charges concerning political subversion indicate Jesus' revolutionary activity.[106] And to Green, the political implications of Jesus' mission surfaced in these charges.[107] He goes a step further and says that Jesus' message had indisputably crossed the Roman political order which was fundamentally a religious violation against the Roman empire-household instituted and validated by the gods, and was at political risk by this religio-political order.[108] For instance, in 6:35, "But love your enemies, do good, and lend, expecting nothing in return," as an alternative household undermines the ethics of Roman household by Caesar that "gifts brought with them expectations of reciprocity."[109] This shows the motive of Luke in portraying Jesus politically in contrast to Caesar. It is very much implicit in the accusations.

On the other hand, the political accusation by the crowd and chief priests, "He stirs up the people by teaching throughout all Judea, from Galilee where he began even to this place," indicates that he stirred up the people from Galilee to Judea. This refers to the scope of Jesus' ministry on the basis of Acts 5:37, that seemed to be a "hotbed of revolutionary activity" and highlights political overtones.[110] Along with this line of thought, it seems that Luke wisely composes this trial narrative by developing it through this issue to bring out the Christological significance of Jesus as a King. Besides, to avoid risk, he sends Jesus to the King Herod, who was in charge of Galilee.

Besides, the presentation of Pilate's question at once like the other evangelists also seem to be the author's design and purpose of composing the trial narrative in focusing on Jesus' Kingship. It should be noted here that all the four evangelists including Luke, in accord, record the enquiry of Pilate as, "Are you the King of the Jews?" But, in Lukan composition, while Luke gives the details of the three political charges on Jesus, among them Pilate picks up only this one. It implies that he also thought of Jesus as his rival. According to Roetzel, the proclamation of a Kingdom in the Gospels presumes a rival claimant, a King. It reflects Pilate's nervousness at the resistance movements.[111] Fitzmyer says that the question is out of Pilate's psychological background due to the multitude's shouting at the time of Jerusalem entry as, Blessed be the King; as well, possibly aroused due to his fear of Jesus as a rival of Rome.[112] The words of the chief priests to Pilate mentioned in Jn. 19:15, "We have no King but the emperor," conveys the political connotation of the title, "King of the Jews."

It may raise the issue of whether it refers to both the King of Israel and the King of the Jews.[113] The triple tradition again in accord, records the response of Jesus as, σὺ εἶπας. It indicates that Jesus doesn't reply directly. But, in John,[114] Jesus clarifies the source of Pilate's question and answers that his Kingship is not of this world. Pilate then concludes to tell him as, "So you are a King." To which Jesus responds again, "You say that I am a King." Jesus' response was a surprise to Pilate. Matthew and Mark record that Pilate wondered; whereas, Luke and John record that Pilate turned to the chief priests and the multitudes and said that he had found no crime in him.[115] Perhaps, Pilate may have intended to avoid judging Jesus and sentencing him to death.

In the second session of Pilate's trial,[116] Pilate called the chief priests, rulers and the people and said to them, "I have examined him in your presence and have not found this man guilty of any of your charges against him. Neither has Herod, for he sent him back to us. Indeed, he has done nothing to deserve death. I will therefore have him flogged and release him."[117] It seems that by using his L source, Luke declares the innocence of Jesus and goes on, continuing the Barabbas episode with others, but briefly.[118]

Though the Barabbas episode is laconic, Luke contrasts the character of Barabbas with Jesus by giving a description of Barabbas, "This was a man who had been put in prison for an insurrection that had taken place in the city, and for murder."[119] Here, Luke depicts Pilate's intention of releasing Jesus whereas, the crowd wanted to release Barabbas[120] and crucify Jesus.[121] Unlike other Synoptics, but like John,[122] thrice[123] Luke depicts Jesus' innocence declared by Pilate, which is clearly a Lukan composition,[124] and pronounces the alternate possibility of releasing Jesus by chastising. Bond comments that the Passion Narrative reaches its climax in Jesus' trial before Pilate itself, where the leaders as well as the people demanded his death by crucifixion.[125] In v.24, in fact it is stated that Pilate released Barabbas and handed over Jesus in accordance with the crowd's will, which is known as *coercitio*.[126]

The judgment of Pilate raises another issue whether the verdict was according to the will of the crowd or according to the will of God. According to Matera, Pilate neither condemns Jesus nor pronounces death sentence; rather, he delivers up Jesus to their will. It may be taken, on the other hand, as Pilate handed over Jesus to them according to God's will since the term παρέδωκεν means deliver up, refers to God's will for his Messiah.[127] Concerning the attitude of the people, Luke uses the term λαός with programmatic function in his composition. In 4:14f & 18:43, λαός praise God and in 21:38-22:2, they are depicted as a threat to the chief priests and the scribes in their plan to kill Jesus. Particularly, they are the ones who were amazed by his miracles and authoritative teaching. But at the end, Luke portrays them as demanding Jesus' death. This seems a twist in Lukan development that is reflected in his composition. D. P. Moessner says that λαός is a smaller group within the ὄχλος to whom Jesus was handed over for crucifixion.[128] However, it shows the scenario of the power of Rome and the change of mind in the people for their survival against the anticipated King Jesus.

Pertaining to the death sentence, D. C. Allison points out that it was "Pilate's decision to crucify Jesus, probably because he perceived him as a political pretender with the potential to stir unruly crowds."[129] But, it seems Luke exculpates Pilate as Matthew, but blames the Jews[130] as the cause for the crucifixion of Jesus. However, the anti–Jewish element concerning Jesus' death is a later development.[131] Matera says that since, as the Roman prefect, Pilate had the legal authority to award the Roman penalty of crucifixion Jesus was crucified under the Roman law by a distinctly Roman form of punishment. Therefore, the responsibility for the death of Jesus cannot be attributed to the historic people of Israel.[132] But, it can be attributed to the historic people of Rome.[133] However, it is obvious that Jesus was sentenced by Pilate because of political accusations; albeit, Pilate's part seems to be a pretension of not sentencing Jesus to death and of *coercitio* or the will of God.

Crucifixion of Jesus, the King

After Jesus was handed over to the people, they led him toward Golgotha, to a place called the Skull.[134] In this event along with all other evangelists, Luke mentions Simon of Cyrene, the one who carried Jesus' cross for him. Vv. 27-31, seems to be a special Lukan material and in that, Luke mentions the people of Jerusalem who accompanied him along with the mourning women. It seems to be another procession like the triumphal entry in which people declared him as King. Instead of people's declaration, in this procession Jesus' utterance of prophetic warning seem to show his courage in facing death as a King. Also the warning to the daughters of Jerusalem parallels the previous warnings in Luke in 11:49-50; 19:41-44 & 21:20-24. Jesus' words concerning Jerusalem's destruction indicate Roman invasion and Jesus' final words to the women calls people to change their mind and attitudes. It may be compared to the socio-political context of baptism as it has been noted in the previous chapter.

At Golgotha, they crucified Jesus along with the two criminals, one on his right and the other on his left. Luke's description of the two criminals reminds the prophecy mentioned by Jesus in 22:37 "For I tell you, this scripture must be fulfilled in me, 'And he was counted among the lawless'..." It indicates that Jesus was crucified with them as a political rebel.

Moreover, if Jesus was only a religious rebel, he need not have been executed by crucifixion. Crucifixion was a Roman punishment practised against criminals, political rebels, and slaves, and this particular mode of death was reserved for those who were observed as a threat to public order of Rome.[135] According to Josephus, crucifixion was "consummately a public affair" and "reserved by the Romans especially for those who resisted the authority of Roman occupation."[136] Jesus' execution by Pilate signifies Jesus as an anti-nationalist who had challenged the Jewish leaders who were controlled by Rome. According to Matera, the crucifixion of Jesus by the Romans primarily indicates that it was a religious-political punishment with the emphasis falling on the political side.[137] R. Bultmann opines that Jesus was accused as 'Messiah' and died due to political misunderstanding.[138] Therefore, Brown says, Pilate ordered Jesus to be executed because he was potentially a menace since people thought him as a messiah or King.[139] According to W. Carter, Jesus was crucified because he was a threat both to the Roman power and Roman Theology in Palestine.[140] J. Moltmann says that the political dimension of the Gospel can be viewed since Jesus was crucified as a 'rebel' "within a world in which religion and politics were inseparable."[141] In all these speculations, since Jesus was crucified by the Roman authority as well as in Roman Cross,[142] it can be considered that Jesus was crucified due to his political revolution.

However, in this event of crucifixion, three prayers are notable in Luke's Gospel, which are special to Luke alone: 1) The prayer of forgiveness; 2) The prayer of the co-crucified criminal; and, 3) The prayer of entrust.

Prayer of Forgiveness: A Heroic Action

Jesus' filial cry in 23:34, "Father, forgive them; for they do not know what they are doing," exhibits Jesus' offer of executioners' forgiveness as a heroic action in accordance with his teaching in 6:27 = Mt. 5:44 concerning the love for enemies. Due to Jewish enmity,[143] and the development of anti-Jewish trends, it was removed from some of the manuscripts like, P[75], ℵ, etc., in later centuries. Some other manuscripts however have this prayer. Besides, in the prayer on the Mount of Olives in 22:40-46, Jesus revealed his filial relationship which reveals him as the anticipated Messiah the King.

Prayer of the Co-crucified Criminal

Jesus' response to the prayer of the co-crucified bandit, in 23:42f "Jesus, remember me when you come into your Kingdom," and the words of granting permission as, "today you will be with me in Paradise," depict his exercise of Kingly power by forgiving his sins and granting paradise.[144] Danker says, "It is a declaration of amnesty, an imperial decree."[145] According to A. W. Zweip, the prayer of the co-crucified criminal expresses the certainty of Jesus' royal authority which continues beyond his death which is the hope of Jesus' Kingship at *parousia* and Jesus' decree denotes it as not a future one, but an instant act.[146] So, this prayer and granting of life in paradise shows Jesus' exalted status of Kingship in Lukan portrayal. On the other hand, the term, σήμερον in Lukan usage[147] also seems to have a sense of messianic salvation.

Prayer of Entrust

The cry of Jesus noted by both Matthew and Mark is omitted by Luke. Instead he adds the prayer of Jesus entrusting his spirit, "Father, into thy hands I commit my spirit!" Fitzmyer says that it points Jesus' "more-than-human condition."[148] Luke cites Psalm 31:5, "Father, into thy hands I place my spirit."[149] During the commendation, unnatural events are noted by the Synoptics: especially darkness, which came over the land. Luke's explanation of 'three hours of darkness' due to the failure of the sun[150] echoes Amos 8:9, where it is pronounced as the punishment for the covenant breakers, who cheat the poor. This kind of oracle is also found in Amos 5:18; Isa. 8:22; Joel 2:2; Zeph. 1:15 and Deut. 28:29.[151] Besides, Luke transposes the rending of the Temple curtain before the commendation of the spirit, while both Matthew and Mark place it after his death. According to Luke, after commending his spirit he died, where as Matthew and Mark depict that with the cry of forsakenness Jesus died.[152] It is clear that Luke depicts it in a royal manner after commending his spirit he died. As well it indicates Jesus' victory over death by handing over his spirit in the hands of God rather than in the hands of his enemies, as mentioned in 9:44; 18:32 & 24:7. Besides, Luke depicts Jesus as the Son of God by the prayer of commitment at the very moment of his death, by addressing God as Father.

Death of Jesus

The death of Jesus is briefly stated by all the evangelists, but it is considered as the basic source for reconstructing the life and purpose of the historical Jesus. According to Dibelius,

> On the border of the Roman Empire, in a small, inconsequential country of the East, and amongst a people of no importance in world politics, there appears a man with the announcement of an impending overturn of the world through the direct interposition of God. In God's name he addresses warnings, promises, and demands to his hearers; under God's commission he performs striking deeds, heals the sick, wins followers; he comes into conflict at the capital with the religious and political authorities and is executed.[153]

The entire scenario behind Jesus' death: the darkness over the earth, the rending of the Temple veil, the declaration of the centurion, the multitude beating their breasts and the witness by the crowds illumine the theological importance of Lukan death of Jesus. The death of Jesus, as the fulfillment of prophecies of the Old Testament[154] is the culmination of the plot surrounded by different units of events in the Passion Narrative of Luke,[155] and it became the key event that was significant in the living experiences of early Christianity.[156] However, according to the Gospels, by seeing Jesus' death, the centurion declares who he is. Both Matthew and Mark record that he declared, "Truly this man was the Son of God!"[157] But, Luke notes that he praised God and declared, "Certainly, this man was innocent." This incident related to the death of Jesus seems to give Luke's theological stand about Jesus' character and his relation to God and the purpose of his ministry, and so of the depiction of his Kingship.

Centurion's Declaration

The declaration of the centurion is one of the major concerns of the discussions in Lukan studies. From a linguistic approach, the demonstrative pronoun, οὗτος refers to the centurion's "perception" of Jesus, the manner in which he dies and the significance of the imperfect verb ἦν which underlines the status of Jesus during his death on the cross.[158] In general, the declaration shows the assessment of the centurion concerning the ontological issue, who is Jesus? through the observation of his function, 'What he did?' Nonetheless, his assessment, pregnant with indispensable meaning beyond his own comprehension, becomes the pinnacle point of the theology of Jesus' death in each Gospel either it is 'Truly, this man was the Son of God' exposed by both Matthew and Mark or 'Truly this man was innocent/righteous,' by Luke. As well, these two varied accounts of the centurion's confession in the Synoptics necessitate the investigation of its theological significance in line with the motif of Luke in modifying the other two Gospels' version.

Luke, from the very outset of his Gospel, points out that Jesus is the Son of God. In the Infancy Narrative, recorded in 1:32-35, Jesus is declared as the Messiah, the Son of God and David's royal descendant; in 2:10-11, his identity is revealed to the shepherds as Christ, the Saviour of the world; and in 2:25-38, Simeon recognized it. His mother's question to him at the age of 12 leads Jesus to speak of his divine sonship. Its climax is seen at the end of Jesus' second question: "Did you not know that I must be in my Father's house?"[159]

Talbert says that in the Infancy Narrative, Luke sees Jesus as the Son of God from his birth as well at his baptism as he shares his real humanity.[160] Mark Coleridge points out the use of the title, Son of God as an Indirect Christology.[161] According to him, it is a shift from theology to Christology and the Infancy Narrative becomes Christocentric.[162] It thus becomes a key title for Jesus throughout Luke's Gospel, shaped by various nuances.[163] While commenting on this title, Dunn says that the image of Jesus as 'the Son of God' is based on how he was regarded during his days.[164] According to Carr, it indicates both directly Jesus' divine origin and divine status, and indirectly as the real emperor.[165] E. Huntress says that the Jewish understanding of the Son of God depicts Jesus as the chosen of God and obedient in his service.[166] As it has been discussed in the previous chapter, it has political nuance.

When we look at the title, Son of God, during the first century CE, it was rooted in ancient oriental religions, in which all Kings were thought to be begotten of gods.[167] In Hellenism, one who possessed some kind of divine power was called θειος ἀνὴρ.[168] It was used for Philosophers and some legendary heroes of Greek myths. In Egypt, Kings were considered as sons of God.[169] In the Roman world too, it was used of rulers. Also, it was often applied to mythical heroes, and historical persons.[170] In the Roman rule, the title θεοῦ υἱός was used for Augustus. As per the Roman imperial theology, the emperor was addressed as the Son of God.[171] So, in the socio-political world of Luke, it seems that they were familiar with the title Son of God and associated it with its political/divine connotations to Jesus the Kingly Messiah.

In Judaism, the title, son of God was used of angels or heavenly beings;[172] to Israel;[173] and to the King.[174] Since this title, Son of God was used in early Christian preaching, it raises the issue, what did the early Christians understand by it when they used it for Jesus? In 2 Sam. 7:14 and the Royal Psalm 2:7, it was a title adopted by a Davidic King.

It shows its roots in the Assyrian royal mythology, but was taken into the Yahwistic theology of Israel. But it differs from the Egyptian royal ideology,[175] in which Pharaoh the King was considered as a god or a divine being. Moreover, in Ex. 4:22b-23a & Hos. 11:1, Israel is spoken of with affection as the son of Yahweh. Even angels are referred to in Gen. 6:2 and Job 38:7, though it is a mythological title. However, this title implies divine favour, divine adoption, and divine power. Yet, in the Old Testament, it never indicates a future, expected Messianic nuance or, the title Son of God never appears in the Hebrew Bible. But, it has several connotations in the biblical world, referring to the King, and referred to the faithful Israelite.

W. G. Kümmel says that Son of God cannot be interpreted as a title for the Messiah at the time of Jesus since there is "not a single, sure piece of evidence" in pre-Christian Judaism to show that it was a messianic title.[176] But, A. V. Collins argues that in pre-Christian Judaism, in the Dead Sea Scrolls of the Qumran community, it was used as a Messianic title.[177] However, in the Lukan Infancy and Passion Narratives, the title, Son of God replicates Hellenistic or Roman background in terms of Jesus' Messiahship, and his function as an alternative King.

Cullmann sees the use of this title for Jesus as it expresses the historical and qualitative uniqueness of his relation to his Father.[178] Naganoolil along with Jeremias points out to Jesus' words as he reveals his filial relationship with God, whom he called the Father.[179] During the trial before the Sanhedrin, the response of Jesus, σὺ εἶπας signifies an affirmative answer.

According to Witherington, the centurion's declaration at the cross, as recorded in both Mark and Matthew, is "a conclusion drawn from Jesus' bravery even on the cross."[180] In Luke, the centurion's confession has not attained the Christological climax as in Mark, but it seems to be the last in the series of pronouncements of Jesus' innocence in line with Pilate's declaration thrice as recorded in 23:4, 14 & 22, and the affirmation of the criminal on the cross as recorded in 23:41. The centurion, by observing the manner of Jesus' death during the happenings of darkness, his prayers, and his conversation with the

criminal, affirms Jesus' innocence. It may raise the issue as to why
Luke replaces the centurion's declaration of both Mark and Matthew.
It seems that in the Lukan writing, there is no need for a confession
from a human centurion as it was needed in Mark, in which, the
messianic secret was disclosed by his declaration, where he is the first
human who perceived Jesus' true identity, which is revelatory through
his death. In Matthew, although the identity of Jesus was confessed
earlier as Christ and Son of God by his disciples, as it is accounted by
Matthew in 14:33 and 16:16, he narrates the centurion's declaration.
Luke drops the title, Son of God from the mouth of the centurion
but he introduces it in the story of the virgin birth, in the lineage
of David as well in Jesus' birth in the backdrop of Caesar Augustus.
Jesus is disclosed as the Son of God at the time of transfiguration. On
the other hand, Luke depicts Jesus as the Son of God by the prayers
of forgiveness and Commitment at the very moment of his death,
through Jesus who addressed God as Father. So, to Luke, there is no
need for a confession from a centurion as it was needed in Mark and
in Matthew.

Moreover, Luke's alteration of the title, Son of God to innocent/
righteous raises another pertinent issue: was it due to his fear/esteem
of Rome that the title 'Son of God' referred to the Roman Emperor?[181]
Or does it show the pro-Roman sentiment of Luke? As it seems to be
the final Roman verdict by the centurion,[182] Talbert explains it further,
as the final verdict for Rome because of his pro-Roman sentiment.[183]
It seems that through his declaration he may be blaming the people
for the atrocious death of Jesus by reiterating the verdict of the
Roman authorities, particularly, Pilate's handing over of Jesus in his
innocence to the people's will as an act of *coercitio*. But, J. A. Weatherly
doesn't agree fully with the pro-Roman sentiment of Luke, as other
scholars viewed it, that prima facie Luke places a certain degree of
responsibility on Herod, Pilate and his Roman soldiers.[184] However,
in line with the pro-Roman sentiment Luke might have been cautious
in using the title δίκαιος instead of Son of God when composing
the Passion Narrative.

In general, while J. Maleparampil, Kingsbury, H. M. Jackson, Cullman, and others see the cause of Jesus' death as messianic,[185] the centurion's declaration seems to have a political nuance. While the disciples of Jesus were with him afraid to declare him so due to the fear of Roman power, would a Gentile centurion, a praetorian for Pilate, and a low grade worker who represents the power of Rome at the execution, dare declare the divine Sonship of Jesus?[186] Was it not against the Roman emperor as well, the Roman theology? To understand this we need to know the connotation of the title used by Romans for their emperors or rulers and the Christian usage for Messiahship.

As it has been noted in chapter 1, according to 2 Sam. 7:14 and Psalm 2:7, sonship is a title of adoption for a Davidic King, which shows its roots in Assyrian royal mythology but differs from Egyptian royal ideology, in which, Pharaoh, the King was considered as a god or a divine being. If we look at the words of the centurion in both Matthew and Mark in terms of grammar,[187] there is no definite article before both the nouns, υιος and θεος. Its meaning without the definite article would have originally been "truly this was a divine man" i.e., a son of the gods in the Greco-Roman context,[188] whereas, M. D. Hooker says that it can be translated either, a son of God or the Son of God; and, the words in the mouth of a centurion could have only the lesser meaning. Mark might have interpreted at a higher level and as an expression of the truth about Jesus.[189] If so, can the declaration be meant as divine man, the emperor?

As it is a conclusion drawn from Jesus' bravery even on the cross,[190] it raises another related issue: was then, the bravery related to an emperor? According to Hooker, 'to a Roman centurion, 'Son of God' would perhaps have meant little more than 'a righteous man.' But, for Mark, his words seem the appropriate response to the death of Jesus to recognize him as Messiah, acknowledged as God's Son.[191] However, it would be viewed since Luke, as a pro-Roman who hesitates to use the title, Son of God along with the centurion for Jesus which refers to the Emperor probably has his own Christological implication in using different title for Jesus.

The declaration can be seen in view of the Roman history of that time, particularly, the anticipation of the people who suffered under the tyranny of Roman imperialism. This perhaps gives a new meaning to it that Jesus is the real emperor who suffers for the people instead of the paradoxical *Pax Romana*. For instance, the political scenario at the time of Jesus' death is portrayed in 23:1-5 through the charges framed against Jesus by the Jewish leaders that he is a revolutionary. Kurichianil comments that people expected a powerful King to re-establish the reign of David and a Messiah to set them free from their bondage of Rome, and a fierce messenger of Yahweh who would ruthlessly wipeout the wicked, as announced by the Baptist.[192] Amidst these socio-political backdrop, the alteration of Luke as δίκαιος seems to be more relevant to his composition of the Gospel with the motif of Jesus' Kingship.

What does δίκαιος mean? Fitzmyer remarks that the centurion would have meant δίκαιος as innocent.[193] Because, the innocence of Jesus had been declared by Herod Antipas, Pilate[194] and one of the criminals on the cross with Jesus,[195] as we see in the Lukan Passion Narrative. Some of the most influential modern translations[196] of the New Testament also support the translation of δίκαιος as innocent. Kilpatrick notices that the idea of innocence fits well into the general theme of Luke chapter 23.[197] W. J. Harrington and Danker also opt for the meaning 'innocent' because of the theme, innocence in Luke 23:4, 14-15, 22.[198] But, R. J. Karris, argues against it by pointing out the immediate context, in which Luke uses δικαίως in 23:41 and δίκαιος in 23:50, which mean respectively, 'justly' and 'righteous,' and questions how Luke suddenly narrowed down the meaning of δίκαιος in 23:47 to mean "innocent"?[199]

Brown prefers just instead of innocent. He argues that the semantic range of 'just' includes innocence.[200] Besides, there is a similarity between Lukan alternative of δίκαιος for Mark's υἱὸς θεοῦ. In Ps. 31:6, the allusion to Jesus' prayer of commending his spirit echoes Wis. 3:1, which says, "The souls of the just are in the hand of God," where, the wicked adversaries destroy the δίκαιος, the παις of God, by saying,

"If the just one [*dikaios*] is the son of God [*huios theou*], He will help him."[201] So, there is antecedence for the alternative use of δίκαιος to the Son of God in a complementary manner.

Liddell and Scott *Greek-English Lexicon* translates δίκαιος as observant of duty to gods and men, just, lawful etc.,[202] According to Matera, Luke uses the adjective δίκαιος throughout the Gospel, in its classical Old Testament sense: the man who fulfills his duties towards God, and in that sense the centurion uses it along with his praise of God, because Jesus accomplished the act of salvation according to the will of God.[203] Further, he argues that the centurion's proclamation of praise advocates the translation for δίκαιος as righteous, because Jesus has completed God's plan[204] and has right relationship with God in keeping God's covenant by practising Torah, the Mosaic Law. It could be evidenced from 1:6 & 2:25 that Zechariah, Elizabeth and Simeon are described as righteous Israelites. Besides, it indicates him as the righteous sufferer in accordance with the psalms.[205] D. Seccombe views it as Jesus' righteousness.[206] According to Talbert the declaration of the centurion in Luke highlights Jesus' vertical relationship with the father in his obedience and his horizontal relationship to the world.[207] However, in the context of crucifixion as a Roman punishment practised against criminals, political rebels, and slaves, the political charges during the trial seem to depict Lukan modification of the centurion's declaration as δίκαιος instead of the Son of God not only due to his pro-Roman sentiment in its historical, cultural, social, political and geographical milieu of the oppressive Kingdom but also, along with his motif, his portrayal of Jesus as the Saviour who has done things in accordance with the will of God in juxtaposition to the Emperor which well fits into the messianic characteristics of Jesus from the beginning of the Gospel.

Eventually, the verb δοξάζειν in Luke for praising God is used in other instances[208] along with the miraculous activity of Jesus. Particularly, two major events of Jesus' life: 1) at the beginning of the Gospel, at his birth the shepherds praised God;[209] and, 2) at the close of the Gospel, during his death the centurion praised God.[210] According to

Luke, the death of Jesus along with the miraculous events of darkness and rending of the temple veil made the centurion to praise God.

Rending of the Temple Veil

In Luke, the event, rending of the Temple veil at the moment of Jesus' death,[211] seems to be a proleptic warning[212] which to S. P. Matthew is an indication of the future destruction of the Temple as divine punishment.[213] According to Green, Luke portrays it as the end of the Temple as, "a sacred symbol of socio-religious power."[214] D. D. Sylva sees God's presence in the temple by comparing 23:45f, where Jesus commits his spirit, and Acts 7:55ff, the opening of the heavens while Stephen commits his spirit.[215] However, the event of tearing the temple curtain at the time of Jesus' death seems to signify the access of every one to the presence of God and in line with Green, it indicates the change of the socio-religious power exercised by Rome.[216] So, according to Luke's portrayal, it may be considered as a reversal act of God through the death of Jesus by symbolizing his Kingship as the plan of God in accordance with the Old Testament promise of a messianic King. However, this may raise the issue, whether the death of Jesus is a divine plan or a Roman punishment.

Jesus' Death as a Divine Plan or Roman Punishment

Luke seems to be accentuating the aspect of Jesus' death as the divine plan or the will of God. By pointing out both Luke's exclusion of Mk 10:45 and 15:34, and inclusion of Jesus' handing over his spirit to the Father in 23:46, Luke does not depict the work of Christ in terms of a sacrifice or atonement but rather, describes it as a pre-eminent act of obedience to the will of God.[217] Besides, the fulfillment of the Old Testament prophecies underlines the Lukan theme of the will of God. According to Fitzmyer, fulfillment in Luke seems to be not only the Old Testament promises but also the things to happen in accordance with God's plan, i.e. "the realization or accomplishment of it."[218] For instance, Jesus' prayer at the time of his sorrow that the will of the Father be done at the Mount of Olives clearly indicates the divine plan.[219] Over and above, Luke depicts Jesus' own understanding of his death through the expressions of the predetermined events. For instance, in 22:22, during the Passover, while foretelling Judas' betrayal, Jesus said, "For the Son of Man is going as it has been determined."

Besides, Jesus' passion predictions comprise Jesus' suffering and death within the divine plan. Luke's usage of impersonal verb δεῖ, seems to underline the inevitability of Jesus' death in accordance with the will of God. It is identified in his own passion predictions and its substantiations after resurrection: 9:22; 13:33; 17:25; 22:37; and 24:7, 26 & 44. It may, perhaps be understood, as the death of Jesus happened as *a* divine necessity. G. Keerankeri comments on it as an early Christian interpretation of the reversal picture of resurrection to transform the scared and dispirited disciples to make them understand his death as the necessity as well as the will of God in the plan of his salvation.[220] But, Kurichianil argues that since they belong to diverse stages of Jesus' ministry and have heard Jesus' words about the things to happen, it need not be considered as the creations of the early church.[221] However, Luke seems to emphasize the death on the cross as it served the divine plan. It can be understood from the Infancy Narrative of Luke as he presents the goal of the Father's plan being realized in the activity of Jesus in human history by addressing Jesus as the Saviour. Yet, it would be better to see how Jesus understands his death in accordance with the will of God.

Jesus' Understanding of his Death

Bultmann's skepticism of Jesus' own understanding of his death; Kessler's ambiguity of whether Jesus saw any special meaning in his death; and, P. Fiedler's evaluation of Jesus' teaching about the Kingdom of God with the concept of his atoning sacrificial death as incompatible,[222] lead us again toward the question, how far Jesus understood his own death in terms of salvation or the divine plan, the will of God. The report of the Theological Committee of the *Evangelischen Kirche der* Union suggests that the saving significance of Jesus' death is elucidated not only out of his death but also from his earthly life, which has been proclaimed by the Christian church as, "Christ paid with his own blood for our sins, redeemed us through his sacrifice, suffered for us the wrath of God, freed us from sin and every power of the devil; that substitution, satisfaction, and reconciliation occurred through Jesus' death."[223] But, Taylor, Karris and others say that Luke does not consider Jesus' death "as a sacrifice or an atoning work."[224] Thus the death of Jesus is always understood theologically. However, one cannot discard the fact that Jesus understood his redemptive work by his imminent death during his life time. There are three reasons: 1) If Jesus would not have understood his redemptive work through his death, why should he pray for the will of God to take place; 2) in 19:10, in the episode of Zacchaeus, he says that he has come to seek the lost and save; and 3) his passion predictions confirm that he understood fully the purpose of his life in this world as a human being. But, the prayer of Jesus at the Mount of Olives indicates it is a Roman punishment although it was a divine plan. In the human life of Jesus, one cannot deny the Roman opposition of Jesus and his teachings. However, it is obvious that Jesus understood his death in accordance with the will of God and divine necessity for the redemption of people and accepted it. Further, the death of Jesus on the cross is interpreted variedly by the scholars based on their theological understanding of it.

Death and Redemption

Scholars like Wilckens, Conzelmann, Käsemann and Dodd argue that Luke has failed to give a direct soteriological value to the death of Jesus.[225] Yet, there are indirect descriptions, which lead to soteriological thought. Kee says that Jesus' death has to be seen as a divine sign of deliverance.[226] For instance, as it has been noted earlier, Jesus' words of forgiveness from the cross in 23:34 and the immediate pronouncement of salvation to the penitent thief in 23:43 imply the soteriological ideology of Luke. Besides, Luke's narration of the crowds returning home by beating their breasts in 23:48 seems to be the action of repentance. Naturally, we may think that it is an action due to the impact of seeing a violent and immature death of a person. But,

Lagrange, A. Valensin, J. Huby[227] and Matera find a sign of repentance by comparing it to an earlier narration of Luke in 18:13, the story of the publican who was beating his breast with humility before God, and was justified. So, they argue that on the basis of Lukan usage of the same language in the earlier episode, the action authenticates the repentance of the crowd.[228]

There is a parallelism in both the contexts of the prayer of the tax collector; and, the praising of the centurion at the time of Jesus' death. In 18th chapter, the context of confession is the temple prayer setting; as well as in 23:48, the centurion's praise of God communicates the sign of a temple prayer accompanied by Jesus' last prayer. However, the death of Jesus in Luke leads to a theology of universal salvation. His salvific activity includes the extension of salvation to persons other than Israelites. Even though the priority of Israel is prominent, Luke depicts the inclusive nature of Jesus' intention of salvation to others by citing the Gentile centurion in 23:47, the crowd in representation of Israel in 23:48, and all his acquaintances including the women from Galilee in 23:49. Yet again, the earlier narration of Luke is more evident in this aspect of universal salvation design. For instance, Simeon's words about Jesus, as salvation is made ready for all people and the revelation for the nations in 2:30-32; the reference to the woman of Zareptah and the Syrian, Naaman immediately after the Nazareth manifesto in 4:25ff; Jesus' entry into the region of the Gerasenes in 8:26-39; the story of the Good Samaritan in 10:30ff; the cure of the ten lepers in 17:11ff etc., include not only an ethnic Israelite salvation, but also a wider perspective of Jesus' along with the salvation of a sinful man like Zacchaeus in 19:2ff, and a sinful woman in 7:36ff, and so on.

Nevertheless, it is conceived that the interpretative imagery of redemption begins from the words of Jesus about his body and blood during the Last Supper: "my body, which is given for you"; and "the new covenant with my blood, which is poured out for you."[229] Subsequently, the blood shedding of Jesus on the cross is viewed as the sacrifice for redemption by the early Christianity.[230] It is the supreme saving act through the innocent, divine victim.[231] By Jesus' words during the

Last Supper, R. Pesch emphasizes Jesus' own understanding of his death.[232] He explains it thus, "Jesus' understanding of his death as the offering of life for humanity is the highest expression of his certainty of God's will of salvation as well as of his self-understanding as the final messenger and mediator of the salvation of God."[233]

R. Kereszty points out, "The dual nature of sacrifice-obedient act and acknowledgment of sin-appears clearly in the Suffering Servant prophecies of Isaiah."[234] But Grundmann argues that the Lukan account of Jesus' death does not have a link with the Suffering Servant theology of expiation because of Luke's variance from Mark, which deals directly with the Suffering Servant of Isaiah.[235] Although, Luke omitted the concept of atonement, mentioned in Mark 10:45, he shows the death of Jesus as a redeeming act.

Death as Foiled Temptation of a "New Adam"

Another aspect of the significance of Lukan theology of Jesus' death is understood by scholars as Jesus, a New Adam,[236] who has overcome all the temptations even at the time of his cruel death. H. Flender points out how Luke consciously links the temptation story with the Passion Narrative[237] and depicts Jesus as the model of human victory over temptations in 22:28.[238] In Luke 4:1-13, Jesus is tempted by Satan in the wilderness, in 22:39-46, in the garden of Gethsemane, and finally in 23:32-49 along with the derisions while hanging on the cross. In 22:53, Jesus describes the context as the assault on the power of darkness. However, Satan's attacks against Jesus became futile.

Besides, Jesus is juxtaposed as the one, who obeyed the divine plan through his death and attained victory, to the disobedience and fall of Adam. Neyrey comments that the soteriological significance is ascribed to Jesus by the implicit portrayal of him as the New Adam albeit Luke doesn't present the death of Jesus as expiation, a ransom, or a sacrifice for sins.[239] Yet, by overcoming all the temptations, Jesus proved his unique relationship with the father by committing his spirit and this is in contrast to the estrangement of Adam from the fellowship of God in the Garden of Eden.

Garrett sees Jesus as a prophet like Moses, who led an exodus as well as the second Adam, who removed the curse.[240] Unlike Matthew,[241] who linked the temptation story with the Passion Narrative, Luke depicts Jesus in the lineage of Adam in 3:38. It shows Luke's theological motif of his Gospel in distinguishing Jesus from the first Adam. M. A. Powell sees it in terms of historical transformation. He says, "Luke presents Jesus as the new Adam in that he is the founder of a new period of history,"[242] by not succumbing to temptation by undermining Satan's dominion over the world. However, Jesus became the prototype in overcoming the temptation and even faced an atrocious death for the salvation of humanity as a martyr.

Death as Martyrdom

Dibelius is the pioneer in proposing the view that the death of Jesus in Luke is the story of a martyrdom.[243] There are three reasons for the prevalence of this idea among scholars: 1) Lukan exclusion of the substitutionary importance of the cross like the other Synoptics; 2) The absence of the view of a suffering Messiah in the Old Testament and in Jewish literature; and, 3) Lukan Passion Narrative retains some common themes parallel to Jewish traditions of martyrdom. Supernatural conflict, divine assistance, and the leitmotif of the innocence of the executed are examples.[244] The highlight of the agony in Luke centers around martyrdom. Thus the appearance of the angel in response to Jesus' prayer together with a description of his wrestling in prayer in 22:43f is considered as a typical experience of a martyr. But, there are differences between the martyrdom of Jesus and others. The Maccabean martyrs died for the law; the Zealots died to defend the sovereignty of the God of Israel; and, others died for certain causes. But, Jesus did not die for a cause but for the people.[245] Karris argues that the assistance of the angel in relation to the martyr's stories doesn't fit here because in Luke there is vagueness and the martyr's condemnation of the oppressors are missing.[246] Here, dying for the people in a political sense and the accusation of Jesus as a political insurgent seems to be the cause of liberation for the people from the tyrannous monarchy as the alternate King depicting a cause. So we cannot reject the idea of martyrdom in Lukan death of Jesus.

In general, Edwards strongly advocates Lukan episode of Jesus' death as the model for martyrs. He says, "In the calmness with which he faces death, it is plain that he is a model for potential martyrs in Luke's church."[247] Theissen and Merz also hold the same view of a model martyr but with a different supportive point that even at the moment of his death Jesus thinks of salvation of the human beings.[248] According to Talbert, Jesus' martyrdom had evangelistic benefits: 1) the conversion of the criminal on the cross; and, 2) a model for Stephen's martyrdom which is recorded in Acts 8.[249] Therefore, Powell places Jesus in the paradigm of the exemplary martyr since his exemplary character is exposed.[250] But Donahue postulates the paradigm of the innocent martyr because Jesus' innocence was proclaimed by Pilate, Herod, one of the criminals at the cross, and the centurion.[251]

Similarly, the paradigm of the prophet martyr is also applicable to Jesus' death. Talbert identifies two parallel streams of martyrdom from ancient Judaism and Greco-Roman milieu: 1) the prophets dying as martyrs at the hands of God's people; and, 2) the faithful among God's people dying as martyrs at the hands of the Gentiles.[252] In Luke's Gospel the evangelist ascribes to Jesus the character of a prophet: the prophetic action in cleansing the temple in 19:43-46; the prophetic vision about the place of the Passover meal in 22:12; his departure in 22:16&18; his betrayal in 22:21f; Peter's denial in 22:34; his words before the Sanhedrin about his glory at the right hand of the power of God in 22:69; and *passim*.

On the other hand, the significance of the death of Jesus as martyrdom is questioned in recent years. H. Thielecke says, "Jesus did not die a martyr's death, as radiant Stephen, under a hail of stones, nor as the noble Socrates in scornfully superior resignation. Rather, his dying was with a helpless despairing cry in the most terrible isolation."[253] Although, Green says about the prevalence of the idea of martyrdom among scholars, his arguments against the view of martyrdom are also noteworthy: 1) if Luke portrays Jesus' martyrdom, how far were Jesus' disciples expected by Luke to follow Jesus' footprints. For instance, in Mk. 8:34, the command to take up the cross has been changed in Luke as an advice to a lifestyle, day by day, with not a reference to the impending persecution; and, 2) several essential details of martyr tales are missing in Luke, particularly, the details in the descriptions of the means of death. For instance, in 22:39-46, unlike the martyrs of Jewish literature, Luke presents Jesus as the one who struggles to face death. So, according to him, the concept of Jesus as a martyr fails to do justice to the richness of Luke's portrayal of Jesus' death.[254] Karris draws a parallel between Luke 22-23 and the martyrdom literature along with the schema of B. Beck[255] and finds it as vague and non-applicable. He puts forward the suggestion that Lukan Jesus is not a martyr because Lukan motif in the death of Jesus is to show Jesus' relationship with his Father in fulfilling his plan rather than martyrdom.[256] Nevertheless, C. P. Vogt points out the intention of Luke in portraying Jesus' death as a model to be imitated, in terms of his patience, compassion, and hope.[257] In a way, both the groups of scholars' argue for and against the view of martyrdom in comparison to the Greco-Roman backdrop. They may be right in their own way of understanding the Lukan death of Jesus. However, we cannot reject the idea of martyrdom in Lukan death of Jesus, which resembles some of the Greco- Roman elements of martyrdom albeit Luke's purpose shows that the death of Jesus took place not as a death of a martyr, but as a saviour King of the world. This is so according to the divine plan of his Father which Luke by his sources and theological composition exposes Jesus' death as an alternative King to Caesar.

Burial

The Burial event recorded by the four evangelists[258] agrees closely regarding the role of Joseph of Arimathea and the nature of the grave. Luke and John however, agree on the description of the tomb as "no one had yet been laid," which Mark omits but Matthew says, a new tomb as well Joseph's own tomb. "A rock-hewn tomb, where no one had ever been laid" illustrates the royal nature of Jesus' burial similar to his royal entry into Jerusalem on a colt on which no one sat. Not only

Luke's emphasis like John indicates the scenario of a royal burial, but also, his interpretation of Joseph as the one who was looking for the Kingdom of God as Mark indicates the consciousness of royalty in the burial of Jesus' body. Besides, Luke's picture of Joseph of Arimathea as a member of the council which might be the Sanhedrin, righteous and waiting for the Kingdom of God signifies Luke's compositional style of including the pious Israelites of the Infancy Narrative: Zechariah, Elizabeth, Simon and Anna, who observed the law and anticipated redemption. It is to be noted that Luke's addition of Joseph's dissent in crucifying Jesus also throws light on the Kingship of Jesus along with Joseph's anticipation of the Kingdom.

The Synoptics note the presence of women at Jesus' burial. By the group present at the time of burial, particularly the women from Galilee, Luke depicts the sympathy of the crowd toward Jesus amidst the issue of survival, albeit in Pilate's trial they are depicted as hostile to Jesus.[259] It indicates acceptance and pursuance of Jesus by his followers till his burial as their King, as depicted by Luke in the triumphal entry. However, Luke's burial sequence and the added reference to the role of Galilean women involving the preparation of spices and ointments, their rest on the Sabbath day, and witnessing the empty tomb on the event of Sunday seem to be the unique composition of Luke to denote the victory of the King in his resurrection.

RESURRECTION NARRATIVE

Many may say that the Resurrection Narrative is a myth and it cannot be accounted for as a historical event. However, our intention is to look at Jesus' Kingship motif of Luke in the composition of the Resurrection Narrative in his Gospel. So the Resurrection Narrative is taken here as a continuous event after the death of Jesus. Luke depicts the crucifixion as a stage toward victory and the resurrection. Chapter 24, the Resurrection Narrative, has five elements: the empty tomb;[260] appearance to the two, at Emmaus;[261] appearance to the eleven in Jerusalem;[262] commissioning;[263] and, ascension.[264] The scene of Jesus' ascension at the close of the Gospel of Luke, and the beginning of his second work, the Acts of the Apostles has the coronation of a King as of its central significance that seems to be in accordance with Philippians 2:6-11.

Massey considers the resurrection event as, "Mission accomplished and handed over to a community."[265] Massey may be correct in the observation of the continuing mission of Jesus. But, historically the Resurrection experience of the Lukan community could be seen in their declaration of "the Lord has risen"[266] which seems to expose the victory of Jesus over Roman power. According to N.T. Wright, by the resurrection of Jesus a new movement came to birth from the state of apparent defeat.[267] R. Williams says that by this apocalyptic act Jesus restored the hope of the people which was under dilemma by His death.[268] It may be defined as a resurrected experience of the community under the victorious Kingship of Jesus in those days.

Empty Tomb

The women who followed Jesus from Galilee became the witnesses of the empty tomb. The women from Galilee represent the continuity between the crucified Jesus, burial and the risen Lord as onlookers.[269] When they went to the tomb at the dawn of Sunday, they found the stone rolled away. Even though all the evangelists say about the event of the empty tomb, both Matthew and Mark say that an angel was inside the tomb; but Luke speaks of two men standing by them in detail and the body was not there. According to Schüssler Fiorenza and Rowan Williams, the empty tomb, an absense exposes that Jesus was not under the possession of a community but he is alive and continued his role for the oppressed community.[270] Besides, in v 6f, Luke reminds the fulfillment of prophecy that he has risen in accordance with his words, that he would be handed over to the sinful men and crucified and be risen on the third day. It seems to be a special material of Luke which indicates the resurrection of Jesus for the continuance of his Kingly functions. The women are depicted by Luke as the first to tell the resurrection event to others. Besides, he depicts that the apostles considered their witness as idle tales, perhaps, as it was unbelievable. However, in the patriarchal society, amidst the gender oppression during that time, Luke portrays the women as the witnesses of Jesus' resurrection. It shows the re-establishment of their position in the society by the life and death of Jesus. So, the event of Jesus' resurrection and Lukan way of portrayal of women depicts Jesus' Kingly position.

Fulfillment of Prophecies

Luke may be emphasizing here the fulfillment of the prophecies in terms of the three passion predictions concerning Jesus' resurrection in two places: "on the third day be raised"[271] and "on the third day he will rise again."[272] Besides, along with the reminding of the prophecy to the women in 24:7f, Luke adds the conversation of the risen Jesus with the two men on the way to Emmaus. From Jesus' conversation with them, mentioned in 24:26, "Was it not necessary that the Messiah should suffer these things and enter into his glory?" It is to be noted that Jesus himself expressed the fulfillment of his prophecy and scripture. However, in the prophecy-fulfillment, the death of Jesus seems to be the basis for the Messiah's entrance into glory albeit the emphasis is on the first part that the Messiah should suffer. Moreover, according to Danker, it is the climax of Luke's portrayal of Jesus through the lips of Cleopas that Jesus is "a prophet mighty in deed and word before God and all the people"[273] in juxtaposition to the political figures whose promises and their deeds are different.[274] Nevertheless, the table-fellowship with the two to at Emmaus[275] indicates his Kingly rule, as it has been already seen in Chapter III, which reveals him as the Lord.

Jesus is the Lord and Christ

After the angelic announcement to the shepherds, in which the birth of Jesus was announced as the Messiah, the Lord, the title ὁ κύριος to Jesus is used by Luke after his resurrection in 24:34 as a sign of proclaiming the victory of Jesus' followers. In Lukan composition of the Gospel, it seems to be deliberate as Jesus was declared as King in the triumphal entry procession by his fans. The title, ὁ χριστός is the post-Easter confession.[276] J. D. G. Dunn sees this post-Easter confession as an impact of Jesus' death and resurrection which transformed his followers to understand the Old Testament scriptures as an "Ongoing Revelation," in light of his Messiahship.[277] Zweip says, "Luke may have felt it appropriate to call the risen Lord 'the Lord Jesus' from resurrection onwards."[278] For the followers of Jesus what they heard during his life time and praised him as King during the triumphal entry procession was confirmed after his resurrection as they believed him as the Lord the alternative King to the Roman Emperor. However, while looking at the composition of the Gospel, it seems that Luke decisively portrays Jesus' Kingship by the titles, ὁ κύριος and ὁ χριστός through his resurrection and the witnesses, as proclaiming the victory, as it was later understood by the early church.

Commissioning and Ascension

At the end of Luke's Gospel, Jerusalem becomes the vantage point of apostolic proclamation of repentance and salvation.[279] Luke only gives the story of Ascension as a historical event in which Jesus was enthroned as a divine King whom the Israelites were anticipating, for instance, Simeon, Anna, Joseph of Arimathea, etc., According to Leaney, by the ascension episode, Luke portrays Jesus as not only the King of Israel, but also as King of the universe.[280] In Acts 17:7, it is told that the risen Lord was considered by the early church as an alternative King of Caesar. According to J. M. Sheridan, the proleptic proclamation of Jesus' Kingship in the Infancy Narrative was recognized and proclaimed after Jesus' resurrection.[281] According to B. J. Malina, the post-resurrection praise of Jesus made obvious to the world about what he did, and he became the community's central symbol of renewal,[282] which seems to be Luke's portrayal of Jesus as King.

Jesus' Kingship is well exposed in the scene of ascension as it marks the enthronement of the divinely chosen messiah-King who fulfills Israel's hopes.[283] It is neither a military action nor an armed deliverance from Rome by exercising power over others.[284] According to R. W. L. Moberly, Jesus is depicted paradoxically as a suffering King who exercises his power through service and sacrifice. Ultimately, his resurrection shows his royalty.[285] In Luke, it could be noticed well that Jesus is shown as a servant King who suffers for the betterment of people. So, along with the expectation of the people who suffered under the tyranny of Roman imperialism, the Kingship of Jesus after ascension perhaps gives a new meaning that Jesus is the real emperor who had suffered and rules for ever for the people instead of *Pax Romana*.

In commissioning the mission of the Twelve, as already seen in the event of the Last Supper in 22:14-30, in which the Kingdom is promised to them, Luke seems to reveal Jesus' Kingship at the end by extending his role to his disciples to proclaim the good news of repentance and forgiveness which are the basic elements in entering into the alternative Kingdom in the socio-political world of Luke.

Summary

In exploring the passion and Resurrection Narratives of the Gospel, one notices the skill of the author in composing the gospel aiming at the culmination of the motif of Jesus' Kingship at the close of the Gospel. His additions and alterations of materials in the narratives seem to expose his intention of portraying Jesus as an alternative King to the Roman Emperor. The special Lukan element portraying Satan's involvement in the conspiracy and betrayal scene depicts Judas' submissiveness to the Roman power by the phrase, εἰσῆλθεν δὲ Σατανᾶς εἰς Ἰούδαν. It further seems to indicate Luke's compositional skill in depicting the Roman Emperor's part in the conspiracy in contrast to the temptation of Jesus in which Jesus could not be made submissive to Rome. From Judas' betrayal, warning of Jesus to Peter in 22:31, and, during Jesus' arrest in 22:53, the use of money and temptations seem to symbolize the power of Roman government. It may be the confrontation between the two Kingdoms of Rome and God's.

The event of the Last Supper seems to expose Lukan artistic composition along with his motif of Jesus' Kingship in setting his final meal and farewell address to his disciples to mark the Kingdom and the Kingship of Jesus as not by rule but by service.

Although, Jesus' prayer on the Mount of Olives shows his strength in divine authority, the Lukan phrase, μὴ εἰσελθεῖν εἰς πειρασμόν of Jesus' words to his disciples indicate the oppressive situation of Rome concerning their survival. The event of striking the ear of the slave of the high priest exposes him as a King not only by his command but also by his healing with the Kingly messianic act of forgiveness. The question during his arrest, "Have you come out with swords and clubs as if I were a bandit? indicates Jesus as an insurrectionist. Jesus' words during that time, "This is your hour, and the power of darkness!" indicate his arrest due to the power and authority of Rome in considering him as an opponent King.

The additions and transposition of mockeries exhibit the skill of Lukan composition of the Gospel in establishing the motif of Jesus' Kingship. Mockery seems to be the final act in the confirmation of Jesus' royal dignity. Herod's mockery with an elegant robe, mockery of the soldiers, inscription over the cross, and the Lukan addition of criminal who rebukes the mocker with requisition of remembrance in Jesus' kingdom, depict the crucified Jesus, as the King of the Jews.

In the Sanhedrin trial, Luke sharpens the Messianic issue through the whole council by asking Jesus, "If you are the Messiah, tell us." It shows their doubt in accepting Jesus as the King Messiah and by the indirect response of Jesus. The council's another pertinent Christological question, "Are you, then, the Son of God?" seems to indicate Jesus as an alternative King in juxtaposition to Caesar. It indicates the compositional skill of Luke from the beginning of the Gospel to the Passion Narrative with the Kingship motif of Jesus: the angelic annunciation to Mary in the Infancy Narrative, in 1:32 & 35, concerning the birth of Jesus in the Davidic lineage and as Son of God; in 4:3 & 9 by the recognition of Satan in the temptation event; in 3:22, the event of baptism; and, in 9:35 at the time of transfiguration. Sanhedrin's appeal to the trial of Pilate indicates their political offence which they had imposed on Jesus. Lukan addition of Herod's trial indicates the political accusations including his deeds and words on the ground of Jesus' nationality and the ministry in Galilee and its challenge to Herod's rule as a counterpart. Lukan portrayal of the accusation of political expediency reveals the revolutionary activity of Jesus along with his fundamental teachings which was against the Roman Empire and its household. However, amidst the three charges, Pilate's question, "Are you the King of the Jews?" signifies the thrust of all the accusations as, Jesus is charged as the King of the Jews against the Roman emperor. The claim for releasing Barabbas depicts the people's mind for their survival under Roman power.

Jesus' death as King through crucifixion makes him an antinationalist of Rome. The prayer of forgiveness and the granting of Paradise to the co-crucified criminal indicate his heroic action and messianic Kingship respectively. By entrusting his spirit, Luke depicts his royal manner of death by handing over his spirit to God than to his enemies. The modification of centurion's declaration by Luke unlike both Matthew and Mark as δίκαιος, indicates the centurion's fear about the power of Rome, but it has the political nuance of Jesus as the saviour who has done things in accordance with the will of God in juxtaposition to the Roman Emperor.

The rending of the Temple veil, according to Luke, indicates the change of the socio-religious power exercised by Rome, and his death in accordance with the Old Testament prophecies for the redemption of the people. Jesus' death happened according to Lukan composition not only in accordance with the will of God and divine necessity for the redemption of the people, but also as Jesus himself understood it as necessary. The significance of his death as portrayed by Luke is considered variously by scholars as he died as a redeemer of the whole universe, a prophet, the new Adam, a martyr, etc., as it is acknowledged in the statement of the problem in this research. But, along with these theological thoughts, this research identifies that amidst the political realities of that time, the accusation of Jesus as a political insurgent and his death according to Lukan composition seem to depict him as the one who was crucified and died as a King since he was an alternative King to Caesar through his reversal teachings and deeds against the tyranny of the Roman Empire.

The burial scene not only indicates Jesus' royalty, as Joseph of Arimathea a member of the council provides him with a new tomb; but also, depicting him as righteous and waiting for the Kingdom of God in line with the Lukan compositional style. Further, in line with that, the pious Israelites in the Infancy Narrative, Zechariah, Elizabeth, Simon and Anna, who observed the law and anticipated redemption in Jesus. It is to be noted that Lukan addition of Joseph's disagreement[286] of crucifying Jesus also throws light on the Kingship of Jesus along with his anticipation of the Messianic Kingdom. The presence of the women at the time of the burial, particularly the women from Galilee, indicate the fan of Jesus' acceptance and pursuance of Jesus till his burial as their King by his followers as depicted by Luke in the triumphal entry.

Lukan reference to the role of the Galilean women witnessing the empty tomb on Sunday seems to be indicate the compositional skill of Luke to denote the victory of the King through his resurrection as well as the re-establishment of their status in the society. Lukan composition of the Resurrection Narrative seems to indicate the Kingship of Jesus, which is portrayed in the resurrection experience of the Lukan community with the declaration of the Lord has risen. It reveals the victory of Jesus against the Roman power, the opponent that crucified him. The Lukan material describing the two to Emmaus reveals the idea of Jesus' disciples before his death about him as 'a mighty in word and deed before God and all the people,' juxtaposing him against the political figures whose promises and deeds oscillate. Further, in the composition of the Gospel, as Luke portrayed Jesus as the Messiah as Lord by the angel at the outset in the Infancy Narrative, the same is confirmed at the close after the event of resurrection by Jesus' followers, the Lukan community.

In commissioning the twelve too, Luke reveals Jesus' Kingship by extending his role to his disciples to proclaim the good news of repentance and forgiveness, which are the basic elements of entering into the alternative Kingdom, in the socio-political world of Luke. Finally, Luke by his story of Ascension as a historical event depicts Jesus enthroned as a divine King whom the Israelites were anticipating. Perhaps, Luke gives a new meaning that Jesus is the real emperor who suffers and rules for ever over the people as a risen Lord instead of *Pax Romana*. It may be seen in his second book, the Acts of the Apostles in 17:7, how the risen Lord was considered by the early church as an alternative King to Caesar.

Endnotes

[1] Lk. 22-24; The events of Jesus' arrest, trial, crucifixion, death, burial, and resurrection are generally accounted as the Passion and Resurrection Narratives.

[2] J. A. Fitzmyer, *The Gospel According to Luke X-XXIV,* vol. 2 (New York: Doubleday, 1986), 1360.

[3] *Ibid.*

[4] G. W. E. Nickelsburg, "Passion Narratives," *The Anchor Bible Dictionary*, vol. 5, O-Sh, ed. by D. N. Freedmann (New York: Doubleday, 1972), 173.

[5] J. D. Crossan, *Who Killed Jesus? Exploring the Roots of Anti-Semitism in the Gospel Story of the Death of Jesus* (San Francisco: Harper Collins, 1995), 10 &139.

[6] J. B. Green, "Passion Narratives," *Dictionary of Jesus and the Gospels*, ed. by J. B. Green and S. McKnight (Illinois: Inter Varsity Press, 1992), 602.

[7] J. R. Donahue, "Passion Narrative," *The Interpreter's Dictionary of the Bible*, Supplementary Volume, ed. by K. Crim (Nashville: Abingdon, 1976), 644.

[8] Lk. 23:2.

[9] Fitzmyer, *The Gospel According to Luke X-XXIV...*, 1366.

[10] *Ibid.*

[11] V. Taylor, *The Passion Narrative of St. Luke: A Critical and Historical Investigation* (Cambridge: University Press, 1972), 119.

[12] H. G. Liddell and R. Scott, *A Greek-English Lexicon*, vol. II: λ-ᾠώδης, revised ed. (Oxford: Clarendon Press, 1940), 1585.

[13] Foerster, "σατανᾶς" in *Theological Dictionary of the New Testament Vol VII, Σ,* ed. by G. Friedrich and tr. by G.W. Bromiley (Grand Rapids: Wm. B. Eerdmans, 1971), 153ff.

[14] διάβολος means slanderer. In Es 7:4 & 8:1 of LXX, it is used as enemy. [H. G. Liddell and R. Scott, *A Greek-English Lexicon.* Vol I α-κώψ (Oxford: Clarendon Press, 1925),, 390.

[15] W. Carter, *The Roman Empire and the New Testament* (Nashville: Abingdon Press, 2006), 17.

[16] K.Yamazaki-Ransom, *The Roman Empire in Luke's Narrative* (New York: T&T Clark, 2010), 97.

[17] Theissen sees the historical evidence of these elements of mountain temptation in the person of Gaius Caligula and his conflict during CE 40 regarding the worship of God or idols, particularly the statue of Emperor. [G. Theissen, *The Gospels in Context: Social and Political History in the Synoptic Tradition,* tr. by L. M. Maloney (Edinburgh: T&T Clark, 1992), 207f.]

[18] Lk. 22:2f.

[19] F. J. Matera, *Passion Narratives and Gospel Theologies: Interpreting the Synoptics Through Their Passion Stories* (New York: Paulist Press, 1986), 158.

[20] Fitzmyer, *The Gospel According to Luke X-XXIV...,* 1367.

[21] M. Borg and J. D. Crossan, *The Last Week: What the Gospels really teach about Jesus' Final Days in Jerusalem* (London: SPCK, 2008), 5.

[22] S. Kim, *Christ and Caesar* (Grand Rapids: William B. Eerdmans, 2008), 191.

[23] *Ibid.,* 147.

[24] The Feast of the Unleavened Bread was celebrated for seven days in continuation to the festival of Passover to recall the event of Exodus (Ex. 23:15; 34:18). Even though these two festivals are distinct, Luke merged them together to denote the death of Jesus during the time of recalling the national liberation. [Matera, *Passion Narratives and Gospel Theologies...,* 156.]

[25] *Ibid.*

[26] *Ibid.,* 190.

[27] Lk. 22:16 & 30.

[28] E. F. Scott, *The Kingdom and the Messiah* (Edinburgh: T&T Clark, 1911), 235-238.

[29] Both Matthew and Mark refer to the blood of covenant which reminds Ex. 24:8.

[30] Jacob in Gen. 47:29-49:33; Joshua in Jos. 23:1-24:30; David in 1 Kgs. 2:1-10 etc.,

[31] J. B. Green says that the divine necessity theme is widespread throughout the Gospel and Acts: Lk. 9:22; 13:33; 22:22, 37; 24:7, 26, 44; Acts 1:16; 17:2f; et al. [J. B. Green, "Preparation for Passover (Luke 22:7-13): A Question of Redactional Technique," *Novum Testamentum* 29/4 (1987): 312.]

[32] D. Senior, C.P., *The Passion of Jesus in the Gospel of Luke* (Wilmington: Michael Glazier, 1989), 17.

[33] Fitzmyer, *The Gospel According to Luke X-XXIV...*, 1391.

[34] Scott, *The Kingdom and the Messiah...*, 236.

[35] Lk. 22:39-46.

[36] J. Massey, *The Gospel According to Luke*, Dalit Bible Commentary, New Testament vol. 3 (New Delhi: Centre for Dalit /Subaltern Studies, 2007), 205.

[37] P. K. Nelson, *Leadership and Discipleship: A Study of Luke 22:24-30* (Atlanta: Scholars Press, 1994), 34.

[38] Cf. Mk. 10:42.

[39] C. J. Roetzel, *The World that Shaped the New Testament* (Atlanta: John Knox Press, 1985), 76.

[40] D. J. Lull, "The Servant-Benefactor as a Model of Greatness (Luke 22:24-30)," *Novum Testamentum* 28/4 (1986): 289.

[41] *Ibid.*, 294 &298f.

[42] Matera, *Passion Narratives and Gospel Theologies...*, 164.

[43] Scott, *The Kingdom and the Messiah...*, 183 & 226.

[44] Matera on the basis of 2 Sam. 15:30-32 points out the Mount of Olives as a place of worship where David went and wept. In Zech. 14:4, the Mount is depicted as a location of future judgement. In Acts 1:6, the apostles on the Mount of Olives ask the Risen Jesus that whether he will establish the Kingdom of Israel at this time. [F. J. Matera, *The Kingship of Jesus: Composition and Theology in Mark 15* (USA: Scholars Press, 1982), 69.]

[45] Lk. 22:39-46; Mt. 26:36-46 & Mk. 14:32-42; Matera, *Passion Narratives and Gospel Theologies...*, 166.

[46] Mt. 26:38; Mk. 14:38 & Lk. 22:46.

[47] V. J. John, "The Role of the State in Jesus' View: A Synoptic Perspective," *Bangalore Theological Forum* 36/1 (June, 2004): 5.

[48] Lk. 10:17ff.

[49] Mt. 26:52f.

[50] Lk. 22:48.

[51] Fitzmyer, *The Gospel According to Luke X-XXIV...*, 1447.

[52] Brown, *The Death of the Messiah*, vol. 1..., 69.

[53] Lk. 22:52.

[54] Lk. 22:31-34.

[55] Fitzmyer, *The Gospel According to Luke X-XXIV...*, 1456.

[56] Foerster, "σατανᾶς"in *Theological Dictionary of the New Testament...*, 158.

[57] Lk. 22:63-65.

[58] Lk. 23:11.

[59] Lk. 23:35-38.

[60] Lk. 23:39-43.

[61] Matera, *Passion Narratives and Gospel Theologies...*, 184.

[62] H. Conzelmann, "History and Theology in the Passion Narratives of the Synoptic Gospels," *Interpretation* 24/2 (April 1970): 191.

[63] Lk. 23:37.

[64] Lk. 23:35.

[65] Lk. 23:38.

[66] W. Horbury, "The Passion Narratives and Historical Criticism," *Theology* 75/620 (February, 1972): 59.

[67] Matera, *The Kingship of Jesus: Composition and Theology in Mark 15...*, 45.

[68] P. Richardson, "The Israel-idea in the Passion Narratives," in *The Trial of Jesus,* ed. by E. Bammel (London: SCM Press, 1970), 7.

[69] G. Theissen and A. Merz, *The Historical Jesus* (London: SCM Press Ltd, 1998), 458.

[70] J. M. Creed, *The Gospel According to St. Luke* (London: Macmillan and Co., 1930), 284.

[71] J. Stalker, *The Trial and Death of Jesus Christ* (Grand Rapids: Zondervan, 1983), 18.

[72] Lk. 22:54-71.

[73] Lk. 23:6-12.

[74] Mt. 26:69-77; 27:1-2 & Mk. 14:66-72 & 15:1.

[75] Mt. 26:57.

[76] Jn.18:13.

[77] Mt. 26:62 & Mk 14:60.

[78] Mt. 26:63.

[79] Mk. 14:61f.

[80] Lk. 22:67f.

[81] To the question of the high priest whether Jesus was the Son of God, Jesus' reply was, "you will see the Son of Man seated at the right hand of power" (Lk. 22: 69. cf. Mt. 26:64 & Mk. 14:62). It is the reference from the Old Testament passages in Dan. 7:13 and Ps.110:1. But, Luke omits the phrase, "coming on the clouds of heaven." According to Cullmann, 'sitting at the right hand' is related to the thought of the priest-King after Melchizedek. (O. Cullmann, *The Christology of the New Testament* (London: SCM Press Ltd, 1963), 88). But in the Passion Narratives, it extends the work of the Son of Man as the divine Judge in a visionary language. M. S. Johnson says that the language about the coming Son of Man depicts the final scenario of human salvation with the supreme authority of Jesus. [M. S. Johnson, *Christology: Biblical and Historical* (New Delhi: Mittal Publications, 2005), 53.]; N. A. Dhal says that Jesus uses the title, *Son of Man* instead of the title Messiah for himself. [N. A. Dahl, *The Crucified Messiah* (Minneapolis: Augsburg, 1974), 31.]

[82] Although the Christian church recognized Jesus' Messiahship, it was never understood by those who crucified him. The Roman charge that Jesus claimed himself as the "King of the Jews" seems equivalent to the saying that he was a political insurgent. Moreover, the fact that Jesus was crucified between two political rebels is a further indication that the Romans viewed Jesus as a revolutionary and a royal pretender. [F. J. Matera, "The Trial of Jesus: Problems and Proposals," *Interpretation*.45/1 (January, 1991): 12].

[83] Lk. 22:69; cf: Mt. 26:64 & Mk. 14:62. Both Matthew and Mark add the phrase "coming on the clouds of heaven."

[84] Lk. 22:70.

[85] Matera, *Passion Narratives and Gospel Theologies*..., 190.

[86] Mt. 26:57-68; Mk. 14:53-65; Lk. 22:54-71 & Jn. 18:13-24.

[87] We cannot absolutely be certain that the exact Aramaic equivalent אָמַרְתָּ lies behind the Greek σὺ εἶπας. But the assumption is probable, and the sense of the Aramaic expression is clear at least to the extent that it does not mean 'yes.'; Cullmann, *The Christology of the New Testament*..., 118f.

[88] R. H. Fuller, *The Foundations of New Testament Christology* (New York: Charles Scribner's Sons, 1965), 110.

[89] The title, Son of God is rooted in ancient oriental religions, in which, all Kings were thought to be begotten of gods. [Cullmann, *The Christology*

of the New Testament..., 271]; in Hellenism, one who possessed some kind of divine power was called θειος ἀνὴρ [Fuller, *The Foundations of New Testament Christology...*, 68]; In the Roman world, it was used of rulers. Also, it was often applied to mythical heroes, and historical persons. [J. A. Fitzmyer, *The Gospel According to Luke I-IX,* vol. 1 (New York: Doubleday, 1979), 205.]

[90] Fredriksen comments Jesus' crucifixion as, "That particular mode of death was reserved for those believed to be a threat to public order of Rome." [P. Fredriksen, *Jesus of Nazareth, King of the Jews: A Jewish Life and the Emergence of Christianity,* reviewed by G. C. Marfin, http/www. Google. com.] Pilate questioned Jesus during the trial, "Are you the King of the Jews?" [Lk. 23:3. cf. Mt. 27:11; Mk. 15:2 & Jn. 18:33]. The real meaning of this question can be understood from the background of Lk. 23:2, which is one of the Lukan independent sources: "We have found this man perverting our nation, and forbidding us to give tribute to Caesar, and saying that he himself is Christ a King." This accusation shows that Jesus is a political insurrectionist.

[91] J. D. Kingsbury, *The Christology of Mark's Gospel* (Philadelphia: Fortress Press, 1983), 121f.

[92] J. B. Green, *New Testament Theology: The Theology of the Gospel of Luke* (Cambridge: University Press, 1995), 67.

[93] Matera, *Passion Narratives and Gospel Theologies...*, 174.

[94] C. Guignebert, *The Jewish World in the time of Jesus* (New York: University Books, 1959), 54f.

[95] S. G. F. Brandon, *The Trial of Jesus of Nazareth* (London: B.T. Batsford Ltd, 1968), 118.

[96] Lk. 23:1-5.

[97] H. W. Hoehner, "Why did Pilate Hand Jesus over to Antipas?" in *The Trial of Jesus,* ed. by Ernst Bammel (London: SCM Press, 1970), 90.

[98] C. H. Talbert, *Literary Pattern, Theological Themes, and the Genre of Luke-Acts* (Montana: Scholars Press, 1974), 26f.

[99] Historically, Herod Antipas ruled the region west of Galilean Sea from 3 BCE – CE 39, the period in which Jesus lived and crucified. [A. Storkey, *Jesus and Politics: Confronting the Powers* (Grand Rapids: Baker Academic, 2005), 31.]

[100] P. Richardson, *Herod: King of the Jews and Friend of the Romans* (Edinburgh: T&T Clark, 1996), 304f.

[101] Carter, *The Roman Empire and the New Testament...*, 5.

[102] R. A. Horsley, *Jesus and Empire* (Minneapolis: Fortress Press, 2003), 41.

[103] B. Kinman, "Pilate's Assize and the Timings of Jesus' Trial," *Tyndale Bulletin* 42/2 (1991): 283. ATLAS.

[104] Mt. 27:11-14; Mk. 15:2-5 & Jn. 18:29-38.

[105] Fitzmyer, *The Gospel According to Luke X-XXIV...*, 1473.

[106] Brandon, *The Trial of Jesus of Nazareth...*, 119.

[107] J. B. Green, "The Death of Jesus and the Ways of God: Jesus and the Gospels on Messianic Status and Shameful Suffering," *Interpretation* 52/1 (January, 1998): 27.

[108] *Ibid.*, 29.

[109] *Ibid.*, 28.

[110] Matera, *Passion Narratives and Gospel Theologies...*, 177.

[111] Roetzel, *The World that Shaped the New Testament...*, 18.

[112] Fitzmyer, *The Gospel According to Luke X-XXIV...*, 1473f.

[113] Does it indicate the divided Kingdoms of Judah and Israel? The Kingdom Judah consisted of two tribes, dominated by the city Jerusalem and Davidic dynasty; whereas, the Kingdom of Israel consisted of ten tribes, which lacked national-religious centre. [T. C. G. Thornton, "Charismatic Kingship in Israel and Judah," *The Journal of Theological Studies* 14/1 (April 1963): 9.]

[114] Jn. 18:33-38.

[115] Lk. 23:4.

[116] Lk. 23:13-16.

[117] Lk. 23:14ff.

[118] Lk. 23:17-23; Mt. 27:15-23; Mk. 15:6-14 & Jn. 18:39-40.

[119] Lk. 23:19.

[120] Lk. 23:18.

[121] Lk. 23:21.

[122] Bailey, Barrett, Boismard, Herekens, Kümmel, F. C. Grant, Parker, Streeter, and Thyen advocate that John had the knowledge of either Luke or the special pre-Lukan Passion Narrative. Whereas, Cribbs and Schniewind advocate that Luke had the knowledge of a pre-Johanine Passion Narrative source or traditions. Hahn, Günther Klein, Maddox and Soards suggest that Luke and John had common knowledge of an independent, oral source or traditions. [Brown, *The Death of The Messiah*, vol. I..., 87.]

[123] 1) Lk. 23:4; 2) 23:14; 3) 23:22; cf. 1) Jn. 18:38b; 2) 19:4 & 3) 19:6.

[124] Fitzmyer, *The Gospel According to Luke X-XXIV...*, 1472; Brown, *The Death of the Messiah*, vol. 1..., 71.

[125] H. K. Bond, *Caiaphas: Friend of Rome and Judge of Jesus?* (Westminister: John Knox Press, 2004), 110.

[126] *Coercitio* is a judgment based on compulsory measure to maintain public order. [Theissen, *The Historical Jesus...*, 457].

[127] Cf. Lk. 9:44; 22:22 & 24:7; Matera, *Passion Narratives and Gospel Theologies...*, 179.

[128] D. P. Moessner, "The 'Leaven of the Pharisees' and 'This Generation': Israel's Rejection of Jesus According to Luke," *Journal for the Study of the New Testament* 34 (October, 1988): 21.

[129] D. C. Allison, Jr., "Jesus Christ," in *The New Interpreters Dictionary of the Bible I-Ma*, vol. 3, ed. by K. D. Sakenfeld (Nashville: Abingdon Press, 2008), 290.

[130] 1) Pilate ordered Jesus to be executed because he was "potentially a menace if people thought he was a messiah or King, and so;" 2) Jesus' followers consider the death of Jesus as the fulfillment of the Law and the prophets particularly, "how the just suffered at the hands of the wicked;" 3) In early Christianity, by distinguishing 'the Jews' from 'the Romans', along with the prejudice of their Gentile background, anti-Judaism[131] elements emerged as "the Jews who killed the Lord Jesus;" and, 4) Finally, the culprit in Jesus' passion was attributed to "the Jews." [R. E. Brown, *The Death of Jesus and Anti-Semitism Seeking Interfaith Understanding*, http://www .Google.com. /paper].

[132] "As long as Christians were the marginalized and disenfranchised ones, such passion fiction about Jewish responsibility and Roman innocence did nobody much harm. But once the Roman Empire became Christian, that fiction turned lethal." [Crossan, *Who Killed Jesus?...*, XI-XII].

[133] In Matthew, the blame is put upon Israel through the people's cry: "His blood be on us and on our children" (Mt. 25:25); by the washing of the hands of Pilate (Mt. 27:24); and in Luke, both the religious leaders and the people. In the book of Acts, it is explicit that the Jews killed Jesus (Acts 2:23; 3:15and passim).

[134] Matera, "The Trial of Jesus: Problems and Proposals"..., 16.

[135] While other evangelists address the place as Golgotha, Luke mentions it as the place called *the Skull*. (Lk. 23:33. Cf. Mt. 27:33; Mk. 15:22 & Jn. 19:17).

[136] M. Hengel, *Crucifixion* (Philadelphia: Fortress Press, 1977), 46; P. Fredriksen, *Jesus of Nazareth King of the Jews: A Jewish life and the Emergence of Christianity,* 2000), 8.

[137] Josephus, *Jewish War* 5.11.1., referred to by Green, "The Death of Jesus and the Ways of God...,"..., 26.

[138] F. J. Matera, "The Trial of Jesus: Problems and Proposals," *Interpretation* 45/1 (January, 1991): 2.

[139] Theissen, *The Historical Jesus...*, 516.

[140] R. E. Brown, "The Death of Jesus and Anti-Semitism Seeking Interfaith Understanding," http://www. google.com/paper.

[141] Carter, *The Roman Empire and the New Testament...*, xi.

[142] J. Moltmann, *The Crucified God: The Cross of Christ as the Foundation and Criticism of Christian Theology,* tr. by R. A. Wilson and John Bowden (London: SCM Press, 1974), 144.

[143] Hengel points out that, "Crucifixion was and remained a political and military punishment." [Hengel, *Crucifixion...*, 86].

[144] Carr, *Luke...*, 366.

[145] R. J. Karris, "Luke 23:47 and the Lucan view of Jesus' Death," *Journal of Biblical Literature* 105/1 (1986): 73; Joel Marcus, "Entering into the Kingly Power of God," *Journal of Biblical Literature* 107/4 (December, 1988): 670f; According to Matera, Paradise refers to King's royal garden. [Matera, *Passion Narratives and Gospel Theologies...*, 186.]

[146] F. W. Danker, "Politics of the New Age According to St. Luke," *Currents in Theology and Mission* 12/6 (December 1985): 343.

[147] A. W. Zweip, *The Ascension of the Messiah in Lukan Christology* (Leiden: Brill, 1997), 150.

[148] Lk. 2:11; 3:22; 4:21; 5:26; 13:32f; 19:5 & 9.

[149] Fitzmyer, *The Gospel According to Luke X-XXIV...*, 1362.

[150] In Ps. 31:5, the Psalmist prays for refuge and protection of God in distress. [P. C. Craigie, *Word Biblical Commentary: Psalms 1-50*, vol. 19 (Texas: Word Books, 1998), 260.]

[151] Matthew and Mark don't make an effort to give any reason for those hours of darkness. [Lk 23:44. cf. Mt. 27:45 & Mk. 15:33]

[152] D. Stuart, *Word Biblical Commentary: Hosea-Jonah,* vol. 31 (Texas: Word Books, 1998), 385.

[153] Mt. 27:45-54 & Mk. 15:33-39.

[154] M. Dibelius, *Jesus,* tr. by C. B. Hedrick and F. C. Grant (Philadelphia: The Westminster Press, 1949), 10.

[155] O. C. Edwards, *Luke's Story of Jesus* (Philadelphia: Fortress Press, 1981), 87; since, the Passion Narratives are narrated with full of quotations of and allusions to the Old Testament, Jesus' death seems to be the fulfillment of prophecy. [Allison, "Jesus Christ,"..., 290.]

[156] M. Gonsalves, *The Passion of Jesus According to Luke: A Narrative Critical Study of Luke 22:29-23:49* (Romae, 2001), 39.

[157] T. F. Best, "The Sociological Study of the New Testament: Promise and Peril of a New Discipline,"
Scottish Journal of Theology 36 (1983): 181.

[158] Mk. 15:39 & Mt. 27:54.

[159] Kingsbury, *The Christology of Mark's Gospel...,* 129-132.

[160] Lk. 2: 49.

[161] C. H. Talbert, "An Anti-Gnostic Tendency in Lucan Christology," *New Testament Studies* 14/2 (January, 1968): 269.

[162] M. Coleridge, *The Birth of the Lukan Narrative: Narrative as Christology In Luke 1-2* (England: Sheffield Academic Press, 1993), 230.

[163] *Ibid.,* 231.

[164] Senior, *The Passion of Jesus in the Gospel of Luke...,* 167.

[165] J. D. G. Dunn, *The Evidence for Jesus* (London: SCM Press, 1985), 1.

[166] D. Carr, *Sword of the Spirit: An Activist's Understanding of the Bible* (Geneva: WCC, 1992), 42.

[167] E. Huntress, "'Son of God' in Jewish Writings Prior to the Christian Era," *Journal of Biblical Literature* 54/2 (June, 1935): 123.

[168] Cullmann, *The Christology of the New Testament...,* 271.

[169] Fuller, *The Foundations of New Testament Christology...,* 68; The philologist W. V. Martitz has shown that the title Son of God should not be associated with the brand of the so-called θεῖος ανήρ, the divine man, because it is questionable whether it was an established type in the first century AD." [M. Hengel, The Son of God (Philadelphia: Fortress Press, 1976), 31.]

[170] J. D. G. Dunn, *Christology in the Making, 1980,* 2nd ed. (London: SCM Press, 1989), 14f.

[171] Fitzmyer, *The Gospel According to Luke I-IX...,* 205.

[172] Borg and Crossan, *The Last Week: What the Gospels...,* 150; Carr, *Sword and Spirit...,* 42.

[173] Gen. 6: 2,4; Deut. 32:8; Job 1:6-12; 2:1-6; 38:7; Ps. 29:1; 89:6 & Dan. 3:25.

[174] Ex. 4:22; Deut. 14:1; Isa. 43:6; Jer. 31:9; Hos. 1:10 & 11:1.

[175] 2 Sam. 7:14. Cf. 1 Chr. 17:13; 22:10 & 28:6; Ps. 2:7 & 89:26f; Dunn, *Christology in the Making...*, 15.

[176] Fuller, *The Foundations of New Testament Christology...*, 31.

[177] Kingsbury, *The Christology of Mark's Gospel...*, 35f.

[178] A. Y. Collins, "Mark and His Readers: The Son of God among Jews," *Harvard Theological Review* 92/4 (October, 1999): 408.

[179] Cullmann, *The Christology of the New Testament...*, 275.

[180] T. G. Naganoolil, "The Christological Titles and Contemporary Jesus-Research," *Bible Bhashyam* 25/4 (December 1999): 258; the only exception in Jesus' prayer without 'Abba' is the cry on the cross: "My God, my God, why have you forsaken me?" (Mk. 15:34. Mt. 27:46). [M. Vellanickal, "The Filial Faith of Jesus: Jesus' Experience as Son of God," *Bible Bhashyam* 11/3 (March-June 1985): 116]

[181] B. Witherington, *The Gospel of Mark: A Socio-Rhetorical Commentary* (Grand Rapids: Eerdmans, 2001), 400.

[182] The title 'Son of God' was intended to denote the superman character of Caesar. [P. H. Bligh, "A Note on Huios Theou in Mark 15:39," *The Expository Times* 80/1 (October, 1968): 52].

[183] P. W. Walaskay, "The Trial and Death of Jesus in the Gospel of Luke," *Journal of Biblical Literature* 94/1 (March, 1975): 93.

[184] C. H. Talbert, *Reading Luke: A Literary and Theological Commentary on the Third Gospel* (New York: Crossroad, 1982), 186.

[185] J. A. Weatherly, *Jewish Responsibility for the Death of Jesus in Luke-Acts* (Sheffield: Academic Press, 1994), 97.

[186] J. Maleparampil, "Unexpected and Unknown but Models of Courageous and Generous Discipleship: Matthew 26:6-13; 27:19; 27:54 and 27:57-61," *Bible Bhashyam* 29/3 (September, 2003): 214; Kingsbury, *The Christology of Mark's Gospel...*, 131f.; H. M. Jackson, "The Death of Jesus in Mark and the Miracle from the Cross," *New Testament Studies* 33/1 (January, 1987): 22; 'At the end, as a historical presentation, Mark articulates the secret and final revelation of the person and work of Jesus.' [Cullmann, *The Christology of the New Testament...*, 294.]

[187] P. H. Bligh joins with Schweitzer's view that the centurion in Mark's

Gospel declares this title in replacing Caesar. He says, "It is in Mark that we have the eschatological storm trooper of Schweitzer invading the Empire of Darkness and establishing in its place the Empire of Light. And it is left to a pagan soldier, a centurion, the backbone of the Roman army, from whom utter loyalty was demanded, who stands looking upward at the lacerated corpse of a Galilean peasant on a Roman gallows, to give the final verdict in the words of the imperial title: 'This man, not Caesar, is the Son of God!'"[Bligh, "A Note on Huios Theou in Mark 15:39"..., 53.] It is countered by Earl S. Johnson that such interpretation could not have credibility because, "A Roman soldier of a centurion's rank and experience would be too sophisticated and would have been exposed to too many gods to make that kind of quick judgment at an execution." [E. S. Johnson, "Is Mark 15:39 The Key to Mark's Christology," *Journal for the Study of the New Testament* 31(October, 1987): 13.]

[188] Mt. 27:54 & Mk. 15:39.

[189] Witherington, *The Gospel of Mark*..., 400.

[190] M. D. Hooker, *Not Ashamed of the Gospel: New Testament Interpretations of the Death of Christ* (Grand Rapids: William B. Eerdmans, 1995), 65.

[191] Witherington, *The Gospel of Mark*..., 400.

[192] Hooker, *Not Ashamed of the Gospel*..., 65.

[193] J. Kurichianil O.S.B., "Jesus' Consciousness of His Passion and Death According to the Synoptic Gospels," *Bible Bhashyam* 9/2 (June, 1983): 119. [cf. Mk 3:7-12; Lk 3:7-9]

[194] Fitzmyer, *The Gospel According to Luke X-XXIV*..., 1520.

[195] Lk. 23:4-12.

[196] Lk. 23:41.

[197] The RSV and NRSV read: "Certainly this man was innocent;" the NAB reads: "Surely this was an innocent man" etc.,

[198] Matera, "The Death of Jesus according to Luke...", 479.

[199] Karris, "Luke 23:47 and the Lucan view of Jesus' Death," ..., 65f.

[200] *Ibid.*, 66.

[201] R. E. Brown, *The Death of the Messiah*, vol. II (New York: Doubleday, 1993), 1163.

[202] Wis. 2:18, cited by Brown, *The Death of the Messiah*, vol. II..., 1165.

[203] Liddell and Scott, *A Greek-English Lexicon*, vol. I..., 429.

[204] Matera, "The Death of Jesus according to Luke...", 481- 484.

[205] *Ibid.*, 485.

[206] *Ibid.*

[207] D. Seccombe, "Luke and Isaiah," *New Testament Studies* 27/2 (January, 1981): 257.

[208] Talbert, *Reading Luke* ..., 219.

[209] Lk. 5:25, 26; 7:16; 13:13; 17:15 & 18:43.

[210] Lk. 2:20.

[211] Lk. 23:44-47.

[212] Lk. 23:45f.

[213] P. W. L. Walker, *Jesus and the Holy City: New Testament Perspectives on Jerusalem* (Grand Rapids: William B, Eerdmans, 1996), 64.

[214] S. P. Matthew, *Temple-Criticism in Mark's Gospel: The Economic Role of the Jerusalem Temple during the First Century CE* (Delhi: ISPCK, 1999), 222.

[215] *Ibid.*

[216] D. D. Sylva, "The Temple Curtain and Jesus' Death in the Gospel of Luke," *Journal of Biblical Literature* 105/2 (1986): 239-250.

[217] cf. Heb. 10: 19f.

[218] Taylor, *The Passion Narrative of St Luke...*, 139.

[219] Fitzmyer, *The Gospel According to Luke I-IX* ..., 180.

[220] Lk. 22:42.

[221] G. Keerankeri, S.J., "The Passion and Death of Jesus and the Problem of Human Suffering," *Vidyajyoti Journal of Theological Reflection* 70/10 (October 2006): 734.

[222] Kurichianil, "Jesus' Consciousness of His Passion and Death..."..., 118.

[223] D. J. Antwi, "Did Jesus Consider His Death to be an Atoning Sacrifice?" *Interpretation* 45/1 (January, 1991): 17.

[224] The Report of the Theological Committee of the Evangelischen Kirche der Union, "Understanding the Death of Jesus," *Interpretation* 24/2 (April, 1970): 139-141.

[225] Taylor, *The Passion Narrative of St Luke...*, 139; Karris, "Luke 23:47 and the Lucan view of Jesus' Death"..., 65.

[226] R. Zehnle, "The Salvific Character of Jesus' Death in Lucan Soteriology," *Theological Studies* 30/3 (September, 1969): 420.

[227] H. C. Kee, *Christian Origins in Sociological Perspective* (London: SCM Press, 1980), 111.

[228] Sylva, "The Temple Curtain and Jesus' Death ..."..., 247.

[229] F. J. Matera, "The Death of Jesus according to Luke: A Question of Sources," *The Catholic Biblical Quarterly* 47/3 (July, 1985): 484.

[230] Lk. 22:19f.

[231] It is seen through the backdrop of the Old Testament: 1) the concept of sin offering and the sprinkling of the blood on the temple altar on the Day of Atonement; 2) the sacrifice in Exodus 24, by which the covenant between God and Israel is made by Joshua; and 3) the idea of the Passover Lamb, which portrays Jesus as the slain lamb. [H. Marshall, "The Death of Jesus in Recent New Testament Study," *Word & World* 3/1 (Winter, 1983):16]. [ATLAS]

[232] M. Heim, "Rethinking the death of Jesus Cross Purposes," *Christian Century* 122/6 (March, 2005): 20. [ATLAS]

[233] R. Pesch, "The Last Supper and Jesus' Understanding of His Death," *Bible Bhashyam* 3/1 (March, 1997): 60.

[234]*Ibid.*, 75.

[235]R. Kereszty, "Toward a Contemporary Christology," in *Crisis in Christology: Essays in Quest of Resolution,* ed. by W. R. Farmer (Michigan: Dove Booksellers, 1995), 341.

[236] Zehnle, "The Salvific Character of Jesus' Death in Lucan Soteriology"..., 443.

[237] It is similar to the idea of Paul about Christ as *second Adam.* Cf. Rom. 5.

[238] Lk. 4:13 and 22:3.

[239] H. Flender, *St Luke Theologian of Redemptive History,* trans. by R. H. and I. Fuller (London: S.P.C.K, 1967), 54.

[240] M. A. Powell, *What are they saying about Luke?* (New York: Paulist Press, 1989), 70f.

[241] Garrett, "The Meaning of Jesus' Death in Luke"..., 11f.

[242] Matthew identifies the lineage of Jesus from Abraham (Mt. 1:1ff.).

[243] Powell, *What are they saying about Luke?...,* 71.

[244] *Ibid.,* 18.

[245] Green, *New Testament Theology...,* 64f.

[246] A. Nolan, *Jesus before Christianity: The Gospel of Liberation* (Darton: Longman and Todd, 1976), 113f.

[247] Karris, "Luke 23:47 and the Lucan view of Jesus' Death,"..., 69.

[248] Edwards, *Luke's Story of Jesus...,* 87.

[249] Theissen, *The Historical Jesus...,* 453.

[250] Talbert, *Reading Luke...*, 224.

[251] Powell, *What are they saying about Luke...*, 68f.

[252] Lk. 23:4, 14, 22; 23:15; 23:41 and 23:47. [Donahue "Passion Narrative,"..., 645.]

[253]Talbert, *Reading Luke...*, 222f.

[254] S. L. Johnson, "The Death of Christ," *Bibliotheca Sacra* 125/497 (Jan-Mar, 1968): 10. [ATLAS]

[255] J. B. Green, "Death of Jesus," *Dictionary of Jesus and the Gospels*, ed. by J. B. Green and S. McKnight (Illinois: Inter Varsity Press, 1992), 160f.

[256] 1) Conflict: the martyr fights against the satanic power and the power of darkness, cf. Martyrdom of Isaiah 4:11-12 and Luke 22:53 and 22:3; God supports the martyr; cf. Jesus is strengthened by an angel as in Luke 23:39-45, God supports the martyr by sending an angel in Dan. 3:25 and 3 Macc. 6:18. 2) Innocence: cf. Luke 23:4, 14-15, 22 and Dan. 6:4-5 and 3 Macc. 3:1-1. 3) Attitude of the bystanders: mockery on the martyr, cf. Luke 23:35-39 and the Martyrdom of Isaiah 5:1-11; the presence of the multitude. Cf. Luke 23:35a, 48 and 3 Macc. 5:24. And, 4) the conduct of the martyr: the martyr suffers for a cause. Even though he draws such a parallelism, he sees this supposed parallels between Luke and the martyrdom literature are formal and not material. [Karris, "Luke 23:47 and the Lukan view of Jesus' Death"..., 68f.]

[257] *Ibid.*

[258] C. P. Vogt, "Practicing Patience, Compassion, and Hope at the End of Life: Mining the Passion of Jesus in Luke for a Christian Model of Dying Well," *Journal of the Society of Christian Ethics* 24/1 (Spring-Summer 2004):147. [ATLAS]

[259] Lk. 23:50-56; Mk. 15:42-47; Mt. 27:57-61 & Jn. 19:38-42.

[260] Brown, *The Death of the Messiah*, vol. II ..., 1422.

[261] Lk. 24:1-12.

[262] Lk. 24:13-35.

[263] Lk. 24:36-47.

[264] Lk. 24:48-49

[265] Lk.24:50-53.

[266] Massey, *The Gospel According to Luke*, Dalit Bible Commentary..., 222.

[267] Lk. 24:34.

[268] N. T. Wright, *Who Was Jesus?* (Grand Rapids: William B, Eerdmans, 1992), 59.

[269] R. Williams, *Resurrection* (Harrisburg: Morehouse, 1982), 23.

[270] T. K. Seim, *Double Message: Patterns of Gender in Luke & Acts* (Nashville: Abingdon Press, 1994), 149.

[271] R. Williams, *On Christian Theology* (Malden: Blackwell, 2000), 192.

[272] Lk. 9:22.

[273] Lk. 18:33.

[274] Lk. 24:19.

[275] Danker, "Politics of the New Age According to St. Luke,"..., 342.

[276] Lk. 24:29-35.

[277] C. A. Evans, "The New Quest for Jesus and the New Research on the Dead Sea Scrolls," in M. Labahn and A. Schmidt (eds), *Jesus, Mark and Q: The Teaching of Jesus and its Earliest Records* (England: Sheffield Academic Press, 2001), 183. (163-183)

[278] J. D. G. Dunn, *New Testament Theology: an Introduction* (Nashville: Abingdon Press, 2009), 21&24.

[279] Zweip, *The Ascension of the Messiah*..., 161.

[280] J. D. Kingsbury, *Conflict in Luke: Jesus, Authorities, Disciples* (Minneapolis: Fortress Press, 1991), 7.

[281] A. R. C. Leaney, *A Commentary on the Gospel according to St. Luke* (London: Adam & Charles Black, 1958), 34.

[282] J. M. Sheridan, "Proclaiming the King – Preaching the Kingdom," *Bible Today* 87 (December, 1976): 996.

[283] B. J. Malina, "Jesus as Charismatic Leader?" *Biblical Theology Bulletin* 14/2 (April, 1984): 60f.

[284] J. Navone, S.J., *Themes of St.Luke* (Rome: Gregorian University Press, 1970), 88.

[285] R. W. L. Moberly, "The Christ of the Old and New Testaments," in *The Cambridge Companion to Jesus*, ed. by M. Bockmuehl (Cambridge: University Press, 2001), 190.

[286] *Ibid.*, 191.

[287] Lk. 23:51.

Chapter - 5

A Reconstruction
of Lukan Christology:
Jesus the King

The study of the *Kingship motif in the Gospel of Luke* so far, has revealed that the motif of Kingship pervades throughout the Gospel either openly or secretly from the Infancy Narrative until its culmination in the Passion and Resurrection Narratives. It is established that the Lukan additions and transpositions of the Markan materials disclose Luke's artistic composition, in reiterating the motif of Jesus' Kingship in the context of the anticipation of the socio-political world of Luke. As a next step in this venture, an attempt is made here to revisit, redefine and reconstruct the Lukan Christology with special reference to the reality of the present Indian context in its diverse cultures and religious faiths across the continents along with the title of Jesus, the King by using insights from the exegetical study done in the previous chapters.

Christology begins in human praxis along with the inquiry of Jesus of Nazareth, who was encountered and interpreted by his disciples.[1] It may be said that the human experience and inquiry not only during the time of Jesus but also the communities followed his death and resurrection till today. So, reconstruction is needed every time as J. Moltmann says, "Christology is essentially unconcluded and permanently in need of revision."[2] In this study of Luke's Kingship motif in the third Gospel, the person and work of Jesus depict that he reformed, restored, renewed, re-ordered, reversed the power and rededicated the oppressed society along with his Kingly attitudes. So, from the findings of the previous chapters, in this chapter the Christology will be reconstructed under two heads: A) Jesus the King: Lukan Christology; and, B) relevance of Lukan Christology of Jesus the King in the Indian context.

Jesus the King: Lukan Christology

While scholars view the crucified Jesus in Luke's Gospel as a martyr,[3] a Saviour,[4] New Adam who has overcome temptations,[5] Son of God, Son of Man, Son of David, Christ the Messiah, Innocent One, and so on, an attempt is made in this section to reconstruct the Lukan Christology along with the sub titles: *a*) The People-centered King; *b*) The Messianic King; *c*) The Alternative King; *d*) The Crucified King; and, *e*) The Victorious King, which represent Jesus the King in Luke's Gospel.

Jesus: The People-centered King

The title, King accredited to Jesus in Luke's Gospel stems out of the socio-political world of Luke. The *Sitz im leben* of the Gospel denotes the eagerness of the society to have a King to redeem them from the existing social oppression of Roman rule. As it has been recognized that the Lukan community, possibly, the Pauline community; the Lukan Jesus, the King could be seen as the King for the betterment of the people. N. T. Wright says,

> If Paul's answer to Caesar's empire is the empire of Jesus,.... It implies a high and strong ecclesiology, in which the scattered and often muddled cells of women, men and children loyal to Jesus as Lord from colonial outposts of the empire that is to be: subversive little groups when seen from Caesar's point of view, but when seen

Jewishly an advance foretaste of the time when the earth shall be filled with the glory of the God of Abraham and the nations will join Israel in singing God's praises. From this point of view, therefore, this counter-empire can never be merely critical, never merely subversive. It claims to be the reality of which Caesar's empire is the parody; it claims to be the modeling the genuine humanness, not least the justice and peace, and the unity across traditional racial and cultural barriers, of which Caesar's empire boasted.[6]

As Wright juxtaposes the Roman Empire with Jesus' Kingship, it is comprehensible from this study that the Kingship of Jesus is people-centered in his attitudes as a benefactor and peasant King as it has been seen in and around the Lukan socio-political world the title King echoed through the ages as a lawful ruler of the people, a head of a state, a sovereign, a monarch, by extension a representative of a group, a shepherd, who sustains the life of the subjects as a benefactor by his own will without a particular geographical stretch and law, one who takes care of the temple, builds great towers and protects his people from his enemies so that they could live happily, and also a Messianic King in the line of King David as it is depicted in the Old Testament and in the Intertestamental literature, a King of the people for their betterment.

According to C. Guignebert, the hope of restoring the Davidic dynasty is based on the glories of Israel during the rule of King David, who unified the nations for the betterment of the people.[7] But, predominantly, the power dynamics of the Greco-Roman Palestine is very much identified, in the first chapter,[8] as an oppressive one by the historic references to the Roman Emperor and the Judean Kings in Luke. The living conditions of the Judeans during that time are a life of political-economic-religious slavery. In this oppressive context, Mol sees Jesus by his person and work as a charismatic leader who appeals to the objectives of the people and protests against a corrupt and hypocritical regime;[9] Malina sees him as a leader who is a restorer of Israel;[10] Theissen, a founder of a renewal movement; and, Horsely, a reformer.[11] But, the researcher sees the Lukan portrayal of Jesus as the people-centered King in the context of socio-economic factors of social rootlessness, poverty and double taxation; the socio-ecological factors of conflicts, socio-political conflicts between the ruler and the ruled, particularly the tyrannical political factors and the resistant movements and the promises of the benefactors and the socio-cultural factors of divisions and distances.

The people-centered activities of the King Jesus in Luke's Gospel are articulated from the annunciation of his birth itself: the good news to the world was announced to the marginalized shepherds who were the outcasts, belonged to the longing community for redemption. Subsequently, Luke presents Jesus as the people-centered King who is empowering the disadvantaged, seeking the lost, reconciling persons across social divisions, calling people to repentance, healing the sick, forgiving sins, and initiating people into the community of God's people. In 4:18ff, the declaration of the Isaianic paradigm of salvation in Nazareth Manifesto; and, in 19:9f, Jesus' words to Zacchaeus, "Today salvation has come to this house.... For the Son of Man came to seek out and save the lost." portray the vision of the people-centered King in his work of saving the people.

John's baptism exposes the political oppressive state of Palestine as well the re-ordering and rededication of the people in the new community who lost their privileges by the sin of worshipping the Roman Emperor. By accepting that baptism, as a people-centered King, Jesus also joined in solidarity with the new community. This attitude of Jesus is further seen in his table-fellowship with others. At the close of the Galilean ministry, providing food for the multitude[12] and at the close of his ministry in Jerusalem, his farewell meal[13] Luke emphasizes his people-centered Kingship. Jesus is depicted not only a host, but also a guest during his journey and the stay in Jerusalem after His resurrection. According to R. Williams,

> The Eucharist, and every 'eucharistic' activity in which the meaning of the material world is transformed from possession to gift, is a sign not only of restoration and peace among human beings, but of the ultimate Lordship of the risen Jesus in which this restoration and peace is grounded. This is the sense in which the Eucharist is a sign of the end of all things, the consummation of Christ's Kingship....[14]

Williams may be describing the life of Jesus after his death and continuing his Kingship in celebrating the Eucharist. But, the reality of new community in Eucharist under the Kingship of Jesus must be understood in the restoration and peace as already established by Jesus during his life time in his participation in the table fellowships as well in the last Supper.

Moreover, Luke's presentation of Jesus' table-fellowship with sinners and tax collectors in 5:27-32; 7:36-50; 19:1-11 and with a Pharisee in 11:37-52 nuance the idea that in praxis Jesus liberated Israel not only from physical repressions such as hunger, sickness, etc., but also from political and social oppression. Yet, in the episode of banquet in a Pharisee's house, Jesus' critic ism on the Pharisees brought hostility[15] and seems that Jesus' table-fellowship invited the sinners to repentance. Although, Jesus challenges the Pharisaic mode of life, he expected the change of life. For instance, in 19:1-10, the repentance of Zacchaeus, and in 15:11-32, the repentance of the younger son explicate the change of life in relation to the table-fellowships. The ἁμαρτωλὸι in Luke are the dishonest people and those who rejected the law. Jesus' intimate table-fellowship with them in Jewish context signifies friendship, intimacy and communion. Jesus gives the reality of life to those who had lost it by their sin. In Jesus' people-centered activity, the dinner table becomes the place where diverse bodies meet; particularly, where people from various backgrounds dine together regardless of sex or social status. Jesus' table-fellowship forms a new way of life along with the vision and articulation of love and service to the outcasts and the marginalized in the socio-political world of Luke. In other words, Jesus established a new form of reformation without any racial barrier through his prophetic action and his proclamation of the Kingly rule of God in praxis.

Besides, in his people-centered activities, he executed the matters as a benefactor King. In 9:51-56, Luke depicts the rejection of Jesus in a Samaritan village due to the prevailing Temple controversy of Jews and Samaritans as he was going towards Jerusalem. Amidst Jesus' disciples demand to annihilate the inhospitable Samaritan village with heavenly fire, his attitude towards the Samaritans by rebuking the disciples shows him as a benefactor King. Subsequently, in 17:12-19, Jesus approves the healed Samaritan who comes to give thanks with an exclamatory remark over against the nine Jews healed from leprosy.[16] Danker says that the Samaritan's thankfulness to Jesus in the Greco-Roman context indicates Jesus as the Great Benefactor.[17] It is again seen in the parable of the Good Samaritan, where responding to the lawyer who asked, "Who is my neighbour?"[18] Jesus appreciates the character of the Samaritan as a benefactor King.

In climax, at the triumphal entry procession, people shouted that Jesus is King, the one who brings peace. Considering Jesus' role in that event, M. Borg and G. Vermes see Jesus as a Galilean Charismatic.[19] But, Lukan portrait gives more significance to the Galilean Jesus not only as a charismatic leader but also a people-centered peasant King. R. Horsley and R. D. Keylor see Jesus in this event as a social reformer, who is engaged in the renewal of the peasant life in order to effect social change.[20] It should be clearly noted that among the Synoptics, only Luke introduces Jesus as "Blessed is the King, who comes in the name of the Lord," which is the title of the pilgrim coming to the Temple now receives a new meaning on the basis of 7:19, where the question of John's disciples resembles the same phrase, and now identified explicitly as King. As Kinman points out it as a counter peasant procession to Pilate's imperial procession[21] that juxtaposes Jesus to the Emperor along with the shouts of people as the King. However, at the end of the procession Jesus depicts his Kingly act of restoring the people from their marginalization and oppressive state as it seems to be a planned peasant procession down the Mount of Olives, riding on a donkey along with the ecstasy of his followers who belong to the peasant class of Galilee. It is to be noted that as the one who belonged to the peasant village of Nazareth and centered his message about the Kingdom of God now led the peasant class people toward Jerusalem and cleansed it.

Moreover, in the procession of the triumphal entry in 19:39, while some of the Pharisees tried to stop the action of the crowd, and in

19:47, as it is said that the leaders of the people, scribes and chief priests were waiting for a time to kill him due to the fear of mutiny indicates the people-centered Kingship of Jesus. While the verb, ἐκβάλλω in Jesus' exorcism means casting out of demons, in the act of cleansing its usage[22] is understood that Jesus in the Temple drove out the demonic control of the Temple in its political, economic, social and religious power for the sake of the people. It shows that as a people-centered King, Jesus re-orders the positions of the people which may be defined as a reversal of oppression. Besides, in comparison to the other Synoptist's usage of the title, the coming one,[23] the Son of David, and the prophet Jesus from Nazareth of Galilee,[24] Luke's usage of the title, King encompasses all those titles and elucidates his Kingly power and authority through his feelings of anger, speech, action of revolution in his people-centered activity.

Jesus: The Messianic King

The expectation of the Messianic King in the Old Testament and the Magna Charta of Davidic Kingship, as it has been established in the previous chapters, is appended in the person and work of Jesus in Luke's Gospel. Predominantly, it is well seen in the introduction of Jesus by Luke as Davidic Messiah and the Saviour in juxtaposition to the Roman Emperor Augustus. Fitzmyer, Coleridge, and Sheeley[25] agree that Luke presents Jesus as the Saviour who is the Davidic Messiah. The angelic announcement of the Davidic descent in the Infancy Narrative not only signifies the Kingship of Jesus but also indicates the Messianic hope that continued to retain the promise of Davidic line in the first century Jewish and Jewish-Christian circles. The angelic words of Gabriel are recorded in Luke 1:32f, as:

> He will be great, and will be called the Son of the Most High, and the Lord God will give to him the throne of his ancestor David. He will reign over the house of Jacob forever, and of his Kingdom there will be no end.

It reminds the promise of the prophet Nathan to David and its fulfillment, as recorded in 2 Sam. 7:8-16. This Davidic connotation is loaded with political overtones because of the Messianic promises. The Davidic descent, courtly languages, and, the political overtones of the reversal of power depicted in the Lukan canticles nuance the Davidic, Messianic Kingship Christology of Luke.

According to Luke, the child of Mary is the Davidic King, who brings joy to the house of Jacob. Though Matthew directly names Jesus as the King of the Jews through the inquiry of the Magi, he doesn't make any reference to the Magna Charta of the Davidic monarchy. Besides, the Lukan special material evidences his motif of exposing Jesus as the Davidic, Messianic King by depicting both Joseph and Mary in the lineage of David in addition to the Magna Charta of the Davidic rule. Jesus' birth is not only traced from the house of David[26] or in the city of David,[27] but also, he was titled as the Son of David. Luke alone mentions the census for which Joseph went to the city of David, called Bethlehem in Judea.

The emphasis of Davidic Messianic King on Jesus is vivid in the recognition of Bethlehem as the city of David in 2:4 & 10f. The poor shepherds are linked very closely with Bethlehem, the city of David. According to 1 Sam. 16:11; 17:12ff & 58, David was a Bethlehemite, hailed from the family of a shepherd Jesse, and tending the flocks. In the Infancy Narrative, Luke has associated the shepherds both to the birth of Jesus and Bethlehem, the city of David. It is to be noted that in Jesus' time, shepherds were considered as dishonest and outside the Law. Particularly, in Luke, they represent the group of sinners, poor and the outcasts whom Jesus has come to save. The Lukan poor shepherds are linked very closely with Bethlehem, the city of David in the Infancy Narrative to show Jesus as a Davidic, Messianic King.

Considering the genealogy, while it follows the Q material, Luke presents a Davidic genealogy of Jesus along with the title Son of God and stresses at the end that he is the Son of God through Davidic lineage along with the inclusion of the lineage of Adam. Within the immediate social and political context of baptism, the lineage of Adam and Davidic lineage along with the political/emperor's title, Son of God depict the scenario: the creation of the world order;

fall of humanity; the united Davidic Kingdom; and, the fulfillment of Messianic prophecy in Jesus in accomplishing the anticipation of Lukan community.

The virginal conception of Mary reflects the Jewish expectation of a Davidic Messiah as it is told in Isa. 11:1f. On the other hand, in 18:18f, Luke depicts Jesus as the Son of David through the voice of a blind man at Jericho. Parsons comments that Luke portrays Jesus through the lens of the Davidic covenant and its associated messianic expectations.[28] So, it is very clear that the person and work of Jesus was realized even by the blind people indicates the presence of the anticipated Davidic, Messianic King amidst them.

Further, in 3:1ff, John's proclamation of the baptism of repentance and as its response, people joining the new community is understood as they were entering into the Messianic Community.[29] As well, in this oppressive socio-political context, Jesus' acceptance of John's baptism depicts Jesus' mode of entrance into the messianic work. Besides, both John and Jesus involve in a revolutionary act against the religious context of forgiveness of sins through sacrifice, which basically belongs to the Temple ideology. John practised the baptism of repentance by denying the temple's role in forgiveness. Later, Jesus forgave sins through his action and pronouncement which caused the conflict with the leaders who in their murmuring queried: Who is he to forgive sins? And in which authority he does these? For instance, in 5:17-26, Luke proclaims the identity and authority of Jesus as the Son of God to forgive sins in response to their question.

In 1:44, the leaping of the child in womb created ecstasy in Mary shows the *Sitz im leben* of an overwhelming joy in attaining the goal. The reference to the jumping of the child in the womb with gladness in vv. 41 & 44b indicates the advent of the Messianic age and probably signifies the perception of the child as the Messiah by Elizabeth. As it is discerned in the second chapter, the *Magnificat* resonates with the political milieu of those days and reflects the community's joy at the arrival of the Messianic King. Luke depicts not only the social salvation to Israel by the Messianic King but also reveals Jesus as the anticipated

Messianic King by the words of Mary. Elizabeth's greeting of Mary in 1:42, and the title, My lord addressed in 1:43, in comparison to 2 Sam. 24:21, seems to be a juxtaposition to the King. The title κύριος applied to Jesus while growing in his mother's womb suggests that he is on a par with Yahweh and connotes him as a Christocentric King. Besides, the words of the angel in 1:30ff, that the child will be given "the throne of his ancestor David," exposes clearly Jesus as the anticipated Davidic King, the Messiah. W. Carter says that the throne of David is depicted by Luke in contrast to Rome's harsh and exploitative rule.[30] Maclaren and Erdman consider that the Magnificat depict the anticipation of the appearance of the Messiah.[31] Particularly it communicates the reversal of position of the powerful against the lowly as a socio-political reversal by the Messianic King even the geopolitics was in favour of the emperor.

The phrases in the *Benedictus* such as: looked favourably, in the house of his servant David, raised up a mighty saviour for us, and prophet of the Most High, explicate the Messianic idea and Kingship in line with the Magna Charta of David as it prevailed in the Old Testament. In 1:74f, Zechariah predicts the complete control of enemies under the Messianic King along with the indication of national-political salvation. 1:78f, the metaphor, the dawn or rising sun is used for Messiah and his redemption.[32] "To give light to those who sit in darkness and in the shadow of death...into the way of peace," in v.79, depicts the prophecy of Isa. 9:1ff, where the Prince of Peace is referred to the redemption of the desolated region of Galilee, Zebulun and Naphtali of the Northern Kingdom ravaged and depopulated by Assyria.

In the canticle *Nunc Dimittis*, the overwhelming joy of Simeon in seeing the anticipated Messiah depicts the fulfillment of the Messianic expectation in Jesus as it is stated in 2:26, "revealed to him by the Holy Spirit that he would not see death before he had seen the Lord's Messiah." While the term, Σωτήρίον in v. 30 denotes the victory in a battle,[33] in the backdrop of the promises made to the Israelites, it means deliverance from the oppressors. The prophecy of Simeon to Mary after blessing the child, "This child is destined for the falling and the rising of many in Israel,...so that the inner thoughts of many will be revealed-and a sword will pierce your own soul too"[34] defines the child's mission of his Kingly role.

Besides, in Luke, the term εἰρήνη has a redactional emphasis and significance of salvation as in Isa. 52:7, the peace the Messiah brings and in Isa. 9:6, called as the prince of peace. In the hymn, *Gloria in Excelsis* it indicates the achievement of God in the birth of the child, which could be understood from the Hebrew word *shalom* which portrays not only the absence of war but also the whole social order of well-being and prosperity, security and harmony.[35] So, this angelic hymn, by declaring peace, depicts the fulfillment of the promises in the Old Testament among the longings of the oppressed Lukan community through the Messianic King. This hymn has resemblances to the shouts of people at the triumphal entry in which Luke openly declares Jesus as King.[36] Both the hymns agree in the usage of the phrase, δόξα ἐν ὑψίστοις. But, they differ slightly in 2:14, where the angels sing ἐπί γῆς εἰρήνη and in 19:38, the people sing ἐν οὐρανῷ εἰρήνη. The former may be heavenly angels' pronouncement of peace on earth which was the longing of the people and the latter, at the time of the triumphal entry, the people perhaps realized the fulfillment of the Old Testament promise and had sung peace in heaven, and expose the chord of Jesus' Christocentric, Messianic Kingship.

In Luke 4:18, Jesus is portrayed as the anointed King at the outset of his mission as the anointed one of Yahweh in the Old Testament. Depicting the inaugural incident of the Nazareth manifesto[37] with a few changes from Mark, Luke's themes of fulfillment, universality of the gospel, and the prophetic role of Jesus in his programmatic mission introduce him as the messianic King. In it, the Jubilee proclamation indicates his re-ordering of the positions of the oppressed. The programme of his mission in the oppressive socio-political context indicates his entrance to the Messianic work and later artistically confirmed as the Messiah, through the inquiry of John the Baptist. It is to be noted that the declaration of the fulfillment of the Old Testament prophecies in the Nazareth Manifesto depicts the dawn of

the new age by the arrival of Jesus:[38] good news to the poor; release
to the captives; recovery of sight to the blind; let the oppressed free;
and, the proclamation of the year of the Lord. Luke's addition of
"to let the oppressed go free" from Isa. 58:6 and the deletion of
intolerant words, 'bind up' and 'vengeance,' directly points to Jesus'
Kingly Messianic act through the worldly Kingship[39] image of invasion.

W. H. Brownlee, E. E. Ellis, J. M. Casciaro, et al.[40] agree that Jesus is
portrayed as the Messiah in accordance to the Old Testament passages.
But, J. D. G. Dunn argues that since Jesus quoted from Isa. 61:1-2,
he accepted himself as a prophet rather than the Messiah. Dunn's
view can not acceptable because at Nazareth, Jesus announces his
Kingly programme of Messianic mission. W. Carter says that Luke
depicts Jesus as the one who offers social vision and challenges the
elite-dominated Rome by citing Isaiah 61.[41] However, in the Nazareth
event, the marginalized, gentiles and neglected groups get attention;
particularly, women and widows. This event depicts Jesus as the
Messianic King challenges the Roman Empire with his Messianic
programme in reversing the conditions of the people who live on
the periphery.

Further, Luke introduces Jesus as the Messianic King through his
acts of exorcism, accounts of healing, performances of revivification
and nature miracles. Healing, exorcism, liberation of the oppressed,
raising the dead and the empowering of women and restoring their
position in the Socio-political world of Luke imply Jesus' messianic
Kingship. Crossan views Jesus' miracles as resistance to discrimination,
exploitation, and oppression out of his Kingly attitude for the welfare
of the downtrodden people in resistance to the prevailing injustice.[42]
The placement of four miracles immediately after the rejection of
Jesus at Nazareth strengthens his mission with authority and power as
a Messianic King in healing and giving life to his people. The healing
of the Gerasene demoniac in 8:26-39 reveals the power of Jesus over
Rome and the destruction of its oppressive structure. The context of
the miracle of feeding the five thousand is an event where the crowd
followed an alternative Galilean Zealot[43] due to the shaky position of

Herod in need of a powerful King. It is vivid in Jn. 6:15 from the realization of Jesus that, "…they were about to come and take him by force to make him King…." It may be viewed that Jesus' miracles transformed the bonded, marginalized human being into a new world of human existence.

In exorcism, the demons declare that Jesus is the Messiah. In 4:31-37, Jesus rebukes the man with the unclean spirit, not to declare his Messianic title, by saying, "Be silent." In the following periscope,[44] after healing Simon's mother-in-law, he healed many. Though it is a triple tradition source, Luke goes beyond in adding the shouts of demons which came out of people, "You are the Son of God!" as the disclosure of Messianic King. Jesus rebukes them and does not allow them to speak. Luke gives the reason that "they knew that he was the Messiah."[45] In all these events, Jesus is portrayed as the Messianic King who has authority over the Satanic forces. Besides, in the healing of the Gerasene Demoniac,[46] the demon haunted person addresses Jesus thus: "What have you to do with me, Jesus, Son of the Most High God? I beg you do not torment me." His command to go back home indicates the restoration and acceptance of the unchained person at home and society. Green says that it conveys the presence of the in-breaking Kingdom of God.[47] According to Ladd, the deliverance from the demon possession indicates the presence of Kingdom of God.[48]

Leprosy healed by Jesus resisted the purity regulations which affected human life on the basis of Lev. 13:45f.[49] By touching the unclean[50] Jesus wanted not only to cure the person but also extended his concern for the affected and accepted him into the society by pointing out the hard-hearted behavior of the society towards the people who were affected by leprosy. In 17:11-19, the faith of the Samaritan shows the transformation by breaking of boundary tension between the Jews and the Samaritans,[51] which is also seen in Jn. 4:20, in the conversation of the Samaritan woman with Jesus concerning the worship place of the Jews in Jerusalem and the Samaritans on Mount Gerizim.[52] It shows his acceptance of the marginalized into the society with his Messianic activity.

Many of the healings by Jesus indicate the full acceptance of those who were socially and religiously marginalized. For instance, the defilement due to menstruation was reversed by Jesus through the act of healing the woman who touched his garment.[53] The miracles among the socially and religiously ostracized people point out the intention of Jesus in reforming the evils of the nation to bring new life to them by the reversal of the old rigid laws on purity regulations.

The healing of the crippled woman in 13:10-17,[54] depicts how the powerless woman for the past 18 years was made straight to stand up. In other words, she was restored into her position. Maloney and Smith explain that the act of straightening up depicts liberation from the oppressive state, i.e., deformed by patriarchy.[55] The words used in v. 11, having a spirit of illness and v. 16, "whom Satan bound for eighteen long years" point out her oppressive state. She must be set free from the bonds of Satan, redefines the Sabbath as the celebration of freedom from slavery and darkness as well states the bondage of her religiously, socially and politically. The way Jesus performed it by calling her over, declaring her cure and laying his hands on her[56] has given acceptance to her in the society. Concerning the healing on the Sabbath, the discussion between the Synagogue leader and Jesus gives two alternative interpretations:[57] 1) violation of Sabbath by breaking the Mosaic Law; and, 2) fulfillment of the Sabbath. Jesus challenges the conventional thinking of Sabbath. And his reinterpretation of the Sabbath and performance depict his Messianic Kingly act.

The verb ἀνορθόω used in the healing of the crippled woman by Luke elucidates the crippled woman's restoration, as it is found in Davidic contexts in LXX, particularly to refer to the establishment of David's throne.[58] It indicates that Luke refers to Jesus as the King who restores the Kingdom by reversing the oppressive state. Ἀνορθόω inclusively refers to the restoration of Israel in Amos 9:11. As the usage of the verb ἀνορθόω in Davidic contexts indicates, Luke portrays Jesus as a Davidic King who restores the life of the people during his life on earth.

The response of Jesus to the disciples of John the Baptist[59] albeit seems to be an indirect answer, the miracles of Jesus authenticate him as the Messiah. The episode of anointing by a sinful woman in Lk.7:36-50 which is set in Galilee in Jesus' earlier ministry, instead of the Passion Narratives as in Matthew and Mark, depicts not only his kingly act of forgiveness but also reveals him as an anointed Messianic King who accepts sinners into his fellowship.

Peter's response, "The Messiah, of God," to the question of Jesus, "What do you say that I am?" discloses the Messiahship of Jesus.[60] Further in the scenario of transfiguration,[61] the conversation of Jesus, Moses and Elijah in their glory is portrayed by Luke as about Jesus' "departure, which he was about to accomplish at Jerusalem,"[62] which is not in Mark and Matthew, and focuses on Jesus' death as the Messianic King. Further, it is developed in 9:35, where Luke again portrays the revelation of Jesus as the Son of God. Here, it should be noted that it is declared to the three disciples of Jesus: Peter, John and James, who were with him in the mount of transfiguration. As a Messianic title implying Kingship, it is disclosed to others in this episode while it was revealed only to Jesus at the time of his baptism.

In 13:31-33, Luke puts forward through the words of Pharisees that Jesus' life is in danger by Herod the tetrarch. In this conversation, Jesus speaks of Herod as a fox. It is necessary to reason, as why Herod wanted to kill Jesus and, why Jesus named him a fox. Although, in 9:9, Herod who beheaded John wanted to see Jesus due to his might and fame, as it is a heightened scenario that a king wanted to see his counterpart who has fans, in 13:31, the report of the Pharisees indicates the contrary view of Herod to kill Jesus. In this episode, v. 32, Jesus' words of praxis, "Go and tell that fox for me, Listen, I am casting out demons and performing cures today and tomorrow, and on the third day I finish my work," indicate that he had to complete his messianic work. In other words, Jesus is juxtaposed as a Messianic King contrary to Herod. Besides, in 20:9-19,[63] the parable of the vineyard and the tenants, Jesus discloses and claims himself as the Son sent by God and they want to kill him. In v. 14b, the tenants words, "This is the heir; let us kill him so that the inheritance may be ours," indicate when the Messianic King is sent, they tried to kill him, so that they could get the Kingdom.

In the interrogation scenario of the triple tradition, while in Matthew,[64] and in Mark,[65] the high priest asks about his Messiahship, in Luke,[66] the interrogator was not the high priest, but the whole council asking, "If you are the Messiah, tell us." The response of Jesus by silence in Luke seems to differ from other Synoptics and depicts him as the messianic King. In all the dealings of Herod with Jesus, Jesus was considered by Herod as his counterpart and sent back to Pilate with the mockery as a King. The two trial secessions before Pilate are recorded by Luke, while the other evangelists[67] record only one. The first session precedes the trial by Herod as recorded in 23:2-5. Jesus is accused of political expediency: 1) he perverts the nation; 2) forbids the Jews to pay taxes to Caesar; and, 3) he calls himself the Messiah, the King. It is to be noted that except Luke no other evangelist gives the details of accusations, by which Luke presents Jesus as a political figure through the details of a real political character and the Messianic King. Further in 23:39-43, the mockery of the criminal and the response of the repented one are from L. Luke concludes it with the addition of another criminal who rebukes the mocker as well as attests Jesus as the Messianic King through his request to remember him in his Kingdom.

In all respects, the presence of the Kingdom is accentuated in Jesus' words, person and action: his parabolic teachings; miracles; hospitality to the outsiders to be insiders; table-fellowship with all kinds of people; forgiveness to the sinners; his Kingly entry into Jerusalem; the cleansing of the Temple; in the compassion of a Samaritan; the faith of a blind man; the repentance of sinners; and by trial Luke emphasizes the Kingship of Jesus in the Kingdom ideology and depicts Jesus as a Messianic King in line with David.

The Alternative King

Luke declares Jesus' birth during the time of Caesar Augustus, who was the Roman Emperor between 27 BCE and CE 14. His might was known throughout his Kingdom and hailed as saviour and god in the eastern Mediterranean world. While comparing Matthew and Luke's Infancy Narratives, both of them introduce Jesus as a King who was born and lived during the period of great Kings: Matthew gives Herod the Great, the Palestinian King as the backdrop and Luke gives the Roman Emperors, Augustus and his successor Tiberius, who were commonly known as the super powers of the 1st century CE. By juxtaposing Jesus, the powerless King to the great Emperors Luke notifies from the beginning of Jesus' life that he as an alternative King will re-order the positions of the marginalized.

The annunciation of Jesus' birth parallels Augustus' birth day and introduces Jesus as an alternative King to Caesar. At the time of Jesus' birth, instead of human proclamation Luke portrays an angel of the Lord announcing the good news in juxtaposition to the message of Augustus' birthday celebration as the good news for the world, "Do not be afraid; for see-I am bringing you good news of great joy for all the people: to you is born this day in the city of David, a Saviour, who is the Messiah, the Lord."[68] As a Saviour King in the socio-political world of Luke who is the alternative King, Jesus was announced to fulfill the hopes of the people which the Roman King Augustus could not. It is well noticeable again in the peace declared by the heavenly hosts in 2:14, which indicates *Pax Christi* against the *Pax Augusta/ Romana*. Brown says that it depicts an implicit challenge to the imperial propaganda of Rome by claiming the real peace of the world in Jesus.[69] J. B. Green and S. Kim[70] also agree that Luke deliberately contrasts Jesus with Augustus by declaring Jesus as the Lord and Saviour who brings peace on earth.

John's valiant speech pleading for repentance and baptism[71] exposes the political oppressive context of Palestine and gives the image of people joining the new community as an act of rededication to God from the sin of worshipping the Roman Emperor. In this context, Jesus' mode of entrance in accepting that baptism indicates the emergence of an alternative rule. It is vibrant in the temptation episode that the Roman Empire expected Jesus to be submissive to the human kingship of Rome rather than God. Luke portrays Jesus not as a power monger but as an alternative Saviour King in juxtaposition to Rome, its theology and rule. Josephus mentions in the history of Judea during the time of Herod about the erection of the golden eagle and its controversy.[72] Golden eagle erected at the front door to appease Rome against the Jewish God, in connection with the Temple theology becomes a nationalistic issue of Jews and Romans. Malina and Neyrey see the oppressive political structure of the Jerusalem Temple as the controlling center of the Jewish social identity, social classifications, and social boundaries as the holy people of God.[73] Hengel depicts the Temple as the seat of political and religious authority of the nation.[74] As an alternative King, Jesus opposed them and established theocracy by not yielding to obey the demand of the devil and Rome.

The use of the title Son of God seems to be plain when it is taken as an independent one; but when it is related to the second test with the indication of the Kingdom, it shows the pun on the title, Son of God in aiming an alternative, liberator King. As per the Roman imperial theology, Roman emperor was the son of god, who was lord and savior, one who brought peace on earth and so on.[75] It is further vivid in the trial before the Sanhedrin and in the response of Jesus to the question of his Sonship.[76] Σὺ εἶπας on the basis of Greek it is an affirmative answer. However, the alternative Kingship of Jesus against the Roman emperor is apparent through this issue of the title along with its political nuance and the council's demand of Pilate to sentence him to death.

Scholars like W. Carter and Yamazaki-Ransom[77] also agree that Satan is depicted to denote the Roman Emperor. Denial of prostration before Satan who has the power and authority to bestow Kingdoms and worshipping him indicate Jesus as an alternative King. In the passion narrative, in 22:3f, the Lukan phrase, "Satan entered into Judas called

Iscariot," indicates the Roman Emperor's part in the conspiracy and the act of Roman power on Judas. Jesus' question, "Is it with a kiss that you are betraying the Son of Man?"[78] portrays Jesus' authority over the event. Jesus' interpretation in v. 53, that it was their time and the power of darkness as an alternative King against the Roman Emperor and critical of the evils of Roman imperial system. It may further be evidenced from the warning of Jesus to Peter in 22:31f, "Simon, Simon, listen! Satan has demanded to sift all of you like wheat, but I have prayed for you that your own faith may not fail...." Here, it is clear that the Roman power wanted to destabilize the Kingship of Jesus along with his disciples.

In the event of transfiguration at the close of Galilean ministry in his departure toward Jerusalem, as a culmination of his disclosure, by the heavenly voice as Son of God depicts Jesus as an alternative King. In the miracle feeding of the five thousand,[79] Luke depicts the crowd as following an alternative Galilean King due to the shaky position of Herod in need of a powerful King. It could also be identified from the socio-political context of that time referred to in Jn. 6:15 from the realization of Jesus that, "they were about to come and take him by force to make him King."

In the calling and commissioning of the twelve disciples[80] by Jesus to proclaim the Kingdom of God,[81] their calling is meant for catching people for a new life. After the event of resurrection, the risen Jesus entrusted them with the responsibility of proclaiming repentance and forgiveness of sin throughout the world. The term metavnoia means to change one's mind; to repent; and, repent and turn away from something.[82] At the end of the Gospel, in 24:47, Luke adds the term, μετάνοιαν to Markan material that the Lord commissioned his disciples to proclaim repentance and forgiveness of sins. F. W. Danker defines μετάνοια as a revolution of the mind in political decision to renounce the political devices that lead to exploit and oppress the poor and the outsider.[83] It may be considered that Lukan Jesus is depicted as an alternative King who is the Saviour and liberator of the people in various strata through his reversal act which is revolutionary.

As a revolutionary act, by accompanying women, Jesus reversed the traditional society of his time, which did not allow them to partake in public activities. It is evident in 8:3b, that women like Mary Magdalene, Joanna, Chuza, Susanna and many others provided their resources. In 10:38ff, Mary the sister of Lazarus is praised by Jesus as the one who chose the better part. The parables of Jesus are concerned with woman: woman hiding the yeast in dough;[84] woman searching the lost coin;[85] and, the widow who confronts an unjust judge in pursuit of justice[86] and depict the transformation of the divine reign among women.

Concerning the poor, Jesus' message becomes the message of salvation, as it is stated in Mary's song as the reversal of fortunes.[87] Blessing to the poor can be understood as bringing a blessing to those who are exploited and woe to the rich who are satisfied.[88] Due to taxation, redistribution, debt, and oppressive economic realities as it has been noted in the first chapter, the poor had become poorer. Luke in his beatitudes adds a series of woes and their significance is spread throughout the Gospel. The rich are condemned in 6:20-26; 12:15-21; 14:12-14, 15-24; 16:19-25 & 19:1-9. In the Nazareth manifesto, by reading Isaiah 61:1f, Jesus reveals the focus of his ministry, particularly to the downtrodden and the people other than Jews by ethnicity and faith[89] by means of his Kingly character. Sheeley comments on the message and ministry of Jesus as, "He transcends the exclusivism of the Jewish people to minister to Samaritans and Gentiles."[90] M. A. Beavis considers Jesus' message as, "the reversal of socio-cultural expectations underlining the message of deliverance for the marginalized people."[91] In 7:29f, in acceptance of the repented, the roles of tax collectors and sinners have been reversed. It indicates the message and the act of Jesus promised a radical social reversal to the poor to be free and fruitful. In the parable of the banquet in 14:16-24, God's Kingdom is indicated as belonging to the poor. In 18:18ff, to follow Jesus meant the criterion was given to the ruler to renounce of one's possessions. It was expected of the disciples too in their calling.[92] These events point to the Kingdom movement of Jesus towards the downtrodden for their betterment. In all these, Jesus assures a complete reversal of economic power in the new era.

In some occasions of conflict, Jesus warned his opponents against their inner blindness and pointed out their hardening of heart. There are sixteen conflict dialogues in which Pharisees play a distinct role: 5:17-26; 5:29-32; 5:33-35; 6:1-5; 6:6-11; 7:29-30; 7:36-50; 11:37-41; 11:42-54; 12: 1; 13:31-33; 14:1-6; 15:1-2; 16:14-15; 17:20-21; 18:9-14. Among them, 11:42-54; 12:1; 16:14-15; 18:9-14 characterize Jesus' criticism of Pharisees and their associates. During Jesus' ministry in Galilee, Jesus is depicted as having the power of the Spirit;[93] authority in words,[94] authority in performing miracles and forgiving sins.[95] Although the audience responded to his authority with amazement,[96] the authority of Jesus becomes an issue of hostility.[97] The authority shown by Jesus in the temple becomes the hub of this conflict. Further with authority, Jesus as an alternative liberator King forgave both the sinners and accepted them into his fellowship while, the tax collectors and the prostitutes were considered as traitors, wicked, sinned, never repented, and betrayed God by disobeying the law. By this act, Crossan considers Jesus as a prophet of Jewish restoration who admitted the wicked into his community without demanding any restitution or obligation to the law.[98] In Luke the acceptance of the sinners by Jesus naturally made them to change their attitudes along with repentance.

The L parables depict Jesus as an alternative King through the concept of reversal of economy, wealth, social systems, religious practices, exclusivism, and the attitudes with the intention of restoration, repentance, transcending geographical and social boundaries, reciprocity, humility, persistent and hopeful prayer and self surrender. They emphasize the community life over against the socio-political situation during that time. The parable of the Good Samaritan in 10:25-37 indicates Jesus as the boundary breaking King and describes the changed social relationship between Jews and Samaritans among the entrenched ethnic controversy. M. Gourgues and Schottroff[99] are of the view that it describes the neighbourly love in responding to the need of others by breaking the boundaries as a reversal of practice. The parable of the friend at midnight in 11:5-8 depicts the reciprocal care and real sharing of life. The parable of the rich fool in 12:13-21 depicts the Kingly warning against apathy of others and clearly explains the socio-economic context of Jesus' time and condemns the attitude of marginalizing the people. The parable of the barren fig tree in 13:6-9, exposes the call to repentance given in its historical and political context referred to in 13:1-5 regarding the atrocities of the Jewish people against a group of Galileans who were murdered within the precincts of the Temple and their blood was mingled with the blood of the sacrificed animals. The gardener's plea shows his gracious mind in giving some more time to change one's attitude as well, marking the political and Kingly attitude of Jesus in conscientizing the people.

The parables of Lost Sheep in 15:3-7 = Mt 18:12-14, Lost Coin in 15:8-10, and Lost Son in 15:11-32 in Luke 15th chapter deal with the repentance of sinners and the joy in Jesus' alternative Kingship. This is also a call for repentance as an act of rededication to the Israelites, who lost their privileges by the sin of worshipping the Roman Emperor. This may be understood as an invitation to the ones who have gone astray to be integrated in the community of true Israel. The sinners here as Luke points out are those who obeyed the Roman Emperor in deviating the Law and theocracy; and, the tax collectors who are the employees of the Roman government. In the parable of lost coin Luke shows the value of life and the lady sharing her joy with the neighbours indicates her restored life. The parable of the lost son exposes the broken family of the father by the loss of a member in his family. The act of repentance indicates the restoration of a family at a micro level as well as all humanity at a macro level along with the bliss of the Alternative Kingship of Jesus.

The parable of the dishonest steward in 16:1-13, a radical scrutiny of the money economy, depicts the reduction of debt and forgiveness of sins in the three fold power structure: master, steward and tenants, provides a relationship system to build up a community. The injustice of the steward is changed by his act of forgiveness as it is considered as justice, and becomes "an expression of totally unexpected grace," that made him trustworthy as an heir of the Kingdom. It challenges the conventional view of wealth as a sign of divine blessing and invites everyone to leave the Satanic rule and follow God. In light of the

Roman Emperor's Rule in the first century Palestine, indicates the rule of an alternative King Jesus. The parable of the rich man and Lazarus in 16:19-31, is a reversal of economic exploitation[100] and demands the repentance of the rich to change their attitude in the earthly life. It is not only a reversal of fortunes, but also the establishment of justice and righteousness of the Alternative, liberator King.

The following parables indicate the oppressive nature of those days and the longing of the oppressed for life which nuances the hope in the rule of alternative Kingship. In the parable of the unprofitable servants, in 17:7-10, Jesus used the prevailing imagery of a slave in Palestine to point out their oppressive state of no reputation, fame or reward but they are expected to do what they are commanded. The parable of the widow and the unjust judge in 18:1-8, though the widow's demand is for justice against her opponent, it is intended to assure hope of justice. The parable of the Pharisee and the Tax collector, in 18:9-14, Jesus' reversal idea justified the Pharisee and the humility and repentance of the tax collector indicates the justice of God.

In the parables common to triple tradition and Q, the additions, deletions and the transpositions of Luke portray Jesus as an alternative King to the oppressive Roman rule. In the triple tradition parable of the sower in 8:4-8 & 11-15 Luke warns people's hardening of the heart and the fear of Roman authority. In 8:13, the term temptation indicates that the people are afraid of Roman authority and tempted to be attached with the rulers. The parable of the mustard seed in 13:18f,[101] indicates the phenomenal growth of the Kingdom, that was originally taken from the Old Testament imagery given in Dan 4:11f; Ezek 17:23 & 31:6. It may be seen as the extensive growth; and, the Q material in 13:20f,[102] the parable of the yeast as the intensive growth, which Luke in line with Matthew indicates as invisible growth. The phenomenal growth of the alternative Kingdom both visibly and invisibly is well portrayed in the parables of the mustard seed as well as the yeast. The parable of the tenants in 20:9-19,[103] is a challenge to political leadership and placed after the question of Jesus' authority. It is obvious that the high priests and the leaders who were in collaboration with Rome were possibly considered to be the opponents, and is a warning to point out their corruption. The parable of the Pounds in 19:11-27 shows Jesus' alternative Kingship against the exploitative Kingship and further, points out the juxtaposition of Jesus against Archelaus and his cruel rule.

In the Q parable of the great Banquet[104] v. 24, "For I tell you, none of those who were invited will taste my dinner" shows the reversal act of Jesus' Kingship in contrasting the practice of hospitality among the upper classes throughout the Mediterranean world, including Israel and the practice of Jesus in bringing up the marginalized and explicates him as an alternative, liberative King. The riddle of Jesus shows a contrast between John the Baptist and a royal person, Herod. Jesus' addressing of the crowd, "What did you go out into the wilderness to look at: A reed shaken by the wind?... Someone dressed in soft robes?... What then did you go out to see? A prophet?"[105] A reed shaken by the wind refers to the reed common in the Jordan desert and on the bank of Gennesaret or the vanishing of John's words and deeds. But, the following parallel riddle, someone dressed in soft robes refers to Herod Antipas by the emblem in the coins of Herod Antipas, reflecting his political programme in the context of people's wavering mind in moving towards the power and authority instead of following the Messianic call of John.

Kingdom of God in Luke's Gospel implies an anti-imperial movement against the secular Kingdom of that time along with the anticipation of an alternative King, Messiah. Jesus' declaration of the Kingdom by forgiveness of debts or sins along with his goal of restoring Israel and his words and actions against the Temple establishment, similar to the covenanters of Qumran imply a political move. The verbs: to enter; to inherit; and to be in, point to God's Kingly rule as it is exercised among people, albeit it is not limited to geographical boundaries. In fact it is a political one because it was a threat to the priestly and Roman authorities who wanted to keep the country in a sound position. It is evidenced from the 1st century CE rabbinic prayers which include the petition for the downfall of the

Roman Empire, considered as the Kingdom of evil.[106] Matera, Houlden, E. Rivikin, Wilson, Winter, Hengel and Sanders explore the truth behind Jesus' mission, as it would have been a threat to the life of the priestly and Roman authorities who sought to keep the country in a stable condition.[107] Besides, the words of Caiaphas,' as John writes in 11:50, "It is better for you to have one man die for the people than to have the whole nation destroyed" indicate the nuance of Jesus' message of the Kingdom of God and their perception on him as an alternative King.

Scholars view Jesus' message of the Kingdom of God differently: Gilbert as not political but ethical and spiritual;[108] C. H. Dodd as a realized eschatology since it has already arrived Kingdom by the words and deeds of Jesus; Jeremias as the progressive eschatology; J. M. Robinson as a proclamation to the present age in concern to the imminent future;[109] W. G. Morrice as the inaugurated eschatology;[110] Crossan as permanent eschatology;[111] Millar Burrows as the universal sovereignty of God combined with the eschatological one;[112] and, G. E. Ladd as, God's presence in Jesus in a new and unique way.[113] But, the Lukan view of the Kingdom of God includes the following concepts: King, reign, Davidic lineage of Jesus, Christ, seated on a throne, Lord, Son of God, and, Son of Man and portrays that Jesus not only the Kingdom-preacher, but also an alternative King in praxis.

Besides both the future and the present state of the Kingdom ideology indicate the change of life during the days of Jesus: 11:2 = Mt. 6:10, "Your Kingdom come" in the Lord's Prayer and 13:29= Mt. 8:11-12, "...People will come from east and west, from north and south, and will eat in the Kingdom of God" 11:20 = Mt. 12:28, "But if it is by the finger of God that I cast out demons, then the Kingdom of God has come to you;" 17:21, "Kingdom of God is among you" and 6:20 = Mt 5:3-6, "Blessed are...poor for yours is the Kingdom of God." The Kingship of Jesus is understood through his saving action. O. Cullmann identifies Lukan Christology in terms of Salvation history;[114] E. F. Scott and A. Ritchl say that the Kingdom had begun to manifest through the life and teachings of Jesus;[115] It may be perceived that the Kingdom is accentuated in the restoration of Israel in praxis by Jesus' healing and forgiveness as a Saviour and liberator who is an alternative King to the emperor.

Considering the triumphal entry of Jesus' procession, it was intentionally a counter to Pilate's procession. To the Jewish subjects of Rome, Pilate's procession indicated Emperor's rule and to the marginalized Galilean Jews, Jesus' procession without any arms indicated God's rule. By this anti-imperial, political event of peasant procession accompanied by action, Luke exposes Jesus as King with the voices of people, as the one who has authority even to drive out the demonic control of the Temple in its political, economic, social and religious power. It signifies restoration of the marginalized and the advent of the Alternative Messianic Rule.

Considering, the question of tribute money to Caesar[116] "Is it lawful for us to pay taxes to the emperor, or not?" it indicates not only the Roman Empire required tribute from the subdued Judea but also Jesus' opposition to that. In Mt. 17:24-27 Jesus condemns the injustice of the Roman tax system by his inquiry, "From whom do kings of the earth take toll or tribute? From their children or from others?" The nationalistic sense along with its own emphasis on faith and religion is explicit in it. Jesus' prophecy along with the condemnation of secular Kingship portrays him as an alternative King. It may be further seen in the phrase "desolating sacrilege,"[117] in the prophetic words of Jesus which denotes the persecution of Antiochus Epiphanes IV during 168-167 BCE, who ordered to erect idols in the altar of the Temple and sacrifice swine and other unclean animals.[118]

Jesus' question to the chief priests, the officers of the temple police, and the elders who had come to seize him, "Have you come out with swords and clubs as if I were a bandit?"[119] indicates that Jesus was considered by the authorities as an insurrectionist. Peter's denial in 22:54-62, depicts the terror of survival and the time of tribulation under Roman rule. The mockery of Jesus indicates him as an inferred King by the popularity of Jesus among the socio-political world of

Luke. "If you are the King of the Jews, save yourself!"[120] indicates not only the helplessness of Jesus against the Roman power, but also the doubtful nature of the soldiers concerning Jesus' Kingship as in 23:11, the Jewish King, Herod sarcastically made him a King by putting on him an elegant robe. Luke by his special material states, "Even Herod with his soldiers treated him with contempt and mocked at him; then he put an elegant robe on him and sent him back to Pilate." It is one of the most significant passages to identify Jesus' alternative Kingship. The robe on Jesus indicates him as a King who is a powerless opponent in front of Herod. In addition to Herod's mockery, in 23:35-38, Luke uses the term, ἄρχοντες, i.e., the rulers scoffed at Jesus. Along with the derision on the cross by the soldiers, the inscription over the cross,[121] "This is the King of the Jews," declares Jesus as the King.

Concerning the trials of Jesus, in Luke, the council raised the pertinent Christological question, "Are you, then, the Son of God?"[122] which is a special Lukan source that indicates Jesus as an alternative King along with the political nuance through this question. In the trial of Herod, recorded in 23:6-12, the special Lukan material indicates that Pilate sends Jesus away to avoid judging him by the accusation of the assembly. Luke portrays Herod as the one longing to see Jesus and that reveals the royal secret of 'who sees whom' not a criminal but they meet as equals. It is vivid that Jesus was considered by Herod as his counterpart, and so sent him back to Pilate mocking at him as King.

In the trial by Pilate as recorded in 23:2-5, that Jesus was accused of political expediency that he perverts the nation, forbids the Jews to pay taxes to Caesar and, calls himself the Messiah, the King. It is to be noted that except Luke no other evangelist gives the details of accusations, by which Luke presents Jesus as a political figure through the details of a real political character. This shows Jesus politically in contrast to Caesar. On the other hand, the political accusation by the crowd and chief priests that 'he stirs up the people from Galilee to Judea,' refers to the scope of Jesus' ministry indicating Luke's Christological significance of Jesus as an alternative King. Besides, the very question of Pilate, "Are you the King of the Jews?" among the three political charges on Jesus implies that he thought of Jesus, as a rival to the Roman Emperor. Although, Jesus' innocence is declared by Pilate, his judgment to crucify Jesus according to the will of people further shows the scenario of the power of Rome and the change of mind in the people for their survival against the anticipated King, Jesus.

Cullmann, Hengel, and Brandon, consider Jesus as a revolutionary whereas, Boff as, the Liberator[123] and, Theissen as a social reformer.[124] But in general, the kind of revolution and reforms he carries out has to be viewed on the basis of Lukan Christology in his liberative actions and teachings of alternative Kingship: friendship, love, grace, mercy, call of repentance by conscientizing the people, emphasizing the welfare of home and community by the subversion of traditional values, establishing justice and righteousness, reversal of values in the Kingdom of God, etc... Particularly, the concepts of reversal of economy, wealth, social systems, religious practices, exclusivism and attitudes with the intention of restoration, repentance, transcending geographical and social boundaries, reciprocity, humility, persistent and hopeful prayer, and self-surrender are emphasized. The table-fellowship indicates the establishment of Jesus' prophetic action of liberation and his alternative Kingly rule in praxis by accommodating all kinds of people.

Jesus: The Crucified King

Moltmann marks the Cross of Jesus as the origin of Christology.[125] In this research, the researcher sees Jesus of Nazareth as a crucified King by his last supper, arrest, trial, crucifixion and death. Jesus did not alter the political, economic, and social structures of that time although he was critical of the evils of the Roman imperial system. But, as it has been discerned in this research, he transformed the society through the liberating acts which the people needed under a Kingly rule.

The Last Supper as an institution and farewell discourse indicates Jesus' Kingship. Green and Donald Senior[126] see the Last Supper as an implication of Jesus' death in accordance to the divine plan and mission. In 22:21-23, the prophecy of betrayal indicates Jesus' knowledge of things related to his death. While sharing the supper, in 22:19, the words of Jesus concerning the bread as body, "which is given for you" indicate the vicarious aspect of his body for others in relation to his mercy and forgiveness. Fitzmyer and Scott[127] see a sacrificial nuance in it in relation to the soteriological purpose in Luke. But, after his death on the cross, the Supper is realized as an act of restoration which leads to a New Community life. Noticeably, the Last Supper is a reversal act in the context of the disciple's desire to be great and Jesus' response about his humble service in contrast to the worldly Kings which exposes him as a servant King who offers himself for crucifixion.

During the betrayal, not only Jesus' question, "Is it with a kiss that you are betraying the Son of Man?"[128] indicates Judas' turn coat attitude under the power of Roman Emperor, but also the subsequent event of arrest with striking forces along with the crowd indicates Jesus as Rome's political rival. The Roman Emperor is pointed out as Satan through the betrayal of Judas and the denial of Peter by their attitudes towards money and survival. Jesus' words of Satan and the power of Darkness indicate the contrast of Jesus against the empire during that time. The staring of the servant girl, her declaration that Peter was with Jesus, and another two men's pointing at Peter as a Galilean also indicate the political rivalry of Jesus' and the emperor.

In the trial, the council interrogated Jesus as, "... tell us if you are the Messiah, the Son of God" and the other pertinent Christological question, "Are you, then, the Son of God?"[129] indicate Jesus as an alternative, Messianic King. These two Christological questions: are you the Messiah? and, are you the Son of God? echo the angelic announcement to Mary in the Infancy Narrative, as in 1:32 & 35 concerning the birth of Jesus in the Davidic lineage and as Son of God; in 4:3 & 9 the recognition of Satan in the temptation event; in 3:22, the event of baptism; and, in 9:35 at the time of transfiguration. So, it is vivid in the Christology of Luke that from the beginning of the Gospel, Luke portrays Jesus as the King and proceeds with it until his crucifixion and death.

With the accusation of Jesus' Kingship, the council brought him to Pilate. In 23:6-12, Pilate sends Jesus to Herod with the accusation of perverting the nation in forbiddance of paying taxes to the emperor. His claim of being the Messiah, a King stirring up people against the authorities by his teaching throughout Judea and Galilee comes to the fore.[130] The trial of Herod indicates Jesus' acceptance of him as the messianic King through his silence. Jesus was considered by Herod as his counterpart and sent him back to Pilate the governor of Judea by mocking at him as a King.

Pilate's trial sessions give the details of accusations and present Jesus as a political figure. Pilate's question, "Are you the King of the Jews?" among the three political charges on Jesus implies that he also thought of Jesus as his political rival. The words of the chief priests to Pilate mentioned in Jn 19:15, "We have no King but the emperor," conveys the political connotation of the title, "King of the Jews." Pilate concludes, "So you are a King." To which Jesus responds again, "You say that I am a King." Bond comments that the Passion Narrative reaches its climax in Jesus' trial before Pilate, where the leaders as well as the people demanded his death by crucifixion.[131] Pilate released Barabbas and handed over Jesus to be crucified in accordance with the crowd's wish. Jesus' execution by Pilate signifies Jesus as an anti-nationalist who had challenged the Jewish leaders who were controlled by Rome.

After Jesus was handed over to the hands of the people, they led him toward Golgotha, the place called the Skull.[132] Luke's mentioning of the people of Jerusalem who accompanied Jesus along with the mourning women in vv. 27-31, and Jesus' utterance of the prophetical warning mark his travel as he faces death heroically as a King in contrary to the triumphal entry in which people declared him as the King. Jesus' words of Jerusalem's destruction indicate Roman invasion, and Jesus' final words to the women call people to change their mind and attitudes parallel the socio-political context of John's baptism.

Matera, Bultmann, Brown, Carter, Moltmann, Hengel,[133] et al. agree that Jesus was crucified due to his political revolution. At Golgotha, Jesus was crucified with the two criminals, one on his right and the other on his left. Luke's description of the two criminals reminds the prophecy mentioned by Jesus in 22:37 "For I tell you, this scripture must be fulfilled in me, 'And he was counted among the lawless'...." It indicates that Jesus was crucified with them as a political rebel because, crucifixion was a Roman punishment practised against criminals, political rebels, and slaves, particularly reserved for those who were observed as a threat to public order of Rome.

Conzelmann says mockery is the last confirmation of Jesus' royal dignity.[134] The method, *anumana* of Saiva Siddhantha points out the mockers: soldiers, Herod, the rulers, and a thief might have either seen or heard the authority of Jesus in his speech and acts with Kingly nature. But, when they actually saw a powerless, voiceless and suffering Jesus, mocked at him as King. The mockery of soldiers, in 22:64f, indicates the popularity of Jesus among the socio-political world of Luke as the messianic King who has the foreknowledge of the events. "If you are the King of the Jews, save yourself!" in 23:37 indicates both the helplessness of Jesus against the Roman power. In 23:11, "Even Herod with his soldiers treated him with contempt and mocked at him; then he put an elegant robe on him and sent him back to Pilate" signifies the identity of Jesus' Kingship. The robe of Jesus indicates him as a King who is a powerless opponent before Herod. In 23:35-38, the rulers said, "He saved others; let him save himself if he is the Messiah of God, his Chosen One!"[135] The inability of saving himself depicts his unselfish action immediately after the saving event of the repentant criminal with authority. It is the place where Jesus' Kingship is highlighted again by Luke. Not only the Jewish rulers' anger on Jesus, but also their hesitation to accept him as the anticipated Messianic King is explicit in it and portrays him as the Messianic King.

The inscription over the cross,[136] Ὁ βασιλεὺς τῶν Ἰουδαίων οὗτος declares the crucified Jesus as the King. Theissen states that it reveals that Jesus was executed as the King of the Jews as the one who wanted to take hold of political power.[137] Creed says that it is noted after, instead of before and as mockery, "a climax and a conclusion" that Jesus is the King of the Jews.[138] Both of them view correctly the inscription over the cross. But along with their views, the researcher sees it as a declaration of Jesus as a powerless, crucified, servant King who is acknowledged by the rulers as well the people through the inscription over the cross. In 23:39-43, the criminal's words, "Are you not the Messiah? Save yourself and us" confirm Jesus as the Messianic King. Luke concludes it with the addition of another criminal who rebukes the mocker as well attests Jesus as the Messianic King through his request to remember him in his Kingdom.

In the event of crucifixion, three prayers are notable in reconstructing the Christology of Luke, which are special to Luke alone: the prayer of forgiveness; the prayer of the co-crucified criminal; and, the prayer of entrust. Although, they crucified him as a rival King against Roman Emperor, Jesus' filial cry in 23:34, "Father, forgive them; for they do not know what they are doing," exhibits his offer of executioners' forgiveness as a heroic action in accordance with his teaching in 6:27 = Mt 5:44 concerning the love for enemies. Jesus' response to the prayer of the co-crucified bandit, in 23:42f, "Today you will be with me in Paradise," depict his exercise of Kingly power by forgiving his sins and granting paradise. By the prayer of Jesus entrusting his spirit, "Father, into thy hands I commit my spirit!" Luke depicts the royal manner he died and indicates his victory over death by handing over his spirit in the hands of God rather than in the hands of his enemies.

In all these above events, the mockeries of soldiers, Herod, rulers, a thief and the inscription over the cross indicate Jesus' caricatured Kingship because of his non-violent attitudes in juxtaposition to the Roman Emperor. During the arrest, stopping the violent act of the disciple, his silence at the time of trial and tolerance of mockeries as well as the hardships and punishments depict him as a powerless King. In his humility, servant attitude and powerless nature, the accusations, Pilate's question, the punishment of death on the cross, and the inscription over the cross portray Jesus as a Crucified King.

The death of Jesus further signifies the life and purpose of the historical Jesus as who was he. The entire scenario behind Jesus' death: the darkness over the earth, the rending of the Temple veil, the declaration of the centurion, the multitude beating their breasts and the witness by the crowds illumine the Christological importance in the death of Jesus. It becomes the key event in the living experiences of early Christianity. By seeing Jesus' death, the centurion assessed and declares who he is. Both Matthew and Mark record that he declared, "Truly this man was the Son of God!"[139] But, Luke notes that he praised God and declared, "Certainly, this man was innocent." His assessment pregnant with indispensable meaning beyond his own comprehension becomes the pinnacle point of the Christology of the Gospel.

Luke drops the title, Son of God from the mouth of the centurion but he introduces it in the story of the virgin birth, in the lineage of David as well in Jesus' birth in the backdrop of Caesar Augustus. As well at his baptism as he shares his real humanity. Jesus is disclosed as the Son of God at the time of transfiguration. According to Carr, Son of God indicates both directly Jesus' divine origin and divine status, and indirectly as the real emperor.[140] As it has been discussed in the earlier chapters, it has political nuance and gives the image of Jesus as an alternative King to the Roman Emperor who was also addressed as the son of god. In Judaism, the title, son of God was used of angels or heavenly beings;[141] to Israel;[142] and to the King.[143] In 2 Sam. 7:14 and the Royal Psalm 2:7, it was a title adopted by a Davidic King. Since this title, Son of God was used in early Christian preaching, it raises the issue, what did the early Christians understand by it when they used it for Jesus?

Along with it, Luke's alteration of the title, Son of God to innocent/ righteous raises another pertinent issue: was it due to either his fear or esteem of Rome that the title 'Son of God' referred to the Roman Emperor? Or does it show the pro-Roman sentiment of Luke? On the one hand, it may be blaming the people for the atrocious death of Jesus by reiterating the verdict of the Roman authorities, particularly, Pilate's handing over of Jesus in his innocence to the people's will as an act of *coercitio*. On the other hand, while the disciples of Jesus were afraid to declare him due to the fear of Roman power, would a

Gentile centurion, a praetorian for Pilate, and a low grade worker who represents the power of Rome at the execution, dare not declare the divine Sonship of Jesus. The anticipation of the people who suffered under the tyranny of Roman imperialism gives a new meaning to it that Jesus is the real emperor who suffers for the people instead of the paradoxical *pax Romana*. Amidst the socio-political backdrop, the alteration of Luke as δίκαιος seems to be more relevant and depicts Jesus' Kingship.

Liddell and Scott *Greek-English Lexicon* translates δίκαιος as observant of duty to gods and men, just, lawful etc.[144] In the context of crucifixion as a Roman punishment practised against criminals, political rebels, and slaves, the political charges during the trial depict Lukan modification of the centurion's declaration as δίκαιος instead of the Son of God not only due to his pro-Roman sentiment in its historical, cultural, social, political and geographical milieu of the oppressive Kingdom but also, along with his motif, his portrayal of Jesus as the alternative Saviour King who has done things in accordance with the will of God in juxtaposition to the Emperor which fits well into the messianic characteristics of Jesus from the beginning of the Gospel. The rending of the Temple veil at the moment of Jesus' death,[145] signifies the access of people to the presence of God and indicates the change of the socio-religious power exercised by Rome. Kee says that Jesus' death has to be seen as a divine sign of deliverance.[146] It is a reversal act of God through the death of Jesus by symbolizing his Kingship as the plan of God in accordance with the Old Testament promise of a messianic King.

Besides, Luke's narration of the crowds returning home by beating their breasts in 23:48 seems to be the action of repentance. Lagrange, Valensin, Huby and Matera find a sign of repentance by comparing it to an earlier narration of Luke in 18:13, the story of the publican who was beating his breast with humility before God, and was justified.[147] Naturally, one may think that it is an action due to the impact of seeing a violent and immature death of a person. But, on the basis of Lukan usage of the same language in 18:13, the repentance of the crowd depicts Jesus, the powerless, crucified King as he continues his Kingly act of bringing people into his fellowship.

Dibelius proposes the death of Jesus as a martyr's death.[148] Edwards, Theissen and Merz, Talbert, Powell, Donahue,[149] et al. agree to it. But, this research finds that Jesus was crucified and died for the people as a people-centered, alternative and messianic King. In a political sense, the accusation of Jesus as a political insurgent depicts his death for the cause of liberation of the people from the tyrannous rule crucified and died as a powerless, servant King.

Jesus: The Victorious King

The Burial event recorded by the four evangelists[150] agrees closely regarding the role of Joseph of Arimathea and the nature of the grave. "A rock-hewn tomb, where no one had ever been laid" illustrates the royal nature of Jesus' burial similar to his royal entry into Jerusalem on a colt on which no one sat. Luke's picture of Joseph of Arimathea as a member of the council which might be the Sanhedrin, righteous and waiting for the Kingdom of God signifies Luke's compositional style of including the pious Israelites of the Infancy Narrative: Zechariah, Elizabeth, Simon and Anna, who observed the law and anticipated redemption. It is to be noted that Luke's addition of Joseph's dissent in crucifying Jesus also throws light on the Kingship of Jesus along with Joseph's anticipation of the Kingdom.

While the Synoptics note the presence of women at Jesus' burial, by the group present at the time of burial; particularly the women from Galilee, Luke depicts the sympathy of the crowd toward Jesus amidst the issue of survival. It indicates acceptance and pursuance of Jesus by his followers till his burial as their King. However, Luke's burial sequence and the added reference to the role of Galilean women involving the preparation of spices and ointments, their rest on the Sabbath day, and witnessing the empty tomb on the event of Sunday depict the unique composition of Luke to denote the victory of the King in his resurrection.

Luke presents Jesus, the Kingly Messiah as a victorious King in the event of temptation as he was victorious over the devil. In Lukan understanding, he didn't submit to the Roman rule for worldly benefits and survival. Even at the time of crucifixion, forgiving the enemies, granting the thief the paradise and committing his spirit depict the victory of the King Jesus. Further, the resurrection of Jesus as a continuous event after the death of Jesus indicates the victory of the King, which is still remembered because the worldly power could not overcome his vision of the Kingdom, a community and the new age, by crucifying him. While the women were at the tomb of Jesus, Matthew and Mark say that an angel was inside the tomb; but Luke speaks of two men standing by them in detail, and the body was not there. Besides, in 24:6f, Luke reminds the fulfillment of prophecy that he rose in accordance with his words, that he would be handed over to the sinful men and crucified and rise on the third day. It seems to be a special material of Luke which indicates the resurrection as Messianic King.

Further, the women are depicted by Luke as the first one to tell the resurrection event to others. In the patriarchal society, amidst the gender oppression during that time, Luke portrays women as the witnesses of Jesus' resurrection. It shows the re-establishment of their position in the society by the life and death of Jesus. So, the event of Jesus' resurrection and the Lukan portrayal of women depict Jesus' victorious Kingship. The empty tomb exposes that Jesus was not under the possession of the oppressive rulers but he is alive and continued his role for the oppressed community as victorious King.

The fulfillment of the prophecies may be seen out of the three passion predictions of Luke in which he mentions Jesus' resurrection in two places: "on the third day be raised"[151] and "on the third day he will rise again."[152] Besides, along with the reminding of the prophecy to the women in 24:7f, Luke adds the conversation of the risen Jesus with the two men on their way to Emmaus. From Jesus' conversation with them, mentioned in 24:26, "Was it not necessary that the Messiah should suffer these things and enter into his glory?" It is to be noted that Jesus himself expressed the fulfillment of his prophecy and scripture. It is the climax of Luke's portrayal of Jesus through the lips of Cleopas that Jesus is "a prophet mighty in deed and word before God and all the people"[153] in juxtaposition to the political figures whose promises and their deeds were different. Nevertheless, the table-fellowship with the two to Emmaus[154] indicates his victorious Kingship. According to N.T. Wright, by the resurrection of Jesus a new movement came to birth from the state of apparent defeat.[155] Massey considers the resurrection event as, "Mission accomplished and handed over to a community."[156] N. T. Wright and Massey may be correct in their observation of the continuing mission of Jesus. But, historically, in the early church, the Resurrection experience of the Lukan community is vivid in their declaration of "the Lord has risen,"[157] which exposes the victory of Jesus over the Roman power. In other words, Jesus as a victorious King restored the hope of the people which was under dilemma by his death. It may be defined as a resurrected experience of the community under the victorious Kingship of Jesus in those days.

After Jesus' resurrection, in 24:34, as a sign of proclaiming the victory of Jesus' by his followers, the title ὁ κύριος to Jesus is used by Luke as it is used in the angelic announcement to the shepherds, in which the birth of Jesus was announced as the Messiah, the Lord. The title, ὁ χριστός is the post-Easter confession. J. D. G. Dunn sees this post-Easter confession as an impact of Jesus' death and resurrection which transformed his followers to understand the Old Testament scriptures as an "Ongoing Revelation," in light of his Messiahship.[158] For the followers of Jesus what they heard during his life time and praised him as King during the triumphal entry procession was confirmed after his resurrection as they believed him as the Lord, the alternative King to the Roman Emperor. Luke decisively portrays Jesus' Kingship by the titles, ὁ κύριος and ὁ χριστός through his resurrection and the witnesses, as proclaiming the victory, as it was later understood by the early church. The victorious King Jesus is portrayed in 24:5 as the living and contrasted against the dead.[159]

At the end of Luke's Gospel, Jerusalem becomes the vantage point of apostolic proclamation of repentance and salvation.[160] Luke only gives the story of Ascension as a historical event in which Jesus was enthroned as a divine King whom the Israelites were anticipating. Leaney says that by the ascension episode, Luke portrays Jesus as not only the King of Israel, but also as King of the universe.[161] In Acts 17:7, it is told that the risen Lord was considered by the early church as an alternative King to Caesar. According to J. M. Sheridan, the proleptic proclamation of Jesus' Kingship in the Infancy Narrative was recognized and proclaimed after Jesus' resurrection.[162] Jesus' victorious Kingship is well exposed in the scene of ascension which is neither a military action nor an armed deliverance from Rome by exercising power over others but paradoxically as a suffering King who exercises his power through service and sacrifice.

In commissioning the mission of the Twelve, as already seen in the event of the Last Supper in 22:14-30, in which the Kingdom is promised to them, Luke reveals Jesus' Kingship at the end by extending his role to his disciples to proclaim the good news of repentance and forgiveness which are the basic elements in entering into the alternative Kingdom in the socio-political world of Luke. From the outset of the Gospel till Jesus' death and also a continuing process, Luke portrays Jesus as a King who restores people from their sin. By commissioning the disciples, Jesus as Messianic King is open to forgive sins and to accept the sinners into his fellowship even after his death and resurrection as a victorious King.

Eventually, this research about the Kingship of Jesus in Luke leads one towards the understanding of Lukan Christology as more relevant to our Third World country of India, in its cultural, political, social and religious context, in view of Liberation. Jesus' socio-economic and political attitude has knocked down the dominant values of imperial oppression empowering the alienated, as it has been noticed all along from the Lukan Jesus' teachings on rich and poor. His positive emphasis on the despised Samaritans, the rival Gentiles; and, the vulnerable women, and his acceptance of sinners along with the prominence of salvation also point to its acceptance and relevance in our own situation.

Relevance of Lukan Christology of Jesus the King in the Indian Context

According to K. C. Abraham, Christologizing means, "to be committed to the struggle for a new social order and to participate in the pains of its birth and in the joys of the new creation."[163] The researcher being an Indian seeks to find out the relevance of Lukan Christology for the people of India in accordance with the time and milieu of people who read the Gospel. While relating Christology to the Indian situation, the first and foremost issue that comes to the mind is, can there be an Indian Christology or Christology relevant to India? That is when the revelation of Lukan Jesus is universal and crosses all barriers of race and culture, can one speak of an Indian Christology as if there are multiple understanding of Christologies in other continents. On this issue, therefore, the phrase Christology relevant to India is preferable, because interpreting the King Jesus in relevance to Indian terms, concepts and cultural forms help the Indians to understand him in the Indian context.

To make Christology intelligible to the people concerned with every culture, their cultural expression can be used as vehicles of thought.[164] K. Y. Beck points out that the Christology in the West is clothed with their political and cultural values and Christ is portrayed as a "dominant ruler like a King, a conqueror, or a colonizer,"[165] whereas, the crucified King, Jesus seems to be a person among the sufferings and struggles of Asians and is viewed as a liberator of the poor, the alienated, oppressed and the discriminated people. So, the Christological open-endedness, therefore, invites us to discover our own particular Christology along with the specific significance of Jesus' Kingship for our third world situation. The historically and culturally conditioned Lukan Christology is relevant to the Indian realities of poor who are broken, mutilated, uprooted, marginalized, and ignored, and as their cry for survival, recognition, and meaning of life and in their anticipation for liberation.

Lukan Christology challenges liberation theology and deals with an option of life for all humankind in the rebuilding of hope for the poor, the dalits, and, the victims of oppression by racial, caste, creed and gender discrimination as well expect the repentance of the oppressors. The Kingship of Jesus relevant to our Indian context will be discussed as follows: a) Jesus the people-centered King: a fellow struggler; b) Jesus the messianic King: an *Avatar*; c) Jesus the alternative King: *Sama Pandhi*; d) Jesus the crucified King: crowned with thorns; and, e) Jesus the victorious King: hope of the powerless.

Jesus the People-centered King: A Fellow Struggler

Luke's Jesus, the Kingly Messiah is understood as an alternative, people-centered and, a benefactor King in solidarity with the people who longed for liberation against the oppressive Roman Emperor. It is vivid in his acceptance of John's baptism. His teachings and life depict him as a King for the betterment of people and benefactor of those who are under political-economic-religious slavery and distanced by divisions. His call for the rededication of people from sin of worshipping the emperor and table-fellowships invites the sinners to repentance and form a new community. The people proclaimed him as the King in the triumphal entry procession. By his people-centered activity he re-orders the position of the people.

In India, Lukan Christology of people-centered Kingship of Jesus may probably change the complex oppressive structure. While religious pluralism and various linguistic differences are on the one hand praised as unity in diversity, and on the other hand it is questionable whether Indians are really united and living in peace in their day to day life. Religious clashes; linguistic clashes; caste differences; class differences; gender inequality; and economic injustice are identified as the burning issues. As *Pax Romana* appeared in Rome in the 1st century CE, the illusionary peace and unity appearances are very much noticeable in India. Indian people are longing for peaceful life. As Luke depicts the birth scene of Jesus with the declaration of peace by the heavenly host, only the Kingly Messiah, Jesus who lives among and with the people could give real peace in the unjust and oppressive context of India.

In the multi-religious context of India, though various religious people are living, the *Hindutva* movement is always a threat to the harmonious living of the people. It leads to exclusivism and particularism. They want to dominate by their ancient Hindu culture. Not only that, it has become a political religion moving forward towards a fundamental and militant Hindu nationalism. According to R. E. Frykenberg, caste Hindus would rule India and with their anti-Muslim motivation, in the near future, and soon a Hindu Muslim riot is expected.[166] Not only with Muslims, but also against Christianity they are mounting up the 'Hindutva' ideology. While constructing the 'Essentials of Hindutva,' V. D. Savarkar, in his Book, *Hindutva: Who is a Hindu?* states, "Jesus died but Christ has survived the Roman Emperors and that Empire,"[167] and further says that Christians belong to Palestine not to India. Following his view, A. Shourie, in his book, *Harvesting Our Soul: Missionaries, Their Design, Their Claims,* offers every reader, an open invitation to counter Christianity in India.[168] It is an ongoing process among the Hindu fanatic movements like RSS. It should be noted that this commotion is not only against Islam and Christianity, but also towards other religions in India. In this situation of apparent peace, only the Kingly Messiah Jesus, as a benefactor, people-centered King who travelled through the enemy village Samaria even though he was rejected there, as we read in Lk 9:51-56, can change their attitude and grant real peace.

Jesus the Messianic King: An Avatar

Jesus' mission and movement constituted both direct and indirect resistance to the Roman imperial order in Galilee and Judea. Jesus' miracles and exorcisms seem to be a restoration of freedom from Roman domination and oppression of the people. While, both the Romans and the religious leaders oppressed the poor, Jesus' poor-centered message spoke of their liberation subjecting them to God's Kingdom. For instance, as it has been noted in the *Magnificat, Beatitude,* and the parable of the Richman, their status is expected of reversal in the messianic Kingship, which is a rule of grace, justice, peace, freedom, and love.

Jesus' birth in this world by the angelic declaration as a Messianic King along with the Davidic descent, and the political overtones of the reversal of power in Mary' song and, the person and work of Jesus in a revolutionary manner reveal him as the Messianic King. His Messianic entry is disclosed by the Nazareth manifesto of good news to the poor, release to the captives, recovery of sight to the blind, etc. His social vision and challenges indicate the inclusive vision of accepting and assuring new life to the sinners, poor, out caste by forgiveness. The mission of healing, exorcism, liberation of the oppressed, raising the dead and empowering of women and restoring the positions of the oppressed and powerless in the socio-political world of Luke imply Jesus' Messianic Kingship. In general, according to Luke, the incarnation of Jesus the messianic King is to save the people from their oppressive state of bondage as saviour and liberator. Phan points out that the repeated failures of political and religious leaders of Israel created the anticipation of decisive coming of God to establish theocracy through the King Messiah.[169]

In this venture, one cannot think of India without taking into account religious pluralism.[170] The Incarnation of Jesus is often understood in relation to the Hindu concept of *avatara*. Thomas states that incarnation is not a mere appearance as *avatara*, rather an articulation of human experiences as recorded in the Gospels.[171] While finding suitable Indian terms to capture, depict and understand Jesus, words may connote different meanings and nuances to Indians.[172] *Avatara* literally means 'descend,' and popularly used to refer to "the manifestation of God in human form" which doesn't mean incarnation, i.e., "becoming human."[173] It could be understood from the doctrine of the virgin birth instead of a manifestation in human form. The term *avatara* etymologically means, "to cross over, to come down or to descend." Normally ten *avataras* of Vishnu are accounted for in Hinduism including Rama and Krishna avataras.[174]

Avatara, according to F. X. D'Sa, is experiencing the pervasive presence of the divine.[175] In the Hindu concept, Krishna *avatara* must be understood from the context of *ksatria dharma*, from the battle described in the *Bhagavadgita*, between Arjuna and the Pandavas, the sons of Dhrtarstra.[176] In terms of establishing *dharma*, Krishna helps Arjuna as "a loving teacher and liberator."[177] The doctrine of *Avatara* signifies the supreme God, Vishnu's appearance in various forms in different times for the sake of liberating the world. *Rama avatara* is described in the epic of *Valmiki Ramayana*, in which Rama is depicted as an ideal King, promoter of ideal human relationships, ideal husband and friend of the weak and the oppressed.[178]

However, concerning the relevance of the term *avatara* for incarnation in India, there are differences of opinion among Indian Christian theologians. R. Boyd and M. M. Thomas say that V. Chakkarai, P. Chenchiah and A. J. Appasamy use it in parallel to the concept of incarnation; whereas, Brahmabandav Upadhyaya, Abhishiktananda and Panikkar don't find this term for a useful Christological reflection.[179] Incarnation of Jesus has occurred only once in history, that too as a human. Jesus was born, lived, died and rose from death. So, the term, *avatara* is inadequate to interpret the incarnation of Jesus except in communicating the presence of God among human beings. On the other hand, Rama is depicted in the epic as a powerful king, who effaced the tribe of Rakshasas, but Luke depicts Jesus as a humble, servant, powerless King who was born from above and fulfilled the Messianic liberation and justice.

Jesus the Alternative King: Sama Pandhi

Against the emperor of Rome and its oppressive nature an alternative King was anticipated by the Lukan community. Exploitation, marginalization and slavery were prevailing and no real peace was among them while pax Augusta/Romana are declared. Amidst the good news to the world during Augustus' birthday, Jesus' birth was announced as Good news to all. Jesus proved him as an alternative King by not accepting the test of prostration before Satan which indicates bestowing kingdom by worshipping the emperor. Catching people for new life, the motto of Jesus which is explicit in the call and commissioning of his disciples and, the command of preaching repentance and forgiveness indicate his alternative Kingship inclusive of everyone irrespective of caste, creed and colour and also the oppressed and the oppressor.

Jesus' revolutionary act of transformation in social system: among women, poor, the exploited and, religious practices; transcending exclusivism and, geographical and social boundaries along with the intention of repentance, restoration, reciprocity, humility, and self surrender depict his alternative Kingship and the new community life of the people.

In India, people are separated by caste, tribe, man and woman within the same caste etc. Due to the varnasramadharma of Hinduism, caste identity is praised. The concept of pollution and untouchables are the customs in it. Ritual purity and the idea of sacred blood on earth are emphasized. Due to this oppressive structure of Hinduism, community life is lost and liberation is needed to come out of this structural exploitation. It is being identified that the Dalits are not only under the oppression of social bondage, but also according to M. C. Raj and Jyothi's writings, they are affected by a wounded psyche.[180] Recognition and acceptance is needed for them in the society, especially for the Dalit women, who are normally addressed as Dalits within Dalits, because they are thrice-alienated, thrice-marginalized and subordinated because of gender, caste and class,[181] they need to be uplifted.

The Song of Mary, the Magnificat discloses the reversal of power in the presence of the alternative King Jesus. Also the miracles of Jesus during his Galilean ministry expose his social acceptance and resistance to exploitation of the marginalized through his messianic authority and deeds. He healed the leprosy affected person,[182] who was considered as unclean by the purity regulations of the religion of those days. By touching him, Jesus extended to the affected person his concern and acceptance into the society. The healing of the unclean woman who touched his garment[183] affected not only by menstruation but also having a wounded psyche, indicates his full acceptance of her into the society in restoring her position. It is also seen in the healing of the crippled woman[184] who was made straight, to stand up in a restored position in the society. Like the Dalits, the Tribals, Backward Castes, Fisher folk, Landless Labourers and so on; as they in India undergo deprivation and separation need human self-understanding of equality, dignity, rights, freedom and the community life.

Another important staggering scenario in India is poverty. Seven decades have passed since independence. Poverty: inequality, deprivation, loneliness, bankruptcy, social exclusion, committing suicide, etc., are the common phenomena in India. It runs from generation to generation as commented by B. B. Malik, "Poverty breeds poverty."[185] Jesus, the Kingly Messiah identified himself in solidarity with the least and the last, the poor and the oppressed in their struggle for seeking human dignity and social justice. In the parable of the Rich man and Lazarus,[186] Jesus condemned the economic exploitation of the lovers of money and preached the reversal of fortunes in the establishment of justice and righteousness in his Kingship. The reversal of fortune is already revealed by Mary through the *Magnificat* in the coming of the alternative Messianic King as a human in the world. In the Nazareth manifesto, Jesus reads from Isa. 61:1f, which reveals the focus of his ministry, a radical social reversal to the poor, where the rich are condemned. Blessing to the poor is one of the central messages of Jesus in Luke. Luke alone adds in his beatitudes a series of woes to the rich and its significance is widespread throughout the Gospel.

Trocmé in light of the concept of non-violent revolution sees Lukan Jesus as the one who revived the Old Testament Jewish custom of "Jubilee."[187] In the Nazareth manifesto, Jesus' programmatic mission includes the proclamation of the Lord's year. Luke portrays Jesus as the one who envisioned a new society based on service and humility along with the non-violent revolution against injustice and oppression. The table-fellowship of Jesus conveys God's invitation to all for God's rule and demonstrates Jesus' praxis of alternative rule. J. Massey sees the Lukan Jesus as one who "offers salvation to all peoples, irrespective of their being rich or poor, high or low, dominant or dominated, ruler or ruled, men or women, black or white, brown or yellow and so on."[188] The table-fellowship of Jesus in Luke may be understood through the practice of *sama pandhi*[189] irrespective of caste, creed, religion and status, by which people of all castes and creeds sit for a meal as equals. On the whole, diversities of issues in India seem to be challenged by the Kingdom values preached and practised by the alternative, egalitarian King Jesus.

Jesus the Crucified King: Crowned with Thorns

Jesus transformed the society with his humble service as a servant in contrast to the worldly Kings. During the trial his silence and the mockery by soldiers, bystanders, rulers, Herod, a thief and, the inscription on the cross indicate his non violent attitudes against the emperor. He exhibits forgiveness to the enemies, granting paradise even at the time of his death his Kingly nature as powerless, crucified servant King. It may be said that his Kingship did not replace the secular power with another similar or sacred power rather it transformed the power. The powerless-cross as it was then even now proves to be so powerful that it can empower countless persons down the ages.[190] The powerless person Jesus is counted as King through his crucifixion and his humility on the cross even at the time of his death. The disfigured, defeated, broken and bleeding Jesus on the cross gives expression to the divine solidarity with the powerless person. T. Balasuriya says that the proclamation of Jesus' Kingdom of God may be understood as a new person, a new society, and new societal values instead of the prevailing values of money, power, prestige, and group.[191] Jesus, the crucified King depicted in Luke seems to be the fellow-struggler with the oppressed and powerless person in the socio-economic and political context of India. The cross and the crucified King remind the painful reality of the suffering people and symbolizes the marginalized and the dehumanized ones as the fellow-struggler.

In contrary to the view of a fellow-struggler who is crucified and crowned with thorns, like the mighty, powerful King Rama, in India,

Jesus' Kingship has been often portrayed. Boff and Beck hesitate to use the title King to Jesus by depicting the immediate interests of the church, which surfaced as political Christology. They blame that the humble image of Jesus which is weak in power was replaced by a political Christ, in terms of power.[192] Boff says,

> Popes and Kings find an ideological base in the title "Christ the King" to justify their own power, which is not always exercised according to the message of Christ and at times is even contrary to it. Without much self-criticism they identify themselves as Christ's representatives in the world. Thus, for example, the title "Christ the King" was understood in terms of the image of the feudal Kings and absolute Romans and Byzantine monarchs. Later, during the crisis of absolute monarchy, Christ the King was understood as the bearer of powers of legislation, execution and judgment.[193]

Beck in line with Boff says that "Christ has been clothed as the dominant ruler such as King, conqueror, or even colonizer."[194] For him, it gives the impression that Jesus is a dominant King over the people. So, he emphasizes the use of Minjung theology's *kenosis of power* as the fundamental Christological statement.[195]

On the other hand, King-Kingdom terminology recalls the past bitter experience of Indian people under western imperialism.[196] India, and other Asian countries except Thailand, as Phan points out, historically experienced negative things under emperors and Kings.[197] Terminologically the metaphor of King to Jesus may strike a chord of the hardship that people experienced under Kings. It is vivid from the above liberation theologians; the title "King" ascribed to Jesus was misunderstood and misused down the ages. However, Third World theologians like, Kuribayashi and Devasahayam rightly point out the difference between the priestly and princely crowns of the Old Testament and Jesus' crown of thorns. Jesus' crown of thorns carries neither glory nor respect rather a mark of mockery and humiliation and dishonor to be the mark of the powerless King of the Jews.[198]

The crucified King Jesus may be understood as one who speaks and has authority which is neither an authority of imposition, nor an armed force, nor an autocracy, but a strange ruler who is a meek servant. It is vivid in the saying of I. Selvanayagam that the confession of Jesus as Lord by the early Christians indicated the declaration of the reversal in the meaning of Lordship that Roman Caesar is not their Lord but, Jesus though a Lord and King who is a slave ready to serve.[199]

Thus, the Lukan King Jesus falls not in line with the dominant King, but with the humble, powerless, servant who is crucified as King. The revolutionary life, message and vulnerable death of Jesus as presented in Luke, which made the authorities of that day to accredit the title King to him, has relevance to the social and political context of the Third World Countries and particularly, to India today, where we face the problems of oppression through power, wealth, so on and so forth for the survival of the fittest. The victimized, vulnerable, humble, mocked and Crucified King Jesus subverts the oppressive rule by his very humility.

Jesus the Victorious King: Hope of the Powerless

Although Jesus was crucified, died, and buried, the resurrection event exposes Jesus as the victorious King not only by overcoming death, but also overcoming the entrenched patriarchal oppression of women. Women came out alone, became the witness of Jesus' resurrection and re-established their position in the social system. It exposes that the worldly power could not overcome the victorious King's rule for the sake of the oppressed community. It further throws light on the hope of the new age under the alternative, messianic kingship.

Accordingly, in the struggles and sufferings of the marginalized, Jesus happens to be a liberator, saviour, powerless, voiceless, servant and, crucified King who still functions as a fellow struggler; whose teachings and practice of the table-fellowship envisage the *sama pandhi*; who is God incarnated not merely as an *avatara* to establish *dharma*, and, a King with the crown of thorns along with the marks of mockery, humiliation, dishonour, and as a slave to serve for the welfare of the people. As a victimized, vulnerable and crucifed King, he subverts the rule of oppression. As a victorious King he is alive and restores the hope of the oppressed.

Summary

In order to reconstruct the Lukan Christology and its relevance to our present context, the Gospel of Luke is taken as an authentic source of early Christian community along with its motif of Jesus' Kingship. The composition of Luke with this Kingship motif encompasses all the Christological titles along with the soteriological significance in the existential reality of the socio-political world of Luke. From the use of titles in Luke, Jesus' person and work is identified on the basis of how he was understood by the Lukan community. However, it is noticed from the overall portrait of Jesus in this Gospel that the socio-political world of Luke considered Jesus as a people-centered King, who was in solidarity with the people in their oppression; a Messianic King who restores the positions of the deprived and the marginalized; an Alternative King to the oppressive Kingship of Rome along with the community's anticipation of liberation; a Crucified King, as he was accused, mocked and executed; and a Victorious King over the Roman power and becomes the hope for the powerless makes everyone to realize his vision of a new community life.

In seeking the relevance of Jesus' Kingship Christology in our Indian context of religious pluralism, linguistic differences, caste disparities, peaceless situations due to Hindutva and other movements and the power struggles even in Christianity, oppressive structures, poverty and so on, in the struggles and sufferings of Indians, Jesus is viewed as a liberator, a fellow struggler, a powerless King but the hope of the powerless, who by the practice of the table-fellowship and eucharist envisage the *sama pandhi*, who is God incarnate not merely an *avatara* to establish *dharma*, but one who lived as a human being amidst the people; and, a King with the crown of thorns along with the marks of mockery, humiliation, dishonour, and as a slave to serve for the welfare of the people. As a victimized, vulnerable and deprived King, he subverts the rule of oppression wherever injustice prevails.

Endnotes

[1] R. Haight, *The Future of Christology* (London: Continuum, 2005), 33.

[2] J. Moltmann, *The Crucified God: The Cross of Christ as the Foundation and Criticism of Christian Theology*, tr. by R. A. Wilson and J. Bowden (London: SCM Press, 1974), 106.

[3] H. Flender, *St Luke Theologian of Redemptive History*, Tr. by R. H. Fuller and I. Fuller (London: S.P.C.K, 1967), 55; A. Nolan, *Jesus Before Christianity: The Gospel of Liberation* (Darton: Longman and Todd, 1976),113f; J. R. Donahue, "Passion Narrative," *The Interpreter's Dictionary of the Bible,* Supplementary Volume, ed. by K. Crim (Nashville: Abingdon, 1976), 645; O. C. Edwards, *Luke's Story of Jesus* (Philadelphia: Fortress Press, 1981), 87; C. H. Talbert, *Reading Luke: A Literary and Theological Commentary on the Third Gospel* (New York: Crossroad, 1982), 222f; M. A. Powell, *What are they saying about Luke?* (New York: Paulist Press, 1989), 68f; J. B. Green, *Theology of the Gospel of Luke* (Cambridge: University Press, 1995), 64f; and, G. Theissen and A. Merz, *The Historical Jesus* (London: SCM Press Ltd, 1998), 453.

[4] R. Zehnle, "The Salvific Character of Jesus' Death in Lucan Soteriology," *Theological Studies* 30/3 (September 1969): 420; H. Marshall, "The Death of Jesus in Recent New Testament Study," *Word & World* 3/1 (Winter 1983):16, [ATLAS]; R. Kereszty, "Toward a Contemporary Christology," *Crisis in Christology: Essays in Quest of Resolution*, ed. by W. R. Farmer (Michigan: Dove Booksellers, 1995), 341; and, M. Heim, "Rethinking the death of Jesus Cross Purposes," *Christian Century* 122/6 (22 March 2005): 20. [ATLAS]

[5] Flender, *St Luke Theologian of Redemptive History...*, 54; Powell, *What are they saying about Luke?...*, 70f; and, Susan R. Garrett, "The Meaning of Jesus' Death in Luke," *Word & World* 12/1 (Winter 1992):11. [ATLAS]

[6] N.T. Wright, "Paul's Gospel and Caesar's Empire," *Reflections* vol 2 (Spring 1999): 61f.

[7] C. Guignebert, *The Jewish World in the time of Jesus* (New York: University Books, 1959), 253.

[8] Chapter I. 2. a. Roman Imperial Rule of Palestine during 1st Century CE.

[9] H. C. Kee, *Christian Origins in Sociological Perspective* (London: SCM Press, 1980), 56, citing H. J. Mol, *Identity and the Sacred* (Macmillan, 1964), 45.

[10] B. J. Malina, *The Social world of Jesus and the Gospels* (London: Routledge, 1996), 131.

[11] D. S. D. Toit, "Redefining Jesus: Current Trends in Jesus Research," in *Jesus, Mark and Q: The Teaching of Jesus and its Earliest Records*, ed. by M. Labahn and A. Schmidt (England: Sheffield Academic Press, 2001), 122.

[12] Lk. 9:10-17.

[13] Lk. 22:14-38.

[14] R. Williams, *Resurrection* (Harrisburg: Morehouse, 1982), 112.

[15] Lk. 11:39-54.

[16] "Were not ten made clean? But the other nine, where are they? Was none of them found to return and give praise to God except this foreigner?" [Lk. 9:17ff.]

[17] F. W. Danker, "Politics of the New Age According to St. Luke," in *Currents in Theology and Mission* 12/6 (December 1985): 342f.

[18] Lk. 10:29.

[19] Toit, "Redefining Jesus: Current Trends in Jesus Research"..., 83; J. D. Crossan, *The Historical Jesus: The Life of a Mediterranean Jewish Peasant* (New York: Harper Collins, 1991), xxvii.

[20] *Ibid.*, 122.

[21] B. Kinman, "Pilate's Assize and the Timings of Jesus' Trial," *Tyndale Bulletin* 42/2 (1991): 283. ATLAS.

[22] Lk. 19:45.

[23] Mk. 11:9.

[24] Mt. 21:9 & 11; in 21:46, Matthew depicts that the authorities wanted to arrest him but they could not, because the crowd regarded him as a prophet.

[25] J. A. Fitzmyer, *The Gospel According to Luke I-IX* (New York: Doubleday& Company, 1986), 309; M. Coleridge, *The Birth of the Lukan Narrative: Narrative as Christology in Luke 1-2* (England: Sheffield Academic Press, 1993), 227; S. M. Sheeley, *Narrative Asides in Luke-Acts* (Sheffield: Academic Press, 1992), 144.

[26] In Lk. 1:27, Luke says that Joseph is "of the house of David".

[27] Mic. 5:1f.

[28] M. C. Parsons, *Luke: Storyteller, Interpreter, Evangelist* (Peabody: Hendrickson, 2007), 152f.

[29] Oepke, "βαπτω" in *Theological Dictionary of the New Testament,* ed. by G. Kittel (Grand Rapids: William. B. Eerdmans, 1964), 537; P. J. Tomson, "Jesus and his Judaism," ..., 30.

[30] W. Carter, *The Roman Empire and the New Testament* (Nashville: Abingdon Press, 2006), 98.

[31] A. Maclaren, *St. Luke* (Grand Rapids: Wm. B. Eerdmans, 1932), 22; C. R. Erdman, *The Gospel of Luke* (Philadelphia: The Westminster Press, 1925), 27.

[32] Cf. Mal. 4:2.

[33] D. Jones, "The Background and Character of the Lukan Psalms," *The Journal of Theological Studies* 19/1 (April, 1968): 40.

[34] Lk. 2:34b-35.

[35] J. Nolland, *Word Biblical Commentary*, vol. 35: Luke 1:1-9:20 (Dallas: Word Books, 1998), 108.

[36] Lk. 19:38.

[37] Lk. 4:16-30; cf. Mk. 6:1-6.

[38] Lk. 4:21.

[39] Cf. Jn. 6:15 &27.

[40] R. Heskett, *Messianism within the Scriptural Scroll of Isaiah* (New York: T&T Clark, 2007), 248.

[41] Carter, *The Roman Empire and the New Testament...*, 20.

[42] J. D. Crossan, *The Birth of Christianity: Discovering What Happened in the Years Immediately After the Execution of Jesus* (Edinburgh: T&T Clark, 1998), 304.

[43] A. Storkey, *Jesus and Politics: Confronting the Powers* (Grand Rapids: Baker Academic, 2005), 86.

[44] Lk. 4:38-41; Mt. 8:14-17 & Mk. 1:29-34.

[45] Lk. 4:41.

[46] Lk. 8:26-39; Mt. 8:28-9:1 & Mk. 5:1-20.

[47] J. B. Green, *The Theology of the Gospel of Luke* (Cambridge: University Press, 1995), 95.

[48] G. E. Ladd, *A Theology of the New Testament* (London: Lutterworth Press, 1975), 76.

[49] Lk. 5:12-16 & 17:11-19.

[50] Lk. 5:13.

[51] R. W. Roschke, "Healing in Luke, Madagascar, and Elsewhere," *Currents in Theology and Mission* 33/6 (December, 2006): 469.

[52] C. K. Barrett, *St. John* (London, SPCK, 1978), 238; Samaritans were neither Jews nor non-Jews. Samaritans used the Pentateuch as their Scripture. Like the Jews, they followed the Israelite biblical tradition. [R. Plummer, "Samaritanism - a Jewish Sect or an Independent Form of Yahwism?" in

Samaritans Past and Present: Current Studies, ed. by M. Mor and F. V. Reiterer (Berlin: Walter de Gruyter GmbH & Co, 2010), 16f.]; the rivalry concerning the worship place is apparent in the conversation of Jesus with the Samaritan woman in John's Gospel. [Jn 4:20.]

[53] Lk. 8:43-48; Mt. 9:18-26 & Mk. 5:21-43.

[54] This event of healing the crippled woman is from the Travel Narrative. But, I group all the miracles together to see the intention of the author in describing them.

[55] L. M. Maloney and E. J. Smith, "The Year of Luke: A Feminist Perspective," *Currents in Theology and Mission* 21/6 (December, 1994): 422.

[56] Lk. 13:12f.

[57] The healing of the dropsical man in 14:1-6 also raises the same issue of Sabbath.

[58] 2 Sam. 7:13, 16, 26 & 1 Chr. 17:12, 14, 42; M. D. Hamm, "The Freeing of the Bent Woman and the Restoration of Israel: Luke 13:10-17 as Narrative Theology," *Journal for the Study of the New Testament* 31 (October, 1987): 28.

[59] Lk. 7:20-22.

[60] Lk. 9:20f.

[61] Lk. 9:28-36.

[62] Lk. 9:31.

[63] Cf. Mt. 21:33-46 & Mk. 12:1-12.

[64] Mt. 26:63.

[65] Mk. 14:61f.

[66] Lk. 22:67f.

[67] Mt. 27:11-14; Mk. 15:2-5 & Jn. 18:29-38.

[68] Lk. 2:10f.

[69] R. E. Brown, *The Birth of the Messiah: A Commentary on the Infancy Narratives in Matthew and Luke* (London: Geoffrey Chapman, 1977), 415f.

[70] Joel B. Green, *New Testament Theology: Theology of the Gospel of Luke* (Cambridge: University Press, 1995), 7f; S. Kim, *Christ and Caesar* (Grand Rapids: William B. Eerdmans, 2008), 80f.

[71] Lk. 3:1ff.

[72] *The Antiquities of the Jews* 17:6. 2f, [W. Whiston, A.M. (tr), *The Works of Josephus: Complete and Unabridged,* new updated edition (Peabody: Hendrickson, 2008), 461].

[73] J. H. *Elliott*, "Temple Versus Household in Luke-Acts: A Contrast in Social Institutions," in *The Social world of Luke-Acts: Models for Interpretation*, ed. by J. Neyrey (Peabody: Hendrickson, 1991), 221.

[74] M. Hengel, *Crucifixion* (Philadelphia: Fortress Press, 1977), 13.

[75] Carter, *The Roman Empire and the New Testament...*, 7.

[76] Mt. 26:57-68; Mk. 14:53-65; Lk. 22:54-71 & Jn. 18:13-24.

[77] Carter, *The Roman Empire and the New Testament...*, 17; K.Yamazaki-Ransom, *The Roman Empire in Luke's Narrative* (New York: T&T Clark, 2010), 97.

[78] Lk. 22:48.

[79] Lk. 9:10-17.

[80] Lk. 6:12-16; Mt. 10:1-4 & Mk. 3:13-19a.

[81] Lk. 9:2.

[82] H. G. Liddell and R. Scott, *A Greek-English Lexicon* (Oxford: Clarendon Press, 1882), 950; W. Bauer, *A Greek-English Lexicon of the New Testament and other Early Christian Literature*, tr. by W. F. Arndt and F. W. Gingrich, 2nd revised ed. (Chicago: University Press, 1979), 513.

[83] Danker, "Politics of the New Age According to St. Luke,"..., 343.

[84] Lk. 13:20f.

[85] Lk. 15:8-10.

[86] Lk. 18:1-8.

[87] Lk. 1:46-55.

[88] Lk. 6:20-26.

[89] Lk. 4:25-27.

[90] Lk. 5:32; Sheeley, *Narrative Asides in Luke-Acts...*, 142.

[91] M. A. Beavis, "Expecting Nothing in Return," *Interpretation* 48/4 (October, 1994): 363.

[92] Lk. 5:11.

[93] Lk. 4:14 & 18.

[94] Lk. 4: 32 & 36.

[95] Lk. 5:20-26.

[96] Lk. 4:32; 5:26; 8:25, 56 & 9:43.

[97] Lk. 5:21-24; 6:11; 7:49; 11:14-16 & 13:13-17.

[98] E. P. Sanders, *Jesus and Judaism* (London: SCM Press, 1985), 203; Crossan, *The Birth of Christianity...*, 339f.

[99] M. Gourgues, "The Priest, The Levite, and The Samaritan Revisited: A Critical Note on Luke 10:31-35," *Journal of Biblical Literature* 117/4 (Winter, 1998): 713; Deut. 6:5 & Lev. 19:18; L. Schottroff, *The Parables of Jesus,* tr. by L. M. Maloney (Minneapolis: Fortress Press, 2006), 195.

[100] Parsons, *Luke: Storyteller...*, 120.

[101] Cf. Mt. 13:31f & Mk. 4:30-32.

[102] Cf. Mt. 13:33.

[103] Cf. Mt. 21:33-46 & Mk. 12: 1-12.

[104] Lk. 14:15-24 & Mt. 22:1-10.

[105] Lk. 7:24ff; cf. Mt. 11:2-19.

[106] P. J. Tomson, "Jesus and his Judaism," in *The Cambridge Companion to Jesus,* ed. by M. Bockmuehl (Cambridge: University Press, 2001), 31.

[107] J. L. Houlden, "Passion Narratives," *A Dictionary of Biblical Interpretation,* ed. by R. J. Coggins and J. L. Houlden (London: SCM Press, 1990), 516.

[108] W. P. Weaver, *The Historical Jesus in the Twentieth Century 1900-1950* (Pennsylvania: Trinity Press International, 1999), 20.

[109] J. D. Crossan, *In Parables: The Challenge of the Historical Jesus* (California: Polebridge Press, 1992...), 23f; G. N. Stanton, *The Gospels and Jesus* (London: Oxford University Press, 1989), 225f.

[110] W. G. Morrice, *Hidden Sayings of Jesus: Words Attributed to Jesus Outside the Four Gospels* (Great Britain: SPCK, 1997), 103.

[111] Crossan, *In Parables...*, 25f.

[112] M. Burrows, "Thy Kingdom Come," *Journal of Biblical Literature* 74/1 (March, 1955): 8.

[113] G. E. Ladd, "The Kingdom of God – Reign or Realm?" *Journal of Biblical Literature* 81/3 (September, 1962): 237.

[114] L. Legrand, "Christological Issues in the New Testament," *The Indian Journal of Theology* 24/3&4 (July- December1975): 73.

[115] E. F. Scott, *The Kingdom and the Messiah* (Edinburgh: T&T Clark, 1911), 150; Stanton, *The Gospels and Jesus...*, 205.

[116] Lk. 20:20-26; Mt. 22:15-22 & Mk. 12:13-17.

[117] Lk. 21:5-24.

[118] 1 Macc. 1:20-50.

[119] Lk. 22:52.

[120] Lk. 23:37.

[121] Lk. 23:38.

[122] Lk. 22:70.

[123] L. Boff, *Jesus Christ Liberator: A Critical Christology of Our Time*, tr. by P. Huges (New York: Orbis Books, 1981), 63.

[124] Toit, "Redefining Jesus: Current Trends in Jesus Research"..., 119.

[125] Moltmann, *The Crucified God...*, 114.

[126] J. B. Green, "Preparation for Passover (Luke 22:7-13): A Question of Redactional Technique," *Novum Testamentum* 29/4 (1987): 312; D. Senior, C.P., *The Passion of Jesus in the Gospel of Luke* (Wilmington: Michael Glazier, 1989), 17.

[127] J. A. Fitzmyer, *The Gospel According to Luke X-XXIV*, vol. 2 (New York: Doubleday, 1986), 1391; Scott, *The Kingdom and the Messiah...*, 236.

[128] Lk. 22:48.

[129] Lk. 22:70.

[130] Lk. 23:1-5.

[131] H. K. Bond, *Caiaphas: Friend of Rome and Judge of Jesus?* (Westminister: John Knox Press, 2004), 110.

[132] Lk. 23:33. Cf. Mt. 27:33; Mk. 15:22 & Jn. 19:17.

[133] F. J. Matera, "The Trial of Jesus: Problems and Proposals," *Interpretation* 45/1 (January, 1991): 2; Theissen, *The Historical Jesus...*, 516; R. E. Brown, "The Death of Jesus and Anti-Semitism Seeking Interfaith Understanding," http://www. google.com/paper; Carter, *The Roman Empire and the New Testament...*, xi; Moltmann, *The Crucified God...*, 144; Hengel, *Crucifixion...*, 86.

[134] H. Conzelmann, "History and Theology in the Passion Narratives of the Synoptic Gospels," *Interpretation* 24/2 (April 1970): 191.

[135] Lk. 23:35.

[136] Lk. 23:38.

[137] Theissen, *The Historical Jesus...*, 458.

[138] J. M. Creed, *The Gospel According to St. Luke* (London: Macmillan and Co., 1930), 284.

[139] Mk. 15:39 & Mt. 27:54.

[140] D. Carr, *Sword of the Spirit: An Activist's Understanding of the Bible* (Geneva: WCC, 1992), 42.

[141] Gen. 6: 2,4; Deut. 32:8; Job 1:6-12; 2:1-6; 38:7; Ps. 29:1; 89:6 & Dan. 3:25.

[142] Ex. 4:22; Deut. 14:1; Isa. 43:6; Jer. 31:9; Hos. 1:10 & 11:1.

[143] 2 Sam. 7:14. Cf. 1 Chr. 17:13; 22:10 & 28:6; Ps. 2:7 & 89:26f; J. D. G. Dunn, *Christology in the Making* (London: SCM Press, 1989), 15.

[144] H. G. Liddell and R. Scott, *A Greek-English Lexicon.* Vol I α-κώψ (Oxford: Clarendon Press, 1925), 429.

[145] Lk. 23:45f.

[146] Kee, *Christian Origins in Sociological Perspective...*, 111.

[147] D. D. Sylva, "The Temple Curtain and Jesus' Death in the Gospel of Luke," *Journal of Biblical Literature* 105/2 (1986): 247; F. J. Matera, "The Death of Jesus according to Luke: A Question of Sources," *The Catholic Biblical Quarterly* 47/3 (July, 1985): 484.

[148] *Ibid.*, 18.

[149] Lk. 23:4, 14, 22; 23:15; 23:41 and 23:47; Edwards, *Luke's Story of Jesus...*, 87; Theissen, *The Historical Jesus...*, 453; Talbert, *Reading Luke...*, 224; Powell, *What are they saying about Luke?...*, 68f; Donahue, "Passion Narrative,"..., 645.

[150] Lk. 23:50-56; Mk. 15:42-47; Mt. 27:57-61 & Jn. 19:38-42.

[151] Lk. 9:22.

[152] Lk. 18:33.

[153] Lk. 24:19.

[154] Lk. 24:29-35.

[155] N. T. Wright, *Who Was Jesus?* (Grand Rapids: William B, Eerdmans, 1992), 59.

[156] J. Massey, *The Gospel According to Luke,* Dalit Bible Commentary, New Testament vol. 3 (New Delhi: Centre for Dalit /Subaltern Studies, 2007), 222.

[157] Lk. 24:34.

[158] J. D. G. Dunn, *New Testament Theology: an Introduction* (Nashville: Abingdon Press, 2009), 21&24.

[159] "Why do you look for the living among the dead?"

[160] J. D. Kingsbury, *Conflict in Luke: Jesus, Authorities, Disciples* (Minneapolis: Fortress Press, 1991), 7.

[161] A. R. C. Leaney, *A Commentary on the Gospel according to St. Luke* (London: Adam & Charles Black, 1958), 34.

[162] J. M. Sheridan, "Proclaiming the King – Preaching the Kingdom," *Bible Today* 87 (December, 1976): 996.

[163] K. C. Abraham, *Third World Theologies: Commonalities and divergences* (Tiruvalla: EATWOT/ CSS, 1995), 235.

[164] V. P. Thomas, "Towards and Indian Christology," *The Indian Journal of Theology* 14/1 (January-March, 1965): 1f.

[165] K. Y. Beck, "Jesus Christ Among Asian Minjung: A Christological Reflection," in *God, Christ & God's People in Asia,* ed. by D. Carr (Hong Kong: CCA Theological concerns, 1995), 12f.

[166] R. E. Frykenberg, "The Sacred in Modern Hindu Politics: Historical Processes Underlying Hinduism and Hindutva," in *Hinduism in India,* ed. by W. Sweetman and A. Malik (New Delhi: Sage, 2016), 109.

[167] V. D. Savarkar, *Hindutva,* 6th ed., (Bharti Sahitya Sadan: New Delhi-1, 1989), 2.

[168] A. Shourie, *Harvesting Our Soul: Missionaries, their design, their claims,* (ASA: New Delhi, 2000), 418.

[169] Phan, "Kingdom of God: a symbol for Asians?"..., 21.

[170] M. Amaladoss, "Images of Jesus in India," *East Asian Pastoral Review* 31/1-2 (1994): 7.

[171] Thomas, "Towards and Indian Christology,"..., 6.

[172] *Ibid.,* 2.

[173] Amaladoss, "Images of Jesus in India,"..., 18f.

[174] J. Parappally, "The Indian Context of Christological Reflection," *Indian Journal of Spirituality* 8/3 (September 1995): 380.

[175] F. X. D'Sa, "Christian Incarnation and Hindu Avatara," in *Any Room for Christ in Asia?* Ed. by L. Boff and V. Elizondo, *Concilium* (London: SCM Press, 1993), 82.

[176] In Hindu Vedic understanding, *ksatriya* is one of the four divisions of labour, from which the King comes to power. [P. Bowlby, "Kings without authority: The obligation of the ruler to gamble in the Mahabharata," *Studies in Religion/Sciences Religieuses* 20/1 (1991): 4.]

[177] Parappally, "The Indian Context of Christological Reflection,"..., 381.

[178] K. A. Abraham, *A Re-examination of the Lordship of Jesus Christ in the search for a Contemporary Christology in Asia* (SATHRI: D.Th. Thesis, 1996), 284ff.

[179] Lin, "Christology and Christologies in India,"..., 12.

[180] M. C. Raj & Jyothi, Dyche, The Dalit Psyche: A Science of Dalit Psychology, (Tumkur: ARC, 2008), 43.

[181] M. J. Melanchthon, "Dalit Readers of the Word: The Quest for Hermeneutics and Method," *Frontiers in Dalit Hermeneutics,* ed. by James Massey and Samson Prabhakar (Bangalore: SATHRI, 2005), 45

[182] Lk. 5:12ff.

[183] Lk. 8:43ff.

[184] Lk. 13:10ff.

[185] B. B. Malik, *Poverty in India – Fundamental Issues* (New Delhi: Mittal, 2009), 70.

[186] Lk. 16:19ff.

[187] Powell, *What are They Saying About Luke?...,* 86.

[188] J. Massey, *The Gospel According to Luke...,* 26.

[189] *Sama Pandhi* is a mid-day meal organized by the Government and social groups in villages to bring unity among the villagers.

[190] P. C. Phan, "Kingdom of God: a symbol for Asians?" *Theology Digest* 47/1 (Spring 2000): 24.

[191] T. Balasuriya, *Planetary Theology* (Maryknoll: Orbis, 1984), 134 referred to by P. C. Phan, "Kingdom of God: A Theological Symbol for Asians?" *Gregorianum* 79/2 (1998): 302.

[192] Boff, *Jesus Christ Liberator...,* 26f.

[193] *Ibid.,* 230.

[194] Beck, "Jesus Christ Among Asian Minjung..."..., 12.

[195] *Ibid.,* 14.

[196] P. B. Santram, "Jesus Christ and the Kingdom of God: A New Testament Perspective," *The Indian Journal of Theology* 29/2 (April–June, 1980): 91.

[197] Phan, "Kingdom of God: A Theological Symbol for Asians?" ..., 299.

[198] T. Kuribayashi, "Theology of the Crowned with Thorns," *God, Christ & God's People in Asia,* ed. by D. Carr (Hong Kong: CCA Therological concerns, 1995), 101-108; V. Devasahayam, "A Theological Response to the Stories of the Discriminated Against and Subjugated Peoples of Asia," *God, Christ & God's People in Asia,* ed. by D. Carr (Hong Kong: CCA Theological concerns, 1995), 133.

[199] I. Selvanayagam, "Who is This Jesus?" *The Asia Journal of Theology* 7/2 (1993): 233.

Conclusion

This book substantiates the fact that Luke, the author of the third Gospel composed it with the motif of Jesus' Kingship, which emerges out of its cultural, social, political, economical, ecological and historical milieu. The relevance of Lukan Kingship Christology to the present day Indian context is helpful to those who aspire for a better understanding of Jesus and the Gospel.

The first chapter, "Anticipation of the King in the Socio-Political World of Luke" exhibits the title King in various Social, Historical, Political and Biblical milieu as it connotes an ideal King who is the representative of a group, a divine being, a benefactor and a servant King. Particularly in Rome, as the emperor was considered as the son of god and worshiped as god. In the Old Testament, in political as well as in *religious* sense it denoted the king as well as Yahweh. In Israel's monarchy and royal history, the tension between theocracy and human Kingship evolved later as a Christocentric Messianic Kingship. The messianic idea can be traced to 2 Sam 7:11-16 and the prophecies of the Old Testament concerning the promise of the restoration of the Davidic rule.

Even in the Intertestamental period, the Dead Sea scrolls and the pseudepigraphical writings give evidence to the prevalence of the concept of the Messianic King. The socio-political world of Luke reveals in ample measure the marginal group of the time, comprising of both the Jews and Gentiles inclusive of the rich, poor, the crippled, blind, lame and guests, in its *sitz im leben* of socio-economic, ecological, political and cultural milieu under Greco-Roman dominance. In their oppressive socio-political structure, they longed to have another King to redeem them from the social unrest. Recent studies in Q also have reconstructed the socio-political world and found the social division in the fundamental structural opposition of the ruling communities in Palestine with their historical regional differences, particularly between Judea/Jerusalem and Galilee, and its eco-related expressions which underline the social and political conflicts of the first century CE.

In the second chapter, "Kingship Motif in the Infancy Narrative," Infancy Narrative serves as a powerful source of introduction to the entire composition of the Gospel is identified. The historic present depicts the backdrop of the oppressive political structure of the Roman rule/empire and introduces Jesus as an Alternative, Messianic/Davidic King and Saviour who brings peace, particularly in the backdrop of the birthday of Caesar Augustus. Lukan special materials give emphasis to the motif of Jesus' Davidic lineage of Kingship. The emphasis given to the virgin birth reflects the Jewish expectations in terms of the human Davidic Messiah as well as the divinely embedded Messianic King.

The courtly language of imperial culture εὐαγγέλιον, σωτήρ, εἰρήνη and χαῖρε, some of the technical terms of Hellenistic thought, indicates the birth of the Messianic/Alternative King in contrast to Caesar Augustus to bring about a new order in the society. The term Saviour connotes the Kingship of Jesus during the time when the emperor was considered as the son of god and saviour by the Roman imperial theology. The term 'peace' juxtaposes *pax Christi* against *pax Romana*. The political overtones of the reversal of power and the re-ordering of positions mentioned in the canticles indicate the birth of Jesus as an anticipated Messianic/Davidic King in contrast to the political oppressive context.

In the third chapter, "Kingship Motif in the Life and Teachings of Jesus," the topographical structure of Jesus' journey from Galilee toward Jerusalem through Samaria, which is peculiar to Luke, exhibits the kingly

motif of Lukan composition: the episodes of the proclamation of John
the Baptist; Jesus' baptism; genealogy of Jesus; and, the temptation
of Jesus expose the historical, socio-political context of the Roman
rule and the oppression in Palestine. In Jesus' Galilean ministry, the
Nazareth manifesto indicates the dawn of the Messianic age along with
his anointing by the Spirit, highlighting Jesus' programme of mission
comprising the jubilee proclamation, fulfillment of the prophecy,
universality of the Kingdom, and his rejection by the Jews. Most of
the miracles with Jesus' authoritative teaching expose the resistance
and reversal of discrimination, exploitation, political oppression, old
rigid purity regulations, Sabbath observances and boundary issues.
Jesus is presented as the King who restores the Kingdom and grants
social acceptance by reversing the oppressive state.

Through the ministry of John and Jesus in Palestinian History
along with Roman History, Jesus is introduced as the one who is
begotten of the Holy Spirit to accomplish the promised Messianic
salvation, and, John as the forerunner who prepares the way for the
messianic King. In John's call for repentance and baptism, the people
rededicated themselves to join the new Messianic community against
political oppression. Jesus accepted baptism as the mode of entrance
to his messianic work, and in that he was declared the Son of God.
The anti-temple behaviour on the part of both John and Jesus by
proclaiming the forgiveness of sin by repentance seems to be a
revolutionary act in the backdrop of the Temple's role and ideology
of forgiveness through sacrifice, which later Luke points out as an
issue of authority.

The proclamation of the Kingdom of God and preaching through
his disciples, the repentance and forgiveness of sin throughout the
world indicate Jesus' vision of the new age of his Kingship. Anointing
of Jesus by a sinful woman is transposed by Luke in Galilean Ministry
fitting to his context to emphasize the forgiveness of sin which is
one of the major characteristics of Kingdom preaching. Besides, the
concept of the Kingdom of God in Roman-occupied Jewish Palestine
implies the downfall of the Roman Empire.

The theme of conflict portrays the hostility between leaders and Jesus. While Jesus' conflict with the Pharisees runs throughout the Gospel, Luke portrays Jesus' hospitality towards them by the act of table-fellowship. Jesus' intimate table-fellowship with people from various backgrounds, dining together regardless of sex or social status invites the sinners to repentance. Through the act of repentance, Jesus expects the rich, leaders, tax collectors and sinners to join his messianic community. It indicates the anticipated Messiah, in praxis liberates Israel not only from physical struggles such as hunger, sickness, etc., but also from political and social oppression. The inclusion of women in Jesus' ministry with the male disciples in the patriarchal society, blessing the poor and, bringing woes on the rich point out the revolutionary and reversal acts of Jesus.

While maintaining the messianic secrecy, Luke discloses to the closer circle of disciples that Jesus is the anticipated Messianic King through the confession of Peter; Jesus' prediction of his messianic suffering, death and resurrection; and, the event of transfiguration. The title, Son of God given to Jesus alone at the time of Baptism is revealed at the event of transfiguration to his inner circle of three disciples. It once again depicts Luke's skill in composing the Gospel from the Infancy Narrative through the travel narrative, step by step, focusing on Jesus' death as a Messianic King as its culmination. Jesus' Davidic pedigree in Lukan composition through the blind man at Jericho seems to be the fulfillment idea of Davidic dynasty through the Messianic King Jesus.

The rejection of Jesus in a Samaritan village explains the ethnic and Temple controversies, and this parallels his rejection at Nazareth due to the inclusion of Gentiles in his programme of mission at the outset of his Galilean ministry. The parables of Jesus, drawn out from the daily life of Palestine, are often used as weapons against the critics and foes in offering forgiveness along with new truths of love, grace and the values of the Kingdom of God. Luke's additional L parables point out the reversal of: economy, wealth, social systems, religious practices, exclusivism, and, attitudes along with the intention of restoration, repentance, forgiveness, transcending geographical and social boundaries, reciprocity, humility, persistent and hopeful prayer, and, self-surrender which seem to be the Kingly aspect of Jesus in uniting the people and building the community life against the socio-political situation of that time. The parables common to Q and the Triple Tradition also indicate the political oppression of the Roman authorities; the phenomenal growth of the Kingdom; and the joy of the Kingdom in living together without any disparity; and challenge the people for their choice of leaders. Lukan usage of both the future and the present state of the Kingdom of God denotes the future hope as well the present reality. The tone of an anti-imperial movement in giving life to the people and strengthening the community life against the oppressive secular Kingdom is noticeable in Jesus' parabolic teachings.

The event of the triumphal entry becomes an indication of the arrival of the anticipated King to lead the society and restructure the social order. Colt, as well as spreading the cloaks on the road indicates his Kingship as a sign of honour befitting a King. Luke's ascription of the title King makes the entry of Jesus explicitly royal. Luke declares Jesus as the King in the procession through the voices of the people in the backdrop of Pilate's procession to maintain the imperial power as well as the Roman imperial theology during the Passover. The Temple act establishes Jesus as the King of the new age. In cleansing the Temple, Jesus suspends the banking operation of the administration system in collaboration with Rome and the emperor worship by driving out its political, economic, social and religious power. It is also noted that the authority of Jesus tested in the temptation episode seems to be a juxtaposition of the supremacy of God against the Roman imperial theology. Jesus is portrayed as the counter King who refuses to be submissive to Rome. While the payment of tax to Caesar indicates people's submission to Rome and exposes that the land, people and the produce belong to him, Jesus nullifies the payment of tribute by hinting that everything including the land belongs to God. The phrase "desolating sacrilege," in the prophetic words of Jesus also denotes the nationalistic sense of Jesus' words against the emperor's idols in the altar of the Temple.

In the fourth chapter, "Kingship Motif in the Passion and Resurrection Narratives" the culmination of the motif of Jesus' kingship is identified. The special Lukan element of Satan's involvement in the conspiracy and betrayal scene indicates the threat, power, as well as Judas' submissiveness to the Roman power in contrast to the temptation of Jesus in which Jesus could not be made submissive to Rome. Roman threat and conspiracy could be identified in it because the scene of betrayal comes only after the cleansing of the Temple, in which the authorities wanted to kill Jesus. Besides, it is evidenced from the warning of Jesus to Peter in 22:31 and during Jesus' arrest in 22:53. Money and temptations seem to symbolize the imperial power of the Roman government. In Jesus' prayer on the Mount of Olives, the Lukan phrase, μὴ εἰσελθεῖν εἰ πειρασμόν of Jesus' words to his disciples indicate the oppressive situation of Rome and the longing of the people for their survival. Even at the trial, the people's voice to release Barabbas and crucify Jesus depicts the same situation.

In the event of striking the ear of the slave of the high priest, Luke depicts Jesus with his command as a King but at the same time portrays him as a healer with the Kingly-Messianic act of forgiveness. The prayer of forgiveness again indicates his vision of Kingship and it is affirmed by the event of granting paradise to the co-crucified criminal and this indicates his heroic action and messianic Kingship respectively.

The question of Jesus to the chief priests, the officers of the temple police, and the elders who had come to seize him as they have come to arrest him as a bandit indicates that Jesus was considered by the authorities as an insurrectionist as well. The handling of the above situation seems to be a literary device of Luke to prove at his crucifixion as he was executed as an alternative King. But, Jesus' words, "But this is your hour, and the power of darkness," in 22:53 indicate the arrest of Jesus due to the power and authority of Rome in considering him as an opponent King. The conferring of the Kingdom, at the Last Supper to the twelve disciples depicts the continuation of Jesus' Kingship after his death. It portrays his royal stature but Luke explains it through the dispute of greatness among the disciples as his Kingship is not by ruling but by service which contrasts the pervasive power of Rome.

The mockeries happen to be the last confirmation of Jesus' Royal dignity. Herod's disdain with an elegant robe depicts Jesus' humble Kingship. The jeering of the soldiers as well as the inscription over the cross discloses the crucified Jesus as the King of the Jews to everyone. Lukan addition of the criminal rebuking the mocker and his request for remembering him in his Kingdom, testifies Jesus as the Messianic King.

The questions during the trials: "If you are the Christ, tell us?" in 22:67; "Then, are you the Son of God?" in 22:70; and, "Are you the King of the Jews?" in 23:3 sharpen the messianic Kingship of Jesus and indicate Jesus as an alternative King against the rule of Caesar. Besides, the political accusations as well, the trials indicate that Jesus was executed with political offence. Herod's trial and his longing expose Jesus' Kingly character. But, Jesus' withdrawal from Galilee and the warning of Pharisees that Herod wanted to kill him seem to reveal that Jesus' ministry challenged his rule as a counterpart by his revolutionary activity. However, the crucifixion indicates that Jesus was considered as an antinationalist, a powerful source of threat to those in power.

Although entrusting his spirit to God at death than to his enemies, the resurrection event proves him as a victorious King over the Emperor's decision. His addressing God as his father indicates his divine Sonship and the centurion's declaration of δίκαιος not only indicates the political nuance of the centurion's fear about the power of Rome but reveals Jesus' Kingship of Messiahship by fulfilling God's will. The rending of the Temple veil, according to Luke, indicates the change in the socio-religious power, and his death in accordance with the Old Testament prophecies for the redemption of the people.

The burial of Jesus' corpse by Joseph of Aremathea, as a member of the council in a new tomb depict him at the close of the Gospel as a righteous one waiting for the Kingdom of God in line with the pious Israelites in the Infancy Narrative: Zechariah, Elizabeth, Simon and Anna, who observed the law and anticipated divine redemption. Lukan reference to the role of the Galilean women witnessing the empty tomb on Sunday exposes the compositional skill of Luke to denote the victory of the king through his resurrection. It indicates the kingship of Jesus, which is portrayed in the resurrection experience of the Lukan community with the declaration, the Lord has risen. It reveals the victory of Jesus against the Roman power, the opponent who crucified him. Through the account of the empty tomb, Luke reveals the resurrection as messianic in accordance with the fulfillment of Jesus' prediction of his death and resurrection. Besides, the L material of the two men to Emmaus reveals the estimation of Jesus by the disciples before his death as 'a mighty in word and deed before God and all the people,' juxtaposes him against the untrustworthy promises and deeds.

In commissioning the twelve, Luke reveals Jesus' Kingship by extending his role to his disciples to proclaim the good news of repentance and forgiveness, which are the basic elements of entering into the alternative Kingdom, in the socio-political world of Luke. Luke by his narration of Ascension as a historical event depicts Jesus as the enthroned King as a divine King whom the Israelites were anticipating. Perhaps, Luke gives a new meaning that Jesus is the real emperor who suffers and rules for ever for the people as a risen Lord instead of *pax Romana*. It can be seen in his second book, the Acts of the Apostles, 17:7, the risen Lord was considered by the early church as an alternative King to Caesar.

On the basis of the exegetical study and the Kingship motif found in the composition of Luke's Gospel, a reconstruction on Lukan Christology is done and the relevance of it to the present context is sought. The Gospel in its socio-political world portrays Jesus as a people-centered King, who was in solidarity with the people in their struggles and sufferings; a Messianic King, restoring the positions of the deprived and the marginalized; an Alternative King to the oppressive Kingship of Rome; a Crucified King, as he was accused and executed;

and, a Victorious King over the Roman power through not only from the temptations but also from death and entrenched oppressions.

Jesus' teachings and praxis along with the table-fellowship make everyone to realize a new rule with the reversal acts in building up of the community life as a visionary and a revolutionary King who is a non-violent, humble, servant, powerless and a crucified King. As it has been stated in the problem of research and dealt with in this research although the scholars view the crucified Jesus in Luke's Gospel as a martyr, saviour, new Adam, Son of God, Son of Man, Son of David, Christ the Messiah, and Innocent One, it is identified that Luke portrays Jesus as an alternative Messianic King who was crucified and victorious through his birth, life, teachings, death and resurrection.

Lukan Christology of Jesus' Kingship relates the social world of Luke to our Indian context of political oppression, caste, religious pluralism, gender disparity, ethnicity, poverty, issues of survival, struggles and, sufferings of the marginalized due to oppression and also among Christians in India. King Jesus becomes a liberator and saviour who is powerless, victimized, and vulnerable deprived King and subverts the rule of oppression. His people-centered Kingship depicts him as a fellow struggler; his virgin birth and messianic Kingship indicate that he is not purely an *avatara* but as one who lived among the people, transformed the society; alternative Kingship by his teachings and practice of the table-fellowship envisage the *sama pandhi* irrespective of caste, creed, religion and status; a Crucified King with the crown of thorns he accepted the mockery, humiliation, and dishonour for the well-being of the people; and, as a victorious King, he establishes hope in the life of the powerless.

The victorious King Jesus remains in the mind and life of people till today. He has become the hope of the powerless. His death and resurrection are remembered and celebrated in Eucharist. His Kingship calls people for repentance and forgiveness of sin as a continuing mission to be the new people and new community without caste, creed and class barriers. He is the humble, servant King who is an alternative to the human oppressive rulers in establishing justice in the society and for the betterment of people. The victory of King Jesus and his continuing mission are portrayed in Lukan writing through Peter's words in Acts 2:36, "Therefore let the entire house of Israel know with certainty that God has made him both the Lord and Messiah, this Jesus whom you crucified."

Bibliography

Reference

Aland, Barbara, et al., ed. *The Greek New Testament.* 4th revised ed. Stuttgart: United Bible Societies, 2001.

Aland, Kurt, ed. *Synopsis of the Four Gospels.* Stuttgart: United Bible Societies, 1972.

Bauer, W. *A Greek-English Lexicon of the New Testament and other Early Christian Literature.* Tr. by W. F. Arndt and F. W. Gingrich. 2nd revised ed. Chicago: University Press, 1979.

Blass F. and A. Debrunner. *A Greek Grammar of the New Testament and other Early Christian Literature.* Tr. by R. W. Funk. Chicago: University Press, 1961.

Brown, F., S. R. Driver and C. A. Briggs. *Hebrew and English Lexicon of the Old Testament.* Oxford: Clarendon Press, 1952.

Charles, R. H. *The Apocrypha and Pseudepigrapha of the Old Testament.* Vol 11. Oxford: Clarendon Press, 1913.

Charlesworth, J.H. *The Old Testament Pseudepigrapha.* Vol. 1. London: Darton, Longman & Todd, 1983.

_____. *The Old Testament Pseudepigrapha.* Vol 2. New York: Doubleday, 1985.

Liddell, H. G. and R. Scott. *A Greek-English Lexicon.* Vol I α-κώψ. Revised ed. Oxford: Clarendon Press, 1925.

_____. *A Greek-English Lexicon.* Vol II λ-ψώδῆ. Revised ed. Oxford: Clarendon Press, 1940.

Whiston A. M. *The Works of Josephus: Complete and Unabridged.* Tr. by William. Updated edition. Peabody: Hendrickson, 2008.

Young. R. *Analytical Concordance to the Bible*. Revised ed. New York: Funk & Wagnalls Co. 1939.

Books & Commentaries

Abraham K. C. *Third World Theologies: Commonalities and divergences*. Tiruvalla: EATWOT/CSS, 1995.

Ahn, Y. S. *The Reign of God and Rome in Luke's Passion Narrative: An East Asian Global Perspective*. Boston: Brill, 2006.

Barrett, C. K. *Luke the Historian in Recent Study*. London: The Epworth Press, 1961.

_____. *St. John*. London, SPCK, 1978.

Becker, J. *Messianic Expectations in the Old Testament*. Tr. by D. E. Green. Philadelphia: Fortress Press, 1980.

Bentzen, A. King and Messiah. London: Lutterworth Press, 1955.

Blinzler, J. *The Trial of Jesus*. Tr. by Isabel and F. McHugh. Westminster: The Newman Press, 1959.

Bockmuehl, M. ed. *The Cambridge Companion to Jesus*. Cambridge: University Press, 2001.

Boff, L. *Jesus Christ Liberator: A Critical Christology for Our Time*. New York: Orbis Books, 1981.

Bond, H. K. *Pontius Pilate in History and Interpretation*. Cambridge: University Press, 1998.

_____. *Caiaphas: Friend of Rome and Judge of Jesus?* Westminster: John Knox Press, 2004.

Borg, M. and J. D. Crossan. *The Last Week: What the Gospels Really Teach about Jesus' Final Days in Jerusalem*. London: SPCK, 2008.

Brandon, S. G. F. *Jesus and Zealots*. New York: Scribners, 1968.

_____. *The Trial of Jesus of Nazareth*. London: B.T. Batsford Ltd, 1968.

Braun, W. *Feasting and Social Rhetoric in Luke 14*. Cambridge: University Press, 1995.

Briggs, C. A. *Messianic Prophecy*. Edinburg: T & T Clark, 1886.

Briggs, R. C. *Interpreting the New Testament Today*. New York: Abingdon Press, 1973.

Brown, R. E. *The Birth of the Messiah: A Commentary on the Infancy Narratives in Matthew and Luke*. London: Geoffrey Chapman, 1977.

_____. *The Death of The Messiah: From Gethsemane to Grave*. Vol I. New York: Doubleday, 1994.

_____. *The Death of the Messiah*. Vol 2. New York: Doubleday, 1993.

_____. *An Introduction to New Testament Christology*. London: Geoffrey Chapman, 1994.

Burrows, M. *Jesus in the First Three Gospels*. Nashville: Abingdon, 1977.

Caird, G. B. *The Gospel of St. Luke*. New York: Seabury, 1963.

Carlston, C.E. *The Parables of the Triple Tradition*. Philadelphia: Fortress Press, 1975.

Carr, D. *Sword of the Spirit: An Activist's Understanding of the Bible*. Geneva: WCC, 1992.

_____. *Re-Reading the Bible with New Eyes*. Bangalore: UTC, 2008.

_____, *Luke*. Thiruvivilia Vilakam. Ed. by K. Hironemus. Trichy: Arul Vaku Mantam, 2013. (Tamil)

Carter, W. *The Roman Empire and the New Testament*. Nashville: Abingdon Press, 2006.

Charlesworth, J. H. *The Old Testament Pseudepigrapha and the New Testament*. Cambridge: University Press, 1985.

Coleridge, M. *The Birth of the Lukan Narrative: Narrative as Christology in Luke 1-2*. England: Sheffield Academic Press, 1993.

Conzelmann, H. *The Theology of St. Luke*. Tr. by Geoffrey Buswell. Philadelphia: Fortress Press, 1982.

Craigie, P. C. *Word Biblical Commentary: Psalms 1-50*. Vol 19. Texas: Word Books, 1998.

Cranfield, C. E. B. *The Gospel According to Saint Mark*. Cambridge: The University Press, 1963.

Creed, J. M. *The Gospel According to St. Luke: The Greek Text with Introduction, Notes, and Indices*. London: Macmillan and Co., 1930.

Crossan, J. D. *The Historical Jesus: The Life of a Mediterranean Jewish Peasant*. New York: Harper Collins, 1991.

_____. *In Parables: The Challenge of the Historical Jesus*. California: Polebridge Press, 1992.

_____. *Jesus: A Revolutionary Biography*. San Francisco: Harper Collins, 1995.

_____. *Who Killed Jesus? Exploring the Roots of Anti-Semitism in the Gospel Story of the Death of Jesus*. San Francisco: Harper Collins, 1995.

_____. *The Birth of Christianity: Discovering what Happened in the Years Immediately after the Execution of Jesus*. Edinburgh: T&T Clark, 1998.

Crossan J. D. and J. L. Reed, *Excavating Jesus: Beneath the Stones, Behind the Texts*. London: SPCK, 2001.

Cullmann, O. *The Christology of the New Testament.* London: SCM Press Ltd, 1963.

Culpepper, R. A. "Luke," *The New Interpreter's Bible.* Vol IX. Ed. by L. E. Keck. Nashville: Abingdon Press, 1995.

Daalen, D. H. V. *The Kingdom of God is Like This.* London: Epworth Press, 1976.

Dahl, N. A. *The Crucified Messiah.* Minneapolis: Augsburg, 1974.

Danker, F. W. *Luke.* Philadelphia: Fortress Press, 1976.

Darr, J.A. *Herod the Fox.* Sheffield: Academic Press, 1998.

Davies, W. D. *Invitation to the New Testament.* London: Longman & Todd, 1967.

Davies W. D. and D. C.Allison. *Matthew: The International Critical Commentary.* Vol III. Edinburgh: T&T Clark, 1997.

Dibelius, M. *Jesus.* Tr. by C. B. Hedrick and F. C. Grant. Philadelphia: Westminster Press, 1949.

Dunn, J. D. G. *The Evidence for Jesus.* London: SCM Press, 1985.

_____. *Christology in the Making, 1980.* 2nd ed. London: SCM Press, 1989.

_____. *New Testament Theology: an Introduction.* Nashville: Abingdon Press, 2009.

Edwards, O. C. *Luke's Story of Jesus.* Philadelphia: Fortress Press, 1981.

Erdman, C. R. *The Gospel of Luke.* Philadelphia: Westminster Press, 1925.

Esler, P. F. *Community and Gospel in Luke-Acts: The Social and Political Motivations of Lucan Theology.* Cambridge: University Press, 1987.

Farmer, W. R. *Jesus and the Gospel: Tradition, Scripture and Canon.* Philadelphia: Fortress Press, 1982.

Fitzmyer, J. A. *The Gospel According to Luke I-IX.* Vol 1. New York: Doubleday, 1979.

_____. *The Gospel According to Luke X-XXIV.* Vol 2. New York: Doubleday, 1986.

Flemington, W. F. *The New Testament Doctrine of Baptism.* London: S.P.C.K., 1948.

Flender, H. *St Luke Theologian of Redemptive History.* Tr. by H. Reginald and I. Fuller. London: S.P.C.K, 1967.

France, R. T. *The Gospel of Mark.* Carlisle: Paternoster Press, 2002.

Franklin, E. *Luke: Interpreter of Paul, Critic of Matthew.* Sheffield: Academic Press, 1994.

Fredriksen, P. *Jesus of Nazareth, King of the Jews.* New York: Alfred A. Knof, 2000.

Fuller, R. H. *The Foundations of New Testament Christology.* New York: Charles Scribner's Sons, 1965.

_____. *A Critical Introduction to the New Testament.* Great Britain: Duckworth, 1966.

Gangatharan, C. *Basic Concepts of Saiva Siddantha.* Madurai: Tamilaji, 1980.

Gonsalves, M. *The Passion of Jesus According to Luke: A Narrative Critical Study of Luke 22: 29-23:49.* Romae, 2001.

Green, J. B. *New Testament Theology: The Theology of the Gospel of Luke.* Cambridge: University Press, 1995.

Guignebert, C. *The Jewish World in the Time of Jesus.* New York: University Books, 1959.

Guthrie, D. *New Testament Introduction. 1961.* 4th ed. Illinois: Intervarsity Press, 1990.

Haight, R. *The Future of Christology.* London: Continuum, 2005.

Hendrickx, H. *The Infancy Narratives, 1975.* Revised ed. London: Geoffrey Chapman, 1984.

Hengel, M. The Son of God. Philadelphia: Fortress Press, 1976.

_____. *Crucifixion.* Philadelphia: Fortress Press, 1977.

Heskett, R. *Messianism within the Scriptural Scroll of Isaiah.* New York: T&T Clark, 2007.

Hooker, M. D. *Not Ashamed of the Gospel: New Testament Interpretations of the Death of Christ.* Grand Rapids: William B. Eerdmans, 1995.

Horsley, R. A. and J. S. Hanson. *"Bandits, Prophets, and Messiahs.* London: Harper & Row, 1985.

Horsley, R. A. *Jesus and Empire.* Minneapolis: Fortress Press, 2003.

Jeremias, J. *The Parables of Jesus.* Revised ed. London: SCM Press, 1970.

Jervell, J. *Luke and the People of God: A New Look at Luke-Acts.* Minneapolis: Augsburg, 1972.

John, V. J. *The Ecological Vision of Jesus: Nature in the Parables of Mark.* Thiruvalla: CSS, 2002.

Johnson, L. T. *Sharing Possessions.* Grand Rapids: Wm. B. Eerdmans, 2011.

Johnson, M. S. *Christology: Biblical and Historical.* New Delhi: Mittal Publications, 2005.

Jung, C. W. *The Original Language of the Lukan Infancy Narrative.* London: T&T Clark International, 2004.

Karris, R. J. *What are they saying about Luke and Acts? A Theology of the Faithful God.* New York: Paulist Press, 1979.

Kee, H. C. *Christian Origins in Sociological Perspective.* London: SCM Press, 1980.

Kim, S. *Christ and Caesar.* Grand Rapids: William B. Eerdmans, 2008.

Kingsbury, J. D. *The Christology of Mark's Gospel.* Philadelphia: Fortress Press, 1983.

_____. *Conflict in Luke: Jesus, Authorities, Disciples.* Minneapolis: Fortress Press, 1991.

Kistemaker, S. J. *The Parables: Understanding the Stories Jesus Told.* Grand Rapids: Baker Books, 1980.

Klausner, J. *The Messianic Idea in Israel: From the Beginning to the Completion of the Misnah.* Tr. by W.F. Stinespring. London: George Allen & Unwin, 1956.

Koch, K. *From Amos to Jesus: Biblical Eschatology and Its Social and Political Implications.* Tr. by J. Gomes. Delhi: ISPCK, 1999.

Koester, H. *History, Culture, and Religion of the Hellenistic Age.* Philadelphia: Fortress Press, 1982.

Kümmel, W. G. *Introduction to the New Testament.* London: SCM Press, 1966.

Laato, A. *A Star is Rising: The Historical Development of the Old Testament Royal Ideology and the Rise of the Jewish Messianic Expectations.* Atlanta: Scholar Press, 1997.

Ladd, G. E. *A Theology of the New Testament.* London: Lutterworth Press, 1975.

Leaney, A. R. C. *A Commentary on the Gospel according to St. Luke.* London: Adam & Charles Black, 1958.

Lesbaupin, I. *Blessed are the Persecuted: Christian Life in the Roman Empire, A.D. 64-313.* Tr. by R. R. Barr. New York: Orbis Books, 1987.

Levey, S. H. *The Messiah: an Aramaic Interpretation, the Messianic Exegesis of the Targum.* New York: Hebrew Union College Press, 1974.

Maclaren, A. *St. Luke.* Grand Rapids: Wm. B. Eerdmans, 1932.

Maddox, R. *The Purpose of Luke-Acts.* Edinburgh: T&T Clark, 1985.

Malik, B. B. *Poverty in India – Fundamental Issues.* New Delhi: Mittal, 2009.

Malina, B. J. *The Social World of Jesus and the Gospels.* London: Routledge, 1996.

Manson, W. *The Gospel of Luke.* New York: Harper and Brothers, 1930.

Marshall, I. H. *New Testament Theology.* Illinois: InterVarsity Press, 2004.

Massey, J. *The Gospel According to Luke.* Dalit Bible Commentary. New Testament Vol 3. New Delhi: Centre for Dalit /Subaltern Studies, 2007.

Matera, F. J. *The Kingship of Jesus: Composition and Theology in Mark 15.* USA: Scholars Press, 1982.

_____. *Passion Narratives and Gospel Theologies: Interpreting the Synoptics Through Their Passion Stories.* New York: Paulist Press, 1986.

Matthew, S. P. *Temple-Criticism in Mark's Gospel: The Economic Role of the Jerusalem Temple during the First Century CE.* Delhi: ISPCK, 1999.

Mattill, A. J. *Luke and the Last Things.* Dillsboro: Western North Carolina Press, 1979.

McKenzie, J. L. *Dictionary of the Bible.* Bangalore: ATC, 1983.

McNamara, M. *Intertestamental Literature.* Wilmington: Michael Glazier, 1983.

Meier, J. P. *A Marginal Jew: Rethinking the Historical Jesus.* Vol II. New York: Doubleday, 1994.

Mettinger, T. N. D. *King and Messiah: The Civil and Sacral Legitimation of the Israelite Kings.* CWK: Gleerup, 1976.

Metzger, B. M. *The New Testament: its Background, Growth, and Content, 1965.* 2nd ed. Nashville: Abingdon Press, 1983.

Moessner, D. P. *Lord of the Banquet: The Literary and Theological Significance of the Lukan Travel Narrative.* Minneapolis: Fortress Press, 1989.

Moltmann, J. *The Crucified God: The Cross of Christ as the Foundation and Criticism of Christian Theology.* Tr. by R. A. Wilson and J. Bowden. London: SCM Press, 1974.

Morrice, W. G. *Hidden Sayings of Jesus: Words Attributed to Jesus Outside the Four Gospels.* Great Britain: SPCK, 1997.

Moule, C. F. D. *The Origin of Christology.* Cambridge: University Press, 1977.

Moxnes, H. *The Economy of the Kingdom.* Philadelphia: Fortress Press, 1988.

Mullen, J. P. *Dinning with Pharisees.* Minnesota: Liturgical Press, 2004.

Muthunayagom, D. J. *The Relationship between Election and Israel's attitude towards the nations in the book of Isaiah.* Delhi: ISPCK, 2000.

Navone, J. *Themes of St. Luke.* Rome: Gregorian University Press, 1970.

Nelson, P. K. *Leadership and Discipleship: A Study of Luke 22:24-30.* Atlanta: Scholars Press, 1994.

Nolan, A. *Jesus before Christianity: The Gospel of Liberation.* Darton: Longman and Todd, 1976.

Nolland, J. *Word Biblical Commentary.* Vol. 35: Luke 1:1-9:20. Dallas: Word Books, 1998.

Parsons, M. C. *Luke: Storyteller, Interpreter, Evangelist.* Peabody: Hendrickson, 2007.

Pereira, F. *Jesus, the Human and Humane Face of God: A Portrait of Jesus in Luke's Gospel.* Mumbai: St. Paul's, 2000.

Plummer, A. *Critical and Exegetical Commentary on the Gospel according to St. Luke.* 5th ed. Edinburgh: T&T Clark, 1922.

Porter, S. E., ed. *The Messiah in the Old and New Testament.* Grand Rapids: William B. Eerdmans, 2007.

Powell, M. A. *What are they saying about Luke?* New York: Paulist Press, 1989.

Ragg, L. *St Luke.* W. C.: Methuen & Co, 1922.

Raj, J. R. J. S. *The "Anointed Ones" in the Qumran Literature.* Delhi: ISPCK, 2005.

Raj, M. C. and Jyothi. *Dyche, The Dalit Psyche: A Science of Dalit Psychology.* Tumkur: ARC, 2008.

Rajayyan, K. *History in Theory and Method: A Study in Historiography.* Madurai: Ratna, 2006.

Rayanna, G. *The Table Fellowship of Jesus (Luke 5.27-32).* Guntur: St. Anthony's Shrine, 2009.

Richardson, P. *Herod: King of the Jews and Friend of the Romans.* Edinburgh: T&T Clark, 1996.

Riches, J. *The World of Jesus: First Century Judaism in Crisis.* Cambridge: University Press, 1995.

Ringgren, H. *The Messiah in the Old Testament.* London: SCM Press, 1961.

Robbins, J. *Prodigal Son/Elder Brother.* Chicago: University Press, 1991.

Robinson, J. A. T. *Redating the New Testament.* London: SCM Press, 1976.

Roetzel, C. J. *The World that Shaped the New Testament.* Atlanta: John Knox Press, 1985.

Russell, D.S. *Between the Testaments.* London: SCM Press, 1960.

Russell, D. S. *The Method and Message of Jewish Apocalyptic 200BC-AD 100.* London: SCM Press, 1964.

Sanders, E. P. *Jesus and Judaism.* London: SCM Press, 1985.

_____. *The Historical Figure of Jesus.* London: Penguin Press, 1993.

Sandmel, Samuel. *We Jews and Jesus.* London: Victor Gollancz, 1965.

Savarkar, V. D. *Hindutva.* 6th ed. Bharti Sahitya Sadan: New Delhi-1, 1989.

Schillebeeckx, E. *Jesus: An Experiment in Christology.* Tr. by H. Hoskins. New York: Seabury Press, 1979.

_____. *Christ: The Experience of Jesus as Lord.* Tr. by J. Bowden. New York: Crossroad, 1983.

Schnackenburg, R. *God's Rule and Kingdom 1963.* Second enlarged ed. New York: Herder and Herder, 1968.

Schottroff, L. *The Parables of Jesus.* Tr. by L. M. Maloney. Minneapolis: Fortress Press, 2006.

Scott, E. F. *The Kingdom and the Messiah.* Edinburgh: T & T Clark, 1911.

Seim, T. K. *Double Message: Patterns of Gender in Luke & Acts.* Nashville: Abingdon Press, 1994.

Senior, D. C. P. *The Passion of Jesus in the Gospel of Luke.* Wilmington: Michael Glazier, 1989.

Sheeley, S. M. *Narrative Asides in Luke-Acts.* Sheffield: Academic Press, 1992.

Shourie, A. *Harvesting Our Soul: Missionaries, their design, their claims.* ASA: New Delhi, 2000.

Shillington, V. G. *Jesus and His Parables: Interpreting the Parables of Jesus Today.* Edinburgh: T&T Clark, 1997.

Sider, J. W. *Interpreting the Parables: A Hermeneutical Guide to Their Meaning.* Grand Rapids: Zondervan, 1995.

Stalker, J. *The Trial and Death of Jesus Christ.* Grand Rapids: Zondervan, 1983.

Stanton, G. N. *The Gospels and Jesus.1989.* 2nd edition. New York: Oxford University Press, 2002.

Stöger, A. *The Gospel According to St. Luke.* Vol I. London: Burns & Oates, 1969.

Storkey, A. *Jesus and Politics: Confronting the Powers.* Grand Rapids: Baker Academic, 2005.

Stronstad, R. *The Charismatic Theology of St. Luke.* Peabody: Hendrickson, 1984.

Stuart, D. *Word Biblical Commentary: Hosea-Jonah.* Vol 31. Texas: Word Books, 1998.

Stuhlmueller, C. "The Gospel According to Luke." *The Jerome Biblical Commentary.* Vol II. Ed. by R. E. Brown, J. A. Fitzmyer and R. E. Murphy. Bangalore: TPI, 1968.

Talbert, C. H. *Literary Pattern, Theological Themes, and the Genre of Luke-Acts.* Montana: Scholars Press, 1974.

_____. *Reading Luke: A Literary and Theological Commentary on the Third Gospel.* New York: Crossroad, 1982.

Taylor, V. *The Gospel According to St. Mark.* London: Macmillan, 1957.

_____. *The Passion Narrative of St. Luke: A Critical and Historical Investigation.* Cambridge: University Press, 1972.

Tenney, M. C. *New Testament Times.* London: Inter-varsity Press, 1965.

Thatcher, T. *Jesus the Riddler: The Power of Ambiguity in the Gospels.* Westminster: John Knox Press, 2006.

Theissen, G. *Sociology of Early Palestinian Christianity.* Tr. by J. Bowden. Philadelphia: Fortress Press, 1978.

_____. *The Social Setting of Pauline Christianity.* Ed. and Tr. by J. H. Schutz. Edinburgh: T & T Clark, 1982.

_____. *The Gospels in Context: Social and Political History in the Synoptic Tradition.* Tr. by L. M. Maloney. Edinburg: T&T Clark, 1992.

Theissen, G. and A. Merz. *The Historical Jesus.* London: SCM Press, 1998.

Thompson, G. H. P. *The Gospel According to Luke.* Oxford: Clarendon Press, 1972.

Trocmé, A. *Jesus and the Nonviolent Revolution*. Tr. by M. H. Shank and M. E. Miller. Pennsylvania: Herald Press, 1973.

Tyson, J. B. *Images of Judaism in Luke-Acts*. Columbia: University of South Carolina, 1992.

Victor, R. M. *Colonial Education and Class Formation in Early Judaism: A Postcolonial Reading*. London: T & T Clark, 2010.

Walker, P. W. L. *Jesus and the Holy City: New Testament Perspectives on Jerusalem*. Grand Rapids: William B, Eerdmans, 1996.

Weatherly, J. A. *Jewish Responsibility for the Death of Jesus in Luke-Acts*. Sheffield: Academic Press, 1994.

Weaver, W. P. *The Historical Jesus in the Twentieth Century 1900-1950*. Pennsylvania: Trinity Press International, 1999.

Williams, R. *Resurrection*. Harrisburg: Morehouse, 1982.

_____. *On Christian Theology*. Malden: Blackwell, 2000.

Wilson, W. R. *The Execution of Jesus*. New York: Charles Scribner's Sons, 1970.

Witherington, B. *The Gospel of Mark: A Socio-rhetorical Commentary*. Grand Rapids: Eerdmans, 2001.

Wright, N. T. *Who Was Jesus?* Grand Rapids: William B, Eerdmans, 1992.

Yamazaki-Ransom, K. *The Roman Empire in Luke's Narrative*. New York: T&T Clark, 2010.

Young, B. H. *Jesus and His Jewish Parables: Discovering the Roots of Jesus' Teaching*. New York: Paulist Press, 1989.

Zweip, A. W. *The Ascension of the Messiah in Lukan Christology*. Leiden: Brill, 1997.

Essays

Balla, P. "What did Jesus think about his Approaching Death." In *Jesus, Mark and Q: The Teaching of Jesus and its Earliest Records*. Ed. by M. Labahn and A. Schmidt. England: Sheffield Academic Press, 2001.

Boring, M. E. "The Historical-Critical Method's "Criteria of Authenticity": The Beatitudes in Q and Thomas as a Test Case." In *The Historical Jesus and the Rejected Gospels. Semeia* 44. Atlanta: Scholars Press, 1988.

Chakkalakal, P. "Women's Discipleship and Leadership in Jesus' Movement: An Indian/Asian Feminist Biblical-Theological Reconstruction." In *Bible and Hermeneutics*. Ed. by C. J. D. Joy. Tiruvalla: C.S.S., 2010.

Chiala, S. "The Son of Man: The Evolution of an Expression." In *Enoch and the Messiah Son of Man*. Ed. by G. Boccaccini. Grand Rapids: Wm. B. Eerdmans, 2007.

Chilton, B. "Jesus, a Galilean Rabbi." In *Who was Jesus?* Ed. by P. Copan and C. A. Evans. London: John Knox Press, 2001.

Davenport, G. L. "The 'Anointed of the Lord' in Psalms of Solomon 17." In *Ideal* Figures *in Ancient Judaism: Profiles and Paradigms*. Ed. by J. J. Collins and G.W.E. Nickelsburg. Michigan: Scholars Press, 1980.

Devasahayam, V. "A Theological Response to the Stories of the Discriminated Against and Subjugated Peoples of Asia." In *God, Christ & God's People in Asia*. Ed. by D. Carr. Hong Kong: CCA Theological concerns, 1995.

Downing, F. G. "Theophilus's First Reading of Luke-Acts." In *Luke's Literary Achievement: Collected Essays*. Ed. by C. M. Tuckett. Sheffield: Academic Press, 1995.

—————. "The Jewish Cynic Jesus." In *Jesus, Mark and Q: The Teaching of Jesus and its Earliest Records*. Ed. by M. Labahn and A. Schmidt. England: Sheffield Academic Press, 2001.

D'Sa, F. X. "Christian Incarnation and Hindu Avatara." In *Any Room for Christ in Asia?* Ed. by L. Boff and V. Elizondo. *Concilium*. London: SCM Press), 1993.

Elliott, J. H. "Social-Scientific Criticism of the New Testament: More on Methods and Models." In *Social-Scientific Criticism of the New Testament And its Social World. Semeia* 35. Decatur: Scholars Press, 1986.

—————. "Temple Versus Household in Luke-Acts: A Contrast in Social Institutions." In *The Social World of Luke-Acts: Models for Interpretation*. Ed. by J. Neyrey. Peabody: Hendrickson, 1991.

Evans, C. A. "Context, family and formation." In *The Cambridge Companion to Jesus*. Ed. by M. Bockmuehl. Cambridge: University Press, 2001.

—————. "The New Quest for Jesus and the New Research on the Dead Sea Scrolls." In *Jesus, Mark and Q: The Teaching of Jesus and its Earliest Records*. Ed. by M. Labahn and A. Schmidt. England: Sheffield Academic Press, 2001.

France, R. T. "Development in the New Testament Christology." In *Crisis in Christology: Essays in Quest of Resolution*. Ed. by W. R. Farmer. Michigan: Dove Booksellers, 1995.

Frykenberg, R. E. "The Sacred in Modern Hindu Politics: Historical Processes Underlying Hinduism and Hindutva." In *Hinduism in India*. Ed. by W. Sweetman and A. Malik. New Delhi: Sage, 2016.

Hedrick, C. W. "Introduction: The Tyranny of the Synoptic Jesus." In *The Historical Jesus and the Rejected Gospels. Semeia* 44. Atlanta: Scholars Press, 1988.

Hoehner, H. W. "Why did Pilate Hand Jesus over to Antipas?" In *The Trial of Jesus*. Ed. by E. Bammel. London: SCM Press, 1970.

Holladay, C. R. "Contemporary Methods of Reading the Bible." in *The New Interpreter's Bible*. Vol I. Eed. by L. E. Keck. Nashville: Abingdon Press, 1994.

Horsley, R. A. "Q and Jesus: Assumptions, Approaches, and Analyses." In *Early Christianity, Q and Jesus*. *Semeia* 55. Atlanta: Scholars Press, 1991.

Hultgard, A. "The Ideal 'Levite', The Davidic Messiah and the Saviour Priest in the Testaments of the Twelve Patriarchs." In *Ideal* Figures *in Ancient Judaism: Profiles and Paradigms*. Ed. *by* J. J. Collins and G. W. E. Nickelsburg. Michigan: Scholars Press, 1980.

Johnson, L. T. "The Christology of Luke-Acts." In *Who Do You Say That I am?* Ed. by M. A. Powell and D. R. Bauer. Westminster: John Knox Press, 1989.

Kereszty, R. "Toward a Contemporary Christology." In *Crisis in Christology: Essays in Quest of Resolution*. Ed. by W. R. Farmer. Michigan: Dove Booksellers, 1995.

Kim. Y. B. "Jesus Christ Among Asian Minjung: A Christological Reflection." In *God, Christ & God's People in Asia*. Ed. by D. Carr. Hong Kong: CCA Theological concerns, 1995.

Kloppenborg, J. S. "Literary Convention, Self-Evidence and the Social History of the Q People." In *Early Christianity, Q and Jesus*. Semeia 55. Atlanta: Scholars Press, 1991.

_____. and L. E. Vaage, "Early Christianity, Q and Jesus: The Sayings Gospel and Method in the Study of Christian Origins." In *Early Christianity, Q and Jesus*. *Semeia* 55. Atlanta: Scholars Press, 1991.

Kuribayashi, T. "Theology of the Crowned with Thorns." In *God, Christ & God's People in Asia*. Ed. by D. Carr. Hong Kong: CCA Theological concerns, 1995.

Longman, T. "The Messiah: Explorations in the Law and Writings." In *The Messiah in the Old and New Testaments*. Ed. by S. E. Porter. Grand Rapids: William B. Eerdmans, 2007.

Mack, B. L. "Q and the Gospel of Mark: Revising Christian Origins." In *Early Christianity, Q and Jesus*. Semeia 55. Atlanta: Scholars Press, 1991.

Malina, B. J. "Normative Dissonance and Christian Origins." In *Social-Scientific Criticism of the New Testament and its Social World*. *Semeia* 35. Decatur: Scholars Press, 1986.

Malina, B. J. and J. H. Neyrey, "Honour and Shame in Luke-Acts: Pivotal Values of the Mediterranean World." In *The Social World of Luke-Acts: Models for Interpretation*. Ed. by J. H. Neyrey. Peabody: Hendrickson, 1993.

Melanchthon, M. J. "Dalit Readers of the Word: The Quest for Hermeneutics and Method." *Frontiers in Dalit Hermeneutics*. Ed. by James Massey and Samson Prabhakar. Bangalore: SATHRI, 2005.

Moberly, R. W. L. "The Christ of the Old and New Testaments." In *The Cambridge Companion to Jesus*. Ed. by M. Bockmuehl. Cambridge: University Press, 2001.

Moxnes, H. "Patron-Client Relations and the New Community in Luke-Acts." In *The Social World of Luke-Acts: Models for Interpretation*. Ed. by J. Neyrey. Peabody: Hendrickson, 1991.

Neyrey, J. H. "Ceremonies in Luke-Acts: The Case of Meals and Table Fellowship." In *The Social World of Luke-Acts: Models for Interpretation*. Ed. by J. H. Neyrey. Peabody: Hendrickson, 1993.

Nickelsburg, G. W. E. "Disserning the Structure(s) of the Enochic Book of Parables." In *Enoch and the Messiah Son of Man*. Ed. by G. Boccaccini. Grand Rapids: Wm. B. Eerdmans, 2007.

Oakman, D. E. "The Countryside in Luke-Acts." In *The Social World of Luke-Acts: Models for Interpretation*. Ed. by J. H. Neyrey. Peabody: Hendrickson, 1993.

Öhler, M. "Jesus as a Prophet: Remarks on Terminology." In *Jesus, Mark and Q: The Teaching of Jesus and its Earliest Records*. Ed. by M. Labahn and A. Schmidt. England: Sheffield Academic Press, 2001.

Orlov, A. A. "Roles and Titles of the Seventh Antediluvian Hero in the Parables of Enoch: A Departure from the Traditional Pattern?" In *Enoch and the Messiah Son of Man*. Ed. by G. Boccaccini. Grand Rapids: Wm. B. Eerdmans, 2007.

O'Toole, R. F. "Luke's Position on Politics and Society in Luke-Acts." In *Political Issues in Luke-Acts*. Ed. by R. J. Cassidy and P. J. Scharper. New York: Orbis Books, 1983.

Paget, J. C. "Quests for the Historical Jesus." In *The Cambridge Companion to Jesus*. Ed. by M. Bockmuehl. Cambridge: University Press, 2001.

Perera, R. "The Task of Rewriting Christology." In *Search for a New Testament Just World Order Challenges to Theology: A Special issue of Voices from the Third World* Vol 22/2. Ed. by K. C. Abraham. December, 1999.

Pieris, A. "Does Christ Have a Place in Asia? A Panoramic View." In *Any Room for Christ in Asia?* Ed. by L. Boff and V. Elizondo. *Concilium*. London: SCM Press, 1993.

Plummer, R. "Samaritanism - a Jewish Sect or an Independent Form of Yahwism?" In *Samaritans Past and Present: Current Studies.* Ed. by M. Mor and F. V. Reiterer. Berlin: Walter de Gruyter GmbH, 2010.

Prabhu, G. S. "The Jesus of Faith: A Christological Contribution to an Ecumenical Third World Spirituality." In *Spirituality of the Third World.* Ed. by K.C. Abraham and B. Mbuy-Beya. New York: Orbis Books, 1994.

Richard, P. "A Theology of Life: Rebuilding Hope from the Perspective of the South." In *Spirituality of the Third World.* Ed. by K. C. Abraham and B. Mbuy-Beya. New York: Orbis Books, 1994.

Richardson, P. "The Israel-idea in the Passion Narratives." In *The Trial of Jesus.*Ed. by E. Bammel. London: SCM Press, 1970.

Rohrbaugh, R. L. "The Pre-industrial city in Luke-Acts: Urban Social Relations." In *The Social World of Luke-Acts: Models for Interpretation.* Ed. by J. H. Neyrey. Peabody: Hendrickson, 1993.

Swartley, W. M. "Politics or Peace (Eirene) in Luke's Gospel." In *Political Issues in Luke-Acts.* Ed. by R. J. Cassidy and P. J. Scharper. New York: Orbis Books, 1983.

Toit, D. S. D. "Redefining Jesus: Current Trends in Jesus Research." In *Jesus, Mark and Q: The Teaching of Jesus and its Earliest Records.* Ed. by M. Labahn and A. Schmidt. England: Sheffield Academic Press, 2001.

Tomson, P. J. "Jesus and his Judaism." In *The Cambridge Companion to Jesus.* Ed. by M. Bockmuehl. Cambridge: University Press, 2001.

Tyson, J. B. "Conflict as a Literary Theme in the Gospel of Luke." In *New Synoptic Studies.* Ed. by W. R. Farmer. Macon: Mercer University Press, 1983.

Walck, L. W. "The Son of Man in the Parables of Enoch and the Gospels." In *Enoch and the Messiah Son of Man.* Ed. by G. Boccaccini. Grand Rapids: Wm. B. Eerdmans, 2007.

Articles in periodicals

Abernathy, D. "A Study on Lk 4, 16-30." *Bible Bhashyam* 27/3 (September, 2001): 223-236.

Abraham, M. V. "Good News to the Poor in Luke's Gospel." *Bangalore Theological Forum* 19/1 (January –April, 1987): 1-13.

_____. "Good News to the Poor in Luke's Gospel." *Bible Bhashyam* 14/1-2 (March–June, 1988): 65-77.

Achtemeier, P. J. "The Lucan Perspective on the Miracles of Jesus: A Preliminary Sketch." *Journal of Biblical Literature* 94/4 (December, 1975): 547-562.

Amaladoss, M. "Images of Jesus in India." *East Asian Pastoral Review* 31/1-2 (1994): 6-20.

Antwi, D. J. "Did Jesus Consider His Death to be an Atoning Sacrifice?" *Interpretation* 45/1 (January, 1991): 17-28.

Asquith, C. M. "Christology of King and Kingdom." *The Living Word* 103/1 (January-February, 1997): 7-15.

Athapilly, S. "Christology and Asian Hermeneutics." *Asian Horizons* 1/2 (December, 2007): 107-135.

Bauckham, R. "The Rich Man and Lazarus: The Parable and the Parallels." *New Testament Studies* 37/2 (April, 1991): 225-246.

_____. "The Scrupulous Priest and the Good Samaritan: Jesus' Parabolic Interpretation of the Law of Moses." *New Testament Studies* 44/4 (October, 1998): 475-489.

Bauer, D. R. "The Kingship of Jesus in the Matthean Infancy Narrative: A Literary Analysis." *The Catholic Biblical Quarterly* 57/2 (April, 1995): 306-323.

Beavis, M. A. "Expecting Nothing in Return." *Interpretation* 48/4 (October, 1994): 358-368.

Best, T. F. "The Sociological Study of the New Testament: Promise and Peril of a New Discipline." *Scottish Journal of Theology* 36 (1983): 181-194.

Betz, H. D. "The Cleansing of the Ten Lepers (Luke 17: 11-19)." *Journal of Biblical Literature* 90/3 (September, 1971): 314-328.

Betz, O. "The Kerygma of Luke." *Interpretation* 79/2 (April, 1968): 131-146.

Beverly, H. B. "An Exposition of Luke 1:39-45." *Interpretation* 30/4 (October, 1976): 396-400.

Bligh, P. H. "A Note on Huios Theou in Mark 15:39." *The Expository Times* 80/1 (October, 1968): 51-53.

Boring, M. E. "Markan Christology: God-Language for Jesus?" *New Testament Studies* 45/4 (October 1999): 451-471.

Bowlby, P. "Kings without authority: The obligation of the ruler to gamble in the Mahabharata." *Studies in Religion/Sciences Religieuses* 20/1 (1991): 3-17.

Broadhead, E. K. "In Search of the Gospel: Research Trends in Mark 14-16." *Australian Biblical Review* 43 (1995): 20-49.

Brown, R. E. "Gospel Infancy Narrative Research from 1976 to 1986: Part II (Luke)." *The Catholic Biblical Quarterly* 48/4 (October, 1986): 660-680.

Burrows, M. "Thy Kingdom Come." *Journal of Biblical Literature* 74/1 (March, 1955): 1-8.

Byrne, B. "Jesus as Messiah in the Gospel of Luke: Discerning a Pattern of Correction." *The Catholic Biblical Quarterly* 65/1 (January, 2003): 80-95.

Carlston, C. E. "Reminiscence and Redaction in Luke 15:11-32." *Journal of Biblical Literature* 94/3 (September, 1975): 368-390.

Carroll, J. T. "Luke's Portrayal of the Pharisees." *The Catholic Biblical Quarterly* 50/4 (October, 1988): 604-621.

Carter, W. "Zachariah and Benedictus (Luke 1, 68-79) Preaching what He Preaches." *Biblica* 69/2 (Fasc., 1988): 239-247.

Chouinard, L. "Gospel Christology: A Study of Methodology." *Journal for the Study of the New Testament* 30 (1987): 21-37.

Clupepper, R. A. "Seeing the Kingdom of God: The Metaphor of sight in the Gospel of Luke." *Currents in Theology and Mission* 21/6 (December, 1994): 434-443.

Coakley, J. F. "Jesus' Messianic Entry into Jerusalem (John 12:12-19 par.)." *The Journal of Theological Studies* 46/2 (October, 1995): 461-482.

Collins, A. Y. "Mark and His Readers: The Son of God among Jews." *Harvard Theological Review* 92/4 (October, 1999): 393-408.

_____. "Mark and His Readers: The Son of God among Greeks and Romans." *Harvard Theological Review* 93/2 (April, 2000): 85-100.

Conzelmann, H. "History and Theology in the Passion Narratives of the Synoptic Gospels." *Interpretation* 24/2 (April, 1970): 178-197.

Cosgrove, C. H. "The Divine Δει in Luke-Acts." *Novum Testamentum* 26/2 (April, 1984): 168-190.

_____. "A Woman's Unbound Hair in the Greco-Roman World, with special Reference to the Story of the "Sinful Woman" in Luke 7:36-50." *Journal of Biblical Literature* 124/4 (Winter, 2005): 675-692.

Cribbs, F. L. "St. Luke and the Johannine Tradition." *Journal of Biblical Literature* 90/4 (December, 1971): 422-450.

Crockett, L. C. "Luke 4 25-27 and Jewish-Gentile Relations in Luke-Acts." *Journal of Biblical Literature* 88/2 (June, 1969): 177-183.

Crossan, J. D. "The Parable of the Wicked Husbandmen." *Journal of Biblical Literature* 90/4 (December, 1971): 451-465.

D'Angelo, M. R. "Women in Luke-Acts: A Redactional View." *Journal of Biblical Literature* 109/3 (Fall, 1990): 441-461.

Danker, F. W. "Politics of the New Age According to St. Luke." *Currents in Theology and Mission* 12/6 (December, 1985), 338-345.

Denaux, A. "The Parable of the King-Judge (Lk 19, 12-28) and its Relation to the Entry Story (Lk 19, 29-44)." *Zeitschrift Für Die Neutestamentliche Wissenschaft* 93/1-2 (2002): 35-57.

Derrett, J. D. M. "Fresh Light on the Lost Sheep and the Lost Coin." *New Testament Studies* 26/1 (October, 1979): 36-60.

Elliott, J. K. "Anna's Age (Luke 2:36-37)." *Novum Testamentum* 30/2 (April, 1988): 100-102.

Erniakulathil, J. "Kingdom of God in the Teaching of Jesus." *Bible Bhashyam* 23/2 (June, 1997): 90-101.

Evans, C. A. "Luke's use of the Elijah/Elisha Narratives and the Ethic of Election." *Journal of Biblical Literature* 106/1 (March, 1987): 75-83.

Ford, J. M. "Zealotism and the Lukan Infancy Narratives." *Novum Testamentum* 18/4 (October, 1976): 280-292.

Freed, E. D. "The Parable of the Judge and the Widow (Luke 18:1-8)." *New Testament Studies* 33/1 (January, 1987): 38-60.

Fuliga, J. B. "The Temptations of Jesus: A Class Struggle." *The Asia Journal of Theology* 8/1 (1994): 172-185.

Garland, J. M. "Signs of Kingship." *The Expository Times* 100/5 (1989): 185-186.

Gnanavaram, "Hermeneutical Issues in Dalit Theology." *Arasaradi Journal of Theological Reflections* 11/1-2 (January-December, 1998): 118-129.

Goudoever, J. V. "The Place of Israel in Luke's Gospel." *Novum Testamentum* 8/2-4 (April-October, 1966): 111-123.

Gourgues, M. "The Priest, The Levite, and The Samaritan Revisited: A Critical Note on Luke 10:31-35." *Journal of Biblical Literature* 117/4 (Winter, 1998): 709-713.

Green, J. B. "Preparation for Passover (Luke 22:7-13): A Question of Redactional Technique." *Novum Testmentum* 29/4 (1987): 305-319.

_____. "The Death of Jesus and the Ways of God: Jesus and the Gospels on Messianic Status and Shameful Suffering." *Interpretation* 52/1 (January, 1998): 24-37.

Hamilton, N. Q. "Temple Cleansing and Temple Bank." *Journal of Biblical Literature* 83/4 (December, 1964): 365-372.

Hamm, D. "Sight to the Blind: Vision as Metaphor in Luke." *Biblica* 67/4 (1986): 457-477.

_____. "The Freeing of the Bent Woman and the Restoration of Israel: Luke 13:10-17 as Narrative Theology." *Journal for the Study of the New Testament* 31 (October, 1987): 23-44.

Hanfmann, G. M. A. "The Donkey and the King." *Harvard Theological Review* 78/3-4 (January-April, 1985): 421-426.

Harington, D. J. "Sociological Concepts and the Early Church: A Decade of Research." *Theological Studies* 47/1 (March, 1980): 181-190.

Hiers, R. H. "Purification of the Temple: Preparation for the Kingdom of God." *Journal of Biblical Literature* 90/1 (March, 1971): 82-90.

Hill, D. "The Rejection of Jesus at Nazareth (Luke iv 16-30)." *Novum Testamentum* 13/3 (July, 1971): 161-180.

Hooker, M. D. "Christology and Methodology." *New Testament Studies* 17/4 (July, 1971): 480-487.

Horbury, W. "The Passion Narratives and Historical Criticism." *Theology* 75/620 (February, 1972): 58-71.

Horsley, R. A. "Jesus and Empire." *Union Seminary Quarterly Review* 59/3-4 (2005): 44-74.

Huntress, E. ""Son of God" in Jewish Writings Prior to the Christian Era." *Journal of Biblical Literature* 54/2 (June, 1935): 117-124.

Ibita, M. M. "Dining with Jesus in the Third Gospel: Celebrating the Eucharist in the Third World." *East Asian Pastoral Review* 42/3 (2005): 249-261.

Iersel, B. V. "The Finding of Jesus in the Temple." *Novum Testamentum* 3/3 (October, 1959): 161-173.

Jackson, H. M. "The Death of Jesus in Mark and the Miracle from the Cross." *New Testament Studies* 33/1 (January, 1987): 16-37.

Jensen, J. F. "An Exposition of Luke 2:41-52." *Interpretation* 30/4 (October, 1976): 400-404.

John, V. J. "The Role of the State in Jesus' View: A Synoptic Perspective." *Bangalore Theological Forum* 34/1 (June, 1004): 1-18.

Johnson, E. S. "Is Mark 15:39 The Key to Mark's Christology." *Journal for the Study of the New Testament* 31(October, 1987): 3:22.

Johnson, L. T. "Making Connections: The Material Expression of Friendship in the New Testament." *Interpretation* 24 (April, 2004): 158-171.

Johnson, S. E. "King Parables in the Synoptic Gospels." *Journal of Biblical Literature* 74/1 (March, 1955): 37-39.

Jones, D. "The Background and Character of the Lukan Psalms." *The Journal of Theological Studies* 19/1 (April, 1968): 19-50.

Jonge, H. J. D. "Sonship, Wisdom, Infancy: Luke II. 41-51a." *New Testament Studies* 24/3 (April, 1978): 317-354.

Karris, R. J. "Luke 23:47 and the Lucan view of Jesus' Death." *Journal of Biblical Literature* 105/1 (1986): 65-74.

Keerankeri, G. "The Passion and Death of Jesus and the Problem of Human Suffering." *Vidyajyoti Journal of Theological Reflection* 70/10 (October 2006): 726-745.

Kilgallen, J. J. "The Obligation to Heal (Luke 13, 10-17)." *Biblica* 82/3 (2001): 402-409.

Kingsbury, J. D. "The Plot of Luke's Story of Jesus." *Interpretation* 48/4 (October, 1994): 369-378.

Kinman, B. R. "'The Stones will Cry out' (Luke 19, 40) – Joy or Judgment?" *Biblica* 75/2 (1994): 232-235.

_____. "Lucan Eschatology and the Missing Fig Tree." *Journal of Biblical Literature* 113/4 (winter, 1994): 669-678.

Klassen, W. "'A Child of Peace' (Luke 10.6) in First Century Context." *New Testament Studies* 27/4 (July, 1981): 488-506.

Kloppenborg, J. S. "The Dishonoured Master Luke 16, 1-8a." *Biblica* 70/4 (1989): 474-495.

Kuhn, Karl A. "The Point of the Step-Parallelism in Luke 1-2." *New Testament Studies* 47/1 (January, 2001): 38-49.

Kurichianil O. S. B., John "Jesus' Consciousness of His Passion and Death According to the Synoptic Gospels." *Bible Bhashyam* 9/2 (June, 1983): 114-125.

Ladd, G. E. "The Kingdom of God – Reign or Realm?" *Journal of Biblical Literature* 81/3 (September, 1962): 230-238.

Landry, D. T. "Narrative Logic in the Annunciation to Mary (Luke 1:26-38)." *Journal of Biblical Literature* 114/1 (Spring, 1995): 65-79.

Landry, D. and B. May. "Honor Restored: New Light on the Parable of the Prudent Steward (Luke 16:1-8a)." *Journal of Biblical Literature* 119/2 (Summer, 2000): 287-309.

Leaney, R. "The Birth Narratives in St Luke and St Matthew." *New Testament Studies* 8/2 (January, 1962): 158-166.

Legrand, L. "Christological Issues in the New Testament." *The Indian Journal of Theology* 24/3&4 (July- December1975): 71-78.

_____ . "The Christmas Story in Lk 2:1-7." *Indian Theological Studies* 19/4 (December, 1982): 289-317.

Light, G. W. "Luke 5:15-26," *Interpretation* 48/3 (July, 1994): 279-283.

Lin, J. V. "Christology and Christologies in India." *Exchange* 14/42 (December, 1985): 1-33.

Loader, W. "Jesus and the Rogue in Luke 16, 1-8A: The Parable of the Unjust Steward." *Revue Biblique* 96/4 (January, 1989): 518-532.

Loewe, W. P. "Towards an Interpretation of Lk 19:1-10." *The Catholic Biblical Quarterly* 36/3 (July, 1974): 321-331.

Lull, D. J. "The Servant-Benefactor as a Model of Greatness (Luke 22:24-30)." *Novum Testamentum* 28/4 (1986): 289-305.

Lyngdoh, C. P. "'God Visiting His People' in the Lucan Texts, Part I." *Indian Journal of Spirituality* 19/2 (April-June, 2005): 135-155.

_____. "'God Visiting His People' in the Lucan Texts, Part II." *Indian Journal of Spirituality* 18/3 (July-September, 2005): 288-312.

Maleparampil, J. "Unexpected and Unknown but Models of Courageous and Generous Discipleship: Matthew 26:6-13; 27:19; 27:54 and 27:57-61." *Bible Bhashyam* 29/3 (September, 2003): 205-220.

Malina, B. J. "Jesus as Charismatic Leader?" *Biblical Theology Bulletin* 14/2 (April, 1984): 55-62.

Maloney L. M. and E. J. Smith. "The Year of Luke: A Feminist Perspective." *Currents in Theology and Mission* 21/6 (December, 1994): 415-423.

Mangatt, G. "The Gospel of Salvation." *Bible Bhashyam* 2/1 (March, 1976): 60-80.

_____. "Jesus' Option for Sinners." *Bible Bhashyam* 18/4 (December, 1992): 208-220.

_____. "Jesus' Prayer." *Bible Bhashyam* 24/1 (March, 1998): 27-36.

Manus, U. C. "Jesu Kristi Oba: A Christology of "Christ the King" Among the Indigenous Christian Churches in Yorubaland, Nigeria." *The Asia Journal of Theology* 5/2 (1991): 311-330.

Marcus, J. "Entering into the Kingly Power of God." *Journal of Biblical Literature* 107/4 (December, 1988): 663-675.

Martin, R. P. "Salvation and Discipleship in Luke's Gospel." *Interpretation* 30/4 (October, 1976): 366-380.

Matera, F. J. "The Death of Jesus according to Luke: A Question of Sources." *The Catholic Biblical Quarterly* 47/3 (July, 1985): 469-485.

_____. "The Trial of Jesus: Problems and Proposals." *Interpretation* 45/1 (January, 1991): 5-16.

Mattam, Z. "The Temptations of Christ. Lk 4:1-13." *Bible Bhashyam* 23/2 (June, 1997): 102-120.

_____. "The Cure of the Blind Man of Jericho (Lk 18:35-43): A Kerygmatic, Patristic and Theological Study." *Bible Bhashyam* 24/1 (March, 1998): 17-26.

Mattill, A. J. "The Jesus-Paul Parallels and the Purpose of Luke-Acts: H. H. Evans Reconsidered." *Novum Testamentum* 17/1 (January, 1975): 15-46.

Menezes, F. "The Mission of Jesus According to Lk 4:16-30." *Bible Bhashyam* 4/3 (September, 1980): 249-264.

Migliore, D. L. "Christology in Context: The Doctrinal and Contextual Tasks of Christology Today." *Interpretation* 49/3 (July, 1995): 242-254.

Miller, R. J. "Elijah, John and Jesus in the Gospel of Luke." *New Testament Studies* 34/4 (October, 1988): 611-622.

Moessner, D. P. "The 'Leaven of the Pharisees' and 'This Generation': Israel's Rejection of Jesus According to Luke." *Journal for the Study of the New Testament* 34 (October, 1988): 21-46.

Moore, K. M. L. "Luke 2:1-14." *Interpretation* 60/4 (October, 2006): 442-445.

Morris, R. L. B. "Why ΑΥΓΟΥΣΤΟΣ? A Note to Luke 2:1." *New Testament Studies* 38/1 (January, 1992): 142-144.

Muthuraj, J. G. "Economic Scenarios of the NT Christianity: A Socio-Economic Reading of Luke-Acts." *Indian Journal of Theology* 38/1 (1996): 49-60.

_____. "New Testament and Methodology – An Overview." *Asia Journal of Theology* 10/2 (October, 1996): 253-277.

Naganoolil, T. G. "The Christological Titles and Contemporary Jesus-Research." *Bible Bhashyam* 25/4 (December 1999): 251-265.

Nevius, R. C. "Kyrios and Iesous in St. Luke." *Anglican Theological Review* 48/1 (January, 1966): 75-77.

Nissen, J. "Christology between the Local and the Global." *Sweedish Missiological Themes* 88/4 (2000): 593-610.

Olsson, B. "The Canticle of the Heavenly Host (Luke 2:14) in History and Culture." *New Testament* Studies 50/2 (April, 2004): 147-166.

O'Toole, R. "The Literary Form of Luke 19:1-10." *Journal of Biblical Literature* 110/1 (Spring, 1991): 107-116.

_____. "Some Exegetical Reflections on Luke 13, 10-17." *Biblica* 73/1 (1992): 84-107.

Owen-Ball, D. T. "Rabbinic Rhetoric and the Tribute Passage (Mt. 22:15-22; Mk. 12:13-17; Lk. 20:20-26)." *Novum Testamentum* 35/1 (January, 1993): 1-14.

Parappally, J. "The Indian Context of Christological Reflection." *Indian Journal of Spirituality* 8/3 (September 1995): 361-412.

Parker, P. "Luke and the Fourth Evangelist." *New Testament Studies* 9/4 (July, 1963): 317-336.

Parsons, M. C. "'Short in Stature': Luke's Physical Description of Zacchaeus." *New Testament Studies* 47/1 (January, 2001): 50-57.

Pathrapankal, J. "The *Nazareth Manifesto* in the Evangelizing Mission of Jesus." *Indian Theological Studies* 43/3-4 (September-December, 2006): 291-308.

Pesch, R. "The Last Supper and Jesus' Understanding of His Death." *Bible Bhashyam* 3/1 (March, 1997): 58-75.

Phan, P. C. "Kingdom of God: A Theological Symbol for Asians?" *Gregorianum* 79/2 (1998): 295-321.

_____. "Kingdom of God: a symbol for Asians?" *Theology Digest* 47/1 (Spring 2000): 21-26.

Plessis, I. I. D. "Once More: The Purpose of Luke's Prologue (Lk I 1-4)." *Novum Testamentum* 16/4 (October, 1974): 259-271.

Plevnik, J. "Son of Man Seated at the Right Hand of God: Luke 22:69 in Lucan Christology." *Biblica* 72/3 (1991): 331-347.

Poonoly, P. "Unique and Universal Saviour? Christology in a Religiously Plural World." *Indian Theological Studies* 45/2 (June, 2008): 159-172.

Powell, M. A. "The Religious Leaders in Luke: A Literary-Critical Study." *Journal of Biblical Literature* 109/1 (Spring, 1990): 93-110.

_____. "Toward a Narrative-Critical Understanding of Luke." *Interpretation* 48/4 (October, 1994): 341-346.

Prabhu, G. M. S. "Good News to the Poor the Social Implications of the Message of Jesus." *Bible Bhashyam* 4/3 (September, 1978): 193-213.

Price, J. L. "The Gospel According to Luke." *Studia Biblica* 7/2 (April, 1953): 195-212.

Rao, O. M. "Jesus: Christ of the Atonement or Christ the New Man." *The Indian Journal of Theology* 24/3&4 (July-December1975): 162-171.

Ravens, D. A. S. "The Setting of Luke's Account of the Anointing: Luke 7. 2-8. 3." *New Testament Studies* 34/2 (April, 1988): 282-292.

Reid, B. E. "Luke: The Gospel for Women?" *Currents in Theology and Mission* 21/6 (December, 1994): 405-414.

_____. "Beyond Petty Pursuits and Wearisome Widows." *Interpretation* 56/3 (July, 2002): 284-294.

Rensberger, D. "The Politics of John: The Trial of Jesus in the Fourth Gospel." *Journal of Biblical Literature* 103/3 (September 1984): 395-411.

Ricoeur, P. "The "Kingdom" in the Parables of Jesus." *Anglican Theological Review* 63/2 (April, 1981):165-169.

Riedlinger, H. "How Universal is Christ's Kingship?-A Bibliographical Study." *Concilium* 1/2 (January 1966): 56-66.

Roberts, J. J. M. "The Enthronement of Yhwh and David: The Abiding Theological Significance of the Kingship Language of the Psalms." *The Catholic Biblical Quarterly* 64/4 (October, 2002): 675-686.

Robinson, G. "Jesus Christ, The Open Way and The Fellow-Struggler: A Look into the Christologies in India." *The Asian Journal of Theology* 3/2 (October, 1989): 404-415.

Roschke, R. W. "Healing in Luke, Madagascar, and Elsewhere." *Currents in Theology and Mission* 33/6 (December, 2006): 459-471.

Ruddick, C. T. "Birth Narratives in Genesis and Luke." *Novum Testamentum* 12/4 (October, 1970): 343-348.

Rudman, D. "Authority and Right of Disposal in Luke 4.6." *New Testament Studies* 50/1 (January, 2004): 77-86.

Salazar, A. M. "Questions about St. Luke's Sources." *Novum Testamentum* 2/3-4 (October, 1958): 316-317.

Sampathkumar, P. A. "The Rich and the poor in Luke-Acts." *Bible Bhashyam* 22/4 (December, 1996): 175-189.

Sanders, J. T. "Tradition and Redaction in Luke XV. 11-32." *New Testament Studies* 15/4 (July 1969): 433-438.

Santram, P. B. "Jesus: The Christ of Mystical Union or the Prophetic Christ?" *The Indian Journal of Theology* 24/3&4 (July- December1975): 126-131.

_____. "Jesus Christ and the Kingdom of God: A New Testament Perspective." *The Indian Journal of Theology* 29/2 (April–June, 1980): 81-91. Seccombe, D. "Luke and Isaiah." *New Testament Studies* 27/2 (January, 1981): 252-259.

Selvanayagam, I. "Who is This Jesus?" *The Asia Journal of Theology* 7/2 (1993): 231-243.

Senior, D. C. P., "The Death of Jesus and the Resurrection of the Holy Ones (Mt 27:51-53)." *The Catholic Biblical Quarterly* 38/3 (July, 1976): 312-329.

Sevilla, P. C. "Problems and Orientations for Contemporary Christology." *East Asian Pastoral Review* 18/4 (1981): 346-357.

Sheehan, J. F. X. "Sacral Kingship and the New Testament." *Bible Today* 82 (February, 1976): 677-682).

Sheridan, J. M. "Proclaiming the King – Preaching the Kingdom." *Bible Today* 87 (December, 1976): 995-1000.

Shirock, R. J. "The Growth of the Kingdom in Light of Israel's Rejection of Jesus: Structure and Theology in Luke 13:1-35." *Novum Testamentum* 35/1 (January, 1993): 15-29.

Stendahl, K. "Thy Kingdom Come on Earth." *American Baptist Quarterly* 14/1 (March, 1995): 14-21.

Sugirtharajah, R. S. "'What Do Men Say Remains of Me?': Current Jesus Research & Third World Christologies." *The Asia Journal of Theology* 5/2 (1991): 331-337.

Swanson, T. N. "The Kingship of God in Intertestamental Literature," *Bangalore Theological Forum* 12/1 (January-June, 1980): 1-25.

Sylva, D. D. "The Temple Curtain and Jesus' Death in the Gospel of Luke." *Journal of Biblical Literature* 105/2 (1986): 243-245.

Talbert, C. H. "An Anti-Gnostic Tendency in Lucan Christology." *New Testament Studies* 14/2 (January, 1968): 259-271.

_____. "Shifting Sands: The Recent Study of the Gospel of Luke." *Interpretation* 30/4 (October, 1976): 381-395.

_____. "The Place of the Resurrection in the Theology of Luke." *Interpretation* 46/1 (January, 1992): 19-30.

Tatum, W. B. "The Epoch of Israel: Luke 1-11 and the Theological Plan of Luke-Acts." *New Testament Studies* 13/2 (1967): 184-195.

Thomas, M. A. "Social Vision of Jesus." *Religion and Society* 39/2-3 (June-September, 1992): 51-59.

Thomas, V. P. "Towards and Indian Christology." *The Indian Journal of Theology* 14/1 (January-March, 1965): 1-10.

Thornton, T. C. G. "Charismatic Kingship in Israel and Judah." *The Journal of Theological Studies* 14/1 (April 1963): 1-11.

Topel, L. J. "On the Injustice of the Unjust Steward: Lk 16:1-13." *The Catholic Biblical Quarterly* 37/2 (April, 1975): 216-227.

Turner, M. "The Spirit and the Power of Jesus' Miracles in the Lucan Conception." *Novum Testamentum* 33/2 (April, 1991):124-152.

Unnik, W. C. V. "Jesus the Christ." *New Testament Studies* 8/2 (January, 1962): 101-116.

Valuparampil, K. "Luke's Version of the Good News to the Poor in a World of Globalization." *Aikya Samiksha* 1/2 (September, 2004): 39-55.

Vellanickal, M. "The Filial Faith of Jesus: Jesus' Experience as Son of God." *Bible Bhashyam* 11/3 (March-June 1985): 113-129.

Walaskay, P. W. "The Trial and Death of Jesus in the Gospel of Luke." *Journal of Biblical Literature* 94/1 (March, 1975): 81-93.

Walker, W. O. "Jesus and Tax Collectors." *Journal of Biblical Literature* 97/2 (June, 1978): 221-238.

Wiles, J. K. "Wisdom and Kingship in Israel." *Asia Journal of Theology* 1/1 (April, 1987): 55-70.

Witherington, B. "On the Road with Mary Magdalene, Joanna, Susanna, and Other Disciples – Luke 8 1-3." *Zeitschrift für die Neutestamentlische Wissenschaft* 70/3-4 (1979): 243-248.

Wright, N.T. "Paul's Gospel and Caesar's Empire." *Reflections* vol 2 (Spring 1999): 42-64.

Zehnle, R. "The Salvific Character of Jesus' Death in Lucan Soteriology." *Theological Studies* 30/3 (September, 1969): 420-444.

Zeller, D. "New Testament Christology in its Hellenistic Reception." *New Testament Studies* 46/3 (July, 2001): 312-333.

The Report of the Theological Committee of the Evangelischen Kirche der Union. "Understanding the Death of Jesus." *Interpretation* 24/2 (April, 1970): 139-150.

Articles in Dictionary

Allison, D. C. "Jesus Christ." *The New Interpreters Dictionary of the Bible I-Ma.* Vol 3. Ed. by K. D. Sakenfeld. Nashville: Abingdon Press, 2008, 261-293.

Collins, J. J. "Messiah, Jewish," *The New Interpreters Dictionary of the Bible.* Vol 4. Me-R. Ed. by K. D. Sakenfeld. Nashville: Abingdon Press, 2009, 59-66.

Donahue, J. R. "Passion Narrative." *The Interpreter's Dictionary of the Bible.* Supplementary Volume. Ed. by K. Crim. Nashville: Abingdon Press, 1976, 643-645.

Eaton, J. "Kingship." *A Dictionary of Biblical Interpretation.* Ed. by R. J. Coggins and J. L. Houlden. London: SCM Press, 1990, 379-382.

Edwards, R. B. "Rome." *Dictionary of Jesus and the Gospels.* Ed. by J. B. Green and S. McKnight. Illinois: Inter Varsity Press, 1992, 710-715.

Fabry. "Qumran." *Theological Dictionary of the Old Testament.* Vol VIII. מֹר-לִכַד. Ed. by J. Botterweck, H. Tinggren, and H. Fabry. Tr. by D. W. Scott. Grand Rapids: William B. Eerdmans, 1997, 374-375.

Foerster. "σατανᾶς." *Theological Dictionary of the New Testament.* Vol VII. Σ. Ed. by G. Friedrich, Tr. by G.W. Bromiley. Grand Rapids: Wm. B. Eerdmans, 1971, 151-163.

Gench, F. T. "Repentance in the NT." *The New Interpreters Dictionary of the Bible Me-R.* Vol 4. Ed. by K. D. Sakenfeld. Nashville: Abingdon Press, 2009, 762-764.

Green, J. B. "Death of Jesus." *Dictionary of Jesus and the Gospels.* Ed. by J. B. Green and S. McKnight. Illinois: Inter Varsity Press, 1992, 146-163.

_____. "Passion Narratives." *Dictionary of Jesus and the Gospels.* Ed. by J. B. Green and S. McKnight. Illinois: Inter Varsity Press, 1992, 601-604.

Houlden, J. L. "Passion Narratives." *A Dictionary of Biblical Interpretation.* Ed. by R. J. Coggins and J. L. Houlden. London: SCM Press, 1990, 515-517.

Hurtado, L. W. "Christ," *Dictionary of Jesus and the Gospels.* Ed. by J. B. Green and S. McKnight. Illinois: Inter Varsity Press, 1992, 106-117.

Kleinknecht. "βασιλεύς in the Greek world." *Theological Dictionary of the New Testament* Vol 1. A-G. Ed. by G. Kittel. Grand Rapids: Wm. B. Eerdmans, 1964, 564-565.

Kuhn. "מלכות שָׁמַיִם in Rabbinic Literature." *Theological Dictionary of the New Testament.* Vol 1. A-Γ. Ed. by G. Kittel. Grand Rapids: Wm. B. Eerdmans, 1964, 571-574.

Lampe, P. "βασίλεις." *Exegetical Dictionary of the New Testament.* Vol 1. Ἀαρων-Ἐνώχ. Ed. by H. Balz and G. Schneider. Edinburgh: T & T Clark, 1980, 205-208.

Luz, U. "βασιλεία." *Exegetical Dictionary of the New Testament.* Vol 1. Ἀαρων-Ἐνώχ. Ed. by H. Balz and G. Schneider. Edinburgh: T & T Clark, 1980, 201-205.

Matera, F. J. "Death of Christ." *The Anchor Bible Dictionary.* Vol 1. Ed. by D. N. Freedman. New York: Doubleday, 1992, 923-925.

Nickelsburg, G. W. E. "Passion Narratives." *The Anchor Bible Dictionary.* Vol 5. O-Sh. Ed. by D. N. Freedmann. New York: Doubleday, 1972, 172-177.

Oepke. "βαπτω." *Theological Dictionary of the New Testament.* Ed. by G. Kittel. Grand Rapids: William. B. Eerdmans, 1964, 529-546.

Rad, V. "מֶלֶךְ and מלכות in the OT." *Theological Dictionary of the New Testament.* Vol 1. A-Γ. Ed. by G. Kittel. Grand Rapids: Wm. B. Eerdmans, 1964, 565-571.

Ringgren. "מֶלֶךְ." *Theological Dictionary of the Old Testament.* Vol VIII. מֹר-לכד. Ed. by J. Botterweck, H. Tinggren, and H. Fabry. Tr. by D. W. Scott. Grand Rapids: William B. Eerdmans, 1997, 347-352.

Seybold. "The Word Group mlk." *Theological Dictionary of the Old Testament.* Vol VIII. מֹר-לכד. Ed. by J. Botterweck, H. Tinggren, and H. Fabry. Tr. by D. W. Stott. Grand Rapids: William B. Eerdmans, 1997, 352-374.

SpicQ, C. "βασιλεία, βασιλειος, βασιλεύς etc." *Theological Lexicon of the New Testament* Vol 1. ἀγα-ἐλπ. Tr. and Ed. by J. D. Ernest. USA: Hendrickson, 1994, 256-271.

Online Article

Brown, R. E. "The Death of Jesus and Anti-Semitism Seeking Interfaith Understanding." http://www. google.com/paper.

Fredriksen, P. *Jesus of Nazareth, King of the Jews: A Jewish Life and the Emergence of Christianity,* reviewed by G. C. Marfin, http/www. Google. com. Garrett, S. R. "The Meaning of Jesus' Death in Luke." *Word & World* 12/1 (Winter, 1992): 11-16. ATLAS.

Heim, M. "Rethinking the death of Jesus Cross Purposes." *Christian Century* 122/6 (March 2005): 20-25. [ATLAS]

Johnson, S. L. "The Death of Christ." *Bibliotheca Sacra* 125/497 (Jan-Mar, 1968): 10-19. [ATLAS]

Kinman, B. "Pilate's Assize and the Timings of Jesus' Trial." *Tyndale Bulletin* 42/2 (1991): 282-295. [ATLAS]

Marshall, H. "The Death of Jesus in Recent New Testament Study." *Word & World* 3/1 (Winter, 1983): 12-21. [ATLAS]

Vogt, C. P. "Practicing Patience, Compassion, and Hope at the End of Life: Mining the Passion of Jesus in Luke for a Christian Model of Dying Well." *Journal of the society of Christian Ethics* 24/1 (Spring-Summer 2004):135-158. [ATLAS]

Unpublished Books

Abraham, K. A. *A Re-examination of the Lordship of Jesus Christ in the search for a Contemporary Christology in Asia.* SATHRI: D.Th. Thesis, 1996. (UTC Library)

Bond, Helen K. *The Historical Jesus: A Guide for the Perplexed.* London: Continuum, 2012. (copy on WebCT, Edinburgh University).

www.ingramcontent.com/pod-product-compliance
Lightning Source LLC
Chambersburg PA
CBHW020637030726
47498CB00002B/258